EXPOSED
DOM NATION #1

Exposed / E. Davies. – 1st ed.
ISBN: 978-1-912245-45-1

EXPOSED

SLATE

"I'll need to see your outfit before I can let you in."

My mouth was too dry, and my palms were too wet. What the hell was I doing here, outside the entrance of Dom Nation? It was marked only with a stylized *DN*, for people in the know.

Thanks to my asshole ex and the scraps of information he'd dangled in front of me like forbidden fruit, I was one of those people.

Crap. Do I really have the balls for this? Maybe Isaac had been right. Maybe I was better off in private, where anyone who showed up at my door was guaranteed to be into me.

Or to want to get into me, which I wanted to believe was good enough.

"Oh, yeah. Of course," I mumbled. Trying to look like I did this all the time, I gave a nervous laugh and lifted my shirt. Beyond the guardian of the dress code, throbbing music drifted through the open door. I wished I could just slip past, unseen.

"Good. And downstairs?"

"D-Downstairs?"

Crap. Was there an extra super-secret zone? A password? I started to hyperventilate. I'd applied by email and they'd accepted me, and nobody had mentioned a downstairs.

"No jeans—it's in the dress code," said the young guy, his voice sharp even if his smile was friendly. "Do you have something else?"

Oh, *downstairs*. I felt like an idiot. Yes, I most certainly did have something downstairs, and it was hot, sweaty, and squished at an awkward angle like a hot dog in a miniature Ziploc.

My leather hot pants felt even more ridiculous than they looked, sticky against my skin. Leather under denim was not a recipe for comfort on a warm spring night.

Fuck. Now I have to drop my pants in public. I kicked myself for not just ordering a kilt online.

Behind me, plain black barriers stretched along the sidewalk, far enough back to make me nervous about how many people would be inside this joint. But I'd come early—hopefully for the only time tonight.

A group of six men approached, all of them twentysomething. They joined the end of the nonexistent line, glancing at me and then slowing their pace. They were laughing, passing around a cigarette. All of them were in leather and rubber and shiny sports gear, broadcasting plain as day where they were going.

Did they come like that on the bus? I had to wonder. *Share a ride? Bike?*

The thought of strangers walking past and doing a double take at the middle-aged guy squeezing himself into sexy clothing made me want to crawl into a gutter and never return. So on the way here, I'd worn my outfit under jeans and a T-shirt. The buckles stood out through my shirt like weird body mods.

I took some comfort: the perky young man in an effortlessly cool silver chain body harness and long, buckled leather trousers had every right to look at me like I didn't belong here. With his lean body and pretty eyes, I wondered how frustrating it was to be stuck checking partygoers at the door.

But his patience and his smile dwindled as the guys behind me approached.

This was it. Time to put up or shut up. My hands shaking, I started to unbutton my pants.

"Oh, no!" He grinned at me and held out a hand. "No public nudity allowed. But if that's your outfit tonight, that's fine." Then the guy *winked,* probably out of pity. I heard a laugh from behind.

Great. I had an audience. Just what I needed.

Mortification bloomed in my cheeks. *They think I'm going in there naked?* No fucking way did I have the balls—or the body— for that.

Holding together the sides of my pants without doing up my fly yet, I was frozen with indecision. Should I rip down my pants and show him that I'd come dressed? Or would he just laugh at me for shyly hiding away under baggy jeans?

"No, I…" I cleared my throat, pulling apart my hands just enough to show a hint of leather in the V. "Shorts. Leather. Short leather shorts. That's my downstairs solution."

Downstairs solution? Jesus Christ. Just go home now, Slate, I thought, my throat tight as I ducked my head to avoid seeing his reaction. *Game over.*

A tiny, self-pitying part of me hoped he'd tell me so. I could fume, call a taxi, stew in indignation, but in half an hour I'd be home with a glass of wine and an episode of *Miss Marple*.

Not trying to indulge the desires I wished to God I could bury, along with my hope of finding a man who shared them *and* wanted more than one soulless night.

"Welcome in," the club guardian said instead, stepping aside and gesturing. "Changing area's to the left next to the lockers."

"Thanks," I mumbled. Shit, I should have brought a bag, but I hadn't known what kind. Gym bag? Tote bag? Locked suitcase? This was an alien world.

As I stepped into the entryway, my heart beat so loudly in my ears that it washed the sound away in a dizzying wave before it returned.

I'm okay, I told myself, keeping my chin up. *Fake it till you make it.*

There were signs everywhere to read. One said *No phones outside the changing room.* The changing area turned out to be a small room that was mercifully empty. I yanked off my T-shirt and jeans and slid my shoes back on. Then I nervously slid my phone inside my jeans, my hand hovering over the pocket.

God, if I got my phone stolen at a kink club, I had no idea how to explain that to my insurance company. I shoved the bundle of clothes into a locker and slid the wristband with its key on. Like a fucked-up adult swimming pool. Speedos would be more comfortable than these shorts.

The dance music was louder toward the right, and I could just see a darkened room with people moving to the music. To the left, though, was the bar.

Oh, God. Yes, please.

I squirmed where I stood, unused to feeling a breeze quite so high against the back of my thighs. A rum and Coke firmly in hand, I ignored the signs pointing to the play areas. I needed more liquid courage for that.

Instead, I escaped to the dance room to watch men dancing to the deep, thumping beat. With nobody watching me, I gradually relaxed and leaned against a wall, nursing my drink.

This was okay. Why had Isaac never wanted to bring me here? I'd asked—but he'd brushed it off.

He'd told me harshly, *I'm all you need.* And how could I argue with that? He could take me apart with his hands, toys, and brutal precision right at home.

Three years later, I'd never been able to switch off the cravings that Isaac had awakened. He'd translated vague longings to reality. I'd always known something was different—wrong, I'd thought often—but it hadn't made sense until Isaac touched me.

I hadn't made sense until Isaac touched me.

Fuck him, I thought for the thousandth time. It was a mantra that saw me through the long evenings when time stretched out into infinity, empty and aching. Sometimes I kneeled on the carpet in my living room, closing my eyes. Remembering.

Regretting.

For years, I'd hated that he'd ever come along and taught me what I *could* be, only to disappear like a wisp of chimney smoke on a winter's night. Off to find some other, prettier hunk of wood to set alight with his blows and his caresses.

Leaving me there, charred and collapsing in on myself and very much alone.

I'd kneeled, and prayed for him to come back, and cursed at him, and stewed in self-loathing for long enough.

Tonight, for the first time in three years, I'd slipped on the harness I'd had to fight to be "allowed" to keep. A gift from a man who had once lavished me with them to keep me on tap. When he'd left, he'd taken everything else.

Even my pride. *Especially* my pride.

But the harness? That was mine. And this boldness was mine, too. We'd never gone to this club—or anywhere public—before. He'd said he didn't like the meat market atmosphere.

Well, beggars couldn't be choosers. Isaac would laugh if he saw me now. I'd never worn so little in public. The harness and leather shorts exposed me. I felt naked, and turmoil writhed through my belly as my body remembered how much it liked that vulnerability.

Steering around strangers, I walked through the arch and toward the dance floor. *Fuck* what he thought. I was at the market because, with a wildness that flooded my senses and filled my lungs, I needed to be—

"Fresh meat."

The voice was masculine, rough. Certain.

It was the voice of a Dom. Like a man woken from the last ice age, my veins remembered the heat of my blood again.

I stiffened from head to toe. My heart hammered against my rib cage as I gripped my plastic drink cup tightly. *Act natural*, I told myself as I turned my head to inspect the man who spoke.

He was in his early forties, with a tight mouth and salt-and-pepper beard. He wore shiny black boots and a leather cap, but nothing caught my attention like the long black whip hung from a loop on his belt.

I gulped, a shudder of inexplicable desire running through my body. He wasn't my type, and after so long, I wasn't even sure *who* my type was anymore. But still, my soul responded to him like a puzzle piece that I could force into the gap, if only I turned a blind eye to my own heart.

Did I care? Would it be awful to pretend I was into him? These years had ground down my pride into dust. I could scarcely afford to turn down compliments, whoever they came from.

His gaze was calm and keen, fixed on my face. One hand crept down to his belt, his thumb hooking into the same loop his whip hung from. "What are you here for?"

I couldn't meet his eyes and pretend—I just wasn't that kind of guy. Maybe I should have been. It would do wonders for my sex life. I looked down past the whip and boots until I stared at the concrete floor, my cheeks hot. "I don't know."

He leaned in and stepped closer. "What was that? Look at me." His voice was gentle, but I was more surprised he hadn't grabbed my chin and *made* me look at him. Was I disappointed? I couldn't tell.

I cleared my throat with a sheepish nod of apology. "I don't know," I said, loud enough to be heard over the music this time. It took longer to drag my gaze back to meet his, but I eventually managed it.

He smiled slightly, a reward for my efforts. "Not me, then. Or you'd know." His tone was graceful and matter-of-fact. Straightforward in a way Isaac had never been. I didn't sense that he was playing a game to beat me down.

Wait—the Dom was talking to me like an equal now, his stance relaxing. This was strange, but the relief was impossible to hide.

I let a breath out, my face creasing in apology. "I'm sorry…?" I trailed off, waiting for a name.

The man paused as if deciding whether I was entitled to the information, and I was almost ashamed to admit it made me prickle with pleasure. Maybe I didn't deserve to know anyone here.

"Seb," the man finally told me, his voice piercing through the beat as it whined, whirred, and turned into another heavy techno beat. "You are?"

I cleared my throat and held out my hand to shake. "Slate."

With an ironic twist to his lips, Seb raised it and brushed his lips to the back of my hand, warm and friendly. I laughed awkwardly and took my hand back, folding it tightly under my other arm as I clutched my drink for dear life.

"As disappointed as I am for my own prospects, I'm glad you joined us tonight," Seb told me like I wasn't crawling up the wall with anxiety. "Don't apologize for who you want or don't want, Slate. Got your eye on anyone?"

I shook my head. "I only just got here."

"Watch out." Seb winked. "Fresh meat brings the sharks. The DMs here are friendly. Holler if you need anything."

I blinked twice at him, surprised that he was offering help. Thank God I knew who DMs were—dungeon monitors—thanks to my Google searches.

My knowledge of the ecstasy of submission started and ended in the bedroom. I was a fortysomething sub who didn't know how to turn down a Dom like Seb, who'd never been on the scene before, but *had* been whipped to tears and broken into tiny, fucked-up pieces night after night.

What did that make me? A fraud? It sure felt like it.

"Th-Thanks?"

Seb chuckled. This time he did touch my cheek lightly. The warmth startled me, and I caught my breath. "Look up, boy," he advised me. "There you are. Let them see those pretty blues."

I blushed, quivering and transfixed where I stood.

"And take a walk around," Seb advised me with another wolfish grin. "You might figure out what you want." Then he turned and melted into the growing crowd of grinding, gyrating, writhing men.

Writhing? My eye drawn to the crowd, I made out the outline of a slender young thing wrapped in an older man's arms, his back pressed against the larger man's chest. His eyes were closed and his lips parted, the light clearly silhouetting the spiked collar he wore, and the leash attached to that collar, and the tight grip his Dom kept on his leash.

The man's other hand was in his underwear, unmistakably gripping the bulge of his shaft.

I gulped hard, not wanting to be caught staring. My own dick was stirring to life, already thickening in the unforgiving confines of my tight little shorts.

I felt nearly naked, my arms folded awkwardly over my chest as I hurried out of the dance area and past the bar to the playrooms.

They were quiet.

The sounds of grunts, cries, and slaps of leather halted me in my tracks. Sweat trickled down my spine suddenly, my throat tight as I stared through the doorway into the half-lit space. Lights close to the ceiling shone up, unobtrusively providing enough light for safety—and to watch.

A throat-clearing behind me reminded me that I was blocking the doorway. "Kind of in a hurry, man. Go in if you're gonna watch. Don't perv from a distance."

"Sorry," I mumbled, averting my gaze and stepping aside. A couple walked past me, both men holding hands and striding like they had a mission.

Did I want to watch?

Yes. Very much.

Whatever I'd said to Seb, I knew exactly what I wanted. Not the act, but the feeling. I wanted to feel humbled, and proud, and utterly helpless. I just didn't know who I could ask, or how.

Excuse me, you're young and hot and I'm not. Want to do me a favor? I promise I'll cum quickly.

No. Even for me, that would be too humiliating. I wanted to be *wanted*, not *tolerated*. God forbid *convenient*.

I swallowed and slipped through the doorway, trying to stay out of the way of the groups of men mingling there. Trying not to stare at anyone too long.

Just a few feet away, a cry of pleasure made me look. A man in a harness and jockstrap was riding another man who reclined on a couch. His head was thrown back in pleasure, his teeth bared. Another man stood next to him, one hand wrapped around the back of his neck, holding him close, swigging at a beer as he talked to the man lying back on the couch.

Like it was all very normal.

I gulped hard and walked past them, ignoring the throbbing in my pants at the crack that rang through the room.

A big, hairy guy was strapped to X-shaped wooden boards, a delicate young man walking back and forth behind him, running the whip over his reddened skin.

That was more like it. But the Dom in question was clearly busy, and from the wedding rings they both wore, for a long time to come. My heart sank and I walked on.

I passed a dark steel cage—currently empty—and found a sling.

That was where my friends in the doorway had hurried. The tall blond was strapped in now, wearing nothing but white lacy underwear. Alongside the tent of his hard-on, the other man slid a bright pink vibrator in, clicked a button, and stood back with a self-satisfied grin.

The begging started immediately, quiet at first and growing louder. Eyes turned to them. Some guys stood nearby and watched with mild curiosity. Others smiled and looked away.

Then there was the thick velvet curtain, and my hopes lifted.

Of course. The darkroom.

I didn't have to worry about *finding* someone. I could go in there...

And wait. On my knees, in the dark, helpless. Whoever wanted to use me would find my hot mouth, and I could beg in the darkness for what I needed without having to look him in the eyes afterward.

I hated it. I wanted it. I hated *myself*.

Did I?

Moans, low and desperate, slid from the darkroom. The sound of spanking, too. A series of grunts, in time with the smacked skin, low and hoarse but quickly climbing.

I swayed toward the doorway.

Fingertips ran up the inside and back of my thigh, to my tight and aching semi. *Shit!* I nearly jumped out of my skin, whirling around with righteous indignation. "What do you think—"

The words died on my lips.

Isaac.

He didn't look surprised to see me. He'd known who I was then. Had he followed me from the bar? From the dance floor? Had he been standing back, watching me, laughing the whole time?

I froze, my pulse throbbing in my ears. His lips moved, but I couldn't hear them. My steadily swelling erection shriveled into nothing. So did my confidence, which had so gradually been growing. And my very will to live.

What in ten fucking layers of Hell was he doing *here*?

I wasn't sure if I wanted to punch him, run away, or scream at him. Maybe all of the above. Or... *Or...*

No! No. I cursed myself out and forced a sneer to my lips. I would never be that desperate again.

"Take it as a compliment," Isaac murmured. "You should be glad for the attention."

And in two sentences, he undid me. I was right back to the man I'd once been, desperate enough to beg at his feet for a scrap of attention like a bone. But older now, even less attractive.

Past my prime. That was what Isaac had told me the day we broke up.

Tears flooded my eyes, and shame closed my throat before I could curse him out. I stepped backward and shook my head, clenching my jaw so tightly my teeth hurt.

"That's right," Isaac said, a cruel smile playing over his lips. "Go home, little boy. You're out of your league here."

I had to leave.

Not because he told me to. Not because of his command—deep and so familiar to obey. But because I was just going to make a fool of myself one way or another, and we both knew it.

I could at least give myself the dignity of a smooth exit. Shame burning through every cell in my body, I turned silently and walked toward the door of the playroom.

I wished to God I could forget the sound of his cruel laugh. I knew it by heart, of course. The rasp to it, the very cadence that played through my fucked-up fantasies, it all came back to me as easy as that.

And that, more than anything else could, made me hate myself.

The man who had broken me and tossed me aside like trash could still issue one order and see me carry it out, and his satisfaction would bring *me* a dark and terrible, self-destructive pleasure.

I barely remembered yanking open my locker, shoving my way past the doorman, turning away from the entrance to the club…

And then fluorescent light made me freeze in my tracks, spilling from a bright pink storefront. It seemed oddly like a portal to another world, surreal and stark in the middle of the empty late-night street.

The banner over the shop read Daddy Cakes. Across the windows were painted cupcakes… and handcuffs, and other BDSM gear like I'd seen in play just minutes ago.

I wanted to laugh, or cry, or maybe both, but my steps took me closer.

The slogan was written on the door, bold and black.

Pig out or chill out—all welcome.

Drawn toward the light like a lost moth, I pushed open the door and walked in. My gaze roved across the space with its cream walls, plushy red chairs, and gold chandeliers. It would have looked at home in the pages of any magazine, except for the whips, chains, and terrifying small metal torture devices artfully arranged on the walls.

A glass display case showed off six varieties of cupcakes, and little tables and chairs were crammed in. Behind the register on the wall was a huge blackboard with the menu. A staircase led around the corner and upstairs with a bathroom sign and an arrow pointing up there.

But my eye was drawn to the corner right under the stairs, which was sectioned off with fairy light–draped railings. A little sign hung on the landing above. Care Corner, it read.

My throat was suddenly tight.

Aftercare. That great myth I'd read about online, daydreamed about, but never earned from Isaac in our two years of off-and-on dating.

Well, not dating. Let's be honest. *Fucking*. That was all I was to him: an object, a play toy, and not in a way that made me feel sexy.

"Can I help you?" The masculine voice shivered down my spine like a dripping of warm honey and leather, silky smooth.

And this time when I turned to look, the spark plugs flashed in my body all at once.

Yes.

The blond man behind the counter, wearing a leather apron and crisp white shirt, looked about twenty-four but oozed a kind of self-assurance in this space that told me he was the owner, not some random employee.

And he was *gorgeous*. Razor-sharp cheekbones, stubble I ached to feel against my inner thighs, green eyes that rooted my feet to the ground, and a straight, soft nose. His cheeks glowed with confidence I wished desperately I could buy like one of his perfect little cupcakes.

Oh, no. I'm a mess, and I'm going to make the worst first impression in front of the hottest guy of the night.

There was no question in my mind that he was a Dom. It was crazy to me—I'd never seen someone so young who carried such a presence with him. I hadn't thought it possible. I'd thought you had to be Seb's age, or at least my age, before you could make me tongue-tied. Apparently not.

My gaze fell to the ground again, fixed firmly on my toes as my cheeks burned hotter than the sun.

Fuck, he was going to judge me for being a scared, sniveling wreck of a man despite the two decades I had on him.

I should just—I should go, I thought. I should leave, and run, and bury the parts of me that screamed for release with anything I could, and pray that the lips of time would draw the sting from my wounds.

But when I turned, choked back my panic, and made a blind and desperate grab for the door handle, his voice rang out again.

"Wait."

There. The note that rang through his voice, in a single syllable, confirmed all my suspicions about him. This slip of a man could wrap me around his thumb in two more syllables, I was sure of it.

I didn't know him from Adam. Was I that desperate? That any Dom who wanted could bring me to heel?

No. No, there was something different flooding my body, and it was utterly unfamiliar. This man—nameless to me—was like a siren. I was under his spell, quivering and awaiting his next command.

"Sit in the Care Corner," the man continued, his voice softening. "You look like you need it. And let Daddy bring you a cup of green tea."

Him? A Daddy? *My* Daddy?

I should laugh. Or cry. Or… leave.

Leave, leave, leave, I told my body, but it wouldn't move. My dick and my heart and the needy, broken part of me had banded together to oust my brain from the decision-making council tonight.

It felt… It felt… holy crap. It felt like subspace.

I'd expected to be in Dom Nation when I slipped into this non-space, this timeless void, this single-minded purpose, this simple ritual of right and wrong, cause and effect, obedience and punishment.

Not in a brightly lit cupcake shop, staring at the black marble underfoot, my nose flooding with the aroma of sugar and spice and… something else that compelled my aching soul with the heady mix of softness and a whisper of danger.

Who knew where this would lead?

Despite the odds, I obeyed.

2

———————

REX

He didn't laugh at me.

Not mean-spirited, not with disbelief, not even in the *all right, I'll humor you just this once* way.

The invisible ropes around my throat went slack, and a smile touched my lips.

This man—this beautiful man with not so much an edge of fear in his eyes as a whole damn blade… he listened to me.

Well, not straightaway. That was only fair. No sub was obliged to listen to any random Dominant around. That was some old-school bullshit I didn't believe in.

He stood there, touching the door handle, head bowed and spirit drawn so tightly in on himself that it would bring anyone to tears. Then, he raised his head and turned, a faraway look in his eyes that I knew. I'd seen it many times before.

This man—this broken man with such deep, expressive eyes and a cyclone of emotions whirling around him—he needed me.

Instinct took the wheel.

No longer was I Rex Black, proprietor of the brand-new Daddy Cakes, nervous and excited about my very first real customer.

I was Master X.

Master X could handle a skittish, frightened, bruised boy; could kiss the tears from his cheeks, the dirt from his knees, and the stain from his soul.

I'd long ago stopped questioning my intuition about a man's… shall we call them, *inclinations*. This man might be twenty years my senior, but there wasn't a shadow of a doubt: he was a submissive.

The second he'd walked in, it was like I'd breathed in a cloud of pheromones. We were polar-opposite magnets, the pull between us stronger than gravity.

And that was why I was certain: however hard he fell, the part of me that was Master X—which was the best part of me— could pull him upright again.

"Here you go." I slid into the seat across from him at the table in the Cozy Corner and then carefully pushed one of the two cups across the table.

The brand-new white cups had small, elegant black roses twisting across them. I wanted custom cups with whips and chains, but they'd have to wait until I had more than one skittish boy of a customer.

His face tilted up at long last, his back straightening as he took the cup. "Thanks," he murmured. He didn't look at me, but at least he wasn't staring at his lap.

Which gave me the chance to examine him up close, and static interest danced along the backs of my hands. My palms itched with the desire to slide them across his rough cheeks and cup his angled jaw as I kissed his small, perfect lips. His eyes were big and a shade of light ice blue that stole my breath.

His hair was short and no-nonsense, a shade of dark blond that was highlighted with gray, and thick stubble I envied crept along his cheeks.

He looked in his midforties, with the laugh lines to prove it, and had square, solid shoulders. Through his white T-shirt, I easily made out the buckles and straps of a harness. Either that or he had some weird-ass nipple piercings.

And he was strong, too—arms with soft, natural muscles, not the kind one avoided carbs to show off. He couldn't be more different from my skinny, caffeine-fueled body. I itched to push him on his back and crawl over him, toying with him like a mouse with a cat.

As if entranced, the poor thing swayed where he sat, palms locked around the hot cup.

"Let me take the tea bag out," I told him. It took several seconds for him to loosen his grip on the hot porcelain, and I stopped worrying about him burning himself. I leaned in to fish it out with a spoon and set it on the saucer. "There you go.

What can I call you?" I asked softly. Might as well start with the easy question.

And, selfishly, I wanted a name to put to this beautiful face and gentle energy. Like knowing it would give me more power over him—power I only intended to use for his good.

But still, the intoxicating voice deep in my gut whispered, *power*.

"Call me?" He sounded faraway, his brow furrowing like I'd just asked him to triangulate our location with Jupiter and the moon.

I winced. He was lost in himself. I needed to start even easier. "Your name, boy," I told him. I didn't lay the emphasis on the last word like I might have if we were next door in the darkened, thumping rooms. I let it slip from my lips, soft and affectionate.

He twitched toward me like a stray in the doorway, guided there by an ancestral memory of human hands filled with kindness, warned away by its own short life.

Gently, I turned my hand up and slid it toward him. "Mine's Rex. I go by Master X in the scene." I wanted him to give me whatever name would make him most comfortable.

Well, no. I *wanted* to wrap my arms around him, pull him into my chest, and breathe into his hair as he clung to me. But for now, I couldn't risk spooking him away.

"Slate." His voice was rusty, like his throat was a gravel road. He cleared it and looked down at his cup of tea like he was seeing it for the first time. After taking a small sip, his voice was smoother. "Just Slate."

"Just Slate," I repeated, letting the word settle on my tongue like déjà vu. A memory of something that hadn't yet come to pass, a silvery fish flashing through the waters as my hand plunged into the river of life—

His palm, scorching hot, came to rest on mine. Lightning jumped between us, a flash of something visceral and hungry and invisible that left a hot aftertaste on my tongue.

Slate. The name scorched through me, bold and unique despite the man who seemed to want to melt into one of the other faceless clones I could find dollar-a-dozen in Dom Nation.

I clamped down my reaction so it was only the smallest twitch. He shuddered and pressed harder, all rough and imprecise and hungry. I closed my fingers softly along the edge of his hand, keeping my touch loose and gentle so he could pull away.

I'd give anything to seize Slate's hand and drag my palm up his arm, a soft and ghostly touch over the hair of his forearms and a hard, raking touch of my nails toward his bicep.

Focus, Rex. The boy needed a different kindness right now.

"Are you coming from the club?" I asked, even though the answer was obvious. I just wanted him to have to speak. It would help pull him out of the place he was in.

"Yeah. Straight from there," Slate said. His gaze was creeping up, on my cup now. I wrapped my hand around it and gradually raised it to my mouth to see what he'd do, but his gaze only tracked the object as far as my chest and then stayed there.

Oh, you've been hurt. Did someone leave you without aftercare? Push a boundary? Didn't any of the DMs spot it? A flash of anger rolled through me. Who was working tonight? I didn't care how long we'd been friends; I'd have words for them.

But, as was my habit in life, I hid every trace of my rage and concern. Subs picked up energy like that and grew nervous. So did others, in business or in friendships. I was the strong one, the in-control one. It wouldn't do to lose it, even for a moment.

"Do you want to talk about it?" I asked.

And finally, like a flash, his eyes raised and his gaze met mine. *Pierced* me to the spot, a storm whipping through the burning, pale, icy blue. Like he was judging whether he could lay his trust in me.

I stayed calm—didn't flinch, didn't look away, didn't even blink.

Seconds passed, but they might as well have been centuries. My world spun around and around again, orienting itself around this boy's next words. All of a sudden, he was the sun and I the planet blessed with his warmth, or cursed with his distance.

Which would it be?

Slate tore his gaze from me, and I felt empty, abruptly wobbling out of my orbit, crashing toward... I didn't know what. My grip tightened around his hand as I fought back the dizzying wave.

Instead, he watched the table again. "It started off nice. They let me in despite being..." Slate waved a hand up and down at himself.

I didn't understand the gesture. *Did he show up in street clothes? Did someone loan him gear? Oh, God. I hope he hasn't run away with it if so.* Although I tilted my head, Slate had moved on, not waiting for my answer.

I didn't want to interrupt the flow now that he was talking. I'd revisit this later.

"I got a drink. That was fine." Slate sounded like he was replaying it all in his head.

This was the part of the movie where they tricked you into thinking it was all going to be okay. I drew a measured breath so I didn't slide to the edge of my seat.

What he needed was calm, so I was calmer than a mountain, absorbing and not reflecting what he gave me.

"Someone talked to me on the dance floor. I think he was hitting on me. Seb."

Shit. Not Seb.

I'd known him for four years, since my twenty-first birthday when he'd watched me handle a sub with precision and delicacy and the cold brutality I was known for back then. He'd helped me grow warmer. Just a little, anyway.

I knew him well. I'd watched him at work with men of all kinds. I counted him one of my close friends. But if he'd scared this boy, I'd move heaven and earth for justice.

My heart pounded despite my outward calm.

Even so, Slate drew a quick breath and looked up at me, suddenly gripping my hand tightly. Like he'd sensed the fury under my skin—the fury so few had ever seen, much less felt.

"It wasn't him," he rushed to reassure me. "It was…"

Then he went silent, pulling back a little. His neck went stiff, and he pressed his lips together. It was like a ghost had slid into the seat beside him and put a finger on his lips.

And I knew.

I don't know how I knew—I just did. There were hundreds of men who came regularly or semi-regularly, and hundreds more who came as tourists, either once in a while or once and never again.

Some of them, I got along with. Others… by unspoken agreement, approaching them felt like oil and water forced through the same tap, so we kept apart. A few made me uneasy, their tastes so far from mine—but anyone who broke the rules, the DMs knew that the owner, Brighton, would throw them out at a moment's notice.

There was only one Dom who came every weekend who made my skin crawl.

Isaac.

There was no real reason why. He was glib and clever, cheerful to everyone, even welcoming to newbies. He'd never broken a rule or intruded on another's scene.

But some primal instinct—an unnameable chill on the back of my neck—had always been *aware* of him when he was around. I didn't like having my back to him, and I didn't laugh at his jokes like most of the others. Even Seb liked him, even Brighton.

Nobody had a bad word to say about him. And that was the craziest reason ever not to like someone, right?

Just like I couldn't explain how I felt about Isaac, I couldn't explain how I'd come to know whose name Slate was about to say, except that I'd briefly jumped a few seconds into the future.

Slate looked up at me, slow and careful, like he wasn't sure if he should run, and time caught up with itself again.

"Isaac."

The lack of surprise on my face—the deliberately sympathetic, unsurprised pinch I allowed in my lips—brought comfort to him. He breathed easier again, like saying the name had helped.

I hoped it had.

Isaac has to be stopped. All my focus shifted to that thought, burning through me like justice's own scales had been placed in my heart.

I didn't let go of his hand, but I rose to my feet.

"Where are you going?" Slate didn't flinch at the sudden movement, but he stared at me. Expectant, seeking, and truly clueless.

"To find Isaac," I said softly, cold and certain. I let the cruelty I'd left behind in those early days bleed back into my voice. "And fix this. And you're coming with me."

Slate yelped and dropped my hand, recoiling into the seat like lava had flowed into my skin, crackling with molten glory. "What? No, I can't!"

Oh, boys. They never knew their own limits. It brought a slight smile to my lips. It was job security for us Daddies, but it never failed to surprise me.

He'd had the strength to leave, to come find me, to spill his troubles. How much harder could it be to fix things?

"Yes, you can," I told him, keeping my hand outstretched. "You need backup, that's all. I'm here."

For you, I mentally added.

How odd it was that just minutes after meeting this man, I recognized the ebbs and flows of his energy like I'd been born to it. Not just because I knew what *boys* needed, but somehow, I knew what *Slate* needed.

"But…" I could see Slate talking himself out of it. The furrows of his brow, the fear in his eyes, it was all written plain as day on his face. He was searching for an excuse.

Patiently, I waited. He'd earned a little patience, after what he'd been through.

"You can't leave your shop," Slate finally said. After he spoke, he sat up, resolute. He even nodded slightly.

What a precious, silly boy. Like such a tiny detail would stop me.

I grinned, showing my teeth like a wolf who'd smelled blood. "Watch me." I turned and strode for the counter, grabbing a paper menu and a Sharpie from next to the register.

I flipped over the menu and wrote.

Back soon. Lick a dick while you wait.

Then I leaned so far over the register I almost cracked a rib, but my fingertips grazed the tape dispenser. I tore off a piece, strode to the glass door, and slapped the sign on it.

"There."

I turned to find that Slate had risen to his feet.

His hands were cupped and locked together the way our hands had been moments ago, but hovering in front of his chest. He twisted them together, dragging his fingertips along his palms and relocking them the other way.

God, he was beyond beautiful in his aching uncertainty, wavering on the edge of obedience to me.

In a flash, I could see it: hands over his head, straining toward me, voice breaking with pleas and passion. The tears I wanted to make fall from those pale eyes were utterly unlike the lost, numb tears that had gathered in the corners of his eyes right now.

"Come," I said, holding out a hand, prepared to wait for him to make up his mind and decide that I could be trusted.

I didn't have to wait. He came. He didn't take my hand, but by God, he came, and I'd never counted myself luckier.

Instead, he stayed a pace behind me, like he was keeping me between himself and the doorway. I could understand that, and I might have even taken a guilty moment of pleasure in it.

I was Slate's protector, his avenging archangel, and I was…

"Not dressed to get in tonight, I see. You—you're back. You're fine, Mr. Exhibitionist."

There was always an edge of rivalry in Tony's voice, and hearing his tone soften as he spoke to Slate made it starker than ever.

Like there was only room for one pretty young Dominant at a time, and letting me in risked his chances of getting lucky after the second shift relieved him later.

Usually I charmed him—and usually I showed up impeccably dressed, with no reason to turn me away, so all I had to deal with was his attitude and not the weight of Brighton's rules.

I sensed he wasn't eagerly seizing the chance to turn me away, though. Some bouncers would have done that, at more pretentious places nearby. He was just commenting. My respect grew one tiny notch.

And I had no time to deal with this shit. As we spoke, Isaac went unchallenged, and the hurt in this man's voice needed to be heard.

"Whoa," Tony breathed.

I hadn't even said a word. All I'd done was straighten up and level my best Dominant stare at Tony. I was used to showing people who I was in a single look: not their coffee boy in the boardroom, nor their sub in the darkroom.

Tony took a step back, like I'd drawn the metaphorical sword of justice I felt weighing down my hand. Still, he hadn't moved aside from the doorway yet.

"We're not staying," I murmured, low. I didn't need to add, *You know me, and you know I'm supposed to be in my shop. I'm not just bringing a boy toy in for a fun time.*

Tony swallowed once and nodded. "See that you don't." He grudgingly stepped to one side, his gaze following each of us as we walked in.

"Whoa," Slate whispered behind me, his voice an echo of Tony's, and while he couldn't see me, I let myself smile.

Yeah. That's what having a Dom around can do.

I was in charge. And it was intoxicating.

But before I made it out of the entryway, a hand closed tightly around my arm, dragging me to a halt. My body tingled with recognition like Slate's biometrics were keyed into the alarm system in my brain.

"Yes?" I turned and looked pointedly down at the hand gripping me.

Slate didn't let go. But seeing as he wasn't *my* sub, I'd allow the misbehavior.

"No," Slate said softly. "You can't get off on this."

I narrowed my gaze, trying to make sense of his words. "I'm not bringing you to the sling to fuck the sadness away," I told him tartly. "Tony would make me get naked, and I don't do that."

"I mean," Slate said, still squeezing my arm like it was the brake on a freight train and he was on the tracks ahead of me, "get off on... on... rescuing me."

What? Indignation bloomed in my cheeks, and it cut a little too finely. Like he'd discovered a truth that even I hadn't realized.

"Excuse us," someone said behind me, which pissed me off.

Slate guided me to the side and stepped close, out of the way. He was closer than he'd ever been—too close, but not nearly enough at the same time.

The air between our bodies swelled, and so did my arousal. Sparks slid through my body, intoxicating and heady. I kept him at arm's length, but only barely.

I glared until the intruders scuttled past and then returned my gaze to Slate. Those pale blue eyes were wide and pleading. His look melted the heat within me—the embarrassment of being caught out with a hero complex.

"That's my call," Slate said softly. "And I say no."

I reeled on the spot. The last thing I'd expected from a shy, scared man who'd been used and left to crawl home on his own was these blazing fierce words. Even moments ago, he'd hardly been able to speak.

And now he was standing up to me?

"Reporting assaults… is critical," I told him. "It's not about *me*." *Okay, maybe it is, a little bit,* I added mentally and winced. A white lie for the greater good. "It's about everyone's safety. The DMs will listen to you. Brighton, the club owner… I know him. He'll listen, too," I told him, my voice rippling as I swore by my honor. "The minute you speak up, he'll be gone forever."

Please listen, I begged him in my thoughts, even if I stayed cool and logical outwards. *You have to listen.*

"You don't understand," Slate hissed, upset creeping into his tone, and I stepped back like I'd been burned.

Hearing the rebuke in his words cut me to the bone more deeply than I could ever have imagined. I choked back the bile in my throat. "What don't I understand?"

My answer, in turn, was sharper than I'd meant it. *Shit. Shit!* I thought. *It's my job to be better than that. Focus, Rex!*

However hurt he was, I had to be steady for his sake.

"You can't talk to the staff. None of them," Slate told me, and my world careened to one side.

It sounded like… *he* was giving *me* an order. My brain reacted like a cat who'd just seen its carrier, screeching to an undignified halt.

My jaw dropped as I stared at Slate, ignoring the next group of men to brush past us, laughing and talking loudly. They might as well have been miles away.

But Slate met my eyes and didn't flinch. "That's my hard limit," he told me, with a hint of a cocky smile on his lips.

My cheeks burned. I felt like I'd been tricked—used, somehow —by this boy who'd pretended to need my help, and now he was just here to arrogantly smile in my face and ignore my rage.

And oh, for a brief but intense few seconds, all I craved was a tool in my hand and a way to make him pay. Surely he couldn't have made up the whole thing just to grab my attention, right?

But no—he wasn't a brat leading me on a merry dance. Under his words, I still heard a wobble of uncertainty. He wouldn't look away from me, his gaze searching. His grip on me never faltered.

Like Slate was gathering the very last of his courage to stare a strange Dominant in the face and defy him.

Christ, I respected him. And I *wanted* him. I couldn't distinguish between the two.

That fire suddenly stirring in his blood called to my own, which roared through my body like a hurricane. I needed to taste that boldness for myself, to undo whatever part of him held it back, and stand in its heart, let it rage around me, revel in its delicate rage…

Breathe. My thought came to me as if from far away. I breathed, and I almost staggered under my own weight again.

I'd been enchanted by Slate before, but now I was utterly ensnared.

"Fine," I whispered.

If he said that was his boundary, I had to respect it. Isaac had clearly broken at least one boundary, and I'd never earn Slate's trust by trampling over them in the name of helping him.

So I had to call Slate on his bluff.

"F-Fine?" The momentary stutter, however slight, made my breath exhale in a whoosh.

Yes. This reaction, this hesitant relief, was honest and raw. No games here.

I nodded once and then touched his fingers, ignoring the crawl of pleasure down my spine at such a simple touch. "Now, before I lose this arm…"

Slate flinched and pulled his hand away whip-quick. "Sorry," he murmured.

But I followed his hand and caught it, squeezing until his gaze returned to mine again. When it finally did, I asked, "What do you need?"

"I…" Slate's brow furrowed, and though he paused for a few seconds, he didn't seem to come any closer to words. Frustrated, he shook his head. "I don't know what I want."

"No," I said and let go of his hand, folding my arms and studying him. God, I wished I could unravel him and lay out the pieces. Get to understand him, then carefully glue him back together. "What do you need?"

There—I saw it. The answer was in his eyes for just a second before his gaze flicked to the left and it disappeared. I was breathless, rapt with attention at the subtlest cue.

Had he ever even sensed it was there, or was he so cut off from his own instincts that it had come and gone without a trace?

Slate shook his head and said nothing, and my throat tightened. He wasn't going to answer. I hadn't earned it yet.

That was, despite the sting to my pride, fair.

I was *not* his Dominant.

Yet, whispered the same voice that had known about Isaac, and because I didn't know what to do with that feeling, I slammed it into a box and locked it shut with everything I had.

Silly, stray passing thoughts.

I knew what I needed: to earn his trust.

"Come sit in the shop with me," I said after a few moments had passed. "Be my good-luck charm."

I needed to get back there, after all, if I wanted to attract my first real customer. Before long, guys would get what they needed and begin to leave the club as others arrived.

"I'm not good luck," Slate mumbled, and I grinned. Was that an obstinate streak? Or was he that wounded? Either way, I could fix that. Given an evening with him, I could help him give himself permission to feel good.

Even without making him cry so I can get off on it, I thought while swallowing a sigh. *Call it an act of altruism. I should be written down as a hero.*

"Whether I get any customers or not, I'm getting lucky tonight." I winked instead, thrumming with pleasure when he smiled. I took a step back toward the doorway, and Tony, and my shop, and held out a hand to him.

"Come, boy," I said softly. But this wasn't a command—it was an offer.

Well, I'll be damned.

He took my hand. He fucking took my hand.

"Yes, Daddy."

And the vulnerability in his voice broke me to pieces. I was supposed to be the strong one, but the shards of me pulsed with something soft and scared and… thrilled.

Overjoyed. Ecstatic. *Correct*. Like it was meant to be.

I'd heard other men—plenty of other men—call me that. None had ever had this effect on me.

Surely I was misremembering. Surely they had, and I'd forgotten. I needed the open air, *now*, or I was going to do something dumb like pull him into me and kiss the words from his lips, or…

I led him outside and tipped my face up to the dark sky and breathed for dear life. I could do this—I must, and I would.

But what I couldn't do in those short few steps between the darkened, pulsing, thumping kink club and my bright, shiny new shop was turn to look at him.

Suddenly, the fear was hot and irrational and heavy in my chest that the moment I did, he'd vanish. All of this would be gone.

He'd disappear, turn tail and run, or worse yet melt away like a figment of my overactive hero fantasies. I'd be back to leaning on the counter, daydreaming and bored and excited and afraid that I'd made a terrible mistake opening this shop anyway.

But the boy's fingers were warm. His broad palm trembled in mine but never pulled away. I pushed open the shop door and finally looked over my shoulder, and Slate was still there.

For the first time, he smiled—and the warmth in his eyes, the dimples in his cheeks, the white flash of his teeth made the careening world find its balance once more.

But I never stopped falling.

3

———

SLATE

"I've never held so many dicks at once." I bounced the plastic bag of tiny penis-shaped candies up and down in one hand. "The small ones are the cutest."

Rex was quick to laugh, his eyes shining with real appreciation for my childish joke. Like I wasn't a burden to have around, but a pleasure.

Thank God I was out of that dreamy, foggy world now. I was a little sheepish about how much of a helpless little thing I'd acted. *A man my age shouldn't need to be coddled by a man his age.* I was ashamed, a little bit, of having been rescued by a Daddy.

Of letting myself be saved when I didn't deserve it.

Regardless of the guilt at the naughty treat, I'd bought a cupcake from him as soon as we got back here, and another cup of green tea. He'd tried to give them to me for free, but I'd insisted.

That had helped. I felt more like a person again, less of a flame waiting for its match—pure unrealized potential, purer for its theoretical state. Schrodinger's danger.

I leaned on the wrong side of the counter. Like I knew anything about running the till. It was a tight space back here, with a batch of cupcakes currently baking in the oven just below the steel countertop. Jars of decorating supplies were arranged along a shelf above my head, and the display cabinet had a list of flavors taped to the back.

Rex stood on the customers' side, a hand on the counter as he watched me exploring the space. His head tilted this way and that as he looked around the shop.

He didn't even seem to notice the way his long fingers stroked the counter—like he was proud. Or possessive.

Like yearning for a motherland I'd never set foot upon, I ached to be the one under his hand, his touch dragging every ounce of shame from my skin.

Filling me with purpose, and perhaps more.

"Larger dicks are available," Rex said.

"Plural?" I teased, looking him up and down like he was the one on show.

A sly little grin appeared on Rex's face. "If required. Mechanical or otherwise."

"One is enough for me," I told him softly. "If it's the right one." Hardly able to believe my own boldness, I met his eyes. But it was far easier when I wasn't in that soft, pliable state, like clay for his molding.

Rex gave me a small smile and then looked away, his gaze distant and his hand going still on the countertop. Didn't say anything, just gazed out the door.

My throat went tight with disappointment. I wanted to know whether monogamy suited him, too. Even if I'd wanted to, I couldn't hide my interest in Rex.

It wasn't just that I was grateful for him stepping in during my hour of need. Something in him called to me, and here I was, answering that call.

But maybe Rex—or Master X, as he'd called himself—was taken. That was a possibility I hadn't considered.

Or not interested right now. Retired from the scene? At his age? It seemed unlikely, but I didn't know how it worked.

All I knew was that he had instincts as strong as Isaac's, and he was ten times gentler. Like a pendulum, I wondered how far he'd swing the other way—when he was clinging to the edge of self-control, another man's pleasure in his hands.

He listened to me earlier, I thought. *I didn't think Doms did.*

I'd tried not to obsess over every detail of the night so far. There would be time for that later. Months and years, probably. I wanted to live in the moment first, before trying to preserve it.

That would make a change.

Rex wandered toward the window and folded his arms tightly. "It's getting busier out there," he murmured, squinting against the darkness outside the glass-fronted shop.

A few customers had wandered in over the last hour, but not many. He'd sold maybe a dozen cupcakes since I'd arrived. I had no idea if that was a busy or quiet night for him.

Was he anxious for more customers? He didn't *seem* anxious.

The oven timer dinged, harsh and sudden by my ear. I jumped, but before I could settle, Rex turned and strode toward me. "Get out or get back," he warned.

It was breathtaking, his sudden and single-minded focus. Having tasted it before, my body recognized it again and thrilled at the sight.

I opted to step back, crunching myself up against the display case to give him plenty of elbow room as he slid his hands into white oven mitts and opened the oven door.

Hot air rushed out, making him simply blink and turn his head away for a moment as I flinched and cowered back.

"It won't hurt you," Rex promised, a smile touching his lips. He set the tray well out of reach and the oven mitts down next to it, stacking them atop one another with precision before stroking them gently.

Even that tiny gesture told me something else about him: there was no careless brutality, like—like *others*. No, this man would be a meticulous and methodical Daddy.

"If you stick around long enough for these to cool, you can decorate one. It calms and focuses the mind."

I couldn't help noticing he hadn't stepped away from me. I was trapped at this end of the counter between the glass display case and Rex, who had placed one hand on the counter on either side of him.

Nowhere to run, and I didn't want to.

I slowly raised a brow at him. Why the hell would he want me to help decorate? Was I cheap labor, or did he want to make me feel better? I was totally unqualified to create anything like the beautiful creations in his cabinet.

"Are you calling me unhinged?" I asked, folding my arms with a pout.

"God, no."

I'd meant to tease him, but Rex's voice was serious. He shifted, popping a hip and leaning on the customer-facing counter, his fingertips still casually brushing the prep counter like he wanted to stop me squeezing past him.

But it was Rex's eyes that stopped me there, the warm gold of liquid honey layered over light brown toast. He scrutinized me like he was trying to pick me apart and put me together all at once.

My heart hammered and I stayed silent, waiting to see what he'd do.

"I've never had a boy defy me like that all of a sudden," Rex told me. "Still waters run deep for you, don't they?"

I licked my lips, my gulp echoing in the quiet air of the cupcake shop. "Yes," I told him. And nothing else.

I didn't even know the layers of crap in my own head. Good luck to anyone else who thought they could sort through it all.

I didn't elaborate—that felt like talking about our personal lives, and we'd both avoided that so far.

Whatever his reasons, Rex was reticent with details. And I didn't want to risk going into it and blabbing about Isaac. That elephant in the room could stay right where it was, thanks very much.

"I was thinking," Rex finally said, spinning on his heel and freeing me abruptly, but trailing a hand along the counter the whole way. "I need to pass out samples. So it might get boring for you."

He doesn't want me in the way. I understood instantly. I'd worked at trade shows to make ends meet in university. If you were busy talking to friends, people wouldn't come and talk to you.

But Rex wasn't thinking creatively enough.

A slow smile spread over my face, and a shiver ran down my spine straight to the tips of my toes.

Suddenly, I was keenly aware of the tightness of my leather shorts and the supple leather stretching across my chest. Warm metal buckles and rings pressed into my flesh just hard enough to remind me of my station.

"Explain yourself," Rex told me, the seductive thread of command weaving into his words.

It was fascinating how he could switch it on so naturally. I might hardly notice, if only that aura didn't almost bring me to my knees. The need to please him. Like a working dog who needed to follow its instincts or a bird on a migratory flight, I knew what to do.

"Do you have a serving tray?"

Still eyeing me until the last moment, Rex slid between the countertops and turned away to dig a tray out from a cupboard.

As he did, I swallowed every ounce of my nerves. It felt like I was straining at the bit, waiting.

When Rex came out from behind the counter, I held a hand out and took the tray as he gave it to me. It was a little larger than a dinner plate, but not by much.

"I could serve for you."

I articulated the words carefully, even though that one little article didn't want to slip out. Serve *for* him. Not serve him.

Right?

Rex held very still, like he'd seen the most rare and precious of birds and he didn't want to startle it away. "What do you mean?" The flicker of hope on his face was unmistakable.

Slowly, maintaining eye contact the whole time, I sank to my knees. It felt like I wobbled the whole way down. Ten or twenty years ago, I could have bounced down in a split second, but now I had to take more care.

I couldn't shake the feeling that I didn't look so much dignified as creaky and ridiculous. But I was this far in, and I had to keep going, even if I was about to humiliate myself.

Dammit, that's not supposed to wake you *up,* I told Slate Junior, but it was a losing battle. I'd known for years that the surest way to get me hard was to make me feel so very small.

A boy, entirely at his master's whims.

My hands trembling, I bowed my head and bent forward, resting the tray awkwardly across the back of my neck and my shoulders.

From here, I could hardly see Rex. My gaze was fixed firmly on the floor as I bent over, humble and quivering with fear that I was about to hear him laugh, or mock me, or say something cutting.

And worst of all—most fucked-up of all—that I was about to *enjoy* my own mortification.

But instead, as I struggled to keep my breathing even and my hands steady around the edges of the tray, all I heard was footsteps soft against the shiny, tiled floor.

Rex stopped just in front of me. "Would you enjoy that?" he asked, a hand brushing against my downturned cheek.

Warm and solid, like a silent promise not to rip me apart with his words and his derision. To strengthen me, instead, by allowing me this submission I so desperately craved.

"Yes, sir," I whimpered, need abruptly slamming into my belly with all the force of a long-silenced confession. The answer left my lips no sooner than it found me.

Until he'd asked, I hadn't realized how much I needed it. I'd come to the club to be used and then melt into the furniture again, overlooked and safe. Not scrutinized and humiliated by the attention I didn't deserve.

And finally, a nail ran along the itch deep in my filthy soul with the promise—even just the chance—of relief.

"Please let me do this," I whispered, my voice rough. I could hardly breathe as I kept begging him mentally, rocking back and forth. *Please, please, please.*

His hand rested on my shoulder, steadying me. When I was still, Rex crouched in front of me, bringing his face almost to mine. I could see his chin now, even as I stared at the floor.

"Yes," Rex told me, speaking with that same precision. His voice had a hint of brutality to it, a cold cruelty that spoke to the fiery, rough pieces of me. Sandpaper to my coarse parts, and blessed relief.

My sigh of pleasure stilled my trembling body. *Yes!* He wasn't going to regret this, I swore to myself.

"But," Rex added, keeping his grip firm on my shoulder, "I'm going to be right here. The moment anyone makes you feel uncomfortable, you stand up. Throat punch them with the tray if you need to. And you come inside. Tell Daddy if *anyone* makes you feel like shit."

I swallowed hard. There it was again: the frozen fire I'd heard in his voice before he dragged me into Dom Nation. For a heady moment, I let myself believe I was worthy of his ferocity.

I bobbed my head, the tray sliding toward the floor as I readjusted it. *No nodding. No reactions at all, or I'll drop all his precious, sweet treats on the ground.*

How still could I stay as I throbbed and groveled with delight?

"And if I give you an order," Rex continued, "you obey me. Immediately." He stroked my shoulder once, languid and slow, and my blood heated up.

I *wanted* him to order me. By God, I'd do anything he asked, right here and now, if only he would. But despite the fierceness of my wanting, he didn't.

"I'm aware of what I'm asking of a boy who I have no claim to," Rex said softly. "So I won't ask anything sexual of you. Understood?"

Fuck. *Fuck*, I wished he hadn't spoken at all! I'd do anything to pluck those words from the air and stuff them back in his mouth.

Didn't Rex understand what I wanted from him? *Needed*?

I *was* unworthy of this attention. He was just humoring me, allowing me to help him out. He didn't want me in all the filthy ways I wanted him to want me.

Not when there were hundreds of young, handsome boys who hadn't yet been broken. Fresh-faced and innocent, unlike me. I was already soiled.

I ought to crawl out of his shop right now, ugly and old, and let the men waiting in line outside Dom Nation laugh at me for thinking I deserved more.

"Yes," I breathed, harsh and hoarse. I was clinging to the scrap of permission I'd heard in his tone despite his words denying me what I wanted so badly. "Yes, Daddy."

Rex's hands glided across the edges of my own, which were still curled around the edges of the tray. Instantly, the hair on my arms stood to attention and heat danced along my spine, like I was a balloon and his touch ignited static shocks.

He guided my fingertips open, coaxing me into releasing the tray, and took it from me. Then he rose to his feet and set it on the counter with a sharp sound.

I stayed where I was, my chin tucked against my chest and ribs crushing into my knees. Like a neat little bundle of razor-sharp longing, and at the heart of it, squeezed between my thighs, my hard-on throbbed in a drumbeat of desire.

Own me, own me, own me, it seemed to beg, and I tightened my thighs around it—twitched with the surge of heat that coursed through me at the tiny, silent, naughty pleasure.

"Stand and strip to your gear," Rex said. His voice was melodic and enchanting again, like a song pulling me into a big, blue wilderness that would flay me alive.

I knew he meant the leather shorts and harness I wore.

I followed it and stood, though I kept my head bowed. My pride made me clamp my throat as my knees wobbled and back twinged, but I made it upright without falling.

My hands rose to my waist as I wavered, wondering what to take off first. Going for my pants first seemed too bold. Shirt it was, then.

It was easier not to look up at Rex, so as I nervously gripped the lower hem of my shirt, I didn't.

The choice was more of a struggle than I'd expected. I wanted to see the emotions written over his face. What did he think of me? Amusement, desire, or studied neutrality?

I was too afraid of what I'd find, so I didn't look. And he said nothing, and the silence—the silence that ticked, ticked, ticked… it was nothing less than agonizing.

Once I'd stripped my shirt off, I had nowhere else to hide. Yet again tonight, I unbuttoned my jeans. But I hesitated. Not just because I wanted to hide the length that pressed into my thigh.

I could hardly bear the gaze, even though I was about to serve strangers in the street. *That* should be what stretched my limit —it was by far the bravest I'd ever been.

But I didn't have to look at Rex to know that he was watching me the way he had earlier, like I was the only thing that mattered. Cool and confident. Letting me let go of everything —giving over my safety and my pride to him for safekeeping.

In here, it was personal, and so much harder than what I was about to do, because Rex wasn't letting me melt away into the walls. No, I was stripping for him.

I sat on a chair to pull my jeans off and put my shoes back on. When I stood up again, that feeling of nakedness returned.

"Good boy," Rex praised softly, cupping my cheek. He didn't make me look at him or say another word. He just touched and let go, moving behind the counter.

I heard him take out a cupcake from the display cabinet with a click and cut it into pieces for samples, humming softly. I didn't recognize the melody, but I smiled.

Once the tray was loaded, never once looking at him, I took it back and followed him out the door. Nerves shuddered through me. Suddenly that bravery I'd been so sure of was faltering.

If I didn't look up at anyone, I could do this. I had to do it. I wanted to do it.

What do you need? Rex had asked.

This. This was the answer.

Come on, Slate. Trust him. Trust yourself.

One foot in front of the other, I walked outside. I risked a glance up at the noise nearby. It was louder out here now, groups of men standing around, talking and partying with drinks.

Nothing explicit outside, of course—but groups of men catching up, some arriving and others leaving. Some smoked and laughed, and others hid drink cups from the guy at the door.

There were at least a dozen, and more in the lineup along the sidewalk, waiting to get in. It was buzzing with activity now. All those eyes. All those men. All my hopes, spilling messily from my soul into my imagination.

The breeze was cool on my thighs and chest and back. The cold had never bothered me, thank God.

Someone called out a greeting to Rex, and he called back, "Hey."

The sharp sounds—the eyes that turned our way—made me shrink back and flinch, my grip painful around the edges of the serving platter. I stared down at the cupcake crumbs like they could save me.

Rex's thumb touched my cheek. His first knuckle dragged along the roughness of my jaw, the tiny, sensual touch pulling me back out of my head.

Focusing my attention on Rex. None of them mattered. *He* mattered. Tonight, he was my Daddy, and he was going to take care of me.

"Kneel," Rex said. It wasn't the cruel command that one fucked-up, broken part of me wanted to hear, but the confidence in his voice swelled my chest with warmth anyway.

Right here on the sidewalk, I did.

Rex swiftly plucked the tray from my hands, helping steady it while I sank down until I was kneeling.

Oh God, I was doing it. Really, *really* doing it.

The sidewalk was gritty and cold under my knees. My joints twinged at the strange position, but I eagerly folded into myself and hunched over. Rex's palm slipped off my cheek as I bent my head too low for him to reach.

I reached up, silently asking, and Rex gave. He slid the cool, metal tray onto the slope of my shoulders.

It felt so tender, giving over my power. But I was safe in Rex's hands. I had to be, right? If I'd misjudged again, trusted a man who hurt me... I'd crumble into the finest dust.

Rex cupped the tray, steadying it and me, guiding my body into a strangely comfortable position. Balanced perfectly, and utterly still. No fidgeting or shrinking away from roaming eyes and Dominant stares.

No matter what happened, I had to hold on. Even if I got used and teased, I'd be unable to move a muscle. That made me so fucking hard it hurt, and I was grateful my position hid my... difficulty.

It drove me wild, knowing this restraint was somehow more voluntary. More taboo. Psychological alone.

So why did I feel it pulsing deep inside, pulsing and red-hot?

His words rang through my head, over and over again. *I won't ask anything sexual of you.*

"Comfortable?" Rex brushed my fingertips, making one more adjustment to the tray before stepping back.

I couldn't look at him *and* ask this of him. Shame stopped my lips. But here...

"You could make it sexual if you wanted," I whispered. "T-Torment me."

I had to hold perfectly still, listen for a reaction. Strain to peer ahead of me, through my lashes. I couldn't see much. Not without moving, which was off-limits.

Rex's boots shifted on the concrete. One crept toward me, between my parted thighs. Nudged—just barely—the head of my cock, outlined clear as day against my painfully tight shorts.

The prickles through my belly, deep down to my very balls, made me gasp.

"We'll see how well you serve tonight," Rex told me, his voice maddeningly calm and quiet.

I whimpered, but all he did was chuckle softly, touch my cheek, and step back.

Arousal bloomed through my whole body, and I trembled in the cool evening air. My knees hurt, grinding into the concrete. And a smile strained at my cheeks, the stress bleeding from me as men came closer, laughed, accepted Rex's offer of a sample.

Ignored my needs and fulfilled their own.

Fuck. *This* was the feeling I'd come here for tonight. And Rex had barely had to lay a finger on me to fulfill it.

I smiled until my cheeks hurt, crouched perfectly still until the tray was empty—and then another. Alone in the crowd, still and obedient in the darkness, my joy stitched together a gulf in my soul.

4

REX

"Watch out. Isaac's on the hunt tonight."

I couldn't show fear. Not with Slate out there on the sidewalk still, waiting for my command to come inside.

"Isaac's always in a foul mood," I told Seb, my voice taut as I kept an eye on Slate outside. I dipped in to ring up customers, but otherwise I'd stayed near him until now. "Tell me something new."

My older Dom friend snorted and tipped his head, acknowledging my point. As charming as Isaac could be to fellow Doms, he flew into tempers. Everyone knew that. And now, Seb sounded unsure—like he was seeing past the façade. "Worse than usual," Seb told me, soft and meaningful. My skin crawled. "He was brutal with Derrick tonight."

Derrick was tough, as subs went. A glutton for punishment. I'd seen him in play-piercing scenes never breaking a sweat. If Isaac had gotten to *him* tonight… precious, shy, sweet Slate had no chance.

The silence drew out as I gazed at the back of the display case, counting cupcakes.

God, I want to tell him. But I didn't even know the story yet. And whatever story it was, it belonged to Slate, and Slate didn't belong to me. I needed to hold that trust until *he* was ready to talk.

More importantly, my boy was still out there on the sidewalk —and Isaac would be leaving Dom Nation soon. I couldn't let Isaac find him. My blood heated up to the danger.

"See you later," Seb told me, looping his arm around his catch for tonight and pulling him along.

The only ones left in Daddy Cakes now were a pair of men who had long ago finished their cupcakes. An older Daddy in a black shirt, his sleeves rolled up, and a twentysomething cub of a boy. They were still sitting at a corner table flirting. I recognized them but not their names.

I slammed the display case closed and announced, "I'm closing." My voice was sharp and loud, to attract their attention.

"What? Why?" the cub asked, turning to look at me.

"We're out of cupcakes," I told them, leveling a glare at them. *We're closing because I said so, boy* was the look in my eyes.

The Daddy looked at the display case and the half a dozen remaining treats in it. He looked confused. "No, you're not—"

"Yes, I am. Because I said so."

My cheeks flushed as I stormed past them to the door. *Great dominance display there, dipshit,* I told myself. *Because I said so? Jesus.*

But I had far more important things on my mind, like relieving my boy of his duties. It was only a shame I couldn't ethically exchange all of his troubles for my load.

I yanked open the door and walked out of the shop toward Slate, who still knelt on the sidewalk. Pity I didn't have time to linger and drink in the sight, because it was more erotic than a whole damn porn shop.

Out here in the open, he was exposed in plain sight, his head bowed. It was enough to take my breath away, just one glance at him.

He was patiently crouching exactly as I'd left him, his broad shoulders steady and strong under the silver tray. To my eye now, he looked like a rock to my ship veering off course, swept by the tide...

Shit. There was no time to dwell on the way he pulled me toward him, because I heard Isaac. A quick scan of the crowd found him in a group near the entrance of the club. He wasn't looking this way, but at any moment, he might.

Standing between him and Slate, I crouched in front of him and pulled the nearly empty tray from his hands. He had to be stiff now. An hour had passed in the blink of an eye. For me, anyway.

I needed to get him to safety.

I put one hand on Slate's shoulder and gripped the tray with the other. I lifted it easily from his tired fingers, pressing my thumb into the stiff muscles of his neck.

God, my *God*, I wanted to reward his beautiful submission. If I were his Daddy, I'd slide him into a hot shower and rub out all the stiffness in his body. Even *that*. Especially that.

Heat surged through me. I wanted to kneel in front of him and pull him into me, kiss the breath out of him.

As I took the tray away, Slate lurched. His hands fell to the pavement, but he stayed where he was, head down. Waiting for orders.

Such a fucking good boy. He deserved sweetness and light and kisses, not the marks I ached to leave along his bare skin. I bit back the whimper that tried to slip free. *Safety first*, I reminded myself.

I didn't know how much time we had before we were noticed. I resisted the urge to look over my shoulder and risk meeting Isaac's eye.

"That's all," I told him, firmly. Leaving no room for argument. "I'm closing. Come inside—now."

He moved slowly, like wading through molasses, so I gripped his forearms to haul him to his feet. It took all of my strength and most of his.

As he stood, I kept my body between him and the clusters of laughing merrymakers. Not because I was jealous. Just so my shy, self-conscious boy didn't melt under the weight of prying eyes.

Fear clamped my throat like loops of rope, and I let go of him abruptly.

No. No, not *my* boy.

He went still and stood where I'd let go of him, and I kicked myself. *Act first, think later, Rex.* He was waiting for my cues, and I couldn't let him down now.

Almost there... almost safe. I opened the shop door and put my hand against his bare back.

Desire surged in me, my palm throbbing at the contact. I wanted to slide my whole forearm across his skin and around his ribs, and pull him back into me until he was locked against my body.

I steered him inside and kept talking, even if I wasn't getting answers. "In you go. Have a seat."

The other couple had left. Good. We were alone. I turned the lock.

Slate sank into a chair, his hands folded in his lap and back straight. He gazed into the distance.

Like he was waiting for me. And—fuck, I could hardly think straight. My fear for his safety from Isaac mingled with my own derision.

Look at you, getting all attached, I taunted myself. *Face it, a boy would only be another project. You don't know how to treat people like anything else.*

Being so new, the blinds were a little stiff, but I hauled the chains quickly and blocked out the large window along the front of the shop. Then I flipped the sign on the door and pulled that blind down, too.

Then I went behind the counter, quickly assembling a six-pack cupcake box and placing the leftover cupcakes into each slot.

"What are you doing?"

"Paying you," I answered, my hands trembling. *Please let me give you something. I can't give you what you seek.*

Slate chuckled, sleepy as his bedroom eyes. "There are other options," he said.

I shook my head, just as much at myself as him. It made me tingle with too much interest when he spoke like that. I'd promised him—myself, too—that I wouldn't ask anything sexual of him.

I'd almost slipped, just that once. My toe nudging the hard bulge of his cock, and the sinfully pornographic gasp of pleasure that had racked his body. I'd wanted to keep going, to test the limits of how steady and still he could hold while I drew him to the edge, right there in public—

But no. Not while he was in God only knew what frame of mind thanks to that *asshole* who'd dared to hurt him.

Letting it continue between us would be a mistake. Because what he didn't know yet was that I was just as bad as Isaac in my own way—the rest of the world just hadn't figured it out yet.

The jokes and laughter that hid the cold brutality and the cravings for unspeakable things, of pain and blood and hurt... I hated them in Isaac most of all because they were a mirror to the parts of me I feared.

No, I didn't fear them. I feared what they would do to *this* boy in particular.

"Are you angry?" Slate asked quietly, startling me. I spun on my heel to look at him, my eyes wide. His face was upturned, seeking answers more than anything.

Christ. Had he sensed my shift in energy that easily? It made my gut churn, thinking of anyone being able to see behind my mask. I'd practiced it for long enough. It had to be a coincidence.

"No," I told him quickly and firmly. "No, boy. I'm not."

A quiet sigh escaped, and a smile touched his lips. He closed his eyes. "Good," he hummed. It sounded almost like he'd been drinking, he was so hazy.

I closed the box and set it on the counter, then came around the end.

Fuck. Slate needed aftercare, and I was too caught up in my own mental crap. I twitched my fingers in a gesture for him to stand up.

He rose without hesitation, his eyes filled with a trust I didn't deserve. Anger sparked in my chest again. *Oh, you sweet boy, but so dumb for trusting me*, I thought, pressing my lips together.

I wrapped my arms around him anyway, squeezing hard. Doing my duty. Pulling him back to Earth from outer space.

He was solid in my arms, like a brick wall. Yet he'd been so fluid, so graceful when he sank to the ground, kneeling for me. That dichotomy fascinated me.

I was the same tough, no-nonsense Dominant all the way through. What you saw was what you got. But Slate? He had layers to him—layers that made me want to dig into him and pick him apart.

It was impossible to ignore Slate's skin on display like a buffet. My palms were hot against his back, and my fingers spread of their own accord. My fingertips pressed in, his muscles shifting and denting under the touch, right under my nose.

The buckle of Slate's harness dug into my rib, and I shifted against him to ease the pressure. My thigh slid between his legs, and his breath hitched as he shivered against me.

It took all my strength to ignore his cues. My instinct wanted to press Slate down against a table and run my hands up his body until he begged for release. I wanted to wring every droplet of pleasure from him, for hours on end.

After a few seconds—the normal length of a hug—Slate's grip loosened awkwardly, but I wasn't fooled. I kept holding him, my hand sliding to the back of his head. Keeping him there, in place.

Waiting.

Slate's breathing hitched, and his weight shifted away from me, and still I held on.

There. He gulped hard, his arms suddenly going around my back again, the stiffness draining away all at once. He was clinging to me, desperately, like I was his last lifeline.

There we go.

"It's okay, sweetie," I murmured, scratching my fingers into his scalp in tiny circles, soothing and steadying him until he was ready. "Take your time."

"I forgot," Slate swallowed hard again, turning his head until his nose pressed into my jaw. Nuzzling softly, like a cat. The intimacy, sudden and startling, shocked me out of my rhythm. "How strange it is. Coming out of that place."

"Yes," I murmured, distant. My heart thumped, fear filling my throat once again. Fuck me, he called to something within me that utterly scared me. Particularly because it didn't *feel* wrong.

It was as natural as breathing right now.

When Slate pulled away from me again, I let him go, my arms falling to my sides, limp and useless.

But Slate's eyes gleamed. "Are you going to invite me home?"

I gulped at the wave of yearning that swept through me at the invitation. Pre-invitation, really. My body and my brain disagreed on the answer, but now that the question was out there, I had to take a side.

Don't ask me that, I begged. *Please, Slate.*

"I'm going to call you a taxi," I mumbled, pinching the bridge of my nose as I searched for the sense of control that hadn't escaped me so completely in years. Where the fuck was it?

Where was *I*?

"Mmhmm?" Slate tucked his thumbs into the waistband of his shorts, his biceps coming forward, framing the ripples of his pecs. His fingers framed... something else completely, which was difficult not to stare at. Below were his bare, strong thighs like tree trunks, and above was his bare belly and chest.

His face wasn't safe to focus on, either. His eyes were wide and hopeful, and his lashes long. So fucking stunning.

"And send you home with something better," I told him. I prayed I didn't sound as shaken as I felt. Who the hell was this boy, to unravel all my tightly wound sense of self? "Cupcakes."

Slate pouted and gathered his clothes, slowly dressing. Hiding his beautiful form under those fabrics ought to be a crime.

I turned away, picking up the box of cupcakes and my phone. I couldn't stand to see the disappointment on his face or the reluctance in his movements.

It was better this way, I knew. I wouldn't want the boy to think *I* could be his Daddy.

The ferocity of my rage he'd so easily whipped up on his behalf, the purity of my desire for his breathtaking submission, and even the sting of my own anger at him for trusting me… nothing in my head made sense tonight.

It scared me, how deep this was. How much I wanted to wrap myself up in his life and fix everything for him. Fix *him*.

Guide and steady and serve him, in the way a Dominant did.

Fuck. I'd *never* thought that before. Lightning ricocheted through my body. I dominated because I needed to. Because it satisfied that fucked-up side of me. I took pleasure, and yes, I gave it, too. But I sure as hell didn't serve *anyone*!

The taxi came mercifully quickly, and I steered him out to the sidewalk, locking up the shop after me. I'd talk to all my friends inside and outside the club after Slate left.

That ought to remind myself who I was, and who I was supposed to be. Who I *had* to be.

We walked to the curb, my hand firm on his shoulder. Close by, from my keenly focused peripheral vision, I saw Isaac.

Shit. I had no time for identity crises. I *was* a Dominant, and Slate *was* my responsibility tonight.

The taxi driver arrived and cracked the window, squinting at the groups of men nearby. "Rex?"

That was us. Good.

Focused and calm, I opened the taxi door, gauging the distance between us and Isaac. He was wandering closer, squinting like he wasn't sure who was with me.

Slate paused like he wanted to talk to me before he got in, but I pressed down on his shoulder to steer him into the taxi. "Move over," I told him, adrenaline flooding my body. My voice grew sharp. "Make some room for me."

It was a split-second decision, and my gut made the decision for me: I couldn't let Slate go home alone.

Slate's eyes widened and he stared up through the semidarkness. Shit. The light in the back seat was on, spotlighting him. But he didn't see that Isaac was there.

If I could protect him from that knowledge...

Fuck. Fuck fuck fuck, hurry up, *you idiot!* But I couldn't rush, or he'd know something was wrong. And Isaac would see me running away, like I was scared of him.

Like hell.

Fighting the urge to slam the door and shout, *Drive,* I elbowed Slate over into the middle seat and slid down, settling the cupcake box in his lap. I shut the door, throwing us into darkness, and clicked the lock as the light overhead faded.

Slate tangled his hand in mine, squeezing with both hands. "Coming to my house?" His voice was sharp and excited.

"Hey."

Fuck. Too late.

Isaac's voice was sharp as he leaned against the driver's-side window, bracing his hands on the sill.

The moment he did, Slate shrank away from him—and me. He didn't let go of my hand, though. His grip grew so tight that my bones hurt.

Isaac was speaking to the driver, not us. Yet. "I think this is my taxi." Then he swung his gaze back to stare me directly in the eye in a cold challenge.

A chill ran down my spine. I wasn't going to get out of this by avoiding him—and I didn't want the consequences to fall upon Slate for anything I might say.

But red-hot anger flooded me as I leaned forward. I swallowed every drop of rage into calm words. "No. It isn't."

I didn't look away. His eyes grew darker, his brows furrowing as his nails dug into the rubber seal of the window.

The driver shrugged and rolled up the window, making him flinch and pull his hands back. "Night, buddy."

Clearly he didn't care about club drama. He had a fare, and that was what mattered to him.

The driver pulled away. "Address?"

I nudged Slate, who unfroze and mumbled an address for the driver.

Part of me expected Isaac to give chase. But of course he didn't. He stood still, and I twisted around to watch him as we pulled away.

Until we rounded the corner, he didn't move a muscle. He just stood there, framed by groups of men and utterly alone, his fists clenched.

Wrong. *So* wrong, the prickle on my neck told me.

Shit, I thought, finally letting out a breath and settling back into the seat as we drove through the silence. *I think I'm wrapped into his life whether I like it or not.*

5

—————

SLATE

A. Daddy. Invited. Himself. Home.

Oh my God, what do I do? I knew I should have vacuumed this week! Will Rex stay? I can lend him pajamas. Do Daddies wear pajamas?

I stared determinedly ahead, never releasing my grip on Rex's hand as my thoughts raced. I might be terrified and clueless, but whatever he was selling, I was buying.

Anything to stop the fear from trailing up my spine and gripping my neck. Prickles along my scalp, the ghosts of fingernails.

He's going to haunt me forever.

No. I wasn't letting myself think about *that* man. I was thinking only about Rex. What Rex was planning for me. How I could charm Rex. Rex, Rex, *Rex*, I *had* to focus on him and him alone.

Or I might just lose it completely.

67

"It's the next right," I said, unnecessarily breaking the silence. I leaned forward, through the middle seats, watching the familiar streetscape change to square houses with perfectly manicured lawns and driveways.

Home, sweet home.

Nobody would ever guess by looking at my little square house with its tidy lawn and pale yellow shutters what had once unfolded within.

No. Think about Rex.

What I hoped would unfold again tonight.

"This house?" the driver asked.

"That's the one."

"Nice place," Rex commented and unbuckled to get out.

I hesitated. Didn't the driver need to be paid? We weren't just ditching the guy, right?

Rex smiled slightly. "It's on my account."

Duh. People who went to the club all the time probably had direct lines to cars. Blushing at my ignorance, I stammered, "Th-Thanks."

As I got to my feet and closed the taxi door, I took a deep breath. I felt discombobulated—like all the parts of me, past and present and future, were ajar and needed to be put back together. I hoped Rex couldn't see that.

I wanted to be strong and independent, as cliched as it felt. Not a scatterbrained and scared little boy.

The taxi slowly pulled away from the curb, and I tilted my chin up like I was marching into battle. I stepped from the sidewalk through the little metal gate in the quite literal white picket fence.

Rex followed close behind, laying his hand next to mine on the gate. Heat flashed between us as if he'd touched me directly, and I yanked my hand back with the surprise. Damn it, why'd I have to do that? It had just been so sudden.

I just gulped and led the way to the porch, suddenly critiquing everything from the layout of my pathway to the hanging baskets along the porch railing.

Digging out my keys, trying not to squirm too much under my layers of leather and denim, I unlocked the door. "Come on inside," I said and then kicked myself—as if Rex was a vampire who couldn't pass my front door otherwise.

"Thank you," Rex said graciously instead, a small smile playing around his lips. He rested just the tips of his fingers between my shoulder blades.

And how my body thrilled to his touch.

He didn't hold a grudge for the gate incident. He wanted to touch me—even if I was a skittish thing. But all he radiated was calm.

We stepped inside. Almost without looking around, Rex said, "Cute house."

Suddenly my throat was tight. Was he on autopilot? Did he invite himself to boys' houses all the time to walk through a script that ended in my agony and his ecstasy?

And if so, did I care? After all, I'd gone to Dom Nation tonight to seek out the very feeling I'd found on my knees on the concrete.

I'd gotten what I wanted. Now it was his turn, right? And I *wanted* him to be pleased. Dammit, I wanted to put aside my own needs and offer every piece of me up to him.

I loved being used. That was the stark truth. So if he was here to say his patter and get what he wanted…

I didn't hate that idea.

God, I did hate these tiny shorts, though. Every wave of arousal that swelled my cock also pinched my head and pinned my shaft against me. If I wasn't careful, I was going to get a Pavlovian response of wincing at every passing boner.

As if he'd read my mind, Rex took his shoes off. "Go get changed," he told me.

He'd left his leather apron back at Daddy Cakes, and now he wore a crisp white shirt with the sleeves rolled up his slender forearms, his black trousers hugging those long, lean legs.

Like a butler who'd sprung out of my very fantasies to torment me. Did that make me the maid? Wait, was that something I could be into?

Right. Get changed, I reminded myself as I realized I was staring again. "Yes, sir," I whispered, experimenting with the words as they fell from my lips.

Seeing how right they felt. How they stirred my blood, yet settled my soul, the very weight of their meaning pressing into my bones.

I think I like Daddy more. How fucking weird is that?

Instead of psychoanalyzing myself, I hurried upstairs. It wasn't that I didn't trust Rex alone downstairs with my stuff. But I wasn't used to having strangers in the house. For all that I trusted him with my body, letting him into my space to look at my pictures and sit on my couch? That was different.

I rushed to my bedroom. I couldn't even pretend to myself that I didn't wish he was following me. I wanted to hear soft footfalls on the steps behind me and a whisper-soft scrape of a palm gliding up the railing.

If I'd been asked at that moment my deepest wish, it would be this: to be the prey bounding ahead of the hunter, hardly daring to look back.

But I rounded the corner, looked back, and my breath rushed out all at once. The stairwell was empty.

Patience, I told myself, frustration welling in my belly. I didn't bother closing the bedroom door as I stripped, tossing my clothes in the laundry basket.

I hesitated, naked but for the harness, my hands resting on the buckle. I pinched the sides in, slowly teasing the metal apart.

What if I go downstairs just like this?

But the Daddy I so wished could be *my* Daddy hadn't ordered it yet, and I wasn't brave enough to see what happened.

I wasn't brave at all.

Hands trembling, I unfastened the harness and pulled it over my head. Then I threw it on the bed, my chest heaving with a silently raging battle of emotions I couldn't place.

No, I knew exactly what they were. I was just terrified of the combination of grief and desire. Mourning who I could have been, and who I'd ended up becoming. Wishing so fiercely that Rex would pick me up and fix me.

But I was just some random middle-aged guy who had let time slip out of his grasp, and Rex still had all the best parts of his life to look forward to.

He's just being kind. Kind, innocent, and naive. If he thought I was a project, he was badly mistaken. He'd never stick around if he knew the truth about me.

That I didn't want a tame, vanilla sex life. And I didn't want a man who'd ask my permission and stick to the scene rules.

I wanted to be used and grovel and beg, but if I could find a way, I wanted to pretend *not* to want it, so that it would hurt even more. I wanted *no* to mean *harder* and *yes* to mean *hurt me,* and what did that make me?

Broken. That was what it made me.

Christ, there was no way of saying that without sounding like a total wacko.

My hands trembled as I pulled on an old T-shirt, then caught myself and yanked it off again, dumping it inside-out back in the drawer. I had company, for God's sake. I should choose something nicer than my paint-stained rags.

Something that Rex would want to wreck.

Hah. Rex, wreck. Does he call himself Rex because he wrecks boys like me? I grinned. However screwed-up it was, I kind of hoped so. That was a great reason to choose the name.

Or his parents had given it to him and it was all quite coincidental. Less interesting and more likely.

Thanking myself for suffering through a recent clothes-shopping mission, I chose my new, navy blue pj pants and a soft white T-shirt.

On the way out of the bedroom, I stopped in the hall mirror and took a long, hard look at myself.

I didn't like what I saw. There was no way around that. Rex was young and fresh-faced and in his prime, and I had deep lines around my lips, a harsh nose, and graying hairs in my stubble. My skin was roughened from sun and wind.

Age had toughened my appearance, unfortunately for me. But it hadn't touched my nature. I was still fragile and helpless and stupidly hopeful that this—this brief thing, this *fling*—might turn into more.

Even if I couldn't hold a candle to everything Rex was, and never would.

"Everything all right?"

I nearly jumped out of my skin as Rex's voice filtered upstairs, sounding close.

"F-Fine, sorry! Sorry, I'm on my way down now." Worry pinched my chest. What if he was impatient waiting for me? Or he needed to know where the bathroom was? Or he'd wanted me to dress down?

I hadn't considered that. There was still time to run and grab my skimpiest underwear.

But Rex peeked around the bottom of the stairwell, his face lighting up in a smile as he saw me. "Oh, it's no rush," he said. "I was just wondering where your mugs are. I found the green tea."

I stared at him dumbly and then hurried down the stairs toward him. "You did?"

"It wasn't exactly hiding," Rex said with a teasing grin, and I blushed. Had I sounded like I was scolding him for rummaging around my kitchen?

Even more anxious, I shook my head. "No, I wasn't implying—"

Rex laughed and held out a hand as I stumbled to a halt at the bottom of the stairs. He wrapped an arm around my waist. "Whoa there. I've got it. Just tell me which cupboard they're in."

"They're, uh, in the second drawer down."

Rex stared at me like I'd lost my mind. "*Drawer?* Who the hell keeps their mugs in a drawer?"

My cheeks heated up as I folded my arms. "I do," I told him tartly. I'd invited him into my home to demean *me*, not my kitchen layout. "Like I just said."

Rex grinned and raised his shoulders in a quick shrug, something of an apology. "Good point. Okay, I'll go make the tea."

My stomach lurched. Isaac had never brought me a drink. Ever. Crap. I was really falling down here. It was my job to serve Rex, not the other way around!

"God, I'm sorry. I should have offered you a drink—"

Rex cut me off with a shushing noise, and I flinched and then held very still as he raised a hand toward me. He pressed his finger to my lips, his eyes alight with something… playful.

It didn't feel like play to me, though.

My whole body rolled in a pleasurable wave. The soft brush of skin on my lips formed a prickle that darted, lightning-sharp and twice as quick, straight through my chest. It settled in my belly, at the base of my cock. Hot and ever-present and impossible to ignore.

I licked his finger, closing my mouth around the tip. His nail scraped the inside of my lip and the edges of my tongue. I dragged my tongue in a circle around it, just once.

"Oh." Rex gave a sudden, rough gasp. Then he pulled his hand away and tilted his head, as if weighing me up.

I held my breath—waiting. *Hoping.* If there was a test, I wanted to pass it. A bar to clear, I wanted to soar over it. If he'd asked me to prove myself, I'd have done it in a heartbeat.

Instead, Rex's expression was inscrutable. "Naughty," he said and then pointed toward the living room. "I'm bringing you tea. Sit there and let me."

He was playing dirty. With that command in his tone, he knew I had little choice but to obey.

Well, that wasn't quite true. I always had a *choice*. I could harden myself in quite a different way than the tent that had formed in my pj bottoms. Swipe aside his words like a wasp zooming around my ears, even.

But I didn't want to, and after all that had happened, I was too tired to resist my urges.

So I nodded and walked to the couch and sat, head in my hands, waiting for Rex to join me again. Listening to him in my kitchen, the quiet rattling and the hum of the microwave.

I'd have to get a kettle sometime. I kept meaning to, but it wasn't like I accidentally wandered down the kettle aisle for fun. I wasn't *that* old. Yet.

Who the hell am I? Who do I want to be?

I had no idea. It wasn't just *Rex* who had shattered those delicate but desperate visions I'd chased to Dom Nation tonight. It was seeing Isaac. And it was meeting Seb. And watching men do things—things I wanted to do—without an ounce of the shame that dripped through my chest like seawater in my lungs.

And... more than anything... it was the minutes, or hours, or maybe decades I'd spent on my knees, giving over my body for a spectacle. A display, yet an invisible one. Where *I* didn't matter, only the position I'd adopted, and the humiliation they'd all witnessed.

I'd loved it. Christ, it made me hard again just thinking about it. My breath caught with the rough *need* that throbbed through me, still thick and unsatisfied.

I shifted, keeping my elbow on my knee, forehead in my palm. I wrapped a firm hand around the hard line of my shaft. Sparks shot through me, and I couldn't breathe.

My blood thrilled with fear and need in equal measure. No— the fear *drove* the need. I squeezed myself, very carefully, my senses suddenly focused keenly on the whereabouts of my guest.

Would he like this? Watching me? Or would he call me pathetic? Would I like that?

If only there were an easy answer: a checklist I could follow. An order of events that made sense.

Instead, I kind of wanted to cry, which was utterly bizarre when I was also holding my own throbbing hard-on as sparks slipped into my brain. Shutting off the common sense, whispering to me that this was a good idea. That I needed it, and after everything I'd done tonight, I deserved it.

That if Rex saw me and he was disgusted by me, he might punish me worse than ever.

Oh, fuck. My cock jumped in my hand, and as much as I dug my fingers into my scalp and choked back my breathing and tried to think of anything else, I couldn't.

Wrong, wrong, wrong. My pulse pounded in my ears, taboo and all the hotter for it.

I should be trying to get rid of this, not indulge myself. I fought with everything I had against the urge to slip my hand in my pants and jerk off until I came in my own pants right here, like some perverted loser.

It was probably only a couple of minutes. Then I heard the footfalls approaching, and I quivered with anticipation, hardly daring to move.

Fuck. If I let go now and sat up, it would be too obvious. *I've made a mistake. Why did I do this?* My own shame only made me grow harder, and I whimpered softly.

I hardly dared to peek through my lashes, but all I saw were Rex's feet again—this time, in socks and not his shining boots.

His steps suddenly halted, just a few feet away. I heard him catch his breath like he'd noticed what I was doing. Covering myself—squeezing myself—riding the line between obscene and considerate, between desperate and ashamed.

My whole body burned and trembled. "I'm sorry," I whispered, two times—no, three times—like it was a ritual. I caught myself rocking forward and back, into my own hand, and went still again, all my muscles tense.

But Rex didn't throw the cup of tea at me or yell. He didn't scoff or laugh.

None of the reactions I'd desired came to pass—and none of those I'd feared.

With two tiny clinks, Rex set the cups on the table nearby. And then he sank to his knees in front of me, his hot palms resting against my shoulders.

So startled I nearly launched myself upright, I jolted and stared at him, my hand still tangled in my own hair, probably looking as half-wild as I felt.

My chest heaved for breath, and the more I sat up, the more it exposed my dilemma. I shrank away from him, mortification staining my cheeks and my soul.

"Tell Daddy what you need," Rex whispered, his hands slipping down my sides. Igniting a wildfire under my skin, fingertips hot and firm, the touch glided all the way to my hips. I trembled, ready to push forward into his grip and beg.

But he didn't go there. His hands slipped past my groin and came to rest against my outer thighs. The whole time, his deep, steady gaze never strayed down to the bulge in either desire or condemnation.

Instead, he looked me in the eye and asked me what I needed. Like he *cared*.

Oh my God, I thought as it hit me like a ton of bricks. *I'm not getting laid. I'm getting* looked after.

My vision was suddenly hot and blurred, and I choked back a sob, but it was too late.

I slumped over toward Rex, and suddenly my cheek rested on his shoulder, and his hand was gliding along my back and neck, through my hair. The soothing touch couldn't hope to mend the pieces inside me, but dammit, it felt *nice*.

Was I allowed *nice* for once?

"I'm sorry," I choked out again, my voice rough and thick with humiliation—and not the kind that made me hard. Instead, my blood rushed to my head, and mercifully, the throbbing in my pants eased at last.

Instead, I fought myself. The unworthy, broken pieces of me recoiled in anger against the tenderness in Rex's hands, while something even deeper and more primal unfurled and pressed close to him, desperate for every touch.

I hated myself for that very desperation, but I'd drink in every drop of comfort Rex offered me.

He never once complained or pulled away. Just as he had in the shop, even when my hold loosened, like he knew I was pretending everything was okay, he kept holding on.

Until I melted, really and truly, into him and gave in.

Young. Small. Lost.

I couldn't work out what I felt, or what I should feel, or why.

I was tired. So fucking tired, and all I wanted was this to make sense. Instead, the more time I spent around Rex, the less sense any of it made.

At last, I felt it—Rex pulling away. That was it. I'd worn out his patience. I'd dithered around for long enough, pretending not to know what I wanted.

Like everyone else, Rex was just going to leave me here, small and alone.

Fuck. My heart hammered and leaped into my mouth. I held tighter, a whimper slipping out of my lips. "Don't go," I breathed out, quick and frantic. "I need…"

Finally, I was too tired to hide the answer from myself anymore.

"I need a Daddy," I whispered.

My feelings about it were irrelevant. I could be embarrassed or angry or defensive about it, but it didn't change what I needed. I could ignore it for years on end, but that wouldn't do anything, either. Just grind me down into the finest dust imaginable.

"I'm sorry," I added, emotion knotting my throat again. "I shouldn't ask you to be… that. To me. I can't. I won't."

But Rex spoke at last, his hands coming to rest on my shoulders. "I'm not waiting for you to ask."

I pulled away, slow and fearful, and met his gaze. "You aren't?"

God, I had to look a pitiful wreck right now. Okay, I'd cried more than a little, and I was wrung-out, and my eyes hurt and my gut felt like a whole hurricane had washed through my soul in the span of a night.

Rex shook his head and drew away from me, but now I sensed he wasn't leaving. So what was he doing?

The answer became apparent a moment later when he pressed the still-warm cup of green tea into my hands, his palms cupping my hands until I had a steady grip.

He'd never left his spot kneeling in front of me. *Isn't that degrading for a Dom?* I wondered. *Does he feel emasculated? God, can't I switch my worries off for three seconds?*

Reflexively, I sipped and then sighed as the prickle washed into a sweet, dulled aftertaste. I looked up at Rex as he spoke.

"For tonight, that's who I am for you," Rex said. "And I'm honored you trust me."

There was something I couldn't place in his voice—not doubt, but something directed at himself. Like Rex didn't think I *should* trust him.

Which was clearly bananas, given everything that had happened tonight, up to and including this very moment.

The cup of tea was gone, and I was exhausted. So tired my emotions fluttered through my grasp, out of control and indiscernible.

It all just felt *loud* right now, and I wanted to hide away from the world.

Rex took the cup and set it on the table, then wrapped his hands around mine. As he stood, he hauled me to my feet, too. "Come," he said softly. "You need to sleep."

"Okay," I whispered.

But my gut lurched with the unwelcome intrusion of a thought. Once the lights were switched off, I couldn't help myself.

Before he could lead me upstairs, I pulled away, veering toward the front door. To my relief, Rex went with me instead of hauling me back on track.

With a shaking hand, I checked the locks and slid the deadbolt across. Then I turned to him in the gloomy, muted half-light of the entryway and spoke to the elephant in the room.

"He knows I live here."

My chest went tight and cold, and suddenly the fearful anticipation I felt upon speaking those words felt *wrong*. It couldn't be more different from the anticipatory fear I'd felt every step of the way with Rex tonight.

I didn't have to say who *he* was. The cringe and shudder that coursed through my whole body spoke for me. I felt it right through to my fingers, laced with Rex's.

But even in the faint glow of the streetlight through the white lace curtain on the windowpane in the door... I saw Rex's lip twist. The same fearless, dominating coldness I'd seen in him earlier was back.

It took my breath away, and I froze like a rabbit caught between two foxes.

"I'm staying the night," Rex said, his tone a command that left no room for argument. Not with him, or even with myself. It was a fact, and that was that.

Then he pulled me toward the stairs, and relief thawed me out. I let him guide me to the bedroom, silently in awe of him.

How could a man not even thirty sound so confident, make snap decisions, and even stare down a wolf like Isaac without a trace of trepidation? I had no idea. Was I just past my prime compared to a young, vigorous, fearless Rex? No. I'd always looked to others to make decisions and hated myself for it.

A real man should be a leader. Everyone said as much. If not in words, in actions. A follower was someone to be scorned and laughed at and used.

And a real man sure as hell wouldn't *want* to be used, right?

I'd expected more awkwardness and anticipation in every moment when we reached the bedroom. This was a man I hardly knew, and he was about to sleep in my bed.

I'd shared my bed with hookups when the itch grew too great, but I hadn't invited any of them to stay.

Instead, it felt easy. The familiarity between us ought to disconcert me, but I was too tired to let it.

I had other things on my mind. Choking back a fresh wave of exhausted emotion, I mumbled, "Do you even wear pajamas?" I pinched the bridge of my nose to keep my breathing under control.

I don't even know that. It's such a stupid question.

Was that demeaning? Should a Daddy always be naked? Or fully dressed? Or was I, in my bone-deep exhaustion, over-thinking every single detail of my existence?

I kind of suspected the latter, so honestly, I didn't blame Rex for glancing at me with a startled expression.

"Whichever answer will make you *not* cry," Rex answered, but there was a gentle smile in his voice, not the hard-edged mockery I'd feared.

It cracked through my runaway thoughts. I laughed, just slightly and softly, and the tension bled from my shoulders and the room.

"Here. I have spares." I winced a moment later. I was wearing the best pair. Crap. I should have thought that through and saved the best for him, not me.

But he didn't look offended at the faded pair I handed over, nor at the way I quickly turned my back to very obviously focus on turning down the bedsheets and fluffing the pillows.

I wasn't sure I could handle seeing him naked yet. It would make him seem vulnerable and human, and I needed his strength.

"Hmm."

The soft word, almost an exhalation, drew my gaze back without thinking.

I blushed as I saw, for the first time, Rex's narrow shoulders and slender chest, each rib pushing a faint line against his pale, smooth skin. He was almost hairless, just a faint fuzz growing in the very middle of his chest, creeping out sideways like a stag's antlers.

Christ. He was *beautiful*.

I shrank back into my pajamas, grateful I'd gone with a shirt and not the gratuitous nudity I'd toyed with earlier.

But he wasn't built at all like me, so my pj pants were way too big for him. There was a gulf between the waistband and his gorgeous flat stomach with just a hint of abs. Rex held out the strings in front of him like reins, and he swam in them.

If I *really* looked, I could probably see… things I shouldn't focus on, if I didn't want Slate vs. Boner, Round Ten.

So I did not let myself look and instead laughed apologetically. "I don't have any smaller."

"Well," Rex said slowly, "I don't usually do this. But I'll sleep in my underwear. Just for tonight."

It was a struggle to hold back my excitement. Not even in a sexual way, just a deeply human and deeply lonely way. I tried to tell myself I didn't crave it, but most nights, that was a lie.

The only times I'd gotten to hold *him* were after he'd exhausted himself using me, and I was bruised and aching all over, but I'd hugged him close and whispered my thanks for breaking me apart with an undercurrent of *please don't go*, and he'd begrudgingly agreed.

Yeah. That was healthy, right?

So I waited for Rex to step out of the pj pants as I slowly made my way to the light switch. When the mattress creaked behind me, I turned out the light and blindly followed my memory toward my bed.

I wasn't used to all my other senses helping me out. The bed shifted under Rex and the sheets rustled, and as I climbed in, the bed dipped nearby me with his weight.

Oh, man.

I gulped, settling the pillow under my head. I scooted toward him, very slightly, and waited for a minute. When Rex didn't pull away, I scooted again.

"Oh, get over here, boy." Rex's voice was soft and amused, cutting through the darkness. He called me that so easily, without ever missing a beat.

I blushed as he called me out. "Yes, Daddy," I whispered as I obeyed.

Soon, he was pressed against me, my chin against his shoulder and my foot between his legs, my knees nestling in the backs of his.

I didn't miss the way he relaxed, letting out a breath and all the tension in his body at the same time. I envied him. If only I could relax that easily.

Dammit, it wasn't fair. The exhaustion was pulling on my eyelids, and yet even if I closed them, I was wide-awake and thrumming with tension that seemed to come from nowhere.

I had to get myself under control—only now, there was nowhere to hide. With Rex pressed against every inch of me, my body was an open book.

Without him there, or even with him on the other side of the bed, I could toss and turn and stew in every damn emotion replaying itself from this evening.

Now, there was the very real risk that my restlessness was going to keep Rex awake, and then his patience *would* wear thin. All I could do was pray that he ignored me and drifted off to sleep.

One of us ought to get some rest, and it wasn't going to be me.

With my face nestling right into his neck, I had to keep my breathing under tight control. Every impulse to squirm or shift around throbbed through me, a little harder than the last to resist.

Nothing seemed to help. Instead, my pent-up energy bounced around me, stuck in an infinite loop of amplification. And still I was too exhausted to even cry about it, but my lungs burned anyway.

I'd been reduced to a wreck at other men's hands, but as the long minutes dragged on, I was trapped in a lonely torture worse than any I'd ever known.

Why couldn't I just be happy that Rex was staying the night? I should feel sexy, or flattered, or excited about what it meant. Yet here I was—suffering through the best thing I'd experienced in years.

How fucking broken was I?

6

———

REX

Slate really thought he was sneaky, didn't he?

I drew on my knowledge of meditation to avoid falling asleep. *Deep breath in, and deeper breath out. Focus.*

The bed was comfortable, and his arms were firmly locked around me, but tension still hummed through his body. Of course Slate was holding me to soothe himself, like his own teddy bear.

That meant no sleep for me until Slate managed it himself. Sub drop could be fierce, especially for the inexperienced.

It was hard to tell how much experience he had—I didn't recognize him from the club, and the details of this house told me he wasn't new to town, but that harness wasn't brand-new, either. It could be another wave of sub drop, or... it could be fear.

How could I possibly sleep with that thought on my mind?

In... and out...

What was Slate afraid of? Or should I say, who?

It was clear that he and Isaac had been intimate, or Isaac had wanted them to be. Slate had frozen like a statue in the taxi, and after getting home, he clearly hadn't wanted to talk about him. Only a warning, or a plea for help, in telling me that Isaac knew where he lived.

Should I have pushed him to talk? No—he had to trust me on his own terms, and he clearly wasn't there yet. Tomorrow, before I left, I'd try to coax the story out of him.

Christ, I wished I could unburden this poor boy's spirit and ease him to sleep right now. He might be older than me, but that part of me I didn't understand had already chosen him. Like a dragon choosing its mate, I'd curled around him all fierce and protective. Not being able to help felt like cutting a piece of my own heart out.

In and out. Just breathe, I repeated my mantra. But I knew it wouldn't make any of this better.

We hardly knew each other. I shouldn't be interested in this intimacy we were sharing. I certainly shouldn't be worrying about his future. I'd just opened my own business, for God's sake. My own life couldn't be further from my mind as I lay still, listening to Slate's breathing hitch and feeling every twitch and subtle squirm of his body.

There he went again, shuffling against the sheets very quietly behind me.

I might have thought it was blue balls, if not for the events of this long night. But there wasn't a boner to be found. And even if there *had* been… I wouldn't be convinced.

However much he seemed to want me to, I wasn't going to take advantage of him. *I* didn't consent to be used in that way. Was it weird to dig my heels in about that? I'd hurt and soothed plenty of boys who wanted, for their own unspoken reasons, what I could give them.

Slate was different.

However much it would make us both feel better for the next hour, I wasn't letting that wild part of me loose from the tight lead I kept it on.

I cracked my eyes open to peer at the alarm clock on the bedside table. It was past two in the morning.

Would this night never end?

My frustration wasn't for a moment directed at Slate. One hundred percent of the blame fell on Isaac's shoulders. If I could turn back time, maybe I would have sent Slate home alone and then ripped Isaac a new one as soon as he was gone.

But then I wouldn't be here, that selfish part of me whispered, *and I like it.* Every inch of Slate's body pressed up against mine, like the missing drumline slotted into the music of my body.

So maybe it was better I hadn't been arrested for assaulting Isaac tonight.

Okay, this is enough.

"Mmm." Decision made, I groaned softly, turning gradually onto my back to give Slate a chance to pull his arm back before I crushed it. When he did, I turned onto my other side and faced him, sliding an arm around him and nudging him until I was the one spooning him.

It felt a little bit silly, like clinging onto the side of a mountain, but he gripped my wrist and pulled my arm tighter around his chest.

"Are you going to be able to sleep at all?" I asked in a whisper as I nuzzled the back of his neck. "When Isaac knows where you are, and that I'm here?"

No dancing around the asshole's name, giving him the power of a shadow slipping through the dark corners of Slate's mind.

Slate's back went stiff, and he caught his breath. It suddenly felt like I was hugging a pile of bricks except that under my palm, the gorgeous, fragile boy's heart thumped as if it was trying to burst through my fingers.

"I'm sorry," Slate whispered, his voice suddenly rough and desperate. "I keep trying to be quiet. I don't want to keep you awake. You've done so much for me tonight."

I dug my nails gently into his chest, prompting a sharp hiss of air, but it interrupted his pleas. "I'm not leaving you," I said, short and simple as that. Every bone in my body wouldn't let me, even if I'd wanted to.

Slate went still for a moment. Then, very gradually, he began to relax in my arms. Just a fraction, but it was enough that I found myself breathing again. I hadn't realized I'd stopped.

"I shouldn't have let him into my head," Slate mumbled, his voice low. I had to hold still to make out the syllables, my nose pressing into his neck and my knees digging into his thighs. "You aren't getting in the middle of anything, don't worry. We're not together, in any way."

The poor guy was still explaining instead of answering me. Apologies came easier to him than admitting to his needs.

And yeah, I could understand that, but it didn't stop me adding another item to the list of reasons I wanted to tear Isaac apart.

"That wasn't what I asked," I murmured. "I don't need to know the nature of your relationship. I saw enough on your faces when we were leaving."

The sigh Slate gave was resigned. He still didn't come up with a straight answer, mumbling something about not wanting to keep secrets.

I waited, running my fingertips in very light circles across his skin, from his heart to his sternum, up to his collarbone and throat. His Adam's apple shifted under my fingertips as I dragged them back down to his chest and pressed my palm against him again.

Grounding him. Reminding him where his heart was—who it really belonged to.

"No," Slate finally whispered. He'd sounded broken earlier, but now he was just tired. Like he'd give anything not to be having this conversation. "No, I don't feel safe here."

Aha. *That* was a problem I could solve, and I leaped at the opportunity to seize it with both hands.

"Then we're going to my place."

Normally I'd be worried about someone getting the wrong impression of me. Or worse yet, the right impression.

If I wasn't bringing a man back to my apartment for sex—and I rarely did, because Dom Nation was perfectly adequate—what was left? Romance? Friendship? No. The neat boxes of my life did not collide, thank you very much.

But there was no way in hell Isaac would know we were there—or be able to get into the building. So for tonight, I'd feel safer bringing Slate to my territory.

I sounded like a lion bringing home its catch, but hey, this was primal instinct. Who was I to question it?

"Yes," Slate murmured, soft and hopeful. "That would help, for tonight. But…"

Here come the walls. I'd expected them. Whatever it took, I'd knock them all down.

I briefly considered knocking Slate out instead and carrying him to my den, but he might end up with a headache. And with the difference in our sizes, it would be less carrying and more sledging. Very undignified.

"It's two in the morning. We'd have to get dressed again and call another taxi. I don't want to drive when I'm so tired, and I was drinking earlier." Slate was rationalizing, coming up with reasons why helping him was too much of a burden. Why he didn't deserve it.

Bullshit.

Luckily, he responded well to a firm hand. So I slid my hand up to his mouth, enjoying the ridges of his collarbone, the soft flesh of his throat, the rough rasp of his stubble… and finally, I pressed my finger against his lips.

"It's not your decision to make," I told him, drawing the finger away to stroke down his arm. "It's mine."

No space for worry or guilt—just obedience.

A whoosh of relief escaped Slate's lungs, and he sagged into the bed all at once. "Okay," he murmured. Pride tingled in my chest and belly, a warm but steady glow. "If you're sure," he added, shifting onto his back and rolling his head to look at me with those worried eyes.

"Up you get. You can go as you are," I told him, shoving my body against his to make him move.

Slate stared at me, even more immovable on his back. I was a wave breaking on his shore. "But… I'm in pajamas."

My lips twitched. Oh, if only Slate knew the half of it. "I've had taxis pick me up in worse states, at later hours," I told him.

Since he wasn't moving, I did. I rolled away from him, ignoring the prickle of displeasure at this brief parting. It was late at night, and I'd been comfortable in bed—that was all it was. Human nature.

Once I was on my feet, I stepped into my trousers, breathing a sigh of relief. It wasn't that I didn't like my body or I didn't trust Slate. I just didn't want it on display.

I called a taxi and then pulled up the blinds so I could see by the streetlight. It was quiet and unsettlingly serene outside. Even though we hadn't slept, it seemed like everything that had happened was yesterday. And, technically, I guess it was.

But more than that, it felt like we were in another world—a second, secret world nestled into our own, and one I cherished. It was just the two of us and the occasional hum of a car engine in the distance.

The night sky was dark and clear despite the rows of street-lights stretching into the suburbs. I shivered at the darkness outside, buttoning up my shirt quickly and tucking it into my pants.

"Are you cold?" Slate came up behind me, draping what was unmistakably his bathrobe over my shoulders. Soft and fuzzy, a deep blue, it stretched almost to my feet, and the sleeves dangled so low I didn't dare put my arms through them.

Speaking of undignified. I didn't need to look like *I* was the boy and Slate the Daddy whose shoes I was trying to fill.

But I was also cold, and I liked the smell of Slate wrapped around me. It was dizzying—or perhaps that was his hands on my shoulders, smoothing out the fabric unnecessarily.

I moaned softly and closed my eyes to enjoy the shoulder rub, but no sooner had I done so than Slate stopped.

"That's the taxi, I think," he whispered.

Damn. Why did late-night taxis have to be so efficient for once? I sighed and slid the bathrobe off my shoulders, turning Slate around to carefully nestle it around his shoulders. "There," I murmured and offered a hand to him. "Let's go."

I led him downstairs, only stopping to make sure I had everything I'd come with.

Except it felt like I'd left something behind, a tiny piece of me still nestled up to him in bed. It felt surreal. Were we wandering around my dreams right now? Would I wake up and find him sound asleep, pressed into me?

But as we stepped out of the house, he pressed himself up against me in a quite different way, flinching at the sound of a car engine nearby.

Fuck. I woke up in a hurry at that, scanning the street. But, of course, Isaac wasn't there.

"It's all right," I told Slate softly and put my hand on his back, steering him straight to the waiting taxi.

Slate let me push him into the back seat, and he scooted over to the middle again to make room for me. I gave the taxi driver my address, and we pulled away from the curb.

"No, it isn't." Slate picked up the conversation in a whisper. "I know it seems like I'm some poor abused guy."

"You don't have to explain," I told him, and I tried to put an arm around his shoulders.

"I want to," Slate told me, bristling with a soft ferocity.

My stomach lurched as I dropped my hand into my lap. I couldn't tell who the anger was directed toward, and I didn't want to risk that it was me for not letting him talk about it. So I bit my lower lip and nodded for him to continue.

At least it was coming out now, one way or another.

"He's not like, an ex who beat me up unwillingly." Slate cast a look toward the driver, and I put a hand on his knee to make him look at me again.

From that peculiar phrasing, I gathered that Isaac had beaten Slate willingly, but the coldness I sensed in him made me wonder. I had to try not to pry. I had to make peace with maybe never knowing.

"I'm not a helpless stray who needs rescuing," Slate continued, still so soft I could barely hear him. His gaze darted around the back of the taxi. "I'm a grown man."

Oof. I squeezed his knee, acknowledging his words. His need to be strong, or at least to appear strong. Nobody liked to feel like a victim. He was embarrassed about me helping him. That wasn't a D/s thing, that was a human thing.

"I know you are," I told him softly. "And I know I'm like, twenty years younger. And I'm diving in and meddling overnight. Feel free to tell me to fuck off."

He huffed a laugh, short and sharp. Irritated. "It's not that."

"What, then?"

Slate was quiet for a time. I watched and waited, keeping every word inside despite how much I wanted to grab him by the arms and shake him and tell him that it was okay not to be okay.

But I could be patient. Watch the beams of light flickering across his face in the dark back seat. Wait for answers.

"You don't know what you're getting yourself into," Slate said at last, turning that breathtaking gaze to me. I could hardly see the icy blue of his eyes, the shadows playing along his nose and hardened jaw.

"Let me guess: oldest son of a Mafia boss."

Slate paused, his brow doing a funny little furl-and-raise thing as his beautiful lips parted. "What?" But he huffed a breath, too, almost a laugh. I'd take it.

"Oh, no. You're a scientist who knows how to stop the end of the world, and the timer is halfway to empty."

"This isn't funny." But Slate's lips twitched, and he looked away, smoothing a hand over his mouth.

I smirked, leaning back in my seat and folding my arms. "You're from the Capulets, and I'm from the—"

"Okay," Slate interrupted, shoving me with his shoulder. Good thing for the seatbelt. I might have hit the car door otherwise. "So it's not like *the stars aren't aligned*. Twerp." Then he cast me a sideways, narrow glance like he was trying to work out whether he was allowed to tease me in return.

I allowed it. He was so fucking cute, after all. I'd let him get away with a lot more than that—but I wasn't telling him. He'd have to find out on his own.

"Then what?" I stayed focused on the important stuff here.

"You *are* twenty years younger." That wasn't really Slate's problem, surely. He cast another look toward the driver.

"So?" I said, tart and crisp as an apple. I folded my arms. "I'm a grown man, too. I'm perfectly capable of deciding I like you. And you're just as deserving of being liked."

Slate turned his head away, gazing out the car window. He was quiet for long enough that I knew I'd struck somewhere close to the truth.

But we were arriving at my building, so I had to leave the conversation there—outside, in the quiet in-between of the taxi—and climb out of the car. I thanked the driver and offered Slate a hand.

He took it, his palm big and hot in mine, and I felt better for it. Once he'd stepped out, I didn't let go.

I felt him draw closer to me as we approached the glass-fronted building. "You live here?"

The questions wrapped up in that one question were too numerous to count, and I didn't care to provide any answers to them. "Yes," I said simply.

I nodded at the doorman, a big blond Swedish guy who stirred from his post behind the desk and hurried over to open the door.

"Evening, Jens."

"Good evening, sir." Jens only glanced at Slate for long enough to not be rude, nodded, and withdrew to his desk, keeping his eyes fixed firmly on the book he'd been reading.

It was rare that I brought company back, and they'd certainly never been in pajamas before. But he knew better than to ask and left me to my own devices—just the way I liked it.

Through the lobby, into the elevator, and up to the top floor, I kept holding his hand. As we rode the elevator, he didn't even look around. He seemed to stare into the distance, until his head nodded forward. Then he suddenly straightened up, trying to hide his exhaustion.

It was totally adorable.

If only I were in the market for adorable, I reminded myself, sharply looking away from him. "Here we are."

The elevator door opened to another door, and I watched Slate for his reaction as I unlocked it, pushing it open.

What if he decided that I was a spoiled rich brat, like so many guys did at first glance?

But Slate hardly glanced around. He didn't even question the elevator door situation. He just kicked his shoes off, loosened the tie on his bathrobe, and pinched the bridge of his nose like he was trying not to fall off his feet.

"The bedroom's this way," I told him, taking hold of his arm and steering him through the sliding door.

He didn't have to be told twice. The moment he stepped down into the sleek, modern bedroom with its floating king-sized bed and smart lighting system, he crawled straight onto the bed, under the covers, and burrowed in on my side of the bed.

My lips twitched with indignation and amusement.

He hadn't stopped to take in the panoramic view, the marble countertops, or even the whiskey display case? Then again, it was hardly the hour for a house tour. At least I didn't have to worry he'd freak out about it all.

"Does Isaac know about this place?"

That was his only question? I jolted back to awareness and shook my head. "No," I answered.

A soft hum was Slate's only reply. He turned onto his side, burying his head in the pillows, and I took a moment to watch him, my heart pitter-pattering in a way I didn't want to think too hard about.

No, he had a second question.

"Coming to bed, Daddy?"

"Hold your horses," I teased.

Slate snorted softly. "Don't want to. At midnight my horses ran away, and all I've got is this pumpkin." He patted the covers somewhere—I assumed over his stomach.

I snorted. "As if." Did he not see how sexy he was? And he definitely wasn't a bear. And if he were, he'd still be hot. God, I had so much to teach him. Or rather, I tried to convince myself, *he* had so much to *learn*. That didn't mean it had to be me teaching him.

I waved a hand over the light panel to set the room lights to dim steadily and then turn off in thirty seconds. I used the time to meander closer to the bed, watching him the whole time. He stayed still, his arm over his eyes, and didn't watch me undress.

So I slid from my day clothes into fresh pj bottoms and then tugged back the covers on the less-familiar side of the bed. The light snapped off, and deprived of my chance to creep on him, I felt my way into the bed.

Slate might be mine now. I was doing more than protecting him tonight. I was… rescuing him.

What did that mean? Was I offering him more than I could really give him? God, I was terrified of what this meant.

But it was the right choice.

"Come here, my boy," I whispered, scooting closer. It took me a marathon to get over to the other side of my huge bed, but he met me halfway.

I hugged my Slate mountain again, kissing the back of his neck and smiling as he finally, truly, relaxed.

He slept like a baby within minutes, and the warm, steadily burning pride in my chest only grew.

I'd done that. I'd taken this poor, lost boy and given him everything he needed tonight. I loved that feeling. Fierce and protective—and a little bit like I owned him. He was *mine* to hold and heal.

It was selfish, I knew, to get off on rescuing him. I'd been embarrassed to be caught at it, but he'd been right. But I had to take my kicks where I could get them.

If he wanted to yell at me tomorrow for kidnapping him to my own little den, for feeling so smug about my big rescue… that was up to him. I hoped he wouldn't.

I stroked his hair softly, petting him, hoping he could feel this comfort in his dreams tonight and not Isaac's cold, cutting gaze.

"Beautiful boy," I murmured, my fingertips gliding from his hair to his shoulder, and down to his chest. I found just the right place to press it, over his heart.

And then I slept, deep and dreamless.

7

<hr>

SLATE

Holy shit. What a bachelor pad.

I stared around me the moment I jolted uneasily out of sleep, immediately sensing I wasn't in my own bed. The sheets were smoother and cooler—like a thousand thread count or something ridiculous—and the light peeking through the blinds was all wrong.

The ground around the bed was recessed, stairs set into the smooth, dark wood floor. There was a wooden dresser down here with sleek silver drawer handles.

In one corner on the upper tier was a large, round chair with a low back. Sitting next to it was a sleek little table connected to a plant pot that held a tall leafy tree of some kind, and a twisted metal lamp that shone over the chair.

Is Rex a reader, then? I wondered, carefully shifting onto my other side so I could look at him. *Or does he just like unique furniture? Like desperate boys?*

The memory of last night made me bite my lip with a pleasurable prickle that tingled across my skin, and once more, I wished I could entice Rex into… something.

I didn't know what I wanted, exactly, but I *definitely* wanted him.

Rex didn't wake, to my mixed relief and disappointment. I smiled down at him, my breath catching at the sight of his soft blond hair and pretty pink lips. He looked even more delicate asleep, which fascinated me.

Awake, his energy was defiant—or maybe it dared me to defy him. He wore that attitude wrapped around him like an armadillo's shell. But it was gone now, leaving him gentle as a sleek little blond otter.

I was fascinated. I wanted to stroke his hair and tuck the sheets around him a little tighter, but I wasn't sure he wouldn't just bite me in his sleep.

Carefully, I eased myself out from between the sheets and wondered if they were made from babies' bottoms or angels' feathers.

Softly, I stepped up the stairs toward the frosted glass sliding door. It glided open almost silently and closed with the faintest *snick* behind me. I breathed a little easier, stepping into Rex's living room.

Holy shit. Had we broken into a movie star's apartment or something? I barely remembered last night. I'd really walked right past… all of this?

Natural floorboards drew the eye to the kitchen, with dark wood cabinets, white marble countertops, and bronze knobs on stainless steel appliances. The backsplash was dark, with recessed lighting overhead. Beyond the kitchen were full-length windows that revealed a breathtaking view of the office buildings I'd never seen from this angle against the gradually lightening sky.

To the left was the living room, with plush carpet, a fireplace, and cozy sofas. The TV on a pivoting attachment in the corner between windows made me smile—it seemed almost unnecessary, with these views.

I felt like I was in a panoramic restaurant at the top of some skyscraper. But instead of ogling the sunrise just yet, I made my way to the kitchen.

I didn't trust myself to cook, but I could make Rex coffee. Or... maybe not.

The silver machine on the countertop looked like it belonged in a hotel lobby or behind the counter at a cafe. It even had a freaking touchscreen.

Did Rex run a hotel for lost boys here? Was the machine going to charge me in quarters? I gingerly touched the dark screen, and it lit up like it expected me to know what I was doing.

That was a bold assumption. I didn't even know what kind of coffee Rex drank. I'd expected a pod coffee machine or something easier than this career-day exercise.

The screen had a whole wheel of options, but it was already set to lattes, so I decided to take a chance. I took a glass mug from the steel pegs above the machine and put it under the dual spigots where I figured the water would come out, but with a metal tube to the right and some contraption to the left, I couldn't be sure.

This was a trial of my wits and nerves.

Was Rex a barista to the stars?

Don't be dumb, I thought a moment later, looking around at the place again. *That wouldn't buy this place.*

Right. Coffee. I fidgeted with the handle of the thing you put the beans into, and then it came off all of a sudden, surprisingly heavy in my hand and sieve-like. Crap. Okay, what did I do with this?

This was where the coffee grounds went, probably. Judging by the touchscreen, the gadget on the left was a coffee grinder, and to the right was a milk steamer. The little metal pitcher on top of the coffee machine made sense, too.

Did I have to put beans into this thing? Feeling like Robinson Crusoe, I gingerly eased the funnel over top of the grinder open and peeked in. *The hopper*, my brain supplied.

Okay, good. There were beans in the hopper.

"I don't hide the family jewels in there, you know."

The voice close by made me yelp, whirling around and flattening myself against the counter as I raised the heavy, sieve-like thing in my hand as if to throw it.

Poor Rex ducked reflexively, just as I caught myself.

"Jesus!" I exclaimed, clutching my chest as I quickly put the metal implement on the counter and sidled away. "Sorry. I just wanted to make you coffee."

Rex's smile was soft, but his usual aura was back—far too mature for his age, and unsettlingly calm. He held his hands out like he was soothing a kitten. "No, my apologies. I startled you."

He was shirtless, which pricked up both ears and something else, too. I bit my lip and tried not to stare at the small, warm pink peaks of his nipples or the faint ripple of abs under his slender, trim waist.

Christ, he was an entire snack.

I shook my head firmly, willing the dizzying wave of arousal away once again. "You're the one walking into your own kitchen, Rex. I'm the intruder here."

"What was the purpose of the intrusion?" Rex's eyes sparkled as he glanced at the LED screen. "Making coffee?"

"For you," I mumbled, rubbing my neck. My gaze flickered down as Rex came around the edge of the counter. "Or I wanted to."

Dammit, he was in lounge pants and not... less, like I'd hoped.

Fine, so I had my fantasies of him walking around naked. All the better for me to entice him, right?

I wasn't *usually* this oversexed and persistent, but Christ, every time I caught sight or scent of this man, everything in me pulled toward him with an inexplicable tug.

Rex moved effortlessly to slot the silver thing under the hopper, ground the beans, and placed two mugs under the twin silver spouts. Then he grabbed the metal pitcher with a flourish and twirled about to open the fridge. He took a carton of soy milk out. "Latte?" he asked. "Soy milk okay?"

"Sure," I answered, a little embarrassed that I hadn't figured the machine myself.

"Phew. I have the temperature set for soy milk. Also, no actual cow's milk in the house."

I laughed. "I'm not picky," I said. "In general." Then I winced, hoping he didn't take it as an insult. After all, I'd picked him.

But then again, every now and then I wondered if I over-thought things. Maybe *everything*.

"This is all too fancy for me," I added in a mutter to cover over that little moment. "I'd just microwave the water if I'd found any green tea lying around."

Rex grinned. "I noticed," he said. "I considered ordering a same-day Prime kettle for you." His voice was teasing, yet gentle—not the cruel daggers of Isaac's words. "I won't let you suffer through microwaved water while you're here."

He stepped closer, one hand outstretched toward my waist—or lower? Time slowed down as my hopes ricocheted into the ceiling.

I froze against the counter, my heart a staccato jackhammer in my ears, but even then, my stupid, logical brain wouldn't let me stay hopeful for long.

Nothing about this gesture was what I hoped it would be.

Sure enough, Rex's fingertips closed around the handle of the drawer next to me. I automatically stepped back, my gaze falling to the drawer as he opened it, and I tried to choke back my disappointment.

Just thinking of him touching me—grabbing my shirt and hauling me in—made me tingle from head to toe. Dressed in my loose pajamas, I needed a moment to recover.

The drawer was full of coffee beans and a wooden tray of tea bag packets.

"Feeling more like a hotel now," I mumbled. At Rex's questioning glance, I added, "I've been trying to decide: home or hotel for lost boys?"

His teeth flashed in a quick grin, his eyes quick to light up. He took out two long, thin metal coffee spoons from a wooden box and closed the drawer again. It slowed and then thumped shut with a muffled click.

"This is what belongs in drawers," Rex informed me, setting each spoon on the counter. "Not mugs."

I clicked my tongue sadly and folded my arms. "Leave my kitchen layout alone."

Rex's fingertips closed around my ear, and he playfully tweaked it, his nail scraping along the lobe. Instantly I went stiff and still, my eyes wide as dinner plates.

Fuck. I had it bad. The tiniest scratch of his nails along my body and everything in me wanted to throw myself at his feet.

"Not giving orders, are you?" Rex asked, his voice low and sultry. Jesus. Talk about mixed messages.

I gulped, making sure I still had the power of speech before I answered. "Wouldn't dream of it," I whispered, resisting the urge to add a cheeky *sir*, even though he kept insisting he wasn't my sir.

No wonder, too. I was out of my league here. Holy crap, I couldn't even make him coffee. He had it all. There was really nothing I could do for him except offer my service, and he didn't seem to have any straightforward answers on whether he wanted that.

Whether he wanted *me*.

I shouldn't need him so badly, right? He was one man—one random man I'd only met last night. Never mind that last night had felt a hundred years long.

"Here you go." Rex passed me one hot glass latte mug, and after one deliciously foamy sip, I sighed with contentment and shook my head. Was there anything he *wasn't* good at? I could let this man spoil me for a long time.

"Thanks."

"Now, come here." Rex didn't wait to see if I'd follow his order. He laced his fingers with mine and pulled me toward the living room.

I gulped hard. Was this an intervention? I didn't want to have to explain that Isaac and I weren't together anymore—or admit to what I'd let him do for so long in my desperation for attention.

But instead of perching at an angle and lecturing me on the sofa, Rex took me to the love seat and sat close to me. Then he wrapped an arm around my shoulders, casual yet intimate.

He doesn't want to tell me off. Duh, Slate, I thought, closing my eyes for a moment to let the sensation of weight across the back of my neck settle in.

I hardly knew what to do except clutch the latte mug to my chest and count my breaths so I didn't make embarrassing excited noises.

"I like to watch the sun rise these days," Rex said softly, between sips of his own coffee.

"These days?" I asked. Was he usually a late riser? If he frequented Dom Nation, that wouldn't surprise me.

Rex hummed softly in response. "I used to work all the time. Dawn 'til midnight."

I took a risk and teased him. "And you don't now?"

I could see the corners of Rex's lips fighting to stay down-turned. "This is different. It's fun."

"So running Daddy Cakes isn't your only job, or…?" I trailed off.

I was hungry for knowledge about him. I felt like I'd glimpsed everything *around* him—his shop, his coffee maker, his very bed—but the man at the middle of it all was still a mystery.

So I didn't know what might be going through Rex's mind as he bristled slightly. "It is," he told me in a voice that left no room for argument.

Had I offended him? Crap. I was walking in a minefield here.

But worse still, I felt the volley of his deflection coming a mile off, and there was nothing I could think of to distract him except to jump up and accidentally spill coffee everywhere.

"How about you?"

There it was. I tried not to groan. "You won't believe me if I tell you," I muttered.

Rex smirked. "Oh, are you the new Bond?"

I snorted at him and elbowed him gently in the side. "Shut up," I told him, prickling with worry that he'd take my words wrong. But he just grinned at me, and I sagged with relief. "No. I'm a dental hygienist."

Here came the joke: *oh no, don't judge me for owning a cupcake shop! I brush all the time!*

But instead, Rex just smiled. "Don't worry. Sugary sweet isn't my style."

Thrown off-balance by my expectations, I just blinked at him. "What is?"

Rex tilted his head back, drained the rest of his latte, and pushed himself to his feet.

It was hard to process the emptiness of my shoulders without that slender arm curled around them. Like without him there, I was just going to float off into space forever.

"Let me give you a ride back home."

Seems pretty sweet to me, I thought, but I'd already pushed him unknowingly once. I wasn't going to test my luck. Not if I wanted to save it up and get lucky later.

Clearly he was trying to throw walls up between us. Normally I would have melted away into a puddle of angst about it. Thoughts like *of course he doesn't like me* or *I don't deserve it* might have carried me off in a great flood of emotions I didn't want and didn't know how to deal with.

But instead, I was intrigued and perhaps miffed. I wanted to know *why* he was resisting me at every turn, and then—just when I gave up hopes of interesting him—he made some move to bring us closer.

"I'll take a ride," I told him, not even bothering to hide the innuendo dripping from my words.

Rex threw me a sideways glance, his lip curling up in a knowing smile and his eyes hooded. Like he was half a second away from calling me over and having his way.

But he said nothing and put his cup in the sink, then leaned on the kitchen island like he was trying to keep a physical wall between us, too. Still, there was something in the way he watched me…

"Come on," I breathed out, leaning forward to put my cup on the coffee table. I rose to my feet, slow and tentative. "I know my own mind. I'm not the mess I was yesterday. I'm me again."

"I didn't like seeing you like that," Rex said softly, leaning further into the counter, pressing his thumbs into the edge of it like he wanted to crack off the whole countertop. "I might not know you, but I know Isaac's effects."

Fuck. Here he was, still getting between me and anything good I might want for myself in my life.

I drew a breath to try to wash away the fury that built in my chest at his name, then let it out. "How long have you known him?"

Rex squinted, his gaze flicking beyond me to the full-length windows over the city. "Four years? Since I started going to DN."

My chest was suddenly tight as I got the confirmation I'd wanted. I wasn't sure I wanted it anymore.

Four? That meant he *had* lied about never going on the scene. So I had to assume he'd been lying about everything else, too. Like me being the only one. I'd just been another hole in his schedule, until I was inconvenient.

I wandered closer, pressing my forearms on the counter as I took a deep breath. The punch in my gut was slow to fade.

"Was he important to you?" Rex asked, drawing my gaze to him. He didn't look unsympathetic. His voice was soft, like he was gentling a scared animal.

I nodded.

"And he hurt you?"

I hesitated. I was afraid of what I was going to unleash if I was truthful, but I was tired of keeping his dirty secrets when it turned out *I* was his dirty secret.

"Yes," I whispered.

Rex's fists went tight on the countertop. He shifted his weight, nostrils flaring and eyes flashing. But instead of being afraid at the anger rolling in a steady wave from him, I was drawn to Rex's outrage on my behalf.

"Then… fuck him," Rex said, his voice thin. "Well, for absolute clarity: don't fuck him. Fuck anyone but him. Get him out of your system. He never deserved you."

There was no chance like the present.

"I want to," I told him, pausing just long enough to catch his gaze. Once he looked at me, I didn't let him look away, my gaze flickering between his eyes. "I want *you*," I clarified.

My hands trembled as I came out and said it. I was risking rejection—directly—for him. Again.

But hell, I wasn't a teen anymore. There was no point in dancing around it. But before Rex could answer, my mouth took over from my brain.

"But you're blowing hot and cold," I told Rex. "I'm here in your house, in your bed, and yet you won't flirt with me for more than ten seconds. You hold hands with me, give me a ride home, let me kneel for you. But you won't let me please you. I don't even need to come. I can just service you. It would make me…" I trailed off, shaking my head.

I couldn't explain how complete I would feel with his cock buried in the back of my throat. The way my dick jumped in my pajamas at the barest excuse. Hell, just begging—because this was begging, no mistaking it—made me flush with a guilty pleasure.

"Slate—" Rex's voice was strangled.

"If you're trying to torture me," I laughed, my voice warbling as I shook my head, "it's working, Rex."

Rex's eyes steadily widened. His stunned expression looked beautiful, lips slightly parted. A pink flush crossed his cheeks. I wanted to kiss the surprise off him, but I didn't even dare lean any further over the counter.

Then his brow furrowed, and he bit his lip hard. He looked so torn that for a moment, I almost felt bad for him. He shook his head slowly.

Fuck. Don't turn me down now.

Even as the weight of his rejection crushed me, I'd get a little thrill out of it, and *that* was not a part of myself I was prepared to accept. Much less think about, even for a moment.

So I let my snark out, distracting myself. "Let me guess," I said tartly. "It's not me, it's you."

A ghost of a smile touched Rex's mouth. He looked fond, almost, as he gazed at me. "No, it is you," he told me.

Wait, what? It was my turn to stare, my jaw dropping as indignation rushed into every nervous space in my heart.

"I don't want to give you what you want if it's not what you need," Rex said, which put a halt to the heat flushing through me. "That's what makes me a Daddy and not just some random, asshole Dom. I'm not here to give kindness to you and take pleasure out of you like an ATM. I'm here to…"

His voice trailed off into a breathy sigh, and at last, he looked away. Fidgeted with the neat row of spice jars on the counter.

"To what?" I prompted, hardly daring to breathe. I didn't know how to tell him that everything he was saying was *exactly* why I wanted him to be my Daddy, or Dom, or both. Fuck.

All of it. Everything he could give me. That was what I wanted from him.

Rex shook his head and pushed himself upright. My heart sank before the words even came. "To drive you back home," Rex told me, with a rigidity that hadn't been in his voice a few seconds ago. Like it was a game plan he was repeating to himself.

He was persuading himself, not me.

"And get to the bakery, and get ready to open again tonight," Rex murmured, tapping his fingers on the counter and moving toward the bedroom. No doubt he was going to get changed or something.

I waited for him, folding my arms like they could hold my heart in place in my chest. But it trailed after him, along with all of my interest. He seemed to bring the oxygen in the room along with him.

"Do you ever take time off?" I asked, raising my voice so he could hear me in the bedroom.

"Maybe I will some weekday soon. After I know when my busy and quiet times are."

I heard a closet door roll open, and the click of hangers. I furrowed my brow. Why wouldn't he already know that? Jesus, the man was a million little mysteries knitted together with a healthy dose of sex appeal.

"When did you open?"

There was a long pause. For a moment, I wondered if he'd heard, and then tried to decide if that gave me an excuse to wander over to the bedroom door and sneak a peek at him dressing.

But he'd been self-conscious last night while getting naked, so I drew a breath. *Down, boy*, I told myself. *Be patient.* Breaking his trust now wouldn't win me any points.

Rex appeared in the doorway in trousers and a button-down shirt, which he was buttoning from the bottom up. "Last night," he told me. For the first time, he looked kind of sheepish.

My jaw dropped. "What? Last night was *opening night*? And you didn't tell me?"

Rex shrugged, not looking at me. He patted down his pockets. "Technically you were my first customer."

That revelation pretty much knocked me out. I stared wordlessly at him until he finally looked at me, his brow furrowing again. Finally, I managed a quiet word. "Dude."

Rex laughed softly and scratched his neck. "Yeah."

"And you spent all that time on me? Did I get in the way?" Christ, if he'd closed early for me or something…

Certainty in his voice again, Rex told me, "No." He strode over to me, closing the gap in a few quick steps.

I only had time to catch my breath before he cupped my face, his thumbs stroking lightly across my cheekbones. "Huh?" I managed.

Great. Real witty rejoinder there. But the hum of pleasure that shot straight to my core—in an animal instinct way, not just a lustful way—made the words on the tip of my tongue take a long vacation.

"Never feel bad about how the night went. This is what I wanted," Rex said, soft and intense. "A place for people to be safe and happy. So as far as I'm concerned, opening night was perfect."

Could he *hear* himself? I ached to shake him by the shoulders and say, *This is why I want you, dumbass!*

Instead, what came out of my mouth was "Do you open up your home to everyone?"

Rex's hands slid from my cheeks to my shoulders. He fidgeted with my T-shirt, straightening the seams on my shoulders like he didn't quite want to let go. "Well, no," he muttered, his gaze sliding to my chest. "I didn't mean to."

I smiled, my hands rising to take his elbows. Then, carefully as I dared, I slid my hands down his until I took his hands in mine. He gripped back, his slender fingers firm and warm in mine.

"I appreciate it," I told him quietly, which didn't even touch on the depth of my gratitude. He'd seen me at my most vulnerable —straight past all my defenses and fears—and helped me like nobody else. "And I want more."

The amused resignation on Rex's face no longer discouraged me. I wanted to push him harder. Otherwise I was going to walk out of his apartment and never see him again.

And that might shatter me into dust.

But Rex didn't discourage me. He just squeezed my hands, watching me. "Why?"

My heart leaped. Now that I'd been given the floor, I had to build my case on the fly. I hadn't expected this.

"We work so well together," I told him. Nobody could argue that. Just a day after meeting, every touch felt natural between us—like we were being pulled together, knitted by some greater external power. "We both hate Isaac. Like you told me to, I want to get him out of my system. And I know who with."

There it was—the smile I'd slowly been coaxing from him, and Rex finally stopped holding it back. My heart lit up. *Yes!* I was getting somewhere. I playfully swayed into him for a moment.

"I can be patient and wait if that's what you want, but..." I licked my lips, my throat suddenly tight. I cleared it. "I don't want to pine after a man who doesn't want me."

Rex huffed, the sound amused yet not annoyed. The curl to his lips told me that. "God, you're persistent," he told me, shaking his head slightly. "I want you, Slate. That's not even a question."

Oh, thank God. I grinned at him, wishing I had the balls to lean in and seal it with a kiss. But I'd wait for him. Whatever was holding him back, I wasn't going to force him.

Fuuuuck, I hated that decision the moment I made it. His lips looked soft, warm, and *right there.*

But I had to prove I could be patient, so I hit him with my cunning plan. "Then give me a ride home now, and I'll repay you by coming by Daddy Cakes tonight to help serve more samples."

Rex blinked at me twice, opening his mouth to say something. Then he blinked again. "Do I get a choice?"

I grinned at him. "Not unless there's a hard limit I don't know about." I let go of his hands and folded my arms. Finally, I felt like I was on firm enough footing to tease him.

I might not know my way around a kink club, how to talk to a DM, or how Daddies were supposed to work, but goddammit I'd spent a whole lifetime being patient. I was a world-class expert.

At last, Rex grinned. I wasn't sure if he was laughing at me or just putting up with me, but if it won me more time with him, I didn't care.

"Okay," Rex finally said. He clicked his tongue and shook his head, turning away from me to grab his phone and keys from the counter nearby. "Come on, then."

I followed in his wake, enormously proud and impressed with myself. I'd negotiated—and I'd won that round!

Of course, waiting at the steel door directly between the apartment and the elevator gave me a lot of questions I hadn't thought to ask last night.

But I just chatted about cupcake flavors, rather than ask Rex why he lived in a penthouse and drove an electric roadster.

There was time to get to know him later, and I worried that asking him that might lead to the wrong impression. Like I was only interested because of what he had.

No—what he had was the mystery. Why he was the person he was? Also a mystery.

But I knew who he was. I'd never even been naked with him, but I knew the most important parts of him.

The drive home was all too quick, and as we pulled up, I still hadn't made my mind up about what to do for my next stage of the plan.

Crap. Time to wing it.

"I'll see you later?" I said, pitching my voice up to make it a question.

I needed his permission for the next step. I had to give him a chance to back out—to say no and slip off into the shadows, where I sensed he liked to stand.

But he didn't, and he just nodded slightly.

And my heart soared. *Oh my God, yes! He does want me!*

Caught up in my joy, I waited too long to go for the kiss I wanted. Instead, Rex leaned in toward me and pressed his lips against my cheek.

Hot and lingering, his breath ghosted across my ear, his grip firm on my shoulder. I ached to melt into him, to turn my head and let my lips meet his. To lose myself in the clash of our mouths and the quickly climbing temperature in here…

It must have only lasted a second. But when he pulled back, there was something real and warm in Rex's eyes.

It matched the warm quiver of delight in my own chest.

"Thanks for the drive," I whispered.

"Thanks," Rex muttered. Then, as if flustered, he cleared his throat. "I mean, you're welcome. See you later, alligator. Oh, God. Just leave now, please."

I burst out in a breathless laugh at this tiny moment of realness —where his walls slipped and he was fragile and human and fucking *perfect*. Rex glared at me, but it only made my giggles worsen.

"I'll see you later." This time, it was a promise.

I grinned all the way to the house, my steps light.

Rex was everything I wanted: firm, confident, and rough, but so charming, too. He seemed to want to be seen as a big, tough Dom, yet he wasn't afraid of being kind and therefore weak.

Now I had all day to practice closing the deal. Chances like this didn't come around every day, and I might never get another.

8

REX

Christ, I could use a drink.

But I was stuck behind the counter of Daddy Cakes, batting my lashes at customers as I asked about their nights. None of them held a candle to the man wandering around outside the club, greeting all with smiles and offers of cupcake pieces.

I wanted to call it quits and bring Slate home right now. But I had to sell out of cupcakes first.

Or did I have to?

I really do, I told myself for the dozenth time this hour. After all, I'd opened Daddy Cakes for a damn good reason. I needed an outlet for the untamable desires I found myself resisting at this very moment.

But holding out as the cabinet dwindled away took every ounce of my patience I'd once thought was so endless. Apparently, there were exceptions. Well, an exception—just one.

Slate.

Honestly, he scared me to the bone. Not because he was the incarnation of evil like Isaac. Slate hadn't done anything wrong. But in the span of one night, he'd blown past every rule I'd ever set myself.

Don't invite them home.

Don't let them see you vulnerable.

Don't get attached.

And most important of all: *Don't fall for anyone.*

All of it crumbled to dust with one big, blue, innocent stare from Slate. It wasn't the fake-innocent stare of an experienced brat who knew how to get what he wanted.

No, Slate was the real deal, under all his layers of self-loathing —no doubt planted there by Isaac for his own amusement. I could rip the bastard limb from limb. I'd known Slate for less than a day, but I'd go to the ends of the earth to protect that innocent, tender vulnerability he'd shown me last night.

My stares out the door of Daddy Cakes mirrored the hungry gazes of my customers into the glass display case. Slate was milling around the crowds filtering out of Dom Nation, offering the serving tray to any and all.

He was dressed the same as last night, but his attitude tonight couldn't be more different. He moved with a newfound confidence to another group of four men, smiling and coyly catching one of their eyes. He laughed at something they said and offered the tray.

One of them put a hand on his arm instead and ran it up his shoulder while the others grinned. I recognized them—Doms, all of them.

I couldn't look away. Deep in my chest, my very soul snarled in a primal rage I had no right to. I *wanted* a monopoly on flirtation. But I was the one insisting at every turn that I wasn't his Daddy, so I couldn't very well get angry now. But inexplicably, every friendly and flirty gesture made me want to storm outside and snatch him away from them all.

Slate sidled away from them with another playful grin and looked right over at me through the glass door. His glance was sly and knowing, a smile playing on his lips. Like he knew how much it irritated me.

Or else he wanted me to see that he was turning them all down.

I should smile or something. Maybe wink at him. *Do* something. But rooted to the spot, all I could do was cling to his gaze like a lifeline.

"Well." Seb's deep voice made me nearly jump out of my skin. He cast a pointed look between me and Slate, then raised an eyebrow. "Running a home for waifs and strays?"

A defensive flush burned through my cheeks. "He's new. He needs… guidance."

Seb smirked knowingly, rubbing a palm over his salt-and-pepper beard, which was just short enough it could still be called scruff. "Needs you, you wanted to say," he told me as he leaned on the counter with an elbow.

I sighed and pinched the bridge of my nose. There was a lull in customers, and nobody at the tables nearby could hear us. "Fine," I muttered and folded my arms. "I invited him home last night."

"So I heard." Seb's deep brown eyes glittered with curiosity. "Why? He's not *your* boy."

I gritted my teeth. It was impossible to ignore the pull in me at those words. I hated them, and hated that Seb was right. Did that mean I wanted Slate?

"I let him sleep in my *bed*," I hissed, shaking my head. "I must be out of my mind."

"Love does strange things to a man." But despite his teasing words, Seb was studying me like an insect pinned to a card.

That trick didn't usually have any effect. A submissive boy might squirm and blush, but not me. Tonight, though? I turned as red as a maraschino cherry.

"Stop," I muttered. "Go directly to jail, do not pass Go."

"Am I wrong?"

"You're a dick," I told him, and I earned an easygoing laugh.

"I am," Seb agreed. "You know that. But am I wrong?"

Ugh, I hated when he pulled this shit. Normally he left me alone to figure out what I needed on my own time. But early on, when I'd been brand-new to DN, he'd pushed me more— forced me to admit what I wanted to do, and it had made me a better Dom.

He was doing the same thing all over again, and we both knew it.

I refused to answer, just looking around the little shop as if I could summon someone to the counter for another cupcake by doing so. But everyone was caught up in conversation or scrolling through Grindr on their phones. Damn it, there was no rescue in sight.

Seb blocked my view by stepping in front of me, making me look at him. "Is he your boy or not? He's out there hustling for you right now," he said, his voice stern but quiet—a scolding note in it.

I bristled. "What's it to you?" *He doesn't have eyes on him, does he?* We might have been friends for years, but I'd fight tooth and nail to keep hold of Slate.

Which was exactly the problem. I wasn't supposed to form attachments like that—not to anyone. Slate deserved someone like Seb in his life, not… me.

The grin spread over Seb's face. "Wow. You've got it bad, X." His casual use of my nickname soothed my ruffled feathers. He'd had my back over the years—he wasn't trying to steal my boy.

Crap. No. Not *my* boy.

Jesus, Rex. Get it together, I thought. Briefly losing my cool, I huffed and pulled my shoulders up in a sharp shrug. "So I want him. So what?"

"You tell me. You're making him parade around out there—"

"Letting him," I corrected him sharply. He couldn't know how Slate had sweet-talked me into it this morning.

"Who's in charge here?" Seb asked. I blushed, but his tone was gentle. "If he's not your boy, stop dicking the poor fucker around. And if he is… well, make sure he knows that."

"Thanks for the unsolicited advice column," I sighed heavily, drawing circles on the counter as I looked out the glass door again.

"Isaac's not around, by the way. But I think you knew that, if you left Slate outside by himself." Seb's gaze was far too perceptive. I'd made inquiries this evening before Slate arrived, and one of Isaac's friends had said he wouldn't be here tonight.

Good. That didn't absolve the guilt that squirmed in my belly about not telling Brighton or the DMs what was going on. This was the worst kind of secret to keep.

"Oh?" I asked, trying to sound casual.

"He flew into a temper last night after you two left. Tony told him to cool his heels and not come back for a couple of nights."

I whistled under my breath, my respect for the doorman growing. He might be scrawny and full of attitude at inconvenient moments, but he never took shit from the real assholes.

"There's no such thing as competition for you. When you want someone, you get them. I've never seen you stumble like this." Seb poked my shoulder. "Close the shop, bring him to DN, and act like a normal human being," he said with a grin. The asshole sounded like he was enjoying this. "You're allowed to have a crush, you know."

Oh, God. Spare me, I thought and flipped him off.

"Think about it." Seb just laughed, then waved as he sauntered for the door.

He sure left me with a lot to think about, like it or not, as I waited for the display cabinet to dwindle away to empty.

It was true that I felt an irresistible attraction to Slate and the desire to Daddy him. To take care of him and put the pieces back together, lift him back to his feet when he was down.

But I also knew I couldn't be the tender and kind man Slate had seen so far—the version of me that he deserved. I was no better than Isaac, fooling him into thinking *that* was who I was.

The bitter, cruel streak that made me so dangerous to be around—I couldn't risk Slate finding that piece of me. And it seemed like he was trying hard to draw it from me.

My patience had run out. I sighed with relief when we were down to the last cupcake. Once nobody was looking, I hid it under the counter.

God. What was I doing? This was a far cry from the version of me that Seb had first met, four years ago.

That Rex—or Master X, really—would have taken Slate's offers. He would have drawn every ounce of agonized pleasure he could from Slate's cries, satisfied himself, left Slate boneless and wrung dry, and fucked off to his own life again.

In a small way, I wished I could be that guy. It would be easier than facing the fact that Seb was right: I had feelings for Slate.

And that made me vulnerable, which was the thing I hated most in life.

I swallowed hard and cleared my throat. "We're closing in a few minutes, guys," I announced. Without waiting for a reply from my customers at the tables, I hightailed it outside.

Slate was resting the near-empty silver tray on his shoulder and laughing with another guy.

It was Derrick. Good. My chest eased with relief, because I'd only ever known Derrick as a sub.

God, I need to get a grip, I told myself. *He's allowed to flirt with other Doms. If he wants that.* There was no telling my gut how to feel about it, though.

"Oh, hey, Master X," Derrick greeted me with a warm smile, his gaze flicking from my leather apron up to my eyes. He was flirting, without a doubt. And he was cute enough, with blond hair and a button nose.

We'd played together before, but I wasn't interested tonight. I almost felt bad about overlooking him, but it was impossible to spare any attention when Slate stood right there, attracting me like a deep earth magnet.

"Hi," I greeted them both. "Slate, we're all done. Come inside."

"Yes, Master X," Slate answered, but his tone was playful. He offered Derrick the last piece of cupcake from his tray and winked. "Nice meeting you."

"You too." Derrick smirked to himself as he looked between us. Good—he wasn't taking rejection hard. "See you around."

I nodded and stepped closer to Slate, placing my hand on the expanse of bare skin between his shoulder blades, my finger-tips just grazing the back strap of his harness. I steered him toward my shop, and we stepped aside to let the last few customers leave.

"That was fun," Slate commented, leaning on the counter as he watched me turn the lock and start cleaning up so I could close up. He was a tall, insufferably gorgeous drink that I couldn't have, and it was maddening.

"Oh?" I grunted and moved to the register to count up the cash.

"You should hire me more often. I work for cheap."

Here he goes again with his flirting. I tried not to smile. He thought he was a lot sneakier than he really was. "Do you, now?"

Sensing his opportunity, Slate leaned in eagerly, betraying the casual attitude with which he'd tried to lean there and tempt me closer. "Oh, yes," he breathed out. "I'm sure we can work out… a fair payment."

"A top-up bonus?" I countered, and when he looked startled, I grinned. "Because you already seem pretty happy having an excuse to let all the guys look at you."

My voice was a lot sharper than I'd meant it to be—tight with a potent fear.

What if he meets another Dom who's better for him? Shouldn't I want that for him?

"Woof," Slate breathed through pursed lips. "I thought those eyes were naturally green."

But he seemed pleased with himself, too. I realized why a moment later. My jealousy was confirmation of his suspicions that I wanted him. Since for some crazy reason he didn't seem to realize how fucking out of character I was acting. And how could he know? We'd only just met.

Goddamn, Slate. Of course I want you, I thought, sighing as his cheeks rounded with a pleased smile. *Too much for your own good.* But he'd run a mile if I told him why I was holding myself back.

"Have a cupcake," I told him instead, brushing past him and ignoring the sparks of pleasure that danced along my skin at the moment of contact. I retrieved the last cupcake from its hiding place and set it on a plate, then handed it over with a napkin.

Slate grinned. "And you said you don't do sugary sweet."

Had I? It took me a moment to remember that conversation, and my laugh was sudden and startled. Slate was much too sharp in mind and tongue to allow me to be the slick, cool, confident Dom most people saw.

"Well, only now and then," I rebutted after a few moments too long, my cheeks burning. "Don't tell anyone." So I couldn't stare at his tongue, which was currently lasciviously drawing around the tips of his fingers, I walked away to close the blinds.

While my back was turned, Slate said, "DN's open for a couple more hours."

Fuck. I lowered the blinds on the windows, meticulously locking one at a time. "Yes…" I answered, my chest thumping. Finally, I cleared my throat as I turned to look at him. "I was thinking that myself," I admitted.

Slate grinned. "Were you also thinking about a drink? And a dance?"

"I was thinking of asking a certain boy for those things," I told him, keeping a straight face. "But it looks like he's trying to give orders again."

Slate's eyes went wide, and he froze against the counter. "No...?" His voice was high and hopeful, like he was trying out the answer that would get him what he wanted.

And what he wanted was obvious. It had been all along. But I wasn't strong enough to resist it any longer.

I walked closer to him, untying the strings of my leather apron. "So, *if* I extended an invitation to a boy," I started softly and paused. I hid a smile at the way he eagerly rocked forward like he was memorizing it all. "It would mean accepting my role as his Daddy for that night."

I was toe-to-toe with Slate now, and I tilted my head back to peer the four inches or so up into his eyes. Slate gulped loudly.

"And in turn, I'd expect that boy to listen to me, and behave."

God. What the hell was I doing? Seb was right—I should send him home and stop stringing him along. I couldn't be his Daddy; he couldn't be my boy.

Sorry, Seb. I can't stop dicking him around. I hated the guilt that swirled in my gut, but I needed just one more adrenaline rush. One more intoxicating night savoring Slate's sweet submission.

Like I deserved it.

Unaware of the turmoil wracking me, Slate was beaming. "Yes, sir," he whispered. He straightened up, pushing away from the counter and standing with his hands by his sides. "I can listen. And obey. And serve. You've seen me do it."

I sure as fuck had. It made electric pulses ripple through my body, straight down to my cock, just remembering him. When I closed my eyes, all I saw was Slate on his knees, offering up his whole body and spirit.

And fuck, I couldn't deny it—I was a little bit angry, too. That he'd so lightly chosen me, not knowing everything he should about who I was. He was naive and gullible. Anyone could see that a mile off.

But if I was taking advantage of him, who was at fault? Me.

I licked my lips, ruthlessly stifled the guilt within, and let the ruse continue—the pure intentions and steadfast force of will I was faking for his sake.

In a heartbeat, I'd have him, I thought, and I dug my fingers into the leather in my hands. Suddenly I wished it were anything else—a whip, a flogger, a paddle, anything I could use to take what he was so clearly offering.

"In that case," I said, my voice low and rough, "come with me to Dom Nation." I grabbed his hand, tingles dancing up my arm to settle somewhere in my chest, my heart thumping.

Slate lurched forward, so quick to follow that he crashed into me like an overgrown puppy. I yelped and braced myself, but his weight threw me off-balance—and we went down.

The floor was waxy and cold under my back, and Slate was hot and heavy on me, his limbs tangled with mine. My self-control had been thin enough before now, but with his weight pressed into me…

Every pulse of blood shot straight down south, and I choked back a groan. My blood pumping and heart pounding, all I could do was gape at him, my mouth opening and closing ungracefully. "Slate!" I scolded.

"Sorry! Sorry," Slate panted, squirming against me and yanking his arm out from under my shoulders. But the grinding motion of his hips against mine only stirred my blood faster.

I choked back a moan, curling my hands into fists and focusing everything I had on the bites of pain into my palms.

Take charge, I reminded myself. Instead of squirming with him, I lay still on the floor and projected a coolness and calm that I wished I felt as keenly as I could imitate it.

"Rule one, boy," I said, watching his eyes widen and breathing hitch as he froze on all fours above me. "Don't throw around your weight unless you want me to throw around mine."

An odd mix of curiosity and worry flashed through his eyes— like he wanted to find out what I meant, but he was slightly afraid.

Good. He had *some* self-preservation instincts.

"Sorry," he whispered hoarsely, his cheeks flushed red. He scrambled into a crouch and offered me his hands.

Is there a dignified way to get out of this? I wondered, still sprawled across the floor and trying to make it look like I belonged there. If I took his hands and he hauled me upright, he might think he could push me around in the future.

Slate impatiently gestured with his hands and then grinned, a wicked spark in his eye. "Well, now I know what the view would be like."

It only took me a second to realize what he meant. And then I couldn't unsee it.

Slate would look *incredible* riding me, his hands bound behind his back, the hard line of his shaft bouncing up and slapping down against my stomach with every thrust, a sheen of sweat gleaming on his brow and trickling down his chest...

Fuck. I was hard as hell, my tip wet and straining against my underwear, pushing a tent out from my trousers. I couldn't hide it, or the way my lips fell apart and my glassy gaze wandered up and down his body.

He grinned at me like he was extremely pleased with himself and wiggled his fingertips again.

"I know what you're doing," I told him tartly, finally accepting his hands to get up. Slate's grip was strong and reliable, making me relax and trust him. He pulled me to my feet so fast and effortlessly that I wobbled before I found my footing.

The mischievous smile vanished, and he looked solemn. "That was an accident. One hundred percent. Sorry, sir. It won't happen again." But his smile never left his eyes.

Slate still held both my hands, and the firm pressure of his warm skin on mine made my cock ache for contact with his body. I wanted to throw my arms around him and press into his thigh. I'd grind shamelessly, denying him release while making him feel every quiver and ripple of my body as I found release against him...

cruel.

Fuck. I was ready. Slate was about to meet Master X for the first time.

I hesitated, my hand on the handle of my favorite, trusty flogger for a long few moments. Then I let go and zipped the bag shut, slinging it over my shoulder. I'd get it out of the bag check later, if…

If. Just *if*.

Slate wants it, that nagging voice at the back of my head said. *So why aren't you going with it?* It was an equation I didn't want to solve. Better to pretend my denial was a fucked-up foreplay.

Because Christ, as I wove through the crowd to pick Slate out in a heartbeat standing by the bar, I wanted him.

The light was strongest here by the bar, and the glow shimmered on his tanned, ruddy bare skin. His understated black-and-silver harness and shorts looked perfect, but he stood awkwardly, one arm folded across his chest like he wasn't used to showing off so much skin.

Yet his harness wasn't crisp or stiff—the supple leather bore the marks of use. And he didn't seem startled by any of the outfits on display.

Who is Slate, really? God, I want to unpick all of his layers and wrap myself in them.

Slate was gazing around the room as if studying everyone, his legs crossed, one toe tapping the ground gently.

I smiled as I came to a halt in front of him. "Hello, boy."

His gaze flickered across me like he was about to turn me down, and then his eyes widened as he recognized me. That brief second made me grin. *He* was *waiting for me.*

But it made me grin even more as his jaw fell open and his cheeks flushed. He tried to speak once, failed, and cleared his throat as he passed me a clear plastic cup. "That's… uh… you look hot," he said, his voice strained. "Sir?"

His eyes were definitely *not* on my face.

"My eyes are up here," I teased him gently. When he quickly looked up with a guilty smile, I winked and took a sip from the cup he'd handed me. "Scotch and soda?"

"Yes. Is that okay?"

"Just fine," I lied as the whiskey kicked me in the nostrils, tonsils, and lungs for good measure. I had to breathe carefully to avoid coughing out the words. If I had a thread of dignity left, I wanted to keep it.

Slate relaxed gradually, eyeing me. "I don't know what to say that isn't a come-on," he admitted at last, clearing his throat as he rubbed his face. "Can we dance instead?"

My brow arched. I appreciated his honesty, and it was hard not to laugh at his sheepish grin. "Come on, then," I said and took his hand, towing him toward the dance floor.

I'd never felt hotter. It wasn't just the way Slate looked at me, but the way everyone else looked at us knowingly—probably thinking, *Master X leading another boy around like a lovesick puppy?*—and I stood even taller. They didn't know the secrets between us.

I pulled him to a halt in a quiet corner of the room that was reserved for dancing—and, of course, the occasional public show.

Then I swung him around until we faced each other, and I started moving to the deep, throbbing beat. It thumped through the air, vibrating my chest, prickling along my skin, under my briefs, straight to the tip of my aching shaft.

If I coughed after sipping my drink, it was easier to hide the soft noises in the thumping music that made the very air tremble around us.

It was a slow, sensual roll, and so were our bodies, moving together as they found a rhythm seemingly without our say-so. It didn't take long, either. By the time I'd tipped back the last of my drink, we were so close I could feel his hot breath against the rim of my ear, his hand gliding so carefully up my side like he wasn't sure he was allowed to touch.

"Latex," he said, hardly audible over the music.

I nodded, gesturing for him to finish his drink. Once he did, I pulled his other hand until he held my sides, and then ran my hands up those strong forearms until I gripped his shoulders.

It felt so right, like our bodies were meeting for a moment that nothing could ever interrupt. It was meant to be, the rhythm of our bodies and hearts.

Nearby, two men ground together, unmistakably caught up in something even more explicit. They were both shirtless, but the darkness of the dance floor hid any other details. One cried out softly, their bodies rocking while the other gripped his head, pulling him close. Unlike at least three-quarters of the room, I didn't recognize them.

Slate's gaze followed mine, and then he gasped softly. He touched my back, fingers tangling in the laces of my corset as he tore his gaze away from them and back to me. "Sexy," he approved, a growl in my ear. "I wish you'd let me unlace this, at least."

"No," I told him. It was a real pain in the ass to lace up, apart from anything else. And I didn't want to get him into bad habits, like exposing me in public. No way.

Slate widened his eyes, pouting, but I just grinned. *Not a chance, boy*, my look said.

Slate gave up and ran his fingertips up to my shoulders instead, touching like he couldn't quite believe I was here for real.

Our bodies pressed together as he leaned into me, and they didn't part again. With every step, we couldn't pull back—we only fell further into one another. As sweat beaded across his chest, our skin glided together, hot and wet.

Fuck. How am I supposed to resist this? Why even try?

I stepped forward until the buckles of his harness pressed against my chest and our hips met. My hard length ground into his thigh, sparks ricocheting through me as my belly flipped with intoxicating arousal. Every muscle in my body was taut.

Slate's hands froze on my back for a moment, and his breath caught. "Oh," he groaned, his fingertips wandering down like he was going to grab my ass. "Master X. Is that a whisk in your pocket, or are you happy to dance with me?"

I choked back a laugh and beat him to it, reaching down to grip his thighs. He quivered in my touch, cupping my ass gently and kneading, but his motions were gentle and distracted. Even now, I controlled him. I trailed my fingertips up his bare skin until I reached the bottom hems of his shorts. I pulled them up just a little, working my fingertips underneath.

Slate whimpered, turning to putty in my hands, and fuck, my resistance was crumbling.

He pulled back, his eyes glassy and lips wet and parted and *right there*.

I was staring, shameless in my wanting, and he held my gaze without flinching away. He looked hungry—desperate, even.

But however hard I wished I could, I couldn't bring myself to close that distance between us. To press a kiss on his lips, and pull him close to me, and tell him how much I wanted him.

Like tectonic plates, my spirit was caught between opposing forces: I was trying with all I had to pull him closer, but another part of me was pushing him away.

I couldn't fathom the idea of giving all of myself to one man— letting him have the power to crush me. I was already vulnerable. I liked Slate, way too much. Every minute I was around him, he intoxicated me. I couldn't peel myself away cleanly. Walking away wasn't an option.

But that only left one route, which made me feel like a cornered animal.

Even through the gloomy light, Slate's gaze was soft and terrifyingly perceptive.

"Come on," he murmured, his breath hot across my cheek. "Walk with me."

I hesitated, my gaze searching his. I found nothing but understanding and curiosity, and it only made shame burn hotter within my chest.

Fuck. I should be the one giving orders here, I thought, biting my lip hard.

I'd envisioned myself confidently steering him around. A neat, clean power exchange—the way it always worked. I'd be the one showing him off, like I'd done plenty of nights with plenty of boys.

What was Master X if he wasn't meticulous and precise and all-knowing? A chill ran down my spine a second later. Shit, that was it: I wasn't Master X tonight, and I didn't know why.

It wasn't Slate, it was me. I swallowed hard and nodded, taking his hand to pick our way through the crowd and through the hallway.

But he didn't stop at the bar. Instead, he led me through the well-lit space toward the playroom.

I caught a breath and dug my heels in, frowning the question at him.

What are you doing, Slate?

Slate's grip tightened on my hand, like he was afraid to let go of me. "We can just look."

But I shook my head slightly, the world spinning around me. Christ, he had no idea what he'd awoken in me, did he?

I wasn't the man who could neatly string him up, dispense a punishment, and send him on his way.

My heart was on the line, and the monster that I kept on its own tight chain deep in my soul was snarling, pulling at the fraying edges of my resistance.

I wasn't myself tonight, and the only reasonable conclusion was that *Slate* was having this effect on me. Wide-eyed and clueless all while pulling me out of my usual routine.

I hated how much I wanted him, and the way my hands shook. I gripped his hand tighter too, our fingers crushing one another's like a weird thumb-wrestling match.

"No," I said, my voice breathless and hoarse.

The disappointment on Slate's face stung, but it wouldn't last long. I already knew what my next words would be.

God help me, I didn't trust myself not to pick Slate apart for all to see. Not to lose control of myself, and let Rex loose in the playroom, until I was the one whose spirit was bared for all to see.

So I gulped and said, "Come home with me."

It was clear what my words meant. *Yes*, I was saying to him at last. Or maybe, *I can't stop myself anymore. You've won, Slate. You've got me. I hope you can handle me.*

Slate's grin would have glowed from miles away. He took my shoulders and scanned my face, his gaze eager, seemingly not noticing the way I tensed up. For a moment, it felt like the power dynamics were all flipped on their head.

Like he was the one with my heart nestled in his hand. I didn't usually fear rejection, but nothing about tonight was the usual.

"Yes," Slate whispered. His fingertips glided up to my neck, and then his palms stopped just short of my neck. Like he wanted to cup my face and kiss me, his gaze intent on my lips.

And I stared at his soft, wet mouth, and tears pricked the corners of my eyes with the sheer *wall* of *want* that hit me, like a wave I hadn't been braced to withstand. It washed me off my feet, my heart slamming in my chest.

More than anything, I wanted to taste him, but not here. Not for all to see. Somewhere for just the two of us. *That* was a thought I'd never had before—not once. I was flying blind, and he was the light guiding me home.

"Let's go," I rasped, stopping by the bag check so we could get our bags. By unspoken agreement, neither of us wanted to waste time changing before we left.

The cool night air did nothing to cool me off, and nobody approached us as we stood alone by the curb and waited for the taxi. Good. Perhaps they sensed the chemistry between us, thick enough to cut with a knife. The air sparked with the same electric storm that ran roughshod through my spirit and heart.

We climbed in the car, and I murmured my address. It was time to go home a different man from the one who had started the day. And Slate would pay for it. I just hoped he knew what he was doing, because for the first time in years... I didn't.

But at long last, I felt *alive*.

9

SLATE

"Wanna see something cool?"

I managed to keep my face straight as I said, "Is it your dick?"

The elevator door had slid closed, and Rex hadn't pressed the button for his floor yet. It was a reasonable guess, and better still, it startled him into a laugh.

"No, that's hot." There he went again, teasing me. But after our time at DN, I finally had high hopes he'd back up his words with actions.

I swayed closer, hooking my forefingers around the straps of his sexy red latex corset. God bless him, the doorman hadn't even blinked. "How hot?" I asked, my voice a sultry purr.

Rex didn't take the bait. He raised his eyes and his voice, speaking crisply and clearly. "Penthouse floor." The elevator set into motion, the movement barely noticeable.

I jolted with surprise, keeping a grip on his corset. "Who the fuck are you, anyway?" I joked, but I was kind of serious, too.

For a guy his age, this setup was insanely good. A career in baking definitely hadn't paid for this place, unless the baked goods came with a little something extra. So was Daddy paying? I didn't think so. Rex was too proud to let me hold him in bed, let alone take others' money.

But oh boy, this young man had layers.

Rex spoke in a husky voice, not brushing me off. "Nobody to be concerned with." Before I could roll my eyes, he grinned. For a moment, he looked his age—a little dorky and very pleased with himself. "Always wanted to say that."

I snorted with laughter and pulled him closer, looping my arms around his shoulders instead. I wasn't sure he'd let me, but he did.

Rex was avoiding the question, but fuck it, he was even more adorable, and I wanted to be on my knees for him. No—well, yes. But not just that. The dopamine flooding my body right now wasn't a sexual kick.

It was a lot warmer and fuzzier, and there was no point in avoiding the label even inside my own head, but I still steered my thoughts away.

Silence fell between us, except for the quiet whir of the elevator rising to the top floor of the building. Suddenly Rex's face was right there, his expression like glass. I ached to take his smooth control apart with the scorching heat of my kisses.

Rex's eyes flicked between mine, studying me once again like a puzzle to be solved, or a philosophy riddle to be answered. Could he ever just dwell in this second, shifting and riding the currents of attraction between us like the tide under a full moon? I ached to find out.

But the elevator slid to a halt and the doors slid open, revealing the steel door of Rex's apartment. I let go of him as he pressed his hand to a panel next to the door and it opened.

Okay, I would have noticed that. He'd *definitely* avoided showing off the first night I stayed here, which was even more fascinating.

This time, I better appreciated the view that opened in front of us—the short hallway opening into that gorgeous kitchen and the living room with its stunning view, the bedroom tucked away behind a thin wall yet sprawling in its own right.

It felt as spacious inside my own heart as it did here. Being here was like cutting all those ties that had held me back from seeking and finding throughout the years. Unlike my own house, there were no ghosts or shadows to slip into the corner of my eye.

"You've been clear what you want from me," said Rex, setting down his bag.

His fingertips trailed down the back of my arm until they rested on my palm. I shivered with anticipation, turning to face him and closing my fingers around his. "Yes...?" It was impossible to keep the hope from my voice.

Rex led me toward the living room, stopping in the vast expanse of floor between his kitchen island and the living room. Then he stopped and looked at me, facing me like he was preparing for battle. "I'm the one throwing up walls."

Understatement, I thought. One corner of my mouth quirked upward in a half-smile I couldn't quite hide. But I didn't need to say it; Rex's smile grew sheepish when he saw mine.

"I can't explain," Rex said.

"Can't?" I echoed, taking his other hand and squeezing it. I swung his hands gently, hoping to diffuse the tension that sparked through his muscles, the hardness of his body which was so clearly on display without so many clothes to hide behind. Then I took the risk. "Or don't want to?"

Rex's brow furrowed. His lips pinched together, and then he huffed quietly, his gaze sliding from mine toward the ceiling. "You won't let me take an inch more than you want to give, will you?"

I couldn't resist. A grin spread across my face. "I didn't think you were the type to take *any* inches."

"Just to be clear, I'm not," Rex told me, looking like he wanted to swat me for my impertinence. But the amusement danced under his words, too. He stepped closer. "And I'm not soft or gentle, whatever you might think."

Yet he wasn't pulling away or shoving me around to prove himself. His touches had been gentle all evening. His words stood in stark contrast to the truth, which made me wonder.

Did he really see himself as harsh and uncaring? Or did he see the other Doms who *were* and compare himself negatively? I ached to know what the hell was running through that layered mind of his.

"I also expect a lot less sass than I seem to get from you." Rex was smiling now, and suddenly a spark of danger was in the air.

A pleasant danger—charged with warning that I wanted to run toward. How the hell this reflex had ever evolved in humans, I didn't know. Surely the idiots who got mauled and *liked* it wouldn't live long.

But fuck, I needed to feel the harsh parts of him like shards of ice dragging across the heat that simmered uncontrollably under my skin.

"That doesn't scare me, just so you know." I smiled back at him, tilting my chin up stubbornly. "I'm tougher than I look. Which is pretty tough." I gave him a self-deprecating wink. I wasn't an idiot. I knew I looked my age—maybe a little old for my age.

Somehow, Rex didn't seem to mind. The comparisons I'd drawn when we first met had fallen away, and it seemed impossible to hold on to them in the face of the energy he brought to us.

"But you like the unexpected," I told him, letting go of his hands. I walked my fingers up both of his bare arms, shivering with delight at the smooth, warm skin under my touch. When I reached his shoulders, I drew the fingertips of both index fingers across his shoulders, like I could frame his spirit in the gesture. "You're not *all* rigid routines."

For all his words, he'd shown me more than he thought about what kind of Daddy he was. I might be gambling with my statement, but the odds were good. After all, he'd adapted quickly to what I offered, like my sidewalk service.

Surprise flickered across Rex's face, and then his eyes narrowed like he was catching control of himself again. "Correct," he murmured, his voice off-kilter. "What else have you noticed about me?"

There it was—a vulnerability he probably didn't realize leaked from his words. I only recognized it because I felt it keenly in my own spirit. For some crazy reason, he was a little bit afraid of what *I'd* seen in him. Like my opinion mattered.

"More than you think," I said, winking to tease him. But I softened it with a gentle smile, too. The razor's edge of power flicked back and forth between us both, a delicate dance.

I let the statement become innuendo by stepping backward so I could look him up and down. As I did, my fingertips trailed over his collarbones and across the red, smooth straps that crisscrossed his chest, straight down to his nipples.

My heart hammered at my ears, the delicate nubs deliciously hard under my sensitive fingertips.

"Even more than I'd hoped for," I whispered, my gaze finally slipping past his chest as I made it clearer than ever what I craved. The bulge pressed against shining black latex, enough of a line pressed into his tight briefs that it was clear he was just as turned on as me.

I'd felt his hard-on when we danced together, straining at my self-control. It was impossible to ignore the urge to lavish attention on him the moment the opportunity arose. So to speak.

If only I could have tempted him into the playroom... but for now, this was better. Our first time—or so I hoped, because my balls would be bluer than the frigging ocean if he sent me home now—it was just for us.

I wanted to be *his*, at last. To give myself just to him. And then he could show me off later, when he finally accepted the power I was offering him.

Rex said nothing, his hands locked behind his back as he stood rooted to the spot. Yet despite my fingertips circling his nipples, he gave no sign of being affected apart from his heavier breathing.

Like he knew that unyielding stare was what I craved.

He inspected me, his head tipped just slightly to one side, like he was weighing up my silent pleading. Judging if I was worthy of him.

Fuck, and there I went—getting hard in my suddenly unbearably tight leather shorts, sparks dancing across every inch of bare skin I suddenly remembered was on display.

Somehow, with him by my side, the rushes of cool air against my chest and back had stopped making me self-conscious the moment I'd gotten into the taxi. Strolling through the lobby in less than I usually wore to the beach had felt like second nature.

What the hell was Rex doing to me?

I squirmed on the spot, my toes curling into the floor as I gulped. His inspection was slow and methodical. In an effort to fan the flames of desperation that licked up my thighs and straight into my belly, I flicked my fingertips across his nipples.

But Rex stepped back with a chiding head shake and fixed me with a stare that kept me from chasing after him. Instead, he walked around me in a slow circle.

I held perfectly still, my pulse fluttering in my throat. I could hardly breathe with anticipation. I wasn't even trying to tense up every muscle in my body for show. He just had that effect on me, the arousal tight and so hot it made me almost burst from the effort of holding back.

At last, after one and a half complete circles around me, Rex's warm palm touched my shoulder blade.

I whimpered, my nipples hard and cock harder as my thighs trembled. If I stared into the huge plate glass windows ahead of me, the night showed his reflection, but only the outlines. I was left to fill in the blanks myself, like the intensity of his stare.

Rex's touch dragged along my back to my bicep and then across the gap to my chest as he came to stand in front of me again. Every fucking inch that he touched lit up like a Christmas tree, begging for more.

Without warning, he turned my trick on me and dragged his fingertip around one nipple, then flicked it harshly with a fingernail.

I gasped and almost buckled at the knees, a hoarse cry escaping as the impact shuddered through me like a lightning bolt starting fires in its wake.

Every inch of me was awake—alive—and hungry.

"Rex," I begged, my voice thin and needy already. The air between us shuddered with unpredictable static. I couldn't tell what he'd do next, but I was transfixed and needy.

And *fuck*, my cock strained against my shorts, tenting the unforgiving fabric. The head was trapped against my thigh, pulsating angrily. But when I reached down to try to adjust myself, Rex smacked my hand away.

The prickle of pain at his sudden, harsh movement made me whimper, and I dropped my hand to my side. Inside my shorts, wetness trickled from the tip of my poor, hard shaft. It just made the leather glide across the sensitive head with every twitch of my cock.

Rex wasn't satisfied with that. "Hands behind your back," he ordered, his voice low and certain. He knew he'd be obeyed despite the discomfort of my arousal and my desperate need for freedom.

Fuck, Rex *was* cruel, and I loved it.

No, cried every instinct that turned away from pain and hungrily desired the shallow, immediate pleasure of getting what I wanted.

Yes, cried my need to be broken down and made into Rex's very own. And, of course, that was the force that would win every time.

My breathing heavy, I managed to ignore my animal desires for long enough to clasp my hands behind my back. I groaned, keeping my thumb tight as a clamp around my other thumb. I poured all my resolve and will into that one simple action.

But Rex wasn't going to reward me for as simple an act of subservience as *that*. I could tell in the appraising gaze he ran over me that this was a test.

Fuck, I wanted him to run more tests. I wanted to write into every cell of my body the memory of this impersonal, objective gaze. Like I was being evaluated.

And I *wanted* to be found wanting.

Isaac had taken all of our equipment—every buckle and clip—save this harness that barely contained my eagerness. I found myself hungry for the stretch of leather around my wrists, the pull against my taut muscles. Strung and helpless: that was the best way to be.

But I sensed already that Rex wouldn't go that far tonight. This was psychological. He wanted to see if I could be an obedient boy. That didn't mean I couldn't surprise him. He ought to see what he was taking on.

So, still keeping my hands clasped firmly behind me, I sank to my knees in front of him. It was an awkward shudder to get those last few inches without my hands for balance, and I dropped heavily onto the ground.

The floor reverberated through my bones, punishingly hard. But I loved that he didn't wince for me—instead, he smiled slightly. Giddy at the smallest sign of approval, that sweet intoxication flooded my veins.

I sank willingly into it, tipping my head back as I gazed up at him. I couldn't keep the adoration and hope from my eyes. In this space where I lived now, there wasn't room for games.

Just shameful honesty, my every desire laid bare.

"Will you be my Daddy?" I whispered. The seconds might as well have slowed to a crawl, my hands shivering against each other, my whole body tense.

One word—that was all that lay between me and bliss.

Despite all his bluster about being cruel, Rex showed the softness he didn't seem to dare to admit. He answered instantly, rather than leave me to dangle in the wind and beg and plead.

"For tonight, yes."

I waited, breath bated, but there were no provisos this time. No doors slammed on the deepening currents between us. No arbitrary rules about what I could beg for.

A night of freedom. And then, who knows?

My grin was pure joy, and Rex's smile softened for a moment as he stepped closer—straddled my knees, his crotch just inches away. I salivated, forced to stare beyond his bulge to his face, trembling head to toe at the smooth heat of his legs against mine.

I wanted to grip his thighs and tilt my head back and let him use me, but I had no idea what he was planning. So I bit back the whimper and pressed my lips together.

Rex ran his hand through my hair, the touch soft. Almost affectionate, if not for the way he tightened his fingers—just for a moment—until my scalp prickled and my throat grew tight.

I made the slightest sound, choked from the back of my throat. But the moment it slipped out, Rex let go and my vision cleared as my body throbbed with disappointment.

More! I wanted to cry out. *Now, Daddy. Please. Please!*

But there was still *something* in the air between us—new and sharp and strange—which hadn't settled yet. I didn't quite dare.

Rex's smooth palm slid across the close-cropped stubble of my cheek. I knew by touch what he was doing. He traced the laugh lines along the corners of my lips and swept a thumb over my ruddy cheeks.

For once, I wasn't ashamed of the face I turned to him. Shame was too precious, too thrilling, to waste on anything that wasn't a choice. Instead, gratitude flooded my veins. Excitement made ten years come off my shoulders.

I was ready for anything.

"Thank you, sir," I whispered. "Thank you, Daddy." I turned my face, pressing my cheek into his hand. Nuzzled it as my eyes slid shut. Without sight, I couldn't drool over the length *right there*, under his shining black briefs.

But Rex didn't let me live in this simple bliss. He pulled his hand away, cupped the back of my head, and pulled my cheek against his bare thigh.

I gasped, struck by ravenous hunger like a man who had suddenly come to his senses after a spell living in his own dreams. As my eyes opened, I found my nose brushing *just* against the swell of his briefs.

I wanted to lick and suck, serve dand obey. His pleasure was my only concern now. The throbbing pulses of my shaft were exiled to a part of my mind that couldn't overpower the need I felt to please my Daddy.

I licked my lips, and my teeth caught the lower lip as I stared hungrily at the dessert he was keeping locked away from me. One thin layer of material was all that lay in the way.

That, and his permission. I didn't dare make this move until I was instructed to do so. But then—*then* I would reward him for giving in to my pleas. I'd close my lips around him, let him fill and fuck my mouth. I was a ready, waiting hole for him to use—

"Slate." My Daddy's voice cut through my half-lucid fantasies.

I swallowed a groan, finally tearing my gaze away to stare at his face again. "Yes, sir?" I whispered.

"I need to know if you have any triggers. Hard limits. Anything you don't want me to touch."

I wanted to scoff at the idea. Who was I to turn down anything he wanted? Isaac had never asked. A tiny voice inside me *knew* I should have more respect for myself than that. But a starving man couldn't afford pride.

Besides, I didn't want my submission to be on *my* terms. That was the whole point. I wanted to be his plaything, and toys didn't get to make the rules.

I shook my head, hoping to please him by the answer. If I didn't, at least I would know I was true to myself.

Rex's brow arched. "Nothing?" He eyed me like he wanted to stop and give me the lecture, but thankfully, he didn't. "We'll work on that later," he informed me.

All that I heard was *later*.

This wasn't it. He wasn't going to use and discard me. As much as I wanted that, it wasn't that simple—I wanted the *same* Daddy to use me at his will.

I wanted a boyfriend, a lover, a partner. A Daddy. One man to find the itch and press his nail into it over and over… not a string of faceless Doms scratching somewhere near the right spot.

And maybe—just maybe—Rex was agreeing to be that man.

A huge, stupid grin spread across my face. I almost swayed into him with my joy and relief, the room spinning around me. "Yes," I whispered my promise, eager. I'd say anything to get *right now* in progress.

"What do you want, then?" Rex asked, petting me like he might a kitten. His nails trailed across my scalp, and my body rippled agreeably as I tilted my head to the side to enjoy the touch.

My words tumbled from my lips. "I want to hurt." I closed my eyes—I couldn't look at him as I said this. Didn't want to risk the reaction, in case it wasn't what I hoped for. "I want to feel like I'm… a small, insignificant thing at your disposal. I want my punishment to be my reward. I want to say no and mean yes. I want…"

My voice trembled and broke, my throat filling with a lump too great to be swallowed away.

"Yes?" Rex whispered.

Fuck, I refused to believe that Rex was the man he thought he was, because his voice now was soft and patient, yet there was no trace of the dangerous smile he'd worn earlier.

I kept my eyes squeezed closed, my shoulders rolling forward. I hunched like I could hide the arousal throbbing underneath me from his gaze. "I think I need to break to feel whole."

My very soul gasped at the open air brushing against the words, and I wanted to curl my next words around myself like a wounded animal. It was the same feeling as walking into Dom Nation wearing just the harness and tiny shorts, vulnerable and exposed.

I pressed my face into Rex's smooth, bare thighs and clutched around the back of his knees. And he held me, his delicate palms still against my head and shoulder. He didn't stroke away the pain in my words—he just held me, secure and unmoving. Yet even without rubbing or touching, his presence enveloped me, folding me into him.

Rex's voice broke through my dizzy trance. "You're safe with me," Rex whispered, and I heard an ironclad promise in his words. "Always. I may break you, use you, hurt you—"

Oh, God, yes! A tide of desire flooded me again, and my cock throbbed at the fleeting fantasies that roared through my soul.

"—but I'll always listen to your needs. Your safeword. Which is...?"

Fuck. I pouted, pressing my face into his thighs a little harder like I could bury myself away from him and refuse to answer.

Rex's tone was sharp. "You're expected to have one, boy. And to answer when you're addressed."

Shit. My heart thudded, and I finally pulled away from his thighs, though it made me tremble. I didn't want to anger him.

"I…" My voice trailed off, unsure. I'd never chosen one with Isaac. Surely he guessed that.

But, as always, Rex was nothing like that man. He was taking care of me. And I was somehow reluctant to *be* taken care of so deeply, but I sensed that Rex wouldn't let me get away with that.

Fine. I'd give him a word. But I'd be damned if I'd use it.

"Pineapple," I mumbled at last, my eyes flicking up to meet his expectant gaze.

Rex smiled, and the anxious flutter of my nerves calmed. "Good boy," he praised softly. "You've earned a reward."

I rocked back onto my heels, my lips parting as I frowned up at him in confusion. Had I? How?

More importantly, hadn't he heard me say that I didn't want to be rewarded, but punished?

But I shouldn't have worried. Rex's sly smile made the prickle of reality fade away again, letting me sink into the fuzzy embrace of this place in my head. Was it subspace? I only knew what it felt like because I knew when I *wasn't* in it—or when something threatened to pull me out of it.

And right now, I couldn't quite think straight, in the best way.

He didn't say a word. My heart thumped, faster and faster, electricity crackling through me as I waited for the word. Or better still, for Rex to move.

I fucking loved being out of control, careening blindly toward a hairpin turn I'd never see in the darkness. And Rex was at the wheel right now. I was helpless. All I could do was cling to this ride for as long as it lasted.

Oh! I sucked in a quick breath, realizing all of a sudden that Rex was *waiting*. Waiting for me to tell him what I wanted my reward to be. Of course, there was the risk that he'd deny me, and I'd love that just as much.

Not my job to worry about that, I reminded myself. Rex was in charge here. All I had to do was be honest about what I needed.

"Can I suck your cock, sir?" I whispered. "Please, Daddy?"

Caught up in waiting to be denied, I didn't expect Rex's answer to be so simple. "Yes."

I gasped. *Yes?* Delight flooded me once I replayed the syllable in my head to be sure I'd heard it, instead of just fantasizing about it. *Yes!*

I hardly dared to believe he was letting me do this. Softly, I ran my hands up the outside of his thighs. I relished the hot, smooth skin gliding under my palms.

Carefully, so carefully, I brought my hands up to the zipper at the front of his latex briefs and eased it down, pulling the metal away from him at the same time so it didn't catch against his skin. Every tiny *snick snick snick* sound of the zipper gliding down its track made me shiver with anticipation.

The zipper ran all the way down to under his balls, but it was barely halfway down before the weight of him sprang free.

And there it was—Daddy's cock. It stood thick and tall, flushed pink at its mushroom-shaped head, and totally irresistible. My mouth watered, and I choked back a moan.

Rex chuckled softly, the noise a siren's call to my ear. "You like that, baby boy?"

Oh, Christ. I lurched toward him, my broad palm closing around the outside of his thigh, thumbnail digging into his skin. I pressed my nose into the crease of his hip. My eyes closed, but it couldn't hold back the tide that flooded my ears and blocked my brain.

Yes! Yes, I am. Yes, I do. Call me that again, please. But the thoughts raced through my brain too fast for words to catch up.

"Mmhmm," I mumbled, my voice hitching into a whimper toward the end of my noise.

"You *do* like that." Rex's voice was a self-satisfied purr, and I loved it. Making him happy. The pride in his voice completed me, told me that I was doing a good job.

Softly, he stroked my head again. My hair was too short to grip except in tiny clumps between his thumb and forefinger, so instead, his nails dragged fiery lines along my scalp.

My body rippled with pleasure unconsciously, my back arching as my mouth fell open. I tilted my face to the sky —to Rex.

I so badly wanted to earn his praise.

"Good boy," Rex whispered. "Now… taste Daddy's cock. I'm waiting for you, Slate. You don't want me growing impatient."

Urgency sparked me to life. I gasped and my eyes flew open, my palms sliding up Rex's thighs. I couldn't stop the grin that crossed my face as I finally curled my fingers under the heavy shaft that jutted proudly toward me.

And then, with all the thrilling trepidation of a first kiss, my lips pressed against the tip of his shaft. My lips parted and his hardness slid between them, over the tip of my tongue.

Salty, musky taste burst across my palate. I was intoxicated, and I was certain my body was pure glass. Rex had to be able to see—even feel—the joy imprinted on me.

I moaned, delighted at the heat pulsing across my tongue as I pressed my head closer to his body and he choked me with the weight of him. I pulled my head back, gasped for breath, and plunged down again.

I *loved* sucking cock. Both of us were vulnerable in totally different ways—yet in the same, shared way, our chemistry finally unchecked and running through the air like a drumline.

Rex filled my mouth, velvety soft but hard as hell. It was all I could do to keep my teeth covered as I gingerly bobbed my head, trying to take him all in, a little more at a time.

I sucked gently, reverential at the connection that pulsed between us. The trust my Daddy showed me, I wanted to repay tenfold. I needed to make him feel like the center of my world —because he was, all of a sudden.

And selfishly, I wanted to prove that I could be his boy and make him happy so I could earn a *next time*.

"Faster than that, boy. I don't have all night."

Oh, fuck. The edge of scorn in his voice was *perfect*. I groaned, my hands sliding around to grip his ass and hold tight. My body burned, a fresh aching wave rolling through my cock, trapped and straining against my stupid little shorts.

I widened my eyes and gazed up as I pulled slowly back, his wet length dragging across my swollen lips. Then he slid free, every vein glistening as I gulped for breath.

No way can I deep-throat him, if he makes me. It was impossible to distinguish desire from adrenaline as I took yet another risk and flicked the tip of my tongue against the slit of his shaft instead.

A shudder coursed through Rex's thighs, and a soft growl warned me that I was playing with fire.

The second time I tried to lick him, my feigned innocence came back to bite me.

"Impudent boy," Rex growled, both hands closing around the back of my head. His nails dug in roughly as he shoved his hips toward my face, his dick forcing its way between my lips and all the way to the back of my throat. "Didn't I tell you I don't like brats?"

There was no apologizing, though. My punishment was already here. He fucked my mouth in sharp thrusts, hard and fast.

Shit! I gasped and whimpered, struggling against his immovable hold as he choked me with his thick length. All I could smell was Rex, and the heat of my Daddy's body slammed against my nose without care.

My eyes flooded, my lungs burned for respite, and the throbbing rhythm of pleasure sped up in my chest. At last, he was *using* me, and holy mother of God, I fucking loved it.

The back of my throat hurt, and in the fractions of seconds between his thrusts, I could hardly breathe without choking on his precum and my spit.

I whimpered and thrashed, trying to apologize in my desperate little noises. But Rex didn't even acknowledge me as he fucked my mouth, forcing his way into my air-starved body however hard I tried to pull away.

The wet, sloppy sounds and his heavy breathing were the only companions to my thin, muffled, wordless pleas. He never stopped or slowed, and neither did he speed up. Like my wishes were irrelevant. Everything that happened to me was up to Rex's every whim.

As if on cue, he groaned softly, and the noise plucked a string deep in my gut, until every muscle in my body was taut with the reverberations of his pleasure.

This was exactly what I'd wanted. Or... I thought I'd wanted. Now that I was granted my wish, I wasn't sure I could handle it. It was all happening *right now*, with no time to think about it. Only animal instinct could suffice.

The cold, merciless edge to Rex's total control filled me with shameful delight like an empty vessel. An object for him to pour meaning into, a star that never shone bright until it was named.

His star. His boy. *His*.

But the unbearable pain between my thighs shook me out of the foggy void where I'd lost myself, planting me back in reality. It was a cold, uncomfortable place where my knees dug into the floor and my back ached.

I'd do anything to escape that prison and bask in the place where Rex was the only thought on my mind. So I fumbled with the front of my shorts, opening them and pulling them down so my aching length could spring free.

Christ, the relief that swept through me! I moaned softly, my shoulders softening and cock stiffening in my hand when the pain eased in my gut.

My animal need, though, wouldn't let me let go now. I kept hold of my length, my fingers a blissful, ridged, softer pressure than the tight seams of my shorts had been.

I lost the battle of wills and stroked myself. Pleasure purred through me, tightening my balls and tickling the head of my shaft until it throbbed along my skin in waves.

I'd barely pulled my hand along myself three times before my mouth was empty, my aching jaw finding relief while my spirit cried out in anxiety at the separation. I couldn't bear to lose Rex's attention, however much it hurt.

"Please," I gasped, shuffling forward as I tried to lick the hard shaft just inches away from my eyes.

But Rex gripped my chin, keeping me back. He spoke in a soft snarl, and all I could register was a danger I craved as much as I feared.

"You may touch yourself as long as you don't come, boy. But you should have asked first."

"I'm sorry." I gulped. And I was, but I was also too far gone to stop now. No transgression could do that. My orgasm was too close, burning too hot in every cell of my body.

I jerked my hand along my throbbing cock for dear life, every brush of my fingers across my skin sending another, stronger wave of arousal pounding through me.

Rex ignored my pathetic movements and spoke over me as if I'd never said a word. "If you don't ask me, boy, how do I know you won't do something *really* bad? Like come before me?"

He let go of my chin and patted my cheek firmly—more of a test than a scolding slap. But the sting reverberated through my cheek, straight to my swollen, still-tingling lips, and down my core to my shaft.

I leaned toward his hand and turned my cheek further away, begging silently for more.

Fuck. He didn't give me what I wanted, and my dick jumped in my hand as I realized that once again, I had to grovel.

Damn it, he'd been listening *way* too well to me, naturally taking charge of me in every way my body craved.

I wanted the harsh sting of his palm on my skin again, the humiliation of an open-handed slap against my skin. I wanted the bite of regret coursing through me in equal measure with the desire that swelled my cock in my own filthy little hand.

"I'm sorry," I whimpered again, closing my eyes as I struggled to breathe with anticipation. I knew he'd hate this excuse. "My mouth was a little full, Daddy—"

Instead of the harsh blow I deserved—expected, wanted, *craved* —the ground itself toppled under me.

No, *I* fell backward, my arms flying to the sides to try to catch myself. My eyes flew open in time to see Rex's foot square in the middle of my chest. In one clean blow, he knocked me sprawling on my ass, and then—as gracefully as if he'd just stepped over a pebble—straddled my sides.

Daddy's beautifully slender foot came to rest on my breastbone, the firm pressure of his toes nestled in the hollow at the base of my throat.

All I could see, staring up at him through the semidarkness of the apartment lit by the glow through the full-length windows, was the underside of his cock jutting out. Rex's shaft was still dripping wet, and my mouth still watered for the taste of him that I was now denied.

I reached for myself, blinded by the force of my need. I didn't dare point it out, but I hoped my Daddy noticed that at least I wasn't stroking myself. It required every ounce of self-control I possessed to keep my fingers from dragging up my skin, sparking every inch of the way. Squeezing myself would have to suffice for now.

The adrenaline rushed through me as I gulped for big breaths of air. Though I could physically knock Rex over in a moment, I was pinned down by far more than physical weight. The energy he wielded by lifting just one finger... the idea was unthinkable. I might have taken risks tonight, but I would *never* dare challenge him so strongly.

And I didn't want to. I wanted my Daddy's authority settling into my skin as it did now, the sting of humiliation as he pressed his big toe into my throat until I whimpered for mercy.

This time, Rex answered my noise. "No backtalk," he murmured, soft and dangerous. His terms and conditions for freeing me, perhaps.

Daddy didn't have to tell me there were no second chances. The imperious gaze told me that he didn't suffer fools, and my provocation would not win me the response I'd hoped.

No brattiness, then. Lesson learned. I quivered, silent and attentive, waiting to see if there was more.

"I'm not in the mood to flog you tonight and make the lesson stick," Rex said.

Holy fuck, I hoped he made the lesson stick next time. But instead, he stayed perfectly balanced as he dragged his toe from my throat down the middle of my body, ever so slowly. Every inch of my skin lit up, and by the time his foot was between my nipples, I bit back whimpers.

At last, I cradled my dick, keeping the top bare so his toe could slide over the hair at the base and down the length… but as soon as his toe connected with my shaft and it jumped under his foot, he smiled cruelly and lifted his foot again, shifting his stance and folding his arms behind his back.

I whimpered, squeezing myself again, but it was a pale comparison to the pleasure that he'd so nearly given me.

Of course he hadn't, though. I didn't deserve that.

"You're going to make me come, shut up, and behave yourself," Rex told me. Every ounce of cold fire he'd tried to warn me about was layered in his voice, and I couldn't bring myself to be afraid. I just wanted *more*. "Remember how lucky you are to be sucking my dick, *boy*."

He snarled the last word, baring his teeth at me.

Fuck. I was prey under his gaze, and I didn't have a hope in hell of getting away.

Any resistance melted, and I closed my eyes. "Yes, Daddy," I whispered, averting my gaze as my cheeks burned. "I'm sorry, Daddy." My voice was thick, embarrassment scorching my veins. "I don't deserve you, sir. Thank you for not flogging me. I'll remember."

"Good." It wasn't praise I could luxuriate in. It was a comment, swift and brutal, that made it clear I'd met his minimum expectations. And then Daddy went silent, waiting for me to keep going. To keep begging him for mercy.

Christ, he didn't just slide the knife in, but he twisted it. And the perverted little slut in me *loved* it.

"Now, unless you *want* me to make you watch me come, wipe my jizz all over your smart mouth, and leave you here on the floor all night with your blue balls..." Rex trailed off.

All I could do was gape, my mouth silently opening and closing as my thighs shook and I squeezed my twitching cock for dear life. *Oh, please, no!*

As much as I craved his harsh treatment, I might lose my mind right here and now if I learned he was going to force me to go without release. There was a *line*, for God's sake.

"Beg me," Rex snarled.

"Yes, Daddy," I whimpered, rolling my head to the side and squeezing my eyes shut as the younger man eviscerated what was left of my pride in two words.

No way in heaven or earth could I do anything but obey. Words spilled from my mouth, unbidden, in a desperate torrent.

"Just let me suck you again, please. I'll take care of myself down here. I won't come without asking permission." I swallowed hard, my words dying in my throat as my Daddy raised his foot to my chest again. This time, his big toe dragged in a circle around my nipple and over it.

Just the tiniest touch sent erotic shudders surging through me. I could have spilled my load on the spot if Rex had kept going, but of course he didn't. Instead, he trailed down the middle of my body again, his head tilted as if in mild curiosity.

Well, holy crap. I'd never been into feet, but right here and now, I finally understood the appeal.

His toes were just as dainty and precise as his fingers, but one step more removed. It had never been more clear: I was a filthy little slut who didn't even deserve his touch.

And I fucking loved it.

"Fuck!" I cried, holding myself upright as his toes glided across the ring of my fingers and finally grazed along my shaft. Pure fire raced along in its wake, all the way to the tip and—as I let my dick fall flat on my stomach—over the wet tip. My cries were hoarse and hollow, I was so desperate. These soft touches weren't enough anymore.

I needed more.

As the noise rang around the sleek room, Rex lifted a brow, his toe pausing. "Yes?" Rex asked.

I squirmed and whimpered helplessly. "Please, please, please, Daddy. Use me, please. Don't just stand there and make me watch. Not tonight. I need to taste you again."

The sooner he finishes, the sooner I can. My dick twitched at the thought, jumping against his foot.

My Daddy smiled, cruel and calm. "Careful, boy," he told me, delight seeping into his words. "You might come all over my foot like the filthy, desperate boy you are. And you don't want to know what's in store if you break a rule. It won't be one of those fun 'punishments'"—he lifted his hands to air quote—"the nicer Daddies dole out."

"Fuck, fuck, fuck." The curse slid from my lips like water pouring from a glass, uncontrollably. The wood floor under me was hot now as I thrashed against it. "No, Daddy. I won't, sir. Please, fuck my mouth. *Please!*"

Rex's foot returned to the floor, and he leaned forward, but instead of offering me a hand up, he grabbed the ring on my harness and hauled me to sit up with shocking strength.

I flailed against thin air, desperately grabbing for his thighs. Adrenaline sloshed through my body—I didn't even remotely have my own balance, hanging precariously from his grip.

Daddy didn't care. He was holding the base of his cock in his other hand, and as I scrabbled against his thighs to grip him tight, he slapped his arousal against my face.

"This? Is this what you want?" He rubbed the tip over my lips and cheeks as I squeezed my eyes shut and gasped for air.

My heart thudded so hard as I tried to straighten up, but he stood at an angle that wouldn't quite allow it. "Yes, sir," I gasped. "More than anything!"

At last, Rex took a step back, letting me sit up straight. "Good boy," he praised, giving me a crumb of joy to cling on to for dear life.

I had to use my hands to brace myself, which—as he no doubt knew—meant I couldn't jerk myself off.

Oh, fuck. I was going to *explode*. My cock was already angrily throbbing at the lack of contact, bobbing desperately in the air, no longer even lying flat on my stomach.

"Suck," Rex growled. This time, he placed me in charge, forcing me to haul all my attention from my own pathetic, worthless orgasm and focus on his.

I had to prove myself. So I sucked hard and deep, choking on his cock as I pushed my mouth down around it. My whole body quivered with the pent-up tension, hard and filled with need from head to toe.

Crap, I might just come hands-free from Rex's rough words and manhandling, from the perfect, pure submission that filled me with purpose for the first time in years.

But my Daddy came first—literally.

I threw myself, body and soul, into this. I groaned and lapped frantically under his cock, then sucked my cheeks in tight as the head of his cock hit the back of my throat.

Rex's grunts turned to groans, his legs trembling and nails biting into my shoulders as he held me upright.

"Going to come in your filthy little mouth, boy," Rex snarled at me. "Fill it up with my hot load. You'd better swallow every drop, you hear me?"

I managed a tiny nod and a choked *Mmhmm* around his shaft as it jerked and jumped, swelled in my mouth, and finally…

Rex blew his load in his mouth, and strings of thick, hot cum hit the back of my throat. At this angle, I could barely catch a glimpse of him, but I did see his head and shoulders thrown back, his whole body an arc like a dancer frozen in slow motion, his rigid self-control finally shattered.

Pleasure written large across his whole body, like he was made of pure stardust, and I could never, ever get enough.

I'd done that. I had! And he'd let me!

I grabbed myself and stroked hard and fast, my hand pumping up and down my shaft. Fuck, *fuck*, it almost hurt how much I needed release.

My body was so taut, my shaft dripping wet already. I forgot the rule until I was so close to the edge I could hardly breathe, and then I gasped.

There was no stopping my orgasm. Not now. It was unstoppably crashing toward me, and I'd only ruin it if I tried to stop. But I needed to ask Daddy's permission! I lurched backward, losing my balance in my brief panic.

But Rex sank to his knees over my lap, swiftly gripping my harness to hold me upright. His other arm locked around my back, his gaze soft and understanding rather than the cold look I'd expected.

I mouthed wordlessly at him, but only a long, desperate groan escaped.

Daddy understood, his eyes dark and hungry. Focused on me. "Now, boy," he whispered, giving me the permission I needed.

And my world collapsed around me.

Nothing existed except Rex, his desires and demands, and any way I could mold myself to suit my Daddy's every whim. I existed for him—to please and serve, to fit him like a glove in both body and soul.

The first spurt of my cum shot so hard it landed on my shoulder, the second coating my chest. Droplets dripped from Rex's forearm where he gripped my harness, and every muscle in my body drew tight along with my balls, my shudders uncontrollable.

I realized I was crying Rex's name, clinging to his forearms, hot wetness building in my eyes. My body hurt in a strange way from the waves of pleasure crashing through me, like every muscle had been on fire and now was limp and spent.

The tide inside me hadn't turned yet, releasing me to the normal world. I was still trapped in the ebbs and swells, clutching Rex but voiceless. It should have ended now, right?

Fuck, I just wanted to feel *good*!

Rex pulled me in, his slender frame taking my weight with ease as I collapsed against him. And there it was at last, unfolding in me—the relief I'd been seeking just waited in his arms.

I sprawled against him as he sat on the floor, my face in his shoulder, my hands gradually rising to his back as he gripped me tight.

My heart pounded. I didn't know what was expected of me now. Isaac had never done this. I couldn't quite breathe. Every loose muscle thrilled with tension, but it hurt to tense up again so soon.

"Shhh," Rex whispered, his hand rubbing a slow circle against my back, like he could hear my thoughts. "Relax, baby boy. This moment is for you."

And that was what I needed. My whole body sagged into him, unquestioning and trusting. Just existing, floating once more in that space that was neither quite here nor there, but in the best of all worlds.

Rex's lips pressed against the side of my head, and then…

We kissed for the first time, and the missing piece of my life slid into place.

It wasn't just any first kiss. It was tender and understanding, his lips grazing mine as soft as a cloud, and then I shifted and gave way to him. I yielded utterly, giving over everything I had, and everything I'd ever be.

Rex never hesitated to strike like a blizzard, harsh and demanding. His lips and tongue were impossible to resist, dragging sharp sparks through me until I whimpered for mercy. I tangled my hands in his hair and clung to him, my lungs burning with the crispness of my Daddy's every move.

But something in my noises or touches melted his iciness, too. Rex yielded to my breathless need and grew soft, uncertain, slow. He let me take over, held still as I caressed his mouth with mine and showed him something I could tell in my very bones he'd never known.

Soft and hard, his and mine, it belonged to us both, and time itself ceased to matter. It lasted for exactly as long as it was supposed to—not a second longer or shorter.

When we pulled away, breath and eyelids heavy, we lingered close together, intimate at last. Our breaths were hot against each other's swollen lips. And my spirit was heavy against him, but he never gave in. Not even once.

I gradually straightened up again, dizzy and drained but back in my own self, strong and alive. More alive than I'd ever been in my whole fucking life.

Certain, as I'd never been of anything, that Rex was the Daddy for me.

Rex rose to his feet and held up a finger. I waited, patient at last, and my Daddy brought me a warm cloth and wiped me down more tenderly than he did himself.

Then he pointed to the bedroom. "Go," he whispered. The word wasn't harsh, though, like earlier, but it also wasn't certain and unyielding.

I hesitated, sensing something raw in him. Something had split open in him, and now he looked at me like a man of his own age, rather than a timeless, implacable force.

"I'll join you shortly," Rex murmured, rising to his feet once more and offering me his hands.

I took them and stood, and I wanted to kiss him. But Rex turned his back, his shoulders heaving with an emotion I couldn't possibly identify. I didn't yet know how to read the every ripple of his expression.

Rex was half a lover, half a stranger to me. And I had the distinct feeling he never let men become his lovers, keeping them at a stranger's distance.

Except me. So far. Fuck, this was it, tonight. The make-or-break moment.

I didn't know if he wanted me to stay the night, but God, I hoped so. I should have stopped and asked right there and then, but I was too raw still. So instead, slowly, I headed for the bedroom, sliding the door shut behind me when Rex gestured for me to do so.

Alone at last, the last of the adrenaline drained, and I stumbled for the bed before stopping with a smile. He had a pair of pajamas on the bed—and they looked new, and in my size.

Like he'd known we would come back here and I'd need them. That gave me a flicker of hope. Fuck. How was I to know what he intended?

I wriggled out of my harness and shorts, laid them on the chair, and clutched the pajamas to my chest.

Just ask him, you fool. Ask if I'm welcome to stay tonight.

The thought brought a tear to my eye again. I wasn't going to put these on and climb into bed if he was just planning on cuddling me for a few minutes and then sending me home. If this was it.

No, I couldn't accept an ounce of pity cuddles if that was all he had left for me. So I clutched the pajamas to my chest and walked, naked and unafraid of my nakedness, to the door.

I gathered my courage—what little I had left, wiped out and exhausted by the best sex I'd had in my life, emotionally naked, terrified of the fear I'd glimpsed in Rex's eyes…

But I paused when I heard his voice, my hand on the groove laid into the door. I didn't *mean* to listen in, it just sort of happened.

"What do you want, cocksucker?"

It was the same harsh tone he'd used in speaking to me just minutes ago, and it ripped me open from head to toe. My mouth fell open. I dropped the pajamas on the floor in front of me, my fingers suddenly numb.

And yet… *and yet*, I tingled with arousal because I *wanted* so badly to be the man he was speaking to—and I had no doubt, somehow, it was a man.

The only doubt was who… oh, and why, but that seemed of secondary importance. I was disappointed that there *was* a who to ask about.

And the jealousy was red-hot, lodged in a tender place in my chest. A knife twisted in my belly, but this time, it wasn't picking through my nerves to find the very best to light up.

Instead, a cold realization set in.

I'd given him everything of me, and what a dumbass that made me. I shouldn't jump to conclusions and assume he was talking to some other boy—the very thought made me bare my teeth. But at the same time, it was far from the only secret Rex was keeping.

That needed to end, if this was going anywhere. Rex wasn't going to become Isaac 2.0. However kind and gentle he was, withholding information was Isaac's game, too.

I needed to know more about him, now.

I'd gone too far, given him too much when we hadn't talked about half the shit we should have. It *felt* like I knew him body and soul because we'd shared orgasms, a first kiss, our very deepest and most shameful desires...

What would it take to get him to call me a cocksucker in that voice, too?

Fuck. Even faced with all the mysteries of Rex's life, *that* was still my biggest concern? Finding a fresh new way for him to humiliate me until I spilled my unworthy seed under his unyielding gaze?

I pinched the bridge of my nose and leaned down to scoop up the pajamas, padding down the smooth steps to the bed so I could slip into them.

I was so screwed-up that there was nothing Rex could say that would scare me. I'd worried over the past day—how the hell could I convince him of that without scaring *him* off first? Well, that wouldn't stop me anymore. This had gone further and faster than I ever intended. If it wasn't too late to save my heart, I could at least save a few scraps of my dignity.

I couldn't let Rex steer me away yet again from asking him who he was—and I didn't just mean in the sense of *why do you live in an apartment fit for a king.*

One way or another, I needed answers, and I couldn't wait one more night.

10

REX

The bedroom door slid closed, and I leaned heavily on the kitchen counter, my heart thudding against my throat like it was trying to bust out. My corset was the only thing holding me together—messy feelings threatened to spill everywhere.

Fuck. My brain was sluggish like molasses. Right here in the no-man's-land between my kitchen and living room, I'd lost the battle of wills.

Is he your boy or not?

Seb had asked me that just tonight. But it felt like weeks ago. As if Slate and I had unlocked a secret extra life hidden between the seconds of the ordinary life that I'd been trapped in before meeting him.

Well, fuck. I had my answer at last.

Slate *was* my boy.

It wasn't even like I needed evidence. My gut just knew. But the evidence was there anyway: he'd never once flinched at the things I did or said. He lapped it up, and came so hard he'd seen stars. He'd taken it all and then some, and for a brief moment, I'd let myself feel like it could all be okay. I'd let down my guard.

Because my heart had told me to.

Duh, you idiot, I told myself. Sex wasn't even the beginning. I'd already invited him to every part of my life: my home, my bed, my shop. He was here, like it or not, and I had to figure out how I felt about it.

I leaned on the counter with both hands, bowing my head over it and pushing my spine straight as I took deep breaths. Slate was *there*, in my bedroom, waiting for me with those innocent wide eyes and that trusting soul that needed me as much as I needed him.

That wasn't even the scary part.

Tonight was just a hint of what we both needed, and I was pretty sure we both knew it. But pushing Slate further meant pushing myself further. Sticking my neck out. Letting the sharp parts out of the pit where I'd locked them away. Taking the risk of having Slate look at me like the monster I feared I was.

I'd gotten that look from boys before. The awe and intimidation and the way they flinched afterward at my touch, their eyes free from the scales of naivety once they knew what I was capable of.

I didn't mind. Or at least, I told myself that. Who cared what a stranger thought, even one I saw twice a week at DN? And when the need was strong enough, they came back to me for more of the ice-edged pleasure I wielded.

But someone who had already seen my home, my life, my very heart? That was a different story. That was a *risk*.

And that kiss.

Fuck me, that kiss! Intoxicating, everything it promised. Ripping me out of my comfort zone. Making my heart do stupid, fluttery things even remembering it.

I raised my knuckles to my lips and closed my eyes, breathing deep and steady.

What had unfolded between us was no doubt too much and too quickly. Yet it also felt like a drop of water to a parched man's throat, too slow and laughably inadequate to my needs.

The room lit up when Slate was in it. And the way he looked at me, straight through my defenses, but he never once raised my guard about it. I'd always hated feeling exposed, but the gentleness in his spirit made me feel safe at the same time.

When he looked sad or tender or vulnerable, I couldn't fathom having the strength—or even the cruelty—not to respond to his needs. Which was rich, for a man who feared his own coldness.

"Fuck," I breathed out and straightened up, wiping a shaking hand down my face. It seemed like the only word in my vocabulary right now.

I'd always told myself that The One didn't exist. He wasn't out there waiting for me. Life was a string of convenient encounters and slammed doors.

But here he was. And I didn't want to fuck it up.

It took a moment to realize where the angry buzz was coming from. My phone was ringing in my bag, which was still on the hallway floor. It was on Do Not Disturb, which meant only people from my contacts list should be able to call me.

I strode over to my bag and fished out the phone, and then I nearly dropped it, snarling at my former business partner's name on the screen.

Christ. What on earth was Logan doing calling me?

I stabbed the screen and raised the phone to my ear, uncorking the unease that bubbled in my veins. "What do you want, cocksucker?"

"One of your freaky little friends dropped by." I could picture Logan's sneer through the phone line, and the pit of my stomach dropped in a familiar lurch. "Don't let it happen again."

Nobody in my life had ever taken the liberty of crossing the streams. Which meant it was someone who had it out for me.

"That would be a lot easier if you told me who the fuck you mean," I bluffed, stalling for more info.

I kept my voice low. I sure as hell didn't want Slate to get wind of this. He was only just settling here, losing the haunted look in his eye. Hearing that Isaac was hunting him down…

No. Better to make the problem go away without him having to know.

"He didn't leave his name. Angry guy. Black hair. Leather jacket. Showed up at the office asking for you."

"I have no idea who it is," I lied, despite knowing exactly who it was. "So I'm gonna assume you're lying and you just wanted to fuck with my sleep."

"I doubt you were asleep, huh?" Logan countered with that ugly note in his voice again. And damn it, I hated that he was right.

My gut churned as I tried to slam the lid on the box of memories that threatened to leak into my life once more. Logan, Jake, and Taylor, the Three Fucketeers.

"Don't make me get a restraining order." I hung up on my threat, not letting him get another word in.

It's Isaac. It has to be. I'm going to rip him apart, and he won't get off on it, either.

My hands still shook as I plugged my phone in, then grabbed a bottle of whiskey and two tumblers. As I slid the cork from the neck, I almost missed the sound of the bedroom door gliding open again.

When I corked the bottle, balanced a glass in each palm, and turned around, I found Slate. He was sitting on my couch and wearing the pajamas I'd left out for him.

Act cool, I reminded myself. My boy didn't know who was sniffing around. He didn't need to.

Slate smiled and patted the couch next to him in an invitation. I felt like I was being led a little bit, which was unusual, but I obeyed anyway and joined him, passing over a glass.

"It's only fifteen-year," I said by way of apology.

"Oh, no." Slate's voice was dry, but his eyes sparkled. "Whatever will I do?" I grinned at his bratty moment, waiting for him to take a sip. When he did, he quickly coughed and covered his mouth. "Jesus."

I laughed and then raised my glass to my lips, letting a few droplets roll over my tongue. They burned, but I knew how to direct them over my palate and into my throat to avoid embarrassing myself. I hid the grimace as it burned a hole straight through my esophagus to my lungs.

Slate eyed me, and then sniffed his glass before he blinked rapidly. "Do you even like this stuff? Or is it part of your Daddy image of always being in control?"

Didn't he know I was in charge here? But it wasn't an attack. It wasn't even a criticism. It was an innocent question, spoken with far too much certainty—like he already knew the answer.

I gaped at him like a goddamn fish. Everything I'd been about to say about the mouthfeel just melted away under his innocent question. "No," I finally admitted, too startled to do anything but tell the truth. "I hated it at first. I just learned how to drink it to impress people."

People like the Three Fucketeers, I added mentally. Had it been worth it? Well, my apartment said yes. My unsettled gut said no.

"Thanks for the devastating honesty," I added as I tried to pull myself together. I wasn't going to dump *that* shit on him when he had so much of his own to deal with.

Slate gave me a quick, beautiful grin, but his eyes were serious, and so was his voice when he next spoke. "Well, I know something's going on with you. And I want to know what it is before we go any further. It's only fair to me."

Apparently orgasm had unlocked a side of Slate I had only once glimpsed—in DN, when he'd stopped me from chasing down Isaac and beating the hell out of him verbally or physically. The quiet strength was back, steely and unyielding. It wasn't born of a flashy command, or a tantrum, but a quiet, steady, earthy resilience.

And if he's thinking about what's fair to him, his self-esteem is better than I've ever seen it, I thought. *I should encourage that.* Totally not self-centered.

But I couldn't lie to myself. It was. A part of me, a scared little part, *wanted* to open up. I'd been sitting on all my self-loathing for months, all alone and lost—tiny and human—in the endless urban view that unfurled in front of us through the huge, dark windows.

Whiskey or whips didn't help as I'd hoped. They only numbed it for a time. Drew a curtain across the shame and the outrage that still bubbled in my chest. Behind it, unless I stayed busy, I could hear the constant hissing simmer in my soul.

But I thought I'd been doing a much better job of hiding it, damn it.

"What makes you say that?" I asked at last. I leaned forward to set aside my glass, then stared out the window instead of at him.

If Slate already *knew* I was screwed-up and he was chasing after me anyway, well... maybe I could afford to let my guard down a little bit more.

"You won't let me close," Slate said, laying out the reasons calmly. "You won't let me see you naked, like that's more vulnerable than having your dick in my mouth. You won't even let me cuddle you. You barely let me tell you when or where to sit down."

I hid both the disconcerting shiver down my spine at his keen observation, and my grin. This boy had teeth. How appropriate. I kind of loved it despite myself.

"And just then, after we cleaned up," Slate went on, laying his hand tentatively on my knee. "You shut down and sent me to your bedroom, but you had pajamas laid out for me already."

I shrugged, eyes flickering to him and then away again. "I was going to make you stay the night. Gotta show you how a coffee machine works sometime."

Slate wouldn't let me distract him. "You've gone beyond the call of duty to take care of one screwed-up boy set adrift. You're thoughtful in so many ways, but you're afraid to be seen as nice, so you tell me you're an asshole."

My stare out the window only increased in intensity, my brow furrowing as something in my chest tensed up. Some Doms would have had him on his knees already for the impertinence, but I didn't *want* to stop him.

"I... maybe that's what most Daddies are like. God knows I don't know," Slate added, his voice finally wavering as he forced a quick laugh. "And I don't know what I'm supposed to do as your boy. All I know is how to kneel and take it and beg for things I don't get."

I looked at him quickly, but he didn't show any signs of being upset. Just determined to unpick me like a puzzle. And I couldn't decide if he deserved to or not, but we were way past that point.

"But I want to know what *you're* like," Slate said, his voice soft. "You made it seem like this wasn't it between us. But before there's a next time, I need to know you."

You really don't, I thought, my heart pounding against my rib cage. *You just need to kneel and take what I give you. Yield to me, and let me run this show.*

But damn it, Slate was right. I couldn't run any longer from it. I'd been hiding everything but the slick exterior I wanted him to see, and if this was going to last for longer than one unforgettable weekend, I had to be real with him, too.

Slate put his glass aside and took my hand, drawing my gaze to his. The deep brown of his eyes caught me, wide and trusting as always. "What should I know?"

A few seconds ticked by as I studied him and tried to unpick the whirling dervish in my head. But I was captivated by that look, and no closer to any answers when I started to speak.

"I met these assholes in college. Didn't know they were assholes, at first. My friends. Worked my ass off with them after we graduated. We started a car-sharing app. It's not big yet, but it's worth a lot of money. Investors and everything. They did the tech and finance stuff. I cracked the whip." I managed a tight smile.

It had been the perfect outlet for me—micromanaging every detail of the startup, keeping those lazy slugs on schedule.

Their ideas were solid, but left to their own devices, they would still be in their parents' spare houses smoking bowls and watching terrible sitcoms.

I was the one who had seen and nurtured their potential, before I even understood what I was doing or why. It had quickly led to me figuring out my own needs, and discovering Dom Nation, and…

Well, it had all seemed perfect. Until it wasn't.

Slate nodded slightly, his grip on my hands warm and his gaze patient.

Christ, here it came. It wasn't going to stop now. All I hoped was that he didn't pity me. How the fuck could I earn his respect—his submission—if he pitied me?

"One day, an investor showed up at Dom Nation. He recognized me. My double life came out. My good old buddies called me a freak and bought me out—hence this place." I waved around, finally tearing my gaze from the sympathetic creases forming on Slate's face.

"Shit," Slate murmured, squeezing my hands.

I shook my head once, briskly. "The real kicker is that I fought them tooth and nail to strengthen our account vetting and add a sexual predator flag we could apply to users. To make it *safe*. And the day they kicked me out, they flagged my account." I snorted harshly, dismissive, but I didn't expect the sting in my chest to be as sharp as it had been that day.

"Assholes," Slate muttered. "No, that's not strong enough. Douchecanoes."

That made a glimmer of a smile pass over my face. I shook my head and finally looked back at him, letting go of his hands and stretching my arms along the back of the couch. "So that's where the money comes from. I'm not some Mafia boss, don't worry."

Slate frowned and nodded, looking uncertain of what to say. "That's still… I'm sorry."

"My old business partner called me back tonight about something," I added and ground my teeth. "God, I wanted to rip him a new one."

Shut up, Rex. Shut up. Don't tell him why.

I'd never been so close to losing control over my impulses. Slate shouldn't even see me upset, much less hear my every thought as it crossed my mind.

Get a grip! I ordered myself. I stood up sharply, pacing across the living room toward the full-length window. Thousands of people living their own little cubicle lives in the skyscrapers that stretched along the city.

I'd nearly been one of them. And now I was, all over again—but in this apartment, as much a trap as a safe haven.

"Hearing his voice again brought it all back," I admitted.

And suddenly I felt even more protective of Slate being dragged back into *whatever* it was with Isaac. No wonder the fear in him had called to me. I wasn't afraid of those assholes— I'd always been the one calling the shots—but my empathy for Slate only grew.

Slate was silent, hands folded between his knees as he leaned forward on the sofa, listening. Letting me control this moment, at least. Whether he knew it or not, that was what I needed.

God, Slate was perfect for me.

But the words were rushing out again. "I bought every lie. I thought our culture was all sparkles and rainbows, like we were a *family,*" I admitted, and my cheeks flushed with embarrassment. My voice was raw. "I just wish I could take back everything."

I laid a hand on the glass in front of me, the cold shiver working its way through my sensitive skin and down my arm as I leaned into the triple-reinforced safety glass.

"Everything I gave them. All the passion and joy and effort and *love* I poured into that stupid company, before it got ripped away from me."

"Is that..." Slate trailed off, his voice almost too soft to hear. Hesitant.

I turned, dropping my hand from the glass and wiping it on my leg. When I caught his eye, he looked frozen as if waiting for permission to say something he knew I wouldn't like.

He's taken enough liberties tonight. What's one more? I raised a brow and nodded for him to continue.

Slate cleared his throat and rubbed his palms together, the nerves shining on his face as plain as day. "Is that why you don't want a boy?"

Hearing it laid out that plainly stung, yet the truth in the words calmed the simmering boil my emotions had been running at for months.

Maybe it was time to stop running from the truth. Because Slate deserved a lot more than my bullshit, and hell, *I* deserved more.

I swallowed hard, but I couldn't look away. The moment was tense between us, as fragile as fine china but as precious, too. The answer was written all over me, wasn't it?

Slate didn't speak. He hardly breathed, every muscle frozen just like mine. There was a deferential air in his expression, like he was about to look away and stare at the floor, ask my forgiveness.

The words wouldn't come out. My brain wouldn't let them. My throat held tight to them, like they were too big to fit in the space between my tongue and lips.

So that's who I am. I drew a deep breath and let it out. *An emotionally crippled freak who uses whips and chains to purge the shit I don't want anyone to see inside me. Who can't look in a man's eyes afterward and be honest for once. He already knows how fucked-up I am, to take advantage of his needs.*

He was the one for me—I'd never been more certain of anything—yet I couldn't even tell him the truth.

Slate cleared his throat softly, and I realized I'd been staring straight through him. But all he said was "I heard a bit of the phone call."

Fuck. Did he know what I was trying to protect him from?

"Which bit?" I asked. At least the subject change helped. The hardness of my muscles had eased, trickling through my body into the solid wood floor under my bare feet.

"The bit where you called him a cocksucker, and my refractory period disappeared."

The relief that washed through me and the glint of humor in Slate's smile shattered the stillness at last. I laughed, the soft and sharp noise squeezing past the ache in my chest.

But I made a note in the ever-expanding list of plans I had for my boy, if indeed I could ever be the Daddy this boy deserved: Slate wanted more of the same.

A lot more.

"Bedtime, I think," Slate said, finally pushing himself to his feet with a groan. "My Daddy needs it."

Me? I didn't even know the last time anyone had said that to me. Noticed, even. Tried to look after me.

Who the fuck was being the Daddy right now, anyway? I needed to step up and play my part.

So I walked toward him and offered an arm, grinning at the picture of the two of us: me in my bright red corset and black zipped briefs, him in his faded pajamas. "Are you giving the orders, boy?"

"No, Daddy." Slate slid his arm around mine and leaned in to peck my cheek, placating. "I would never."

"Good."

There were no words for the way I glowed with the firm pressure of his hand, his arm brushing mine as I led him to the bedroom like it was a cocktail party and all eyes were on us.

It felt right. Holy God, help me, it felt *right*.

When we reached the bedroom, Slate let go of my arm and moved for my side of the bed again. He made a show of pulling back the covers and arranging them, making it clear that he wasn't looking at me. Respecting my limits.

I wriggled out of my corset quickly anyway, tugging on a fresh pair of underwear. Maybe he was right that I needed to be more vulnerable. But Daddies weren't vulnerable. They were strong and unyielding and generally had their shit in order.

Somehow, Slate was getting the messiest possible version of me and he wanted *more*? Jesus, it seemed just as improbable as suddenly starring in a Broadway musical about filthy darkrooms and perverted desires.

I shook my head and climbed into the other side of the bed. I turned the lights out, but as I turned to face my boy, I nearly banged my nose into his. He was facing me this time.

"Oof," I whispered in surprise.

"Come here," Slate murmured. "Your turn for a hug."

I frowned, wishing I could see his expression in the darkness.

Was he *trying* to be the Daddy now? Discovering some latent top deep inside, bursting free just because I was a tiny little twinky thing? He wouldn't be the first so-called sub to try that.

"But you need aftercare," I reminded him. It had been *my* foot on *his* throat not that long ago.

"And I want to make my Daddy feel good," Slate murmured back through the darkness, utterly disarming every argument I had. He shifted against the bed, a small and eager movement. "Please?"

Despite myself, I smiled slightly. "A lot of people would think you were trying to Daddy me right now."

"I'm not a lot of people," Slate said, and I felt his shrug against the sheets. His breath was warm, ghosting across my cheek. "I just want to give you what you need, sir."

Did I need his comfort? In a way, yes. Okay, not just *in a way*. Totally. But I also didn't want his pity-cuddles. The bond between us wouldn't last long on that foundation.

I cleared my throat. It was a lot easier to speak truth to the darkness, without the weight of his expression and his every movement. "I don't want you to think less of me."

"You promised me earlier that I was safe with you," Slate murmured. "It's only fair I promise you the same thing, whether you believe it or not. I'll never hurt you or judge you for what you need. Sensing what you need, serving you... that's what makes me a boy."

Funny he should say that. I was just thinking that that was what made me a Daddy. But now that he said *that*, something else altogether occurred to me.

I needed a man to break into pieces before I could feel whole. And holy shit, that was far more shameful to admit, even to myself.

I pushed it aside. Slate was right. I needed this, and if I tried to deny it, to make him force comfort on me… then *I* was the one placing myself in submission, wasn't I?

I rolled onto my side. I faced the right way, but on the wrong side of the bed—like this was meant to be.

But Slate didn't put his arm over me, and indignation flared in me for a few hot seconds.

Is he going to make me *beg? Because that really would be my last straw.*

Then I realized it was just me being a dumbass. Slate was waiting for permission.

So I granted it. "Come here," I murmured.

"Yes, sir." Slate slid toward me as fast as lightning, his body so eager that the arm that circled my rib cage was almost trembling.

I smiled to myself and ran my fingers down his bare skin, soothing the frenetic energy I felt under his skin. "Good boy."

I was enveloped by those strong arms and the warm skin behind my back.

For the first time in a long time, I felt small, but in a very different way. Not the empty coldness of staring out at all the offices and apartments of the starless city sky. Not the humiliation of a man trying to challenge my authority.

Warm, personal, safe.

Slate's lips pressed the back of my neck. "Your safeword?" he whispered.

"Mine?" I exclaimed. If I'd had any more energy, I might have recoiled so hard his nose would be in danger again.

"I'm pushing you out of your comfort zone, too," Slate murmured. "I want you to feel as safe as I do."

I drew a long, deep breath and shook my head slightly. For a guy who claimed to have so little experience, his intuition was some freaky powerful shit. "If I tell you to stop, you can assume that means stop," I told him. "I don't have that desire to make *stop* mean *more*."

"That's much handier than me," Slate said with a self-deprecating little chuckle. "Okay. Thank you, Daddy."

It was the exact right thing to say, and I lost any doubt about his submissive instincts. He knew how to handle me. I just wasn't sure if I should be pleased or terrified of that fact.

"Yes," I murmured. "And thank you."

Slate squeezed me gently, his thumb stroking one of my ribs in a way that threatened to lull me to sleep on the spot. "How's this? As awful as you imagined?"

A tiny, exhausted giggle escaped me as I shifted around to find a comfortable place for my arms. "It's not the worst," I whispered back.

Slate chuckled. "Good night, my Daddy."

My Daddy. It was very clear he was looking for more than just my earlier promise—which seemed laughable in retrospect—to be his Daddy just for tonight.

Yeah. I could promise him a hell of a lot more than that.

"Good night, my boy," I whispered. And then I let go of everything, and allowed Slate's warm breath on my skin to tease me free from my body like wind on a dandelion, and send me to a deep and dreamless sleep.

11

SLATE

"Today's selection of our finest toothbrushes." I held out five different colors of toothbrush and offered my young patient an outrageous bow. "Please, accept one with our compliments."

Hannah giggled and folded her arms, pretending to scrutinize them. "I thiiiink…" She trailed off. Then she hummed, squinting at them as she made this very important choice. "Purple," she finally decided.

I shuffled the others into one hand and offered her the purple toothbrush. "Very good choice," I said with a serious nod.

"Purple's my birthstone," she informed me.

"Ah! Matching." I nodded to her. "I'm lucky if my socks match in the morning."

She squinted down and then giggled, clutching her toothbrush to her chest. I swapped a grin with her mother, who looked slightly more optimistic about her chances of getting the eight-year-old to brush every night.

"You're all done, then. Well done today," I told her, offering a hand for a high five. "You were really brave."

Hannah high-fived me and beamed. "See you, Mr. Slate!" Then she scurried for the doorway and cast her mother an imploring look. "Come on, Mom. I have art class."

My lips twitched in amusement at her busy schedule.

Diane grabbed both of their jackets and stood up. "Thank you," she said, the relief clear on her face. "My dentist growing up was… well, nothing like you guys. I'm glad you're here for her."

I nodded, understanding instantly. One bad experience could scar for life. I specialized in kids and nervous clients—anyone who needed more time and patience. It was so rewarding helping people get the care they needed, especially when I could set them up for life with positive impressions.

Sure, I did get bitten a little more than my colleagues, but that meant unexpected afternoons off now and then.

"My pleasure," I said, showing them to the door and holding it for them both. I waved back at Hannah and then turned my attention to tidying up the room. I liked to be ready for the first appointment after lunch. That way, I could enjoy every minute of my break guilt-free.

By the time I made it to the staff room, Pam was already there, clogging the air with her awful tuna salad.

"Jeez," I groaned, theatrically clapping a hand over her mouth. "Is it tuna day again already?"

"Sorry," Pam said, but she grinned at me as she stuck a fork into her bowl and carried it to the table. "I could do tuna casserole next time."

Okay, that was worse. "Oh no," I told her, wagging a finger. "Not in our microwave."

"See?" Pam winked and made a big deal of brushing her hand through her shoulder-length curls. "A girl needs her omega-3s. Also, didn't you bring in that broccoli casserole last month…?"

Damn it. She had the memory of an elephant. I held up my hands and surrendered, then grabbed my lunch box from the fridge. "Fine, fine," I laughed. "No hot fish."

"Even I have limits," Pam agreed. "Oh, by the way… I heard Hannah telling everyone her teeth are happy now." She winked at me. "Anyone would think you'd make a great dad."

"This again," I groaned. Usually I patiently told her the time wasn't right for me. We'd kept up that back-and-forth for five years now. But today, I blushed as I settled at the table, meticulously arranging everything I'd packed. "Is that so?"

Does Rex want kids one day? Or will I be enough to keep him busy? That was enough to keep me daydreaming all day. I cleared my throat and cracked the seal on my bottle of sparkling water.

Pam was instantly suspicious. "You're looking radiant. What's his name?"

"You should be a detective, not a dental hygienist," I complained, but my smile crept across my face anyway as I opened up my sandwich container.

"Spill," Pam insisted. "If I told you about Greg's mole, you can tell me his name."

I nearly choked on my water, and she gave me a helpful slap on the back.

Pam was one of my few friends, and I'd been bursting to tell *someone* all weekend about this. I so rarely had good news of my own to share—no kids' achievements to brag about or exciting new cars to drive into work. And certainly no boyfriends to show off.

"It's Rex," I said. "We saw each other Saturday and Sunday."

"And? Is it serious?" Pam's fork hovered over her tuna salad as she watched me like a straight guy watched football.

"Pretty sure we're… dating now?" I offered up, my own sandwich halfway to my mouth and all but forgotten. *Is that what you call it? Would he be okay with that? Oh, God, I only just got him to admit he's serious. I don't know the protocol here.*

"Whoa," Pam gasped, stabbing her fork in her salad and reaching out for a high five. I transferred my sandwich into the other hand so I could meet her palm with mine. "You move fast!"

I laughed. "I've got a fraction of the dating pool options and a lot of pent-up feelings. Of course I fall fast."

Pam's curiosity was far from satisfied. "How old is he? What does he do? Is he cute? Of course he is. Do you have photos?"

I carefully chose the question to answer from that assortment. "As of Saturday, he runs a cupcake shop. It just opened."

Pam stared at me and then snorted so hard she coughed. "A—A cupcake shop? Well, at least you can give him free dental exams..." She grinned, letting her expression fill in the rest of what she wanted to say, but we were *technically* at work.

I rolled my eyes. "I know."

"What's it called?" Pam dug in her pocket for her phone.

I should have seen that one coming. "Oh, God. No."

"Fine," Pam muttered and started tapping at her phone. "Cupcake shop... Saturday... new..."

I couldn't stop her googling, so I wolfed down my sandwich at top speed and hoped for an escape.

"Daddy Cakes?"

My expression had to be a dead giveaway.

Pam squinted and tapped at her phone. "And it's got a theme of... and it's next door to..."

"Shh," I urged, glancing behind us at the door. We got up to some rowdy conversations, but I didn't want the others to hear.

"*Dom Nation?*" Pam exclaimed, her voice practically a squeak. "Slate!"

I said nothing. Nothing at all. Bit my lip, in fact, and stared at the table, my cheeks red-hot.

Pam was one of my closest friends, because after thirty the only way you made friends was at work. She knew about me and Isaac—sort of. She knew about the failed first dates I'd been on, and my last few years pining after a man who didn't want me.

But I'd never quite filled her in on the finer details. I'd danced around them so she'd thought he was a homebody who liked to drop by my place for Netflix and cuddling.

I hadn't been able to bring myself to tell her. After all, what I did in the bedroom was my business, right? So maybe I'd dialed up the romance a little bit. Or a lot. Made up a few dates on special days, so it wouldn't seem so weird. Like a relationship based only on sex and pain.

My gut crashed into my heart, and my palms were sweating.

"I've been trying to tell you to get back on the market for what, two years now?" She scoffed. "And all the time you were just waiting to be old enough to be a Daddy!"

My head snapped up so fast I might have actually lost consciousness for a second. *Wait, what?*

Pam grinned wickedly at me. "And you've found yourself a boy at last, huh? He's younger, isn't he?" When I nodded, she giggled. "Don't look so embarrassed. I'm happy for you! You look so good today, like there's a weight off your shoulders."

I was way too stuck on the idea that she thought I was a Daddy. Me, of all people! "Uhhh…" I mumbled, clutching my sparkling water for dear life. "Thanks."

"You should have told me." She clicked her tongue. "I'd have set you up with my gay friends who are his age, not yours. Now I know. If this doesn't work out…"

I bristled. *That won't be necessary.* I couldn't fathom a world in which I didn't move heaven and earth to *make* it work out between us. There was simply no other option.

Rex was mine, and I was Rex's, and that was that.

She smirked. "Jealousy is adorable on you. I can't wait to meet him."

Crap, I could picture her showing up at the cupcake shop one night only to see the side of me I'd never been brave enough to speak up about…

"No," I gasped, mortified. "I'll introduce you some other way. No showing up at Daddy Cakes, please." *Or especially Dom Nation.* It occurred to me that she was taking this way too easily. She wasn't into the scene herself, was she…?

But I couldn't fathom the idea of one of my good friends seeing me like that. Not just submissive or humiliated, but *loving* it. How would anyone look me in the eye afterward, here at work or hanging out at the movies, without laughing?

Pam put a reassuring hand on mine for a moment and nodded, calming me from my genuine moment of panic. "Okay." Then she winked. "Slate! Your backbone is showing. Is that an order?"

"Oh, Lord," I groaned. "Lunch must be over now, right?" I snapped the lid on my sandwich container. I stood up so quickly the blood rushed from my head.

Pam's delighted laughter followed me out the door. I rushed back to my exam room to tidy up the toy box and open the next patient's notes.

But despite the anxious buzzing of my nerves, the worry that my secret was out, and most of all the incredulity that anyone would think I could be a good Daddy…

I was also happy. The weight off my shoulders was more than me moving on from Isaac and finding something good for myself in life. It was one less secret I carried—the biggest secret I had. And Pam hadn't even batted an eye.

Maybe the only person I hurt with my silence and my secrecy was myself. And maybe Rex saw that, and he could help. I needed Daddy's help: his tenderness and his roughness in equal measure.

I just had to survive one long afternoon before I could talk to him again, and it had never felt longer.

By the time I pulled into my driveway, I'd replayed my favorite moments of the weekend—up to the moment he'd seen me to the penthouse elevator with a kiss—so many times I felt like a scratched, looping CD.

We might as well have spent a year together, for everything we'd said and done and felt in those few short days. But now the real world had intruded on our little bubble. It felt like my perfect weekend with the perfect Daddy had been one long daydream.

At least, until I got home and found two neatly stacked boxes next to my front door, hidden behind one of the square planters of pansies. And I recognized the design of the top box. It was smaller, but still black with white roses.

Just like the six-pack cupcake box Rex had left on my counter. Did he know I'd already eaten all six cupcakes—and hardly anything else—while daydreaming about seeing him again? My heart fluttered with hope.

I picked up both boxes gingerly, shifting them into the crook of one arm and tucking the cupcake box against my chest to unlock my door. The bottom box was plain cardboard and a lot heavier. *Is it a giant cupcake?* I wondered. *Because I'll definitely sit down and pig out on it for supper.*

Once inside, I headed straight for the couch and set the cupcake box on the table, since I already knew what it was. I slashed the top box with my car keys and tore the flaps open like a kid on Christmas Day.

And then I laughed, pulling a stainless steel electric kettle free from its foam packaging and setting it on the table to admire.

I turned my attention to the cupcake box, relieved to see the treat inside was in perfect condition. I pulled it free from the cardboard lining and gasped. Across the white creamy surface, red frosting ropes crisscrossed the surface, knotted together at four points.

Rex had talented fingers indeed, and I couldn't help wondering if that talent extended to real-life ropes, too.

"Jesus," I whispered. But something else caught my eye—a slip of paper tucked into the cupcake box. I gingerly set my Daddy's creation aside, eagerly fishing out the note.

Make yourself a cup of tea and text Daddy about your day.

-X

"Ohhhh my God," I breathed out, and before I thought twice, I raised the note to my nose to sniff it.

Wait, what the hell? I stifled a giggle. Ten words in Rex's very own handwriting and I became a total weirdo. What was I expecting to smell besides ink, anyway?

But the effervescent joy bursting from me was impossible to contain. I was made of glass, my spirit shimmered so brightly. I was awake and alive all of a sudden, my fingers tingling. Even after a long workday, I felt refreshed and renewed like it was a whole new day. And then there was the big, happy, stupid grin I couldn't wipe off my face.

My Daddy knew just what I needed.

The giddy rush that flooded through me wiped away any doubts I'd had about the weekend all being a finite daydream.

"Okay," I said out loud to calm myself down. "Right. Okay. Let's plug this in. Come on, Slate." I picked up the kettle and walked to the kitchen, plugged it in, and then paced back and forth several times to burn off the energy sparking in me.

I could leap mountains, climb tall buildings—or was it the other way round? Whatever. I could fucking fly if I had to.

The kettle took the place of pride on my kitchen counter as I filled it with water from the tap, flicked the switch, and stood back, hands clasped by my chest. I stared at it like Rex himself was in there, heating up the water with his magic touch.

Oh, God. I've never felt like this before. Isaac had made me feel stupid fluttery feelings, sure, but he'd never given me the chance to soar on them before dragging me down, reminding me of my place.

But now? I could imagine a future with Rex—a commingling of our lives, a perfect niche in each of our hearts for each other.

And this little gesture spoke volumes. I was more than a convenient weekend distraction for Rex. I'd finally broken down his walls last night, and he hadn't hated me for it. Far from it. He'd looked relieved at finally sharing the most tender parts of himself.

The feeling of holding Rex simmered in my chest and thighs and forearms again, just like he was right there with me.

Suddenly I wasn't worried about being too old, too new to the scene, or too ugly to be Rex's boy. I'd never felt more fresh-faced and beautiful as I had with him.

"Oh, God help me," I murmured. When my cup of tea was ready, I went back to the living room to compose a text and admire the cupcake in its place of pride on my table. I couldn't imagine eating it, but I figured I was supposed to.

Hi, Daddy! I got your gifts. Thank you xxx

I kept typing, trying to figure out how to tell him about my day. It was so fizzy and wonderful in my brain that it was hard to focus. I couldn't tell if it was a good idea to tell him every-thing, like the fact Pam thought I was a Daddy now. *Not* telling him everything seemed impossible.

Work was fun today. I was so happy today that my friend at work pried the details out of me. (Not all of them, don't worry!) She found out about Daddy Cakes and um... she thinks I'm the Daddy now...?!

I sent the message, took a photo of the cupcake, and finally allowed myself a bite once I peeled off the wrapper.

Oh, God, it was soft and delicious with an unexpected tart cherry pop on my tongue. Were the ropes flavored? So clever.

My phone buzzed and I nearly dropped the cupcake as I eagerly grabbed it. I gasped but caught the cupcake just in time to keep myself from smearing the top all over my chest.

"Well done, Slate," I muttered, but grinned.

A crying-with-laughter emoji greeted me first and then a message.

Oh, Slate. I don't mind if she has the wrong impression so long as you know who's in charge.

He was typing again, which seemed dangerous. I squeaked, put down the cupcake, and typed as fast as I could.

I do, Daddy!

Then there was a pause before another message.

Good boy. So you were as happy as me today, I take it.

I beamed. Rex was just as lovestruck as me, was he? God, that made me happier than anything so far. I was a cupcake getting layers of happiness slathered all over me.

Yes, Daddy. All because of you this weekend. And coming home to your treats was the best part of the day. Is there anything I can do for you tonight?

I bit my lip, hoping he got the gist of my last sentence. I'd never truly sexted anyone before—not even the prick whose name should not be associated with Rex's—but I'd learn, for Rex's sake.

Tell me if you liked the cupcake. It's my new flavor combo.

I eagerly put my phone on my knees and picked up the cupcake for another bite. Then I caught my breath as an idea occurred to me. After stabbing at my phone a few times, I held it at arm's length, wiped a finger through the red-and-white frosting, and pressed the button to record a video.

I tried not to feel silly as I closed my eyes. I just pretended Daddy was standing right there, his crotch right at the level of the camera. And I swirled my tongue around my icing-laden fingers, sucking them deep into my mouth with a sensual moan for good measure.

Then I hit the button again and grinned, sending the video straight to Rex in response.

Will he like it? God, I hope so. It might be bratty, trying to turn on my Daddy while he was too busy to come over to me. I stared at the phone, transfixed and waiting for a response as I lapped at my fingers to clean off the rest of the icing.

My phone screen lit up with an incoming video call.

I stifled a giggle and cleared my throat before I answered, trying with everything I had to look cool and not like I was about to faint from excitement.

"Hi," I greeted as soon as the image of Rex loaded on my screen.

"Hi, what?" Rex raised his brow sternly at me. He was at Daddy Cakes, the counter behind him littered with baking ingredients and dustings of flour.

I hadn't wanted to push him *too* hard. Before now, I'd had to work to earn his agreement to Daddy me. But it seemed like everything had changed last night. He wasn't just a Daddy for me, he was *my* Daddy.

There went the stupid grin again, lighting my face up in the thumbnail in the corner of my screen. "Hi, Daddy," I added, shy and soft. I could barely look at him, my cheeks hot with pleasure.

Rex's soft chuckle made me look up, but his gaze was still stern. "Hello, my naughty boy," he greeted. "You've made Daddy far too happy at work. You know that, don't you? You were trying to turn me on."

I blushed, but my guilt was written all over my face. Instead of apologizing, I grinned. "It worked?"

Rex's brows snapped together. "Far too well, boy. Unfortunately for you, there are consequences for trying to top from the bottom."

A gasp escaped as I sat up straight. I had no idea what that meant, but *possibly* he was referring to the fact I'd been hoping to entice him into sexting. "I—"

Rex cut me off and held up a finger. "I wasn't done speaking."

Oops. I was digging myself an even bigger hole, wasn't I? I squirmed apologetically as I mimed zipping my lips.

"You told me yourself, my boy: you want *me* to choose when you're going to please me. You need your Daddy to decide when he wants to play with you. You can't go trying to taunt and tempt me whenever you like and not expect consequences. Especially when you know I'm at work," Rex told me sternly.

Oh no! Or… yes? Consequences! I nodded slightly and quivered with anticipation, barely breathing.

"You're not allowed to come without asking permission, remember," Rex reminded me. "You do remember that rule, right? It's not just when we're together."

Whoa. I gasped. Good thing I hadn't had time to linger in my shower that morning, but I'd really been looking forward to a long, hot bath tonight. *You can't just…!*

But he could, and he was.

One hand slid down my stomach, over the zipper of my trousers, and settled on the growing bulge. I squeezed my throbbing semi, wishing it didn't send such delicious sparks through me. The knowledge of what was forbidden somehow made every sensation even more raw and irresistible.

This was the biggest ask anyone had made of me, and suddenly obedience didn't seem as easy or as fun.

"Are you touching yourself right now?" Rex demanded, suddenly harsh. His voice made my cock pulse with delight, growing under my palm.

"Yes, Daddy," I whispered, freezing. "I'll—I'll let you watch. I'll wait for your permission before I come. Is that okay?"

Rex clicked his tongue. "I told you: that's topping from the bottom. I won't allow it. *You* don't want it. You want to be told what to do, not given free rein. So… your Daddy says no."

"No?" I wasn't allowed to touch myself, or I couldn't come? Because fuck me, I hated the idea, but I *loved* it at the same time, in a way that made my chest dance with stars and sparks.

"You can touch yourself all you like," Rex said. His smile was self-certain, like he knew perfectly well I would obey him, however much I resented it. "But you aren't allowed to come tonight. And if your slutty little cock does it anyway, you're going to tell Daddy the truth. And the punishment will be a lot worse."

How much worse? I was dying to know, but I was afraid to ask. My mouth was dry as I suddenly licked my lips, adrenaline flushing through me. I kind of wanted to run and hide, but there was no escaping my Daddy.

Even if I hid, I wanted him to find me.

"It won't feel good for you," Rex purred. His voice was slow, sweet and smooth like honey. Damn it, my Daddy was *enjoying* this. "You know how pretty you'd look crying? Because I've fantasized about it all day."

Fuck. I gulped, frozen on the couch. I was torn between wanting to hang up and run very far and fast, and wishing he could burst in the door and do it right now. I wanted Daddy to scare me into submission, use me for his own ends, leave me a crying mess... and then gather me into his arms and forgive me.

I wanted it so badly I couldn't breathe.

My voice was thin and breathless. "Y-Yes, Daddy. I'll be good." I squirmed, grinding my desperate shaft against my palm. Suddenly it felt like I might burst.

If he kept talking dirty like this, I feared I'd get my wish right away. So with all the self-control I could muster up, I pulled my hand away from myself and sat on it instead with a soft whimper, my eyes sliding shut.

Don't touch yourself, I commanded myself. It would only make it worse, not being able to finish. Better not to go there at all.

Then it struck me: Daddy was giving me an all-day taste of what I'd done to him.

"Oh," I groaned, my toes curling into the floor as my thighs tensed and released. I jiggled one foot, wishing there were some way I could relieve the pressure.

Rex smiled innocently. "Having trouble there, my boy? Struggling to obey?"

I gulped and shook my head as hard as I could. "No. No, sir. Not at all. I'll do anything you tell me."

"Yes," Rex breathed out smugly, savoring the word. "You will."

I pressed my hand against my face, my grip so tight on the phone that my knuckles hurt. "You aren't going to make me wait until the weekend, are you, Daddy?"

I swear I wasn't trying to direct him. I just needed to know if I was going to lose *every* night to dreams of Rex and urges that I couldn't satisfy.

"No," Rex said, chuckling softly. "I'm going to take you on a date one night this week." At last, the commanding tone faded in his voice, and he gave me a sheepish smile. "Something... romantic."

Oh my God, I've actually died and gone to heaven. My body flushed with a whole new kind of heat, my chest suddenly full of butterflies like every cheesy movie I stayed up late to watch.

"You… you are?" I asked softly, ducking my head. "I don't deserve *that*." I'd never believed *I* could deserve a place in one of those stories, but here I was.

Rex sharply corrected me, "Yes, you do. When I want to scratch the itch inside you that needs scratched, I'll tell you that you don't deserve things. That's not true. You *do* deserve to be romanced, and I don't want to hear you say otherwise. Understand?"

I could barely speak, my gaze fixed on my lap. At least the tide of emotions that had flooded my body distracted me from the fading pressure in my pants. *Don't cry*, I told myself, but his words made me feel small and vulnerable in the best way possible.

"Well?" Rex prompted at last.

"Sorry, Daddy," I finally whispered and looked up at the screen. "I do deserve your…" *Love*, I wanted to say, but I was afraid. "Romance."

"Yes," Rex said firmly, like it was never even in question. "So, keep your schedule clear."

"I will," I promised, breathless. I could hardly feel my lips, my heart still hammering at my rib cage. He just casually said things I'd never known I needed to hear.

"Good boy," Rex added, soft and deliberate. He was giving me permission to bask, and so I did, my shoulders easing into the back of the couch as the tension bled from my body.

"Now, shoo and let me focus, sweetheart," Rex added, his eyes flicking offscreen as he frowned slightly. Then he turned bright red and stared right at the camera like he couldn't quite believe the word had left his mouth.

Oh, it *had*, and we both knew it. I beamed so wide I could swallow the whole world. "Bye, Daddy," I chirped.

"Bye!" Rex's cheeks were a funny shade of red. He hung up so fast that I burst into breathless giggles.

Then I got a text from him with just one emoji—two little red hearts revolving around each other. After a minute of searching my emojis to send him the exact same one in response, I smacked my forehead. I could just copy and paste it, duh. So I did, sending the response with a trembling hand before laying my phone on the coffee table next to my cooling cup of green tea.

I stared at it until the screen went black, but with no response from Rex, I could finally catch my breath and try to pretend I wasn't floating into the stratosphere with happiness.

I glanced around the living room like anyone else could even be here, grabbed a pillow and stuffed it against my mouth, and squeaked in a deeply undignified fashion. When I was done squirming with joy, I set the pillow aside again and stood up, pacing back and forth along the carpet.

I deserve Rex. Even as I thought it, I barely believed it, but Rex clearly wanted me to, so I was going to start practicing now. *I deserve his romance and his love and his attention. I deserve to be a good boy for my Daddy.*

For more than one reason, it was going to be impossible to sleep tonight. And for the first time in so long, it was no longer because I was writhing in the hollow emptiness that shame left in its wake. No—the kind of shame I felt with Rex was full of rich joy, and it left me light and breathing easier.

I grabbed the cool cup of tea and headed for the kitchen to make another, whistling the whole way there.

Yeah. Sleep wasn't happening anyway. I might as well fill myself with green tea, the remainder of the cupcake, and endless replays of my Daddy's words.

12

REX

I was never going to live this one down.

Distracted by Seb letting himself into the cupcake shop—I'd left the door unlocked—my mouth had moved without my express permission.

"Now, shoo and let me focus, sweetheart," I'd said, before realizing what had come out of my mouth. Endearment, plain and simple. A sign of affection I'd never let myself feel for a boy, much less *say*. In public, too.

Heat flushed my cheeks, crawling down to the very pit of my stomach. *I don't have anything to be embarrassed about*, I told myself, but it fell short. I'd spent *years* cultivating my reputation, after all.

After hanging up as fast as I humanly could, I finally looked at Seb. He was grinning enormously as he leaned on the display cabinet, wearing the suit and tie that meant he was on his way to some late meeting.

"Evening, sweetheart," my so-called friend said, batting his lashes at me.

I gave him a look that let him know there were sharp knives behind this counter. "Asshole."

"No, I'm happy for you." Seb's eyes glinted as he smoothed his hand over his face like he was trying to stroke away the smile lines. "Love looks good on you."

My heart just about stopped. *No, he did not,* I thought. I gave him an incredulous look, but he wasn't joking around. He must not understand everything he was implying by using *that* word.

It was just a phrase. A thing people said when they approved of their sad, long-single friends getting un-single.

"I didn't ask your opinion, actually," I said with a smirk. "I wanted to talk about something else."

Seb only swooned harder against the display case. "Not the depths of his eyes and the—" I unrolled the top of the flour bag under the counter, and he held his hands up, stepping back. "Okay! Not on this suit, man."

No point in beating around the bush. "I want to know how I should go after Isaac." I let a moment pass as I scrutinized him, making sure he wasn't about to tell me they'd become best buddies while I opened up the shop.

Seb's brow wrinkled. "I've never known either of you to sub."

"Not *that* way," I groaned. "I mean, I think he's harassing me. But everyone loves him. They won't believe it without proof."

The jokes faded from Seb's eyes, and he immediately grabbed a chair, turning it around to sit and face me. "Are you serious? What's happening?"

I allowed myself a moment of gratitude for my friend before explaining. Not all the details, of course. Barely any of them. Just that someone had shown up at my old workplace, I was pretty sure it had to be him, but I wasn't given a name or face, so I had no proof at all.

Seb raised a brow. "You're sure it's not some boy's jealous boyfriend?"

"Slate would *never*." My words were an ice-cold warning, but fire sizzled in my belly. He wasn't a cheater. Not on his life.

Seb blinked at me. "Whoa," he said, sounding startled. "I didn't mean *his* boyfriend. Is he the only one in the picture, then?"

He wasn't asking to be curious or tease. He still had his serious voice on. So I ground my teeth and snipped, "Yes. And the guy who showed up had black hair and a leather jacket."

"That's what he often wears," Seb agreed, rubbing his chin.

I nodded, hoping we were on the same page now.

"What are you going to do about it? Because I'll help you hide the body, but…"

I smiled, but my gut roiled. This was the part I couldn't quite come to terms with. What *was* I supposed to do?

I couldn't let Isaac rampage around my life, trying to find out more about me. And telling Slate would only make him feel guilty—or worse, unsafe.

I was the Daddy. It was my job to deal with this, and I already knew how.

"I want to talk to Brighton," I said. "Even though I don't have evidence yet… there are things he should know."

"Okay. Let's go," Seb said, checking his watch, not even questioning my decision. "I've got a few minutes before I have to leave. I saw his car, so he should be in."

A few minutes later, it was déjà vu all over again.

"And you think it was Isaac even though he didn't leave a name? Why?"

Brighton leaned back in his office chair, his hands clasped in front of him as he frowned.

He couldn't look more different from the dark office with its red-paneled walls and plush velvet chairs. He wore a fluffy pink sweater and skinny jeans, bright blond hair swept to one side, dangling gold earrings, and black heeled boots.

Brighton always looked like a twink who'd gotten lost on the way to the cocktail bar, but I knew better than to be fooled by the appearance. He was tough as nails. I just didn't know how to get him on my side without breaking my trust with Slate.

I chewed the inside of my cheek. I'd been over the words endlessly in my head, and I still couldn't find quite the right ones.

"There wasn't much of a description, but it matched him. I can't reveal the rest without violating others' privacy," I said carefully. "But if I told you what I know… Isaac should never darken the door of this place again."

Though I acted as cool as ever, nervous energy bubbled in my gut. Brighton liked Isaac—as everyone did. Without any evidence, I sounded like I was holding a grudge.

Maybe I was, but it was extremely well-founded.

Brighton couldn't act on "an unknown man showed up at my workplace, and I think it was Isaac based on a hair color and a jacket," though.

So, even more cautiously in the stillness of the office, I offered up another crumb. "I have reason to believe he's played outside the rules—just not within these walls, to avoid being caught. And he might have broken the rules within the club once, too."

"This isn't something you've witnessed, Master X," Brighton surmised, his gaze narrowing as he examined me, leaning forward. "But you know someone who has."

"No, and yes," I said with a sharp nod. "I'm sorry, but that's all I can tell you right now."

"My DMs missed something." Brighton didn't sound pleased, and it made me exhale with relief, because he clearly believed me. His eyes flickered to Seb, who shifted uncomfortably. "You don't know anything?"

"I'm afraid not," Seb said gravely.

Seb didn't DM every night—and not on the night in question. I itched to defend him, but I'd start saying too much if I tried. The fact he was accompanying me had to be enough.

All I had to go on was a scrap of an interaction between Isaac and a taxi driver. I'd never even seen anything with my own eyes, and that made me helpless.

There was no worse feeling in the world.

Brighton blew out a quiet sigh and fidgeted with one of his earrings. "Very well. I can't launch a formal process on a gut feeling. But I'll pull him in for an interview when he comes in next weekend. If he doesn't admit that it was him…"

I knew what he was saying. *There's nothing more I can do without evidence.* Communities could be destroyed by jealous Doms competing for sex, attention, or—most of all—love.

"Thank you," I told him and stood up. Seb shadowed me. "That's all I can ask."

"I trust you. You've never stepped outside the rules—never even tried to skirt them. I'll take your word, if push comes to shove. Let's hope it doesn't."

I nodded, but I had the feeling it wouldn't be that easy. Isaac could just deny being the one to show up, and unless I could convince the Three Fucketeers to give me CCTV footage, that was that. Isaac would win, and he'd get to revel smugly in it.

"Thanks, Brighton. See you."

The place was still quiet at this hour, with just a few guys sitting at the bar and—by the sounds of it—others enjoying the whole playroom to themselves.

Seb pulled me into the dance floor, which was half-lit and empty this early. On a Monday, it would be the quietest spot in the building even later in the night. It looked like a weird corporate event space, except that the tables were bolted down. Even with all the lemon cleaner in the world, there was no shaking that unmistakable tang of sweat and sex.

"Did that go how you imagined it?" Seb asked.

I snorted and shrugged. "What more can I ask from him? He's right. He can't just start acting on whispers."

Seb rested an elbow on the table and inspected me, saying nothing. He had the same air of quiet authority in leather, a suit, or a T-shirt and jeans.

The scrutiny shouldn't have bothered me. He was the closest thing I had to a mentor, but I didn't belong to him. I sure as hell didn't answer to him, nor did I have to explain myself.

But guilt squirmed in my stomach nonetheless, and I didn't meet his gaze.

Maybe I shouldn't have come to Brighton. I wasn't *technically* breaking Slate's trust, but…

"So, how about you?" I changed the subject with all the grace of a ballet-dancing buffalo.

"You mean, do I have a hot little thing hanging on my every word?" Seb snorted. "No way."

I grimaced sympathetically. I'd always assumed I'd be in the same boat for years to come. And then, overnight, everything had changed. "But you're going on the DN cruise."

Brighton had commissioned a small cruise ship for a gay kink cruise sponsored by Dom Nation. The usual crowd was going, but there was plenty of space for kinky fuckers from across the country. The week aboard had been the talk of the club for the last year.

I swallowed my envy yet again. I couldn't go—my shop might have started as a fun diversion, but it had also eaten a lot of my money, and I really did want to make it a success. Randomly closing for a week wasn't an option.

"Brighton's trying to get me to DM for at least one day," Seb said, laughing as he shook his head. "I'm such a sucker I'll probably say yes."

"That leaves, what, six days to wander a boatload of hot guys." I bumped his shoulder with mine. "Leaving your mark."

Seb gave a crooked grin. "Yeah. But life's not *just* hookups. As I suspect you're finding out."

He had me there. I shrugged, my gaze quickly darting away again. Until now, I'd held myself back from the possibility of finding love. Seb did the same thing in his own way, often pushing away guys that I privately thought would be a good match for him.

"How about you set a goal of finding someone to take on the cruise with you?" I suggested, grinning. "Rather than holding your breath and waiting to meet someone."

It wasn't like the extra cruise fare would be a problem for him. And maybe the time limit would make him start seeing things differently than just letting guys drift past him. Slate might have drifted out of my life if he hadn't doggedly worked his way into my heart.

No, that's not true. I bit back a smile. I'd seen something special in him, as much as it terrified me. I started off hot and cold but ultimately wouldn't have let him go. Indeed, I hadn't.

"That's a good idea." Seb looked way too surprised as he said that.

I snorted. "Gee, thanks. I have them, now and then."

Seb grinned. "Once in a blue moon, I'll give you that. You're still not going, are you?"

I shook my head. "I don't even know how Daddy Cakes will be doing by that point. I'm not covering expenses yet, but it's only been two days. I think I'll need to open days during the week, and at night on weekends and special parties."

Honestly, I looked forward to it. Without this structure in my life, I'd just be wandering around my apartment waiting for Slate to finish work every day.

"Sensible," Seb nodded.

I snorted. "How do people know how to grow businesses, anyway?" I could micromanage the daily stuff, but I'd always relied on my so-called friends to dream big.

Brighton's laugh startled me into turning around. "By trying and failing a lot," he told me with a wink. "Just like relationships. If you need advice, let me know. I'd make a shitty Dear Abby, but I'll help you with accounting."

"Thanks," I said with a laugh. "I'll keep you in mind."

"Speaking of which," Seb prompted, elbowing me.

Shit. I should have sworn him to secrecy. I did *not* want to tell Brighton about my new boy right now—he wasn't stupid. He'd connect the dots, and Slate's secret would be out.

It might already be. Another guilty itch to add to the whole mess of guilty prickling under my skin.

"No news on that front," I told them both briskly, giving Seb an extra look that I hoped he could interpret.

Don't you dare tell him.

Seb nodded slightly; message received loud and clear. "I'd better take off for work," he told both me and Brighton. "I'll catch you later."

As he headed for the front door, I tried to smooth my own ruffled feathers. "And I've got to get back to baking."

"Hope this week goes well," Brighton said.

"Thanks." I took off for the cupcake shop, walking fast so Seb didn't stop me for any more questions.

I let out a breath when I made it to Daddy Cakes. This time, I turned the lock on the door and pulled down the blind on the door.

Peace and quiet and solitude. Just me, my baking, and a whole peaceful evening to spend singing along to the radio.

And, of course, the guilt that wouldn't quite leave the back of my mind. Perhaps I shouldn't have gone after Isaac at all. But I hadn't spilled Slate's secret. I was acting on my own behalf. Going to someone's workplace was so far out of line.

Shit. What if he showed up at Slate's workplace, too? Okay, now I was verging on paranoia. Isaac's beef was with me, no doubt for "stealing" his property.

I scooped up my box of food dyes and set them out on the counter in rainbow order. It helped me order my thoughts and calm down.

If Isaac went after Slate, I had to trust my boy would tell me and let Daddy handle it. Slate knew that was what I was here for. To help him, no matter what.

At last, there was a thought to make me smile. I *had* a boy—and God, it made me proud to call Slate mine. I wished I could share that news with all my friends. I hated keeping secrets. And since I didn't want to play with any other boys... well, everyone else would notice my singular focus soon.

Just a little longer, I told myself and plucked the bottle of red dye from the end of the lineup. First, I'd frost the cherry cupcakes my boy had approved yesterday. Once Isaac was gone, I'd tell Slate the good news, and then he'd come around to trusting Brighton, the DMs, and maybe the whole club.

Then we could be another of those happy couples in Dom Nation most weekends. Slate would be safe from Isaac's prying gaze, and I could show him off like the boy toy he wanted to be.

"Soon," I murmured to myself and set the other bottles aside, grabbing steel bowls from under the counter.

Good things were coming soon.

13

REX

I could walk into a room of investors and cold-pitch them, and I'd be sweating less. But here I was, just staring at my boy over a white tablecloth and candles as the Italian restaurant slowly revolved.

This was the sort of place old rich guys took their bored wives, or business partners came to make those all-important connections. We were seated in a quiet part of the restaurant, at a romantic table for two.

Slate was fascinated by the ever-changing skyline. He kept glancing out and staring, craning his neck to see more.

"You only have to wait fifteen minutes and you can see the view behind you without breaking your neck," I teased.

Slate blushed as he looked at me again with a little laugh. "Sorry," he murmured.

But I just smiled at him. It was cute, watching him get flustered. "I like that you're enjoying this."

"Are you?" Slate asked, wide-eyed and innocent.

Oh, boy. Apart from the constant jiggle of my leg under the table and my deep-abiding anxiety that I was charting a course through regions unknown…

"Yeah," I said with my usual confident smile.

I'd never taken anyone on such a traditional romantic date, but it had felt important. Daddy Cakes had been so quiet yesterday night that I didn't care about being closed for another weeknight. Weekends would be busier, and other things mattered more right now. Slate deserved to be wooed properly, and more importantly to know that he deserved every bit of it.

I wanted the world to see the way I looked at him: like he was my future. But I'd spent all evening sweating like crazy because I didn't want to screw this up.

"Good," Slate said with a soft smile. "This is all so new to me…"

The waiter who had just cleared away the dishes reappeared with dessert menus and offered them. "Dessert, sirs?"

"No, thank you. We've got plans," I said, winking at Slate. I knew exactly where his mind would go, and even though I didn't mean that precisely… I didn't mind embarrassing him a little more.

He turned bright red and cleared his throat. "Thank you," he added before giving me a wide-eyed stare once the waiter walked away.

"Finish your wine," I told him. "Or don't. We're not going home yet."

Slate's pretty, full lips parted, his bright white teeth flashing in a smile. "Really?" He sounded amazed, like he couldn't imagine what else there was to enjoy tonight. Then he tipped back his head and finished the last sip of his wine, setting down his glass. He pushed back his chair slightly, almost vibrating with excitement like he was ready to spring to his feet.

I love seeing him eager as a puppy. I luxuriated in the thought and imagined myself scratching my fingers along his scalp later, pulling his quivering body against mine as he moaned… *Romance first*, I reminded myself and cleared my throat.

When I'd planned the evening, I'd pulled every classic idea from my scant knowledge of movies and pop culture. Ergo, three-course Italian meal and now rooftop stargazing with champagne.

It worked in the movies, right?

"Yep," I told him with a self-satisfied smile. "Let's go."

He waited in the entrance lobby while I paid—which earned me a curious stare from the staff, which was rather irritating since they were clearly expecting the older man to pay. But I brushed it off and led him to the elevator. When he tried to hit the ground floor button, I pushed his hand away and pressed the top floor instead.

"Oh," Slate breathed out, his whole face lighting up again as he figured out the plan. "I've never been up here."

"Better late than never," I told him and slid my hand into his. "You'll like the view."

Slate leaned into me like he was about to say something risqué. "I like all the views you've shared with me," he said.

I didn't comment, but I grinned to myself. So far, so good. I hadn't horribly screwed up the dinner conversation, wine etiquette, or any one of the thousand romantic moments that had passed between us already tonight.

Come on. Nail the landing, Rex, I urged myself. My grip tightened on Slate's fingers.

The elevator pinged softly, and the doors opened to the semi-darkness of the viewing deck.

"I'll go get us champagne," I told him, brushing my hand gently across his back.

"Uh-huh." Slate's gaze was fixed on the huge windows, which showcased an even better view of the city than my apartment. He wandered toward the window as if spellbound.

I grinned and hurried to the bar. I'd managed to sneak a bouquet of flowers upstairs with the judicious use of tipping, and they ought to be waiting behind the bar now.

This was it. This was the moment.

My heart thudded. By the time I reached the bar and a black-shirted bartender swooped in to serve me, my throat seemed to be blocked by a frog. I gulped hard and said, "Hi. I'm Rex. I'd like two glasses of champagne, and also, I called about the flowers…"

"Ah!" She gave me a conspiratorial wink and pulled the slim bouquet out from under the bar. Just half a dozen red roses wrapped in black ribbon. Nothing *too* fancy. Yet. I could save those ideas for the proposal. Oh, God, that thought made my heart flip in my chest again. "Lucky lady."

My lips twitched. "He is," I agreed, doing my best to be solemn. Many men would take offense if she'd assumed otherwise. I didn't want to embarrass her, but I couldn't help the laugh that threatened to burst out.

"Oh, of course. Sorry, sir." I just grinned to show her all was forgiven. "Lucky gent," she corrected herself as she poured two glasses of champagne. "Is it an engagement?"

"No. I'm asking him out. I mean, we're… sort of official. But I want to make it really official."

She smiled warmly and placed the glasses in front of me. "Good luck. Not that you need it."

"No. Thanks." I ruffled in my wallet and handed over more than enough to cover the glasses plus the trouble of hiding away the roses.

This presented me with something of a problem. I couldn't very well carry both glasses in one hand without spilling champagne. But I wanted to surprise him. Dammit, so much for all my careful planning.

I could shove the flower stems in the back of my pants, but they might slide down, and nobody needed ass flowers.

The bartender saw my dilemma. "I'll bring the drinks over," she offered, whipping out a small serving tray and balancing them.

"Thank you. I seem to have forgotten my spare hand at home." My joke couldn't quite cover the nervous waver in my voice, though.

Shit. Who the hell was *this* man occupying my body? Certainly not the Master X who effortlessly handled even the stubbornest boys, or Rex who didn't break a sweat about production deadlines.

No, I was Tyrus Black, the scared young man under the veils Slate had so patiently drawn back. The man who had walked away from his own family to be the man I *needed* to be—starting by coming out at sixteen and sealing the deal by leaving for the big city where I'd always imagined my future and fortune awaited.

Well, I'd found both. And I was scared shitless to lose my chance at a future shared with Slate.

Don't be ridiculous, I told myself as my moment for dawdling ran out. The bartender was stepping out from behind the counter, and it was time to lead the way.

Time to put up or shut up—and I was never one to shut up.

As I joined Slate, the bartender presented our drinks. He smiled and thanked her, taking a glass just as I did. And—as I'd hoped—he didn't even notice what was in my other hand.

"To us," I murmured, holding out my glass.

Gently, he tapped the rim against mine. "To us," he agreed, his smile warm and welcoming.

And my shoulders sank, the stress evaporating at that one easy expression. I knew his answer already, but I had to ask. So, after we'd each sipped, I cleared my throat and shuffled in front of him, blocking his view of the city.

"Slate," I murmured, holding up the slim bouquet.

He blinked as if he wasn't sure they were for him, then looked around. "Rex...?" His voice was soft, rising at the end and trailing off.

"Can I call you my boyfriend—my partner?" I asked softly. Should I be down on one knee? No, then everyone would think I was proposing. *A thought that ought to scare me more than it does.* "Whatever word you like. Nobody else but us. Just you and me, boy."

Slate beamed at me, his gaze sliding between the flowers and me. He looked dizzy, overwhelmed with emotion, so I had to press them into his hand for him to take them.

"You can call me your boy, and anything else you want," Slate whispered back, a dusky blush rising over his cheeks. He gulped. "Yes. Yes. Now kiss me before I faint, Rex."

A rush of relieved laughter escaped, and I crowded up close to him, tilting my chin up. I had to rise onto tiptoe to press our lips together, and the moment I did, I felt like I could keep going—until my feet lifted from the floor, until we flew together.

Under the starlight and over the twinkling lights that stretched behind me, up and up, all the way past the moon. Find ourselves a dark little patch of the universe, a place to nestle together and make our home. Forever.

When we finally pulled away, my heart still hammered in my chest. The relief was an intoxicating rush that made me completely forget about the glass in my hand, the view behind me, or anything else. I was just standing on the spot, staring at Slate and grinning like a loon.

Slate kept gulping, raising the roses to his nose now and then, his gaze fixed on the skyline. Like he wasn't quite sure what to say. But the smile never left his face, and I knew he was happy.

"Come here," Slate finally whispered and gently nudged me to turn around. Then he wrapped one arm around my side—the one with the roses—until they nestled against my chest.

We fit perfectly together like this, him and me.

"Are you okay?" Slate finally murmured.

I laughed and shook my head slightly. "Of course. I just spent all night trying to make this perfect, and I haven't really planned anything after this point. I suppose I was so worried that…" I trailed off and laughed sheepishly.

It wasn't very Dominant to admit that I'd been scared shitless that he only wanted a Daddy for a little while. Someone to fix him up, sort him out, and send him on his way a newer, better man. Or worse still, take all the best parts of me and make them feel like a curse.

But no—this was *Slate*. It was crazy, but I'd trust him with anything.

Slate's voice was very quiet behind my ear. "Never doubt I'll always say yes, Rex." He crushed me against his chest for a moment, like he couldn't find any other way to show me the intensity of his emotions. "Before meeting you, I never imagined this." His voice turned hesitant, the words dripping from him. "I know you don't want to hear about him. But… can I tell you something?"

"Anything," I promised, inwardly bracing myself.

"Isaac never did anything like *this* with me. And boyfriends before him never did anything like—well, the other things we do. The naughtier things." My lips twitched as he tried to find a way to refer to kink in public. "I didn't think I could have both at once. Him and me... we didn't technically date. *I* called it dating, but to him, it wasn't."

I could imagine. My jaw tightened, and despite my best efforts, I knew I was going stiff in his arms with the adrenaline that flooded me. I ached to make Isaac pay for what he'd done to my sweet boy.

"I knew I needed a Daddy because I needed someone to be cruel to me. And I thought that's what a Daddy's like. I didn't think I could be a boyfriend *and...* a boy, you know?" He stuttered a bit, like he wasn't quite sure how to convey his meaning.

But I understood perfectly.

"Thank you for telling me," I murmured, covering his hand with my own. It was warm and rough, and my fingertips danced over the wrinkles of his knuckles. "And trusting me."

Being his Daddy was a responsibility I'd never take lightly. And that started by being honest about what I'd done.

"I have to tell you something," I said softly.

Slate went still, listening closely behind me. "Mmhmm?"

"Isaac stopped by the front desk at my old workplace. I think he's trying to blackmail me, hoping I'm closeted and ashamed or something. Letting me know that he could go to them and out me as a..." I trailed off. *Kinkster? Dom? Freak? Same difference, to the Three Fucketeers.*

Slate was suddenly stiff as a board. "What?"

I pressed my hand firmly against his. "I don't have proof that it's Isaac since they wouldn't give me CCTV, but there's no other reason for anyone to do that. So I went to Brighton and told him that Isaac's threatening to out me. They take their members' privacy seriously. Someone outing anyone in the scene to their family and coworkers is taken as seriously as outing them as gay."

"Is it?" Slate's voice was faint. The cellophane around the roses crunched gently.

I tried to turn in his arms and see him, but Slate's arm was too tight. He clung to me like a teddy bear, suddenly vulnerable. So I stroked his arm lightly, soothing him.

"You're going to be safe," I promised. "When you talk to Brighton, you just have to tell him what Isaac did to you. It's enough to get him banned from Dom Nation."

"But what if he gets angry...?" Slate gulped loudly.

"That's not your problem," I told him, boldly confident. "It's Brighton's." I had no idea how I could keep him safe when we weren't together, except... well... But I'd find a way. Anything for him. "But I'll be there for you when you're ready."

A few moments passed before Slate took a deep breath, his chest swelling against my back. Then he let it out and relaxed, his arm loosening. "Okay. When I'm ready?"

"Of course," I repeated myself. After all, I didn't have secrets anymore. Isaac had missed his chance to fuck up my life. I'd done that all on my own. But I was going to make sure he paid for what he'd done for Slate.

"You make me feel precious," Slate said, soft and wondering. "Is that crazy?"

I chuckled softly, squirming in his hold until I could turn my head sideways. Shit, he was tall when we stood like this. I craned my neck up. It was the worst angle *ever* for a kiss, but he grinned and indulged me in a peck on the lips.

"You *are* precious," I told him, turning ahead again. At last, I could focus on the tops of the buildings that stretched into the distance, lit in shimmering squares of light. "Having you in my life gives me a… purpose I didn't realize I was missing."

How the fuck had I coped before him? Suddenly, it didn't seem like such a crazy risk to put everything—my heart and soul—into one man. One boy. My chest ached with bittersweet joy. I'd gone around my whole life *not* knowing what this was like? And if I'd passed by Slate one night and never looked twice… I would have missed *this*?

Thank God. I hadn't believed in the universe aligning, and fate, and all that shit. But now? How could I believe anything else? Slate had been meant to walk in that night—my very first customer.

I could barely breathe, even though his arm was loose around my side.

"Take me home, Daddy," Slate begged me in a whisper. "Do anything you want. With you, I feel safe. I want to go further than ever before. I want you to erase every memory of *him*. I want my body to know only you."

I drained my glass, called a cab, and took the chance to rub the wetness from my eyes.

This. This is all I need for things to be perfect.

———

The moment I pushed open the door of my apartment, Slate darted ahead of me. He paused only long enough to kick off his stiff, formal shoes before striding for the kitchen, roses clutched to his chest.

"I hope you have a vase."

"Of course I do." Did I? I sweated for a moment before remembering—Seb had bought me flowers to celebrate getting the lease on the shop. "In the bottom cupboard," I told him and followed at a leisurely pace.

Slate set the flowers on the counter and opened the cupboard, bending over. His pants were already tight around that magnificent ass, and when he bent over? Well, that gave me the ideal view.

Then I realized Slate was grinning at me from between his legs. Busted. "You deliberately put it there," he accused me.

"I do what I like. Now get the vase and stop fooling around, or I'll be tempted to test your stamina," I ordered.

I couldn't help myself, though. Moth to a freaking flame. I walked toward him, my palms already burning with the need to touch him.

Slate shivered. "Yes, sir. Right away, sir." He took his time sorting through the pots and boxes in the cupboard.

So I reached out with a single fingertip, drawing it up Slate's inner thigh and over the mound of his balls, the fabric tight across his groin. He rocked forward, stumbled—almost fell, but caught himself on the counter as a low cry tore from his throat.

"I hope my boy has been good," I whispered and folded my hands behind my back. "Anything you need to tell Daddy?"

Slate clutched the vase like it was made of gold, shut the cupboard with his knee, and shook his head. He leaned heavily into the counter. "No, Daddy. I learned my lesson."

"Which is?" I shifted my weight until I stood evenly, my hands cupping my elbows. I wanted the weight of a whip at my side, but I knew I projected the same energy whether I had one there or not.

"No giving orders. No distracting and tempting you. No bottoming from the top. Wait. No. Topping from the top. From the bottom. Topping from the bottom. That's it." He kept talking faster, his tongue tripping over itself as he grew more flustered. "I-I learned the lesson, Daddy. I promise."

Apparently he hadn't learned after all, then. I grinned and let him see all my teeth, joyous desire flooding me at Slate's nervous gulp.

"No, boy," I corrected him, stifling the joy that threatened to soften my words as I remembered how real it was now. How official. "I decide when you've learned your lesson."

"S-Sorry," Slate whispered.

But that wasn't enough. I needed to make it stick—make it sting.

"Bend over."

Slate's eyes went huge. He set down the vase a good arm's length away, sensibly, but stared at me. "R-Right here?"

Oh, he'll learn to obey. But he'll take training.

I stepped forward, grabbed his bicep and his hip, and forcefully spun him around. "Here," I hissed, letting the savagery bleed into my words. "And now." I shoved a flat hand up his back, pressing him down against the counter.

He buckled but went down, resting his forehead against his folded arms on the counter.

"When your Daddy tells you to do something, you do it," I snarled. If he couldn't master the simplest rules of being a boy... *No. He'll learn*, I reassured myself. "Understand?"

"Yes, Daddy," Slate whimpered. I could hear it in his voice—the slightest of changes, but clear as day to my ear now. The way his muscles loosened and his body relaxed, while tensing up in anticipation of his punishment.

I smiled and drew back my hand for one slap on the delicious mounds of his firm ass. It wasn't going to sting, especially through the muffling layers of fabric, but it would get his attention.

Slate grunted and rocked back toward my hand, spreading his feet on the floor for balance. He kept his head down, his breathing shallow. Sharp-edged, like the knife of anticipation that danced along my skin.

At last, I was still and steady. Certainty anchored me and slowed my thoughts. I, too, was sliding into another state of mind: the pure, utter focus on Slate's every twitch and gasp.

I imagined this was how subs felt, too. Both of us gave in to instinct. No decisions or thinking. This was all the feeling mind—the animal brain that knew what it needed, if not why. Blissful escape.

Another glancing blow landed on the irresistibly soft, rounded ass hugged by the thin fabric of his trousers. Tingles ran through my palm, dissolving at my fingertips.

Time disappeared. It ceased to matter. All I cared about was drawing Slate at exactly the right pace through the stages of bliss, from the earliest touches straight through the ecstasy that awaited at the end. And this was just the foreplay.

I lived for his shallow breaths, the tiny grunts of pain and pleasure, and the rocking of his hips as he swayed forward with the impact of each blow, then fell back onto his heels again.

"Please," Slate gasped, and I nearly stopped breathing to hear better. "Please, Daddy."

Oh, those two words could have been spoken as a joke, but not right now. They came straight from Slate's subconscious, finally free to run rampant. They were perfectly chosen to reverberate straight through me.

"Yes, boy?" I brought my palm down hard, across both cheeks.

"Agh!" Startled, he jumped onto his toes and squeaked. His breathing heaving, he settled onto his feet again. "Ow, it hurts."

"What hurts, my boy?" I circled him, standing directly behind him now as I ran my hands from his lower back over his ass, squeezing gently on my way past, then tickled his thighs with my fingertips.

Slate's gasp became a squeak of protest, but his whole body vibrated as he fought to hold still. "M-My cock, Daddy. It's so hard."

Oh! He remembered! I grinned, gliding my hands up his upper thighs as I stepped closer. I rocked my hips into his, pressing the hardness in my trousers against his thighs and grinding until sparks shot straight into the pit of my belly. "Is it?"

"F-Feel it yourself," Slate begged. "I swear. It's too tight. Can I get it out?"

I didn't want to spoil him. I liked the idea of keeping his swollen shaft confined a little longer, but he was demonstrating his lesson already learned so well…

"All right," I whispered, rolling my hips in slow, fluid movements to drag my hard length back and forth along his thighs. Already, I could imagine our bodies heaving together without clothes in the way, my cock buried to the root inside him.

His body hot and tight, squeezing around my shaft as he whimpered and begged for more. Thrusting into the slick little hole, my nails biting into his neck to keep him pinned on the bed. Slamming against him, pounding him fast and hard to satisfy my own urges while he begged for mercy…

Fuck. I reeled at the intense visions dancing in front of me. My carefully developed patience threatened to unravel with this boy under my hands. *Slow down there, Rex.*

My fingertips danced along his waistband until I embraced him around the waist. I peeled his shirt off, tearing at the buttons until they gave way. I unbuttoned and unzipped his trousers, then tugged them down. In one fluid movement, I knelt and helped him step out of them, then tossed them aside. One sock at a time came off next.

Almost there. The view got better and better, but I was hungry for more.

Slate's bare thighs were covered in dark fuzz, strong as tree trunks yet trembling under the slightest touch. He stood perfectly still, letting me inspect the curves of his ass in his tight, navy blue boxer briefs.

"Gorgeous, boy," I breathed out. "You make Daddy so hungry." I squeezed that round bottom again, pushing the cheeks apart and stretching the fabric just over where I knew his tight little hole awaited. I could just imagine it pulsing and fluttering with the anticipation that lent every moment a crisp, desperate edge.

"Need you, Master X," he moaned, his butt flexing under my touch. He flinched and trembled, like he was afraid of the very desires that heated his blood. "Daddy. *My* Daddy."

Christ. My throat went tight again with some unfamiliar emotion—a sort of tender viciousness, like I loved him so much that I needed to break him apart to prove it.

It was terrifying, yet impossible to escape. Sucking me in, a maelstrom of the parts of me I'd locked away for so long. They mingled within me now, as this moment unfolded. There was no tearing them apart or denying them. No more.

"I'm here, my boy," I breathed out. Tearing myself away from the hot glide of his smooth back against my palms was like Velcro mixed with superglue. But I had to, for both of our sakes.

I wasn't done yet. I needed to see the impact of my fingers on Slate's skin the way I felt the impact of my words on his soul.

When I stepped to the side again, the erection straining at the front of Slate's underwear was impossible to miss. So were the reddened marks along his upper thighs where I'd laid a few well-placed swats.

So I grabbed for the elastic of his waistband and hauled his underwear down. Slate kicked the fabric aside himself, then spread his legs. The muscles in his back rippled, his spine straightening and then arching. In front of him, his erect manhood pointed up toward his stomach, bobbing heavily up and down with every move.

"Better," I decided and pulled back my hand, delivering a single swat to the left side of his precious, spankable bottom.

Slate's cry was loud and sharp, ripped from him. "Ahhh!" He looked startled, his eyes flying open as his head snapped back. "Jesus!"

I smiled, dancing my fingertips over the spot. "Different without clothes in the way, isn't it?"

"Yes, Daddy," Slate whimpered. "Good, though. Very good."

"I don't care if *you* find it good," I told him, letting harshness bleed into my voice again. I pulled back my hand for a harder slap on the other cheek, emphasizing the last word.

"Oh! Fuck!" Slate's ass contracted under my hand as red blossomed across the pale skin. His whole body shuddered.

There would be other chances to fall into a rhythm, spanking him over my knee, pushing my fingers into him, pumping hard before pulling out to spank him again. Torturing him sweetly until he squirmed and gasped and finally came, his body on fire and cries falling from his lips.

Tonight, though, I just wanted him to get a taste of the punishments that lay ahead of him. I was satisfied with how he reacted. He was *very* spankable—responsive to me and obedient, yet not whining. Nor did he hide his reactions or play tough.

Perfect.

"Stand up," I told him, my tongue loosened by the fire running through me. I was in my element now, fully dressed and powerful as I stood behind the shivering, naked boy. I'd never felt stronger, and my shaft swelled in answer. "Face me."

Slate gulped, his eyes wide and hazy. He swayed, standing and staring at me. His hands folded in front of his boner like he was shy all of a sudden, his gaze sliding downward. "Yes, Daddy?" His voice was barely a whisper, his toes curling into the floor.

Fuck, he was adorable. His very energy was so precious that I wanted to absorb it into mine—wrap myself around him and be his shield, yet turn my claws on him to draw out the painful release he so desperately wanted, yet feared right now.

"Look at you," I taunted, folding my hands behind my back and tilting my chin up. It was a power stance, the authority radiating from me like a fucking sun. Slate reacted like any natural sub, keeping his gaze fixed on the floor. Trembling. Waiting.

Good. Very good.

"Y-Yes?" Slate whispered.

I grinned. To the untrained ear, he wanted to hear that he was beautiful, but I knew better. "Hard already. Trying to hide it. What a desperate little slut you are."

Slate trembled, but he couldn't quite hide the twitch of his cock behind his palms without touching it—and he knew that was forbidden. "N-No—"

"Hands to your sides," I ordered, cutting him off.

Slate whimpered softly, hesitating as heat crept down his neck and up his cheeks. His face flaming red, he finally unfolded his hands and let his hands fall, his fingertips twitching nervously through the air. His breathing came in short, shallow bursts.

"See?" I whispered. God, I wished I had a crop or a whip in my hand. Something to touch his throbbing erection, draw along the length…

Wait. I was in the kitchen. *Perfect.*

My eyes roved the countertop, and then I found it—the dark wooden spatula. I reached for it, and his eyes darted up. Then he gasped, the sound harsh in the kitchen.

"Did I say you can look up?" Quick as lightning, I slapped his thigh with the implement, and I wasn't gentle. The red mark appeared instantly, and his cry rang across the walls of the kitchen.

He clutched at the counter to stay upright, but his cock pulsed in front of my eyes, desperately twitching in midair. "N-No, sir," Slate whimpered, fixing his gaze on his own aching dick again.

I grinned, drawing the tip of the spatula along his balls, up the center of his shaft toward the tip. "Look at this," I hissed, pausing to ever so gently touch the corner of the tip of the spatula against the leaking slit, picking up his precum. "Do you think you can hide it? I know how much you're enjoying this. Pretending not to want it. What a horny little slut." My lip curled as I stepped closer. "Filthy, *filthy* boys like you need a Daddy, don't they?"

Slate froze, his fingers stiff and nails pressed into his thighs as he stared down. "Y-Yes, sir?" His gasp rose at the end, like he wasn't sure if he was supposed to agree with me or beg for mercy. Like he wanted to do both.

I grinned. *God*, watching him come undone was going to be the best treat of my life. Dessert at home really was better. "Have you been saving yourself for Daddy, the way I told you to?"

Slate's gulp was audible. His throat bobbed. I narrowed my eyes, homing in on any guilt I might be able to pick up on. "Yes, sir," Slate whispered. "I—I touched myself, when we were on that video call. That was it. Except… I woke up this morning and I was so hard…"

I tilted my head and waited. "Yes?"

"I was dreaming about you," Slate babbled, his words coming fast and desperate. "I'm sorry, Master X. I couldn't stop it. But I didn't come, not at all. And then I had to get up, so I had to touch myself to take a leak. Y-You know how it is," he begged, gulping as desperation bled into his voice. "But I didn't—I didn't go any further. I swear."

Idly, I drew the tip of the spatula up and down his shaft once more before patting the head of his pulsating erection with it. I decided he was telling the truth. "Good boy. Telling the truth is important. Right?"

Slate bobbed his head, his chest heaving. "Yes, Daddy."

I smacked the side of his hard cock with the spatula, smiling as Slate's knees nearly buckled.

Slate's cry was sharp, desperate. He clung to the counter to stay upright. His eyes were wide as he gulped for breath. "Ahh! N-No, please! I-I followed your rules, Daddy. Why punish me? I've been a good boy."

"Because punishment *is* your reward, you dirty boy. I remember you telling me you don't *want* to be rewarded," I said patiently, swatting him lightly again. "If you've changed your mind, do let me know."

Slate gulped, anxiously shifting his weight from foot to foot, but said nothing. His eyes followed the movement of the spatula in my hand as I twirled it about.

I smiled, suspicions confirmed. He was having the time of his life. "I thought so." The wood in my palm was wonderfully warm. As much as I wanted to leave him covered in marks, I had other ideas, too. So I flicked the flat of it against his balls. Just lightly enough that it was an erotic slap, not a sucker punch… but an unexpected one.

Slate nearly went down on his knees, his head thrown back and body arching as every muscle tensed up. "*Fuck!*"

"That's right," I growled. "Too fragile for me, aren't you? Breakable little boy. In over your head with a cruel Daddy like me. Are you afraid?"

Slate's head bobbed in silent desperation, his whole body tense. Waiting for the next strike, eager despite himself. Another droplet trickled from the slit of his cock, leaving a slick trail as it ran down along his length.

My teeth bared with my wolfish grin. There was no stopping me now. I had what I wanted in my sights, and my teeth sunk into Slate, and I was never letting go.

"Good." He was lucky I was feeling merciful—romantic, even. I set down the spatula and folded my arms behind my back again. "Now, on your knees."

Slate dropped hard to the floor. He hit it so hard I had to hide my wince, but he didn't even seem to notice. He crouched there on hands and knees, his head tentatively rising until he stared at my feet. I could tell he so wanted to look up at me—but I denied him again.

"Crawl," I ordered. My pulse fluttered nervously at my neck. Every command was a test of his boundaries, figuring out how deep his need for humiliation ran.

Pretty fucking deep, apparently, because Slate gasped and scrabbled forward at the speed of a dog who'd heard its treat bag. "Where, Daddy?"

"Here." I grinned, stepping aside, casually laying a hand on the back of his head. I walked slowly by his side, leading him to the bedroom but tempering his pace.

I wanted him to really think about every slide of his skin against the ground, face-first and so close to the ground. Then I let go of him, hands behind my back, waiting to see if he'd look up.

Slate stopped once or twice, gathering his breath and his wits, his head turning toward me like he wanted to reassure himself that I was there. But he didn't peer up at me.

Good. He's learning fast. I allowed myself a moment of tenderness in the privacy of my own head. *He's going to be so much fun.* I hadn't looked forward to anything so much since…

Well, *ever.*

I slid the bedroom door closed behind us.

"You can get up for this part," I told him. I didn't want him tumbling down the steps, even if it was only a foot or so down to the level of my bed.

Gingerly, Slate gathered all of his limbs and pushed himself to his feet, quivering as he walked down the steps and then stood there, perfectly still.

You could hear a pin drop between us. I had his focus, utterly and completely, and it made the circuits in my brain slide into place like he was the missing spark plug in my life.

Fuck. Fuck, he *was.*

"Look at me," I whispered, hoarse with desire and raw emotion I couldn't possibly stop to process right now.

Slate's gaze flicked eagerly up my body, lingering for a moment at the bulge in my pants, all the way to my face. I waited until our gazes were locked before I let myself grin, wide and wolfish. Slate gulped hard, his nostrils flaring.

I licked my lips, looking him up and down in return—but not the same way. No, I looked at him like a predator with a rabbit in its sights. "I need to ruin you tonight, my boy," I told him. "Need you to fall apart at my hands. Break you into pieces."

I stepped onto the topmost of the two steps down, and he flinched backward.

The hunt was on. I snarled at him, delighted in the primal surge of desire that shut off every circuit in my brain, and stepped forward again.

Slate's will broke. He scrambled backward, whimpering as he tried to stay out of reach. "No, Daddy," he begged, but I heard the thrill of *yes* in his voice. It made my cock stretch painfully under my trousers, wet against the satin that secretly lay beneath. "Please. Don't break me. I-I can't... you can't..."

There. His mistake. "I can't?" I repeated in a low rumble and stepped forward, sharply grabbing for his arm. It was a gesture intended to miss, to let him get away, but to show my intentions.

Slate nearly fell onto the bed, then grabbed the bedpost and scrambled around the end of it, like he was trying to shelter behind it. "No, I didn't mean—Daddy, no!"

I growled and surged forward, sprinting for him as he ran backward and we fell into a game of cat and mouse. He dodged this way and that with surprising nimbleness given his broad shoulders and height, the sturdiness of his body.

And I let the frustration well up in my chest, layers building upon layers, sharpening my anger and my savagery.

"Enough," I growled, cornering him by my dresser. I surged forward, seizing him by his wrists and hauling him toward the bed.

Slate struggled, but not hard. He didn't throw even half his weight into it, and my pride stung. Did he think I couldn't handle him really fighting back? That was yet another lesson to teach him.

"N-No," Slate begged, but I bent him over and shoved him face-first onto the mattress. I locked his arm behind his back with one hand, the other on the back of his head as I leaned over and spat on his back. *So there*, I might as well have been saying, reveling in my victory.

Then I pressed my erection, barely contained by layers of satin and polyester, against his ass and shoved hard, and suddenly his knees gave way and I was the only thing holding him down against the bed.

The cry that fell from Slate's lips and reverberated through his body was genuine, shocked yet delighted. "D-Daddy...!" He twitched, his shoulders pulling up.

I let go of his head and raked my nails down his back. I drew them from the wet heat between his shoulder blades straight down his spine, leaving four red-hot scratches in the wake.

And this time, I wasn't gentle.

Slate's cry verged on an animalistic scream of defeat and rage, but he didn't dare fight back, either. He arched into his punishment, his face pressed into the bed as he quivered under my touch.

This had finally shifted from gentle foreplay to the battleground of my desires: harsh and real, far too raw to plunge straight into. *This* agonized ecstasy was what I craved. I lapped at it like life force to a vampire.

And I hadn't realized until this moment that I was starving.

Every instinct in my body wanted to take, claim, and *hunt*. But I stopped, digging my heels into the floor like that would help me rock away from him. It didn't, but it grounded me.

This was the moment. The *real* test of whether we, as a together-We and not just a Daddy and boy coming together, would work. Long term. Maybe forever. Because I couldn't live without this, as twisted as it was, and if Slate couldn't take it…

This was the moment where some Doms—terrible Doms, shithead abusers like Isaac—would simply never ask, so they never had to hear an inconvenient answer. But I'd sooner throw myself off this building here and now than be *that* man.

So I steeled every ounce of courage and resolve I had, fear bubbling as hot as lava in my throat and blooming across my cheeks, stinging in the corners of my eyes. "Red? Yellow? Green? Pineapple?" After all, I couldn't trust that he remembered his safeword right now.

It took Slate a moment to stop panting for breath, gulp, put together his voice again. It might as well have been a century, every millisecond a painful reminder that what I needed was *not* normal, and for some—for many—it would be going too far…

But Slate's response, despite the hazy and broken way syllables slipped from his mouth, was clear. "Greener than your eyes."

A big, fluttery, stupid grin crossed my face. My grip on his arm loosened for just a second. *He knows the color of my eyes without even looking at me*, I thought, and I let myself gulp for fresh air to quell the wildfire in my chest. Except, of course, that wasn't how fire worked.

It danced to life, spreading to the very top of my head and the tips of my toes, until I was full of a restless, quivering joy. Relief—pure relief, sweeping through my tense muscles with strangely agonizing speed.

This would work. *We* would work.

I gulped hard and shook my head. Slate needed me on the top of my game. Giddy, gooey, romantic Rex—a character I'd never met—couldn't possibly bring that. So all of *that* would have to wait until later. Preferably much later, when nobody could hear or see the vulnerability of this moment of joy.

"Please," Slate begged, and it was just what I needed to sharpen my focus again. Then he struggled, just a little bit, against my grip. Trying to pull his wrist free so he could wrestle me. "No, Daddy." But his voice was light and wry—playful despite the ferocity of my rage raking his bare skin.

Fuck. My worries dissolved, and I was Master X again. My boy was strong as iron, and he needed me to be even stronger.

So I shoved back against him, overpowering him with simple physics. Hauling him up the bed, one limb at a time, until he was flat on his front and splayed like a starfish, and I crouched over him all hungry and raw.

I bit back my irritation once again at the gentleness with which Slate pushed back against me. I wasn't the breakable one here. My boy really had a lot to learn about me.

I reached under the pillows, yanking out the handcuffs I'd left hanging around one bar of the headboard, down the back of the bed and under the pillows. Almost invisible, yet ready for just such a moment.

These were well made, to say the least. If he wouldn't fight back against me, let him try his strength on them.

Slate gasped sharply and went still. "What? No, please…!"

I grinned. It gave me enough time to work unhindered, threading the leather through the buckle of one cuff and fastening the catch. He'd come to his senses by the time I grabbed his other wrist, but it was easy to bend his arm just the right way that he couldn't resist. I fastened up the other cuff and checked that the chain was still threaded around the bar of the headboard. "Yes, boy?"

"B-Bu-Th-Wh—" Slate stuttered and then whimpered. His wrists were bound by a six-inch chain, however hard he pulled at them. He twisted, trying to see me. "I-You just…!"

"Yes," I told him, shoving his face back into the pillows. That went some way to teaching him *that* lesson. "I did."

Then I straddled Slate's thighs, moaning at the way my bulge pressed against the firm mounds of his ass. I loved the view of his naked, sprawled, and utterly helpless body.

His resistance dispensed with, I could pay attention to other matters. I was still fully dressed, and as much as I appreciated that contrast, it was time to give him a treat.

Slowly, I peeled myself away from him, grinning at his protesting moan. Slate whispered, "Don't go…!"

Don't worry. I'm not just leaving you there. But I didn't blame him for thinking that. "No chance. Look." I stood up by the side of the bed, rolling my shoulders back and unbuttoning my suit jacket.

With my permission, Slate wriggled and twisted onto his side until he could see me. His expression lit up in quiet, grateful delight. "Ooh. A show."

I moved slowly, making sure every single ounce of his attention was fixed on me by the time I had my jacket and shirt off. Then I ran my hands across my thighs, my heart pounding with anticipation.

I let my trousers fall to the floor, stepped out of them, and stood still by the side of the bed as he twisted against the tight bonds to see as much of me as he could.

My rock-hard cock had burst free from the silky satin pocket. Slate gulped, his mouth falling open at the sight. I followed his gaze down to my erection and the thin black strings that stretched over my inner hips, framing the satin cup that hung loosely around the base of my cock.

I hooked a finger around the edge of the thong, pulling it over my tip again to form a tent and hide it from view. Not that it could hide very well. The satin stretched across the rounded head, showing off every detail.

God, I'd never make it as a sub. Not even for a second. I could barely stand the anticipation, and I was the one deciding how long to make it last.

A slow smile spread over Slate's face. He couldn't seem to tear his gaze away. "Daddy," he gasped, licking his lips. "Let me… let me taste you. Please."

"Oh, you will," I promised and gave him a wicked grin. I raised one knee and balanced on the bed, pushing my hips forward.

Just out of reach.

As much as Slate struggled against his bonds, panting and pushing his tongue forward, he couldn't *quite* run it over the hot, hard line of my shaft. Then he stopped and sharply whimpered, raising a pleading gaze to my face. He'd realized what I was doing.

"Yes?" I whispered, honey sweet.

"You *are* cruel," Slate whispered.

But he wasn't afraid. Not disgusted, or exasperated. His voice rang with the awe of a man standing in a grand cathedral, or turning his gaze to a whole universe stretching infinitely above him, or a grove of ancient trees touching the sky.

I grinned, totally satisfied with myself. The pleasure was razor-edged and dangerous, and it intoxicated me utterly.

At last, he believed me.

"Yes," I whispered, stroking his hair with such gentleness that he flinched. "I am, boy."

Suddenly, I gripped the back of his head and pushed my hips forward, forcing my satin-covered cock against him. I ground against his cheeks and lips without care. Rubbed my bulge over his face, taunting him.

Slate whimpered, trying to kiss and lick whenever my cock touched his full, hot lips. "You're so fucking hot. I need you so much it hurts. Let me suck you, please. Please, Daddy? Please, please, please…" He trailed off, gasping for air.

I smirked, but I finally allowed it. "You like seeing your Daddy's cock? Tasting it?" I reveled in the power I held over him, the unashamed eagerness with which he lapped at my bulge.

"Mmhmm," Slate whimpered, vibrating through my shaft. My body went tight with a dizzying flush of need and ecstatic bliss. At last, after an evening of squirming against the smooth satin, the wet heat of his mouth on just the other side of that one thin layer was unbearably arousing.

"See? I knew you were a filthy little slut," I growled, digging my nails into his scalp as I shoved my cock against his mouth. "Daddy's about to fuck your face, and there's nothing you can do about it. You can't even touch your pathetic little hard-on. What a worthless little toy you are. A *thing* for me to use, aren't you?"

Slate nodded eagerly, his breath harsh as I shoved my underwear down, freed my cock with one quick flick of my hand. The pink, flushed shaft stood proudly in the air.

"Daddy's going to fuck your holes any way he feels like, all night. Leave you tied up for my pleasure."

I wouldn't, of course. Basic safety. But the words worked. Slate groaned hungrily even as he begged me for mercy, shaking his head hard. "No, please… please, I need to come!"

I grinned. "That wasn't a suggestion," I told him and bent over to slap his ass hard as a reminder of all his many lessons tonight. "*I decide when you deserve to come.*"

Then I shoved my cock between his lips. He tightened his cheeks and ran his tongue under the head, but this was no time for foreplay. I was ready for him *now*. Both my hands went to the back of his head to hold him steady as I pulled back and thrust forward. Started to fuck his waiting mouth.

The heat of him seemed to engulf my whole shaft—my whole body, even, filling up with restless sparks. Energy I needed to take out on something, and boy, did I ever.

I pounded his gorgeous, wet mouth as he tried to catch his breath. He groaned and whimpered, tears leaking from the corners of his eyes as I dug my nails into his scalp and bared my teeth.

I claimed the spoils of my victory over the helpless boy I'd cornered and pinned down. My prey, my love, my very own.

My balls and even my whole body tightened, my muscles hard as a brick wall. I struggled to breathe, to hold myself back. There was no possible way. I was too far along, too engulfed by the fantasy playing out in this moment.

My helpless, broken boy. *Mine.*

Slate gulped, like he wanted to say something, but his mouth was far too full. The sight of him thrashing against his bonds, his words gagged by my very own erection, squirming helplessly against the bed like he was trying to please himself the only way he could…

I couldn't hold back anymore. Fuck. So I pulled back, still gripping his head with one hand as my fingers closed around the sensitive skin and my whole body throbbed.

It was too much at first, every inch of me too sensitive and wet. The tingles in my chest were gone, replaced by a painful lightning strike. But within moments I was back to quivering on the precipice of ecstasy.

"Yes…!"

I barely realized the cries spilling through the air were my own until it was too late. My back arched, my hand tightened on my shaft, and a harsh, raw cry reverberated to my very soul. Fuck, I was losing the battle. My mouth fell open, and with one final cry, the blinding blackness of ecstasy struck.

Moments later, I forced my eyes open as heat pulsed through my shaft, dancing under my fingers. The first streak of my mess landed on his nose, just between his eyes, all the way up to his hairline. My hand slowed on my stiff skin as it grew sensitive, but I had a lot more of my load to spread across his whole face.

I grinned at the sight, smearing the last few drops across his cheeks as they trickled from the tip of my shaft.

Fuck. I'd seen plenty of hot sights, but nothing like this: Slate's helpless face upturned toward me, mouth open and tongue out as if to desperately receive my load while I denied him even that taste. Covered him in my mess, reminded him who the fuck was in charge.

I stroked my thumb along his cheek, wiping a fingerful of my jizz into his lips. Slate gasped but eagerly licked my finger clean, and I repeated it. Then I grabbed a tissue, gently cleaning off his face.

"Safe for you to open your eyes now," I told him with a wicked grin to myself, finally giving myself one last stroke and squeeze as I softened.

Slate's eyelids fluttered open, his mouth still hanging open and cheeks flushed. He was fucking *gorgeous*, every Dom's wet dream and daytime fantasy. The sheen of sweat against his forehead and the faraway bliss in his eyes…

"Thank you, Daddy," Slate whimpered, and I just about broke inside.

Perfect, perfect, perfect was all my heart could tell me, in a tempo so loud and fast I couldn't possibly ignore it.

And one more thing.

Love this. Love him. Love us.

Yeah. It was impossible to name this heat between us as anything else. It wasn't fading now that I'd gotten my kicks. Far from it—it burned brighter than ever, in a way I was utterly unfamiliar with, which fucking floored me.

Just like in the restaurant, I was back to scrambling for my senses. But there was one more task left, and I could do that. Yes. I latched eagerly to the thought and slid onto the bed next to him, pulling my satin thong back up over my softening cock.

I bent my head and pressed my lips to the tip of Slate's cock, suckling the droplets of intensely musky, salty precum.

With no warning or chance to prepare himself, Slate cried out and thrashed, but the chain between his cuffs was a little too short to let him turn on his back. So he was trapped on his side, his body twisted and trembling with the strain.

"Fuck!" Slate whimpered, and I sucked my cheeks in and bobbed my head.

I swallowed him right to the base, sharply swiping my tongue under the tip as I went. Then I pulled back, bracing myself with a hand behind his ass, and bobbed my head hard and fast.

There was no mercy even in the way I sucked him off, no chance to linger and enjoy the moment. I could feel his approaching climax crashing toward him in the way his cock swelled in my mouth, and his whole body tensed up as stiff as a board. His cries went from full-throated to harsh, short, tense.

And now... my final trick.

"Daddy...! D-I'm—" Slate gasped, his voice harsh. "Oh my God!" He no doubt thought I was going to swallow his load and treat him to the orgasm of his life.

But he hadn't really met me if he thought that. I held my breath, not just because of the impending orgasm, but paying attention to every tiny flinch and gasp.

"Yes...!"

I pulled my head back just as Slate spilled over the edge, my hand flying to his hip to hold him still as his whole body thrashed forward and back with the shock of the sudden absence of pleasure.

And as his eyes flew open and the scream ripped from his throat, I *grinned* down at him.

Ruined his fucking orgasm at exactly the right moment.

"Fuckfuckfuckfuuuuuuuck-no-please-fuck-Daddy-fuck-*please!*" Slate's lungful of air rushed out of him, but it was too late now. His cock was pulsating, spraying the bed in front of him with the heat of his release but none of the pleasure.

I reached for his cuffs before he was even done, anticipating what was about to happen. I fumbled with the catches and straps, loosening the cuffs and letting them fall to hang around the bedpost again.

Slate choked up, curling in on himself as tears flooded him, his hands balled into my chest and the bedsheets, and he *cried*.

I curled myself around him, one hand on his chest and the other on his back, holding him so tight against me that it felt like we might just merge into one. My breathing was labored, too, emotion ripping through me.

Not guilt, though. Nor was it simple, uncomplicated pleasure. It was a mind-altering, potent brew of *yes* and *no*. I couldn't bring myself to regret what I'd done. It was exactly what Slate needed, like it or not.

And deep in my soul, like a rainstorm in a desert, his tears filled a void in me that I had no other way of reaching.

"I know," I whispered, pressing my lips into his hair.

Slate only choked and pressed his face into my chest, his thighs shaking helplessly. I swallowed hard, squeezed my eyes shut, and waited. Held him. Stroked him gently.

"Beautiful," I whispered. "You're so beautiful. Such a good boy. You deserve the best things in the world, honey." And more words—of reassurance and praise, everything I sensed he needed. Words to soothe the very needed stings my earlier words had left in his soul.

He drank them in, pressed close to me. A minute passed, and a few more. His tears and trembling slowed until finally a sluggishness overtook him. Gradually, he slipped out of subspace into the pure exhaustion I'd expected.

All the tension gone from his body, Slate finally pulled back and murmured, "Thank you, Daddy." His smile was dizzy, and relief tinged my cheeks. "I... I didn't know... but I needed that." His voice rose in wonder. "How? Why? That shouldn't..." He gulped for air. "But it feels good..."

I was right. I closed my eyes for a moment, and God, I basked. "Good boy," I whispered again, opening my eyes to meet his smile with my own. This one was tender, though. Nothing like earlier. "You've made your Daddy very happy."

"Please do that again. Especially if I tell you not to," Slate murmured. He only now seemed to realize he was free, gradually uncurling and rolling onto his back. "But not tonight. Next time tonight, I get to come for real, or I might go insane."

I chuckled, but I couldn't imagine a better chance to tell him what I needed to next.

"Okay, my boy," I agreed. "On one condition."

Slate's eyes flew open. He looked indignant as he stared at me, like he couldn't believe I had the nerve.

I grinned, holding his look without flinching. "You get to come when we talk about your limits. Because I won't let you pretend you don't have any just because you trust me. Or because you want me to be happy."

Slate blinked once or twice, and at last there was the tinge of sheepishness to his eyes that told me I was right.

"I've broken you tonight—for the better, I think…"

Slate nodded hard, eagerly, and pushed his hand into my chest, fingers curling like I was wearing a shirt he could grip.

I chuckled softly. "But I barely pushed you tonight. There's so much more we could do. I need to know what will truly break you, because I *can't* come back from that. And I can't let you let me do that. Understand?" I stroked his cheek tenderly.

Slate pouted, but I leaned in and pressed a kiss on his lips. Heat burst between us, a sweet and mellow thing. And his resistance finally melted as his lips softened against mine. He let me suck his lower lip for a moment before pulling back with a chuckle.

"You win," he whispered. Well, duh. "Let me think about it for a minute. Unpick… *him* from things. Figure out what I need."

There was no question who he meant. *Calm*, I told myself, as I had to every time that asshole came up. I nodded slightly, so as not to scare him. Then I squirmed, pushing him with my shoulder further onto the bed as he laughed and scooted over to make room for me.

I stripped my underwear and tossed it aside before I could think twice about it.

There. I was naked. Was that so bad?

No. No, I wasn't afraid of being vulnerable anymore. Slate had just let me break him to pieces, and hell, I'd just shown him my most raw parts, too. A little skin felt like nothing now.

Slate's eyes widened, and then he smiled, saying nothing. He wrapped his arm around me and aggressively cuddled.

Our bodies skin to skin, nothing between us anymore, a long time passed and yet felt like no time at all. And it was... definitely not the worst.

At last, Slate pressed his lips against my neck. "Everything we did today is good," he told me. "Chase me down. Spank me, slap me, scratch me. All over. Anywhere. Leave marks."

I grinned and pressed my nails into his back playfully as he moaned his approval.

"Whips, paddles, anything," Slate continued, breathless, and I noticed that his shoulder was forward. His arm twitched. My eyes widened and I pulled back enough to see his hand wrapped around his semi-erect cock.

This time, though, I didn't interrupt. My beautiful boy had endured everything I'd thrown at him tonight, so I let him show off for me.

"Tie me up, order me... and toys are good." Slate's breathing turned harsh. He went silent for a minute, his eyes squeezed shut and lips parting. The fantasy playing out over his face was fucking enchanting to watch.

It was my turn to be flooded with an utterly reverential kind of heaven on earth. I kissed his lips gently, top and then bottom, and said nothing. Waited. Listened and learned.

"Call me your slut. All the things you did. I'm so small and helpless, Daddy. I like it when you make me cry. Surprise me. Want—want no to mean yes…" His hand pumped himself hard and fast now as his lips moved without words for a moment.

"Yes," I breathed, staring at him. Memorizing every fucking moment.

"I don't want to be in charge. I want you to be in control of everything. Body and soul. All of me, Rex. Please…" His voice rose, his hand shuddering and slowing as his eyes suddenly flew open.

"I've got you," I breathed out, my whole body burning right along with his. And at last, at long last, my beautiful boy got to come without shame or rules. Just him and every single drop of the ecstasy he so richly deserved. "You can come, my beautiful boy," I purred.

Slate practically levitated off the bed, his back arching and feet pressing into the bed. Climax seemed to hit him even harder this time, having been denied pleasure before.

I was enraptured, unable to look away. I heard my future in his every gasp, and saw it in every hard line of his body. There was no denying myself or him any longer. And I wasn't afraid of it now. How could I be?

"Oh, God," Slate finally gasped and collapsed into my arms, nuzzling me. "All of that. Yes. That's what I want."

Me too, I thought as I swallowed hard. There was one big thing missing, though. "And… in public?"

I couldn't give up the whole life I'd built in Dom Nation—the people I knew, the joy I found in playing with a boy in front of a hungry crowd, knowing he was mine and mine alone...

"I don't want others touching me," Slate murmured, pressing his lips into my shoulder. "But I want to try it in public. Never done it before. I think I'll like it. We'll see, hm?"

"Good," I whispered and stroked his hair, pleasure and pride swelling my chest at my beautiful, *beautiful* boy. Every single thing he'd said he wanted, I'd make come true—and then some. "Good boy."

"Mmhmm," Slate whispered, burrowing into me. His breathing grew slow and steady, so I took charge of wrestling us both under the covers, turning out the lights, tucking us both in.

I didn't expect him to still be awake when I joined him in bed and curled myself around him, holding him close to my chest. "And you?" he whispered. "What do you need the most?"

I shook my head slightly. It all boiled down to one simple thing. "I need to have you," I told him. What else was being a Daddy? "To be cruel and break you, over and over. Take care of your every need. Put you together again, a little better every time. And when problems happen, Daddy will deal with them."

"Mmmm," Slate murmured agreeably. "Like Isaac."

That started with making sure Slate knew that he was worth a lot more than being someone's toy. That he was loved, too, not just wanted and discarded in turn. Even if he chose to yield control to me... the first and last choice was always his.

And I was never going to let him down. I never wanted him to suffer again. Not at anyone's hands but mine, anyway. And judging by tonight, mine knew how to make him feel loved, too.

"Like him," I agreed. "Everything's going to be okay," I murmured, just as much for my own benefit as his.

"Okay," Slate whispered. "Yes, Daddy."

And then he was out like a light, and I closed my eyes and pressed my face into the back of his head.

My beautiful boy was going to be safe. Forever. Nothing less.

14

SLATE

"Slate. You came." Rex's eyes sparkled with quiet amusement. He held the steel door open, and I giggled as I stepped through.

How could I resist?

"No, Daddy," I told him, my heart rate already speeding up. He was impossibly handsome in a closely tailored suit. Did he just wear it all the time, or was he ready to go out like this? I gave him an innocent smile. "I've been very good this week."

I sauntered out of the elevator, but before the door had even closed, Rex had snagged me around the waist with one surprisingly strong arm. "Good boy," he told me. "Now, give Daddy a kiss."

Obediently, I bent over and closed my eyes. A shiver of contentment coursed along my skin, heating me straight through. Just having my Daddy's arms around me steadied me and made the world feel like it was the right way up.

Rex's lips were soft against mine, but there was no deception in the gentleness. We both knew perfectly well what was on the table tonight. Or *whom*.

Me.

Tonight was the night: we were going to Dom Nation together. And this time, we weren't sticking to the dance floor. I was finally going to get to live out the scene of my dreams.

"Tea?" Rex offered, ushering me to the couch.

I nodded and settled on the couch, watching him move around the kitchen and his damned complicated coffee maker. Nothing made me happier than letting Daddy take care of me after a long week.

"How are you feeling?" Rex asked once he'd pressed a cup of tea into my hands and wrapped an arm around my shoulders. I only realized I was quivering when he squeezed me against his side.

"Er..." My nervous laugh was more air than voice. Tension thrummed through my body, plucking at my nerves like a too-taut bowstring. "Fine?"

Rex fixed me with a piercing stare. "Are you telling Daddy a lie? If you're trying to find a way out of this, that's the wrong way to go about it."

I flushed with embarrassment. "N-No, I'm not," I promised, hanging my head. "I'm sorry. But I... I guess I'm nervous." God, none of the other subs I'd seen at Dom Nation had looked anxious. They'd all been relaxed and happy and... well, confident. I was faking it. They'd instantly spot me, a shaking mess, and wonder what the hell I was doing among them.

Rex pulled his arm away from my shoulders, and for a moment, my heart jumped into my throat. *Is he mad at me for being nervous?* I twisted my hands together in my lap and looked at him, but his expression was inscrutable.

I wanted to break the gaze, but I was pinned down now, helpless once again. How the crap could he do that with one stare? I wished I could stare at my lap and apologize for being so scared and new to everything, but I was silent.

His next words punctured my apologies. "Listen to me," Rex told me softly, those dark green eyes flickering between mine like he was watching a sports match. "It's more important than anything else that you're able to tell me how you feel—*truthfully*—the first time I ask. It's the most important thing I'll ever ask of you. Without knowing you can do that, I can't do anything with you."

I swallowed hard, my nails digging into the smooth porcelain of my teacup as a chasm opened in my world. His statement wasn't *intended* as a threat, but it sure felt like one. But I pushed back against the overwhelming urge to beg and grovel. This wasn't foreplay—it was serious.

"I understand," I murmured. I was rewarded with a warm tickle that crept along my neck as Rex let out a breath and relaxed against me.

"Now," Rex told me, "tell Daddy what you're feeling."

These few simple words shattered me like a crystal, until my lungs were all fragments and my very blood hurt with the rush of emotion that flooded me. It took everything I had to swallow back this tide.

At last, I managed one word. "Scared."

He didn't laugh at me or scoff and roll his eyes. He didn't even chuckle quietly until I wanted to crawl into a hole. Instead, he just gazed at me, calming me with the smoothness of his voice. "Why?"

A rush of images assaulted me.

Seb and his muscled, leather-bound friends casting us sideways glances and wry smiles, like they were indulging me by allowing me close.

Rex leaning close to correct me on some kind of important etiquette I hadn't even known applied, shattering the moment.

Isaac watching us, the cruel smile never faltering from his lips as he saw me floundering out of my depth.

"I'm not… your usual boy," I muttered.

Rex paused and shook his head. "There *is* no usual boy." No doubt he was about to give me a lecture on how anyone could play any role—but that wasn't what I meant.

"*Your* usual boy," I repeated, with emphasis on the more important word. "And everyone else will know it."

Rex paused. "Ah."

Just this week, Rex had made me feel things I hadn't even known I *wanted*. It was undoubtedly the best sex of my life. But that was here, where nobody could think poorly of him as a Daddy just because he'd chosen a boy—and boyfriend —like me.

"Slate," Rex said quietly, and the pure fire in his voice made me freeze and pay attention. "I don't give two shits what anyone else thinks. Especially, but not limited to, Isaac."

I drew my knees onto the couch, pressing my heels in front of my butt as I wrapped my arms around them. It was a silly gesture for a grown man, but it made me feel better. "He's going to be there."

It wasn't a question. From how he'd acted perfectly at home, and how well Rex seemed to know him, I had no doubt he was a regular. Probably had been the whole time he'd been lying his ass off to me, telling me I was the only one.

Oh, fuck. That means he could have exposed me to God knows what! The chilling realization made me go still. The selfish, arrogant, abusive asshole.

But how much of it was my fault for seeking the pain he offered?

Rex's arm slid around me, like he knew what I was thinking. I pressed the side of my head against Daddy's shoulder, pushing my knees onto his lap and letting him hold me.

Safe. I was safe here, his grip warm and tight. Rock-solid.

He said nothing, like he was waiting for me to say more. And at first, I didn't know what to say. But then the threads of my discontent began to knit together, and I burrowed into him. "I don't believe in myself."

"I know," Rex said softly. "But do you trust your Daddy?"

I nodded before he'd even finished the sentence. "Always."

No wonder I'd wanted to be his boy from the moment we met. I'd sensed that only he could give me that certainty I needed, wrapped both in soft tenderness like right now and in glittering coldness like I hoped was coming later.

"*I* know you're capable of this," Rex said. "You don't have to do anything except tell me what you want, and then listen to me as I give it to you."

I nodded slowly. I could do that: follow his rules and lose myself in the helplessness I so needed, when rational thought slipped away and I lived in the space between pain and pleasure.

What *did* I want to try first? I only knew a fraction of what was possible, yet the options already made me dizzy.

"I want…" I trailed off, finally looking up at him.

Rex gazed down at me, his hand rising to stroke my hair gently and cup the back of my head. "Yes?"

It was Daddy's job to teach me what to do, protect me from Isaac, and even to decide when I got to come. All I had to do was relax and obey him.

The knowledge made me sink into that familiar, cozy cloud of bliss. From the outside, perhaps it would sound impossible to feel this kind of ecstasy at the simplest touch, but I couldn't explain it.

God, it was hard to say out loud, but Daddy was listening so carefully that the words just spilled out without the shame I usually felt woven into these desires.

"I want you to whip me," I whispered. "Tie me up and hurt me until I beg you to stop. Break me." My chest was full now, just imagining how that would feel—being an object for his amusement, a toy at his every whim.

Rex nodded slowly, thoughtfully. "Flog, not whip," he told me. "And you'll pick out the flogger before we leave," he told me.

I gulped. I didn't know one whip from another, but Daddy could help guide me. "Okay."

"And what about sex?"

I quivered, my skin lighting up as my cock grew thick in my trousers at how much control I was handing to Rex. He could display me—make me lose all control and spiral into ecstasy until I spilled my load in front of everyone. Or just use me for his own pleasure, leaving me aching hard and not allowed to do a thing about it.

"I'm yours to use," I reminded him, my mouth dry. "Or not. No matter what I beg for, it's up to you. As long as I get to come later...?"

My gorgeously mean Daddy hadn't let me come even once since our incredible night of sex. I couldn't pretend I didn't love being at his mercy, but I couldn't wait much longer. Otherwise his sheets were going to be a mess in the morning, and they looked expensive.

Rex chuckled deeply and ran his hand down my back until four fingers slid under my waistband, tickling at just the top edge of the crack between my cheeks. "Daddy will decide whether you deserve it, then," he said.

I grunted, heat pulsing along my cock at the touch—his finger-tips not quite far enough into my pants to touch my sensitive little hole, but my nerves on fire as if he were. I pushed my hips forward toward him. I could just about straddle his thigh and grind… but he pushed me onto my feet instead.

"Where are we going?" I barely stifled the noise of protest.

"Where I tell you."

Fuck. Rex's voice had slid from gentle questions to a darker surge of instinct now, that raw animalistic side of him seamlessly taking over.

I responded automatically, ducking my head and shrinking into myself. "Yes, Daddy," I whispered and locked my hands behind my back.

Rex took a moment to admire me, staying seated in front of me. Then he smiled, a wicked little expression on his face, and leaned forward to kiss the tent at the front of my trousers. "Good boy."

The sudden warm pressure against my throbbing shaft made me pulse with pleasure. His praise rang around my body, making me feel all warm and soft in all the places that weren't my dick. That was hot and hard.

"Fuck," I hissed, my toes digging into the floor as I rose onto them with the control it took not to thrust greedily toward his face.

But Rex pulled away again, standing up. "Come."

The week had dragged along—especially the evenings remembering everything that had taken place in his bedroom.

Which it looked like we were going to right now.

I shouldn't have been surprised when he pulled open what looked like a closet door only to reveal a very different closet than I'd assumed lay behind that door. It wasn't a clothes bar and some shelves—it was a flat pegboard, and things I hadn't even imagined hanging from pegs set into dark red velvet.

It was the classiest, raunchiest sight I'd ever seen.

My jaw dropped and all I could do was stare at it—the unidentifiable metal objects methodically laid out across two shelves, and the whips, and the hooks to one side from which hung his familiar red latex corset as well as other things.

"Well?" Rex stood to my side, one hand on my back between my shoulder blades as he showed off the collection that was no doubt his pride and joy.

I hadn't even expected to be greeted by three floggers hanging in a row, all of them eye level with me, much less the rest of it. "Um..." I reached out automatically for the whip with a twisted leather handle and thin strips, each knotted toward the end.

Rex chuckled quietly. He reached out and pushed my hand from the one I'd chosen to the one hanging next to it instead. This one had thicker, more velvety strips hanging from it. "That one," he murmured and kissed the side of my neck. "For now."

"Yes, Daddy," I whispered, trusting his judgment. Carefully, I unhooked the loop from the peg. It was heavier than I'd expected, and I gulped hard, turning to offer it to Rex right away. It felt like I shouldn't be allowed to hold this tool.

Rex accepted it from the bottom up, lazily coiling the strands in his hand before he took the handle from me. "Good boy," he murmured. "Now... I have another suggestion."

I narrowed my eyes at the metal gadget I strongly suspected wasn't for pie crusts, even if it looked like a crimper. If I started trying to guess at everything in here, I'd be here all day, so I tore my eyes off the closet of wonders and looked at him. "Mmm?"

Rex was holding a single, padded strip of leather, too long to be handcuffs but too short to be much else besides...

"I'd like to collar you tonight. It would mean nobody can flirt with you besides me. It's a signal that you're taken. It's a serious commitment, however. I understand if you're not ready..." Rex's brows drew together. "Slate?"

My jaw was hanging open as I stared at what he was holding, mesmerized by the thin strip of black leather and metal D-rings. The moment he'd said *collar*, my brain had all but shut off. God, how I wanted Rex to lead me around the club by a collar and leash, the ultimate sign of control.

But Isaac had made me wear a collar sometimes, too. He hadn't said anything about it being a sign of commitment.

"What kind of commitment?" I managed and braced myself on the wall next to Rex's sex closet.

Rex licked his lips. Wait. Was he nervous?

I stared at him, fascinated by every little shift and twitch in his expression. It looked like he was deciding what to tell me. And, well, I was the newbie here. I had to take his word for it.

But I trusted him to tell me the truth, no matter what.

"Some people—especially in the old guard, traditional leather community—see collaring almost like a wedding." Rex almost tripped over his words to continue before I could say anything. "I'm not saying… I mean, that's never been my scene. But you should know how some people will see it."

Oh, my God. He was adorable right now, and I held my breath. I didn't want to startle him off, or make him retreat into the big, bad Daddy persona he used to hide so many of his feelings.

"Okay," I whispered. "So what does it mean for you and me?"

"That you're mine." Rex's answer was swift and certain. His assertive words sent a tingle rushing up my spine until my scalp prickled. "That nobody can touch you, flirt with you… without my say-so. And I don't intend to give anyone that permission. You're mine to show off, not to share."

I barely hid my grin. He remembered everything I'd said, of course. "Yes, Daddy," I whispered, sidling closer to him. "Collar me, please."

Rex licked his lips and bit the lower lip, a flush sweeping his cheeks. His breathing grew quick and shallow as he eagerly raised the leather to my neck. The padded inside was cool across my throat.

Animal instinct made me want to pull away and growl—make him work for it. I stiffened and he paused, looking up at me.

But I drew a deep breath, said nothing, and held still. My chin raised, I stared him down, proud and bold.

I don't care what anyone else thinks. I'm his, and he's mine.

A smile touched Rex's lips. He stepped behind me, his slender fingers working on the buckle. Then I gulped for breath as it suddenly tightened and his finger slid between the material and my skin. It eased a moment later.

"Two fingers of room," Rex murmured, resting his lips against my shoulder. His breath was warm through my cotton T-shirt. "Perfect. One last thing."

I gulped as he reached in a little drawer for a small padlock, perhaps half an inch big. One key was in the lock already, with another dangling from a ring.

"Now," Rex murmured, taking me by the shoulders and turning me to face him. When the younger man locked our gazes, he didn't let me look away. One hand stayed on my shoulder as he balanced the lock in his palm. "Tell me you want this. That you want to be mine, officially."

I smiled as my brain flooded with so much *yes* that it was the only word I could think or say. *Come on*, I urged myself. How was I supposed to think of smart, sexy things to say when he did *this* to me with one simple command?

"Yes, Daddy," I whispered, then cleared my throat. "I want to be yours. Officially."

I quivered on the spot as Rex reached up to thread the shank through my collar. With one quiet click, it was closed, and he took the keys out. "Done," Rex murmured. "Now, nobody takes this off but me. Understand?"

I couldn't imagine *wanting* to take it off, but I nodded anyway. "Yes, Daddy."

Rex's eyes shone with a very different triumph than I'd ever seen when Isaac looked at me. He looked pleased and proud, bursting with excitement, and frankly, I'd do anything for him to smile like that again.

"Then let's get changed. It's time to show you off, my boy."

"*Yes*, Daddy," I whispered, my fingertips rising to trace across the smooth leather that marked me as his.

At last, I was going to be exposed and broken in front of more people than ever, but I'd never felt so utterly safe. From the moment the collar closed around my neck, my nerves had settled. *Rex* was in charge here. All I had to do was obey.

This was the moment I'd been waiting for all my life, and I couldn't wait.

———

"Check you out."

The snarky little thing was back at the door again in the same silver chain body harness as before. But this time, instead of scrutinizing me, he was smiling like an old friend.

"I'd rather you didn't." Rex's hand closed around my shoulder, and suddenly he seemed to stand six inches taller.

It was clear the door guy was just being friendly. There was absolutely no need for that tone. And I fucking loved it.

I barely held in the giggle until we stepped into the building, and then I clutched Rex's waist. "Oof. Look at you go, Daddy," I whispered. "I like the jealous side of you."

We were barely inside, and I was so excited I could hardly think straight. The nervous anticipation felt good now, and it all kept coming back to the band of leather around my neck. As I walked, I could hear the padlock clicking against the metal ring that kept my collar closed.

I belonged to *Rex*—Master X, my Daddy, my love.

Nobody and nothing else could faze me, even getting changed. Although I paused by the window, Daddy didn't want to wait at the bag check. He just led me straight to the playroom, his stride even and certain.

And Daddy knew best. No bag check, then.

I squeaked under my breath and followed him, trying not to breathe down his neck with excitement. I was close to naked in my little leather shorts and harness and collar, and Daddy wore his sexy red corset. I was the only one who knew that under his black latex briefs was a little black satin thong.

God, I was buzzing with a happy excitement I'd never known.

Rex handed me his duffel bag, and I clutched it to my chest like it was made of gold. I knew what was inside because I'd sat on the bed watching as he meticulously packed it: lube and condoms, gloves, some kind of balm in a dark blue unlabeled tub, the flogger I'd chosen, chains and handcuffs and metal clips galore...

"Wait," he told me simply, and I nodded, watching him walk over to Seb, who stood against the wall with a bright vest. He must be working tonight, then.

I couldn't help peeking around the room at everything that was going on. One man bent over a complicated-looking black bench while another stood behind him, raising his open palm. There was a sharp crack of skin on skin, and the kneeling man gave a glorious cry of surprise.

I squirmed where I stood, hardly able to wait another second to be in his shoes, with Rex behind me and guiding me the whole time.

"Come. It's time," Rex told me softly, taking the duffel and laying one hand on my back as he rejoined me.

"Yes, sir," I whispered, not questioning him. Daddy knew that the longer I waited, the more sick with nerves I'd be. Right now I was excited in the best possible way.

I didn't even care if Isaac saw me. If he tried anything, Rex would get him banned. That made the creep powerless, and his presence didn't matter to me anymore, so long as Rex was here with me. I had a *real* Daddy who had earned my trust and love and shown me how strong I could be—not just a wolf in Dom's clothing wearing the name of Daddy to beat me down.

My heart thumped as Rex guided me to a large X-shaped cross of black metal and shiny steel rings. I'd seen these in videos, but I hardly knew how they worked. Luckily for me, I didn't have to worry about that.

I stood obediently next to my Daddy as he set down his duffel and sorted through the contents.

"The rules," Rex said, swiftly standing up when he was satisfied everything was ready for him. "Listen closely."

I nodded and locked my hands behind my back.

"You don't have to be silent—noise is fine—but no screaming." Rex's eyes glittered with amusement. "Save that for home later. It's not polite to interrupt others."

Ooh, yes, sir! I nodded.

"If Seb or another DM comes up and addresses you, they're checking to make sure you're safe. I can't answer them for you. All you need to tell them is red, yellow, or green. Or you can use your safeword—or just say *safeword*, that works, too." Rex rubbed my back, walking his fingers down my spine. "Apart from them, you don't need to worry about anyone else. You only listen to me. Okay?"

I nodded, knowing what he was really saying. *Isaac doesn't matter.* Then I hesitated, wondering if that meant he was here. The thought made me prickle with annoyance.

Rex's hand stopped in the small of my back. "I asked Seb about him, too. You should know that he's here tonight. Are you still okay going ahead with everything?"

I nodded before he'd even finished his sentence. *If he thinks it's safe, then I'll do it. It's my fantasy tonight, and he can't get in the way of my life anymore.*

"I told Seb, and he's the best DM here. I trust him with my life and yours," Rex told me, his voice still soft enough for me alone. "If *he* or anyone else stalks us, Seb will move them along."

I was starting to feel like a bobblehead doll, but I nodded again, not sure what I should say.

"Are you ready?" Rex whispered. I heard a soft clinking and realized that he was holding the cuffs he'd used on me once before.

Oh, God. This was really happening! "Yes, Daddy," I whispered, turning my face to him.

Rex softly smiled at me. His heels made him about the same height as me, so all he had to do was lean in to brush our lips together. "I've got you," he whispered.

I closed my eyes and sighed, the stress bleeding from the muscles between my neck and shoulders. "Yes, Daddy."

Rex's strong hands guided me up to the frame, and then he raised one hand at a time. I paid close attention to his movements, quickly figuring out that my wrists and ankles would be clipped down to leave me spread-eagle. Now I knew what I could play at resisting next time.

I kept my eyes closed until all four of my limbs were restrained, my body suddenly taut. There was enough room for me to pull a few inches away from the bonds, but that was it.

When I opened my eyes again, I took in the situation. The cross was exposed to the open air, which meant that I could see across the room.

No sign of Isaac, though. I just saw Seb standing there against one wall, impersonally scanning the room like he was memorizing the details. He made eye contact with me and nodded slightly, giving me just the ghost of a smile.

I can do this.

I closed my eyes and sighed, shifting my weight as I tugged at my wrists. No way I could get loose from these cuffs. But unlike usual, I wasn't already drifting into that place where my own body seemed unreal.

This is all just too new, I thought. *I'll relax. Come on, Slate. Chill.*

I yelped and rocked against the cross with surprise at the tickling sensation against my back. Then I realized it was the strands of the whip against my skin as Rex dragged them gently upward to my shoulders, then let them trail back down my body again. They went over my ass, where I barely felt them.

Would Daddy untie me to strip me? I wanted to feel them better. The tickles resumed against my bare thighs, down to the backs of my knees and shins, and back up my body again.

I ground my teeth with impatience. I needed the stinging pain, not this gentle foreplay, to slip away from my thoughts.

"You like that?" Rex whispered. His fingers tightened in the hair at the back of my head, and then he leaned in so only I could hear him. "You're going to like it even more in a moment, my beautiful little pain slut."

Oh, yes! That described me to a T! "Yes, sir," I whispered, my throat suddenly dry. "Please…"

Rex chuckled. "I'd ask if you mean *please, yes*, or *please, no*, but it doesn't make a difference, does it?"

Crack. In a split second, he pulled back and lightning-thin bolts sprang across the skin of my middle back. And holy fuck, I went taut from head to toe with the pleasure that followed in its wake. I hadn't felt a flogger in far too long.

"Oh!" I cried out softly and closed my eyes tightly, waiting for the pain to pick me up and tug me gently down that river of pleasure like a tiny, helpless dinghy in the ocean's swells.

It didn't find me. Not yet.

No sooner had I caught my breath than another stroke landed across my shoulder blades, and then my lower back. Even through my shorts, I felt the muffled impact of the tails against my ass and then my thighs.

Fuck, yes! As red-hot lines etched themselves into my skin, the tension gradually sank from me like a lead balloon, leaving me floating. But however much I thrashed and gave my Daddy little cries of encouragement, I couldn't let go entirely.

I peeked through my lashes to see if people were watching.

No, I couldn't fool myself. To see if *he* was watching. And I couldn't even tell if I wanted or dreaded it.

No sign of him.

I gasped as rough hands fumbled with my waistband, but there was no escaping. "Daddy! No, I'll be…"

"Exposed?" Rex breathed out, his voice coming in short, harsh pants over my shoulder. He embraced me, shoving his hands down the front of my shorts, and suddenly he was cupping my half-hard shaft, squeezing it tightly between his palms. "Exactly where I want you."

However much I gasped in protest, Rex pressed up against me, the buckles of his corset digging into my bare back.

Gently, he rolled my stiffening cock back and forth between his palms in the confined space, every drag of friction against the sensitive shaft painfully erotic.

I threw my head back into his shoulder and cried out. Surely to God he wasn't going to make me finish in my shorts! Even for him, that was cruel.

I wasn't sure if I was relieved or disappointed when he pulled his hands free again.

My eyes flew open just as the flogger's bundle of tails landed along my back. And I made direct eye contact with the very man whose name had been in my mind for far too much of this scene.

In a split second, the image of Isaac imprinted itself on my brain, and closing my eyes *now* wouldn't make a difference. He was there in the H-style harness I'd once been so attracted to, the flogger that had once hung from my dresser knob at his waist.

I didn't grow faint or sick like the last time I'd seen him. Instead, defiance bubbled in my chest, hot and fierce—but it burned away any trace of the blissful foggy tendrils of subspace that had been wrapping around me.

The next lash against my thighs felt twice as hard—brutal in a *bad* way for the first time. I cried out louder than I'd meant to, throwing myself against the cross to try to squirm away.

Just before I closed my eyes, I saw it:

Isaac smiled. Thin, cruel, and... pleased. Fuck! Holy fuck, my gut roiled in an instant. I *hated* the idea that I'd given that worm a single ounce of pleasure—now or ever.

Icy regret flooded my veins, melting away my hard-on, making me shudder and gasp for breath.

"Is everything okay?" In the blink of an eye, Seb was somehow standing next to me, tall and calm and speaking only to me even though his friend—my boyfriend—stood by his elbow.

Fuck. How had he picked up on the first moment of trouble? No wonder Isaac had kept me away from anyone who could have helped me.

Stop thinking about him, damn it! God, I hated myself and my stupid brain that couldn't seem to let go of that man. My eyes stung with heat.

Seb was waiting for my answer.

I gulped for breath and peeked for just a moment—but Isaac had melted into the crowd again. I closed my eyes again and hissed, "Green," as I pulled against the wrist cuffs. "More, Daddy. Now. Now!"

If there was one way to earn punishment, it was trying to top from the bottom. And I wanted it—I wanted the blows, even if they felt too harsh, without the pleasure that had been making my shaft throb until a minute ago.

Rex hissed quietly. "You know that makes me want to stop," he taunted me sharply. And then the fronds of the whip left my body, and I gasped, pushing back against the bonds.

Seb stepped back, melting into the scenery. Good. Good, I was losing track of my surroundings. But that wasn't enough. I wasn't *floating* away, I wasn't disappearing until nothing except Rex meant anything.

"No, please," I gasped. If he didn't hurt me *now*, I was going to lose my shit. And nobody needed to see that. "Daddy. Please, I need—please," I gasped. I couldn't remember the right words to use, if there were any.

Maybe it was the desperation in my voice that won him over, but thank God, something did. Another sharp lash landed across my back, and I gasped, tears of gratitude springing to my eyes.

"*My* boy," Rex whispered, punctuating it with another stroke. "*My* decisions. *My* pleasure to give or withhold."

"Yes, Daddy," I whimpered, my body tensing with anticipation between each of the rhythmic, heavy lashes. "Yes, sir. I'm sorry. Don't hurt me, please, sir…!"

"I'll hurt you," Rex whispered, and suddenly my left thigh stung, and I yelped. "If I damn well want to." Another blow on my right thigh.

My knees buckled, and now the cross supported my weight. I cried out, but words were fleeing from my mind.

And still—still, at the edge of my endurance—I couldn't find the blissful release I so desperately needed.

My chest tight, my throat filled with a sudden lump, all I could do was fight back against every blow. My cock was hard but no longer throbbing with desperation for Daddy's touch.

As abruptly as he started, Rex ran the tails of the flogger down my back, and then both his palms met my skin, rubbing every burning-hot patch of skin like he was soothing the sting from them.

I tensed up, resisting. I didn't want it to be over!

"Good boy," Rex whispered, his arm looping around my waist. "My beautifully good boy. My sexy fucktoy, and my gorgeous boy. You did so well for your first scene. You're fine now, love."

The words blurred into each other as I fought the knowledge that it was over. How could I get him to give me more? Fuck, I couldn't face reality again just yet.

I choked back frustration as Rex unbuckled the cuffs and rubbed each limb. I stood on my own but leaned against the cross as Rex wiped it down, ignoring the room whirling around me. After the whole week waiting, my balls were heavy with need, my cock thick. I could find the mood again. I just had to entice Rex into more.

Rex turned to me, and I seized my chance.

"Fuck me," I whispered against Daddy's lips, crowding up to his hot, tight body. Then I pressed my mouth against his neck, flicking my tongue against skin where I knew it would drive him crazy. My nails dug into his hips as I pressed my cock into his thigh, desperately grasping for the arousal I knew should be running along my skin. "Right here, Daddy. I need you. Fuck me. I'm ready for you. Feel this? How hard I am for you?" I blinked back tears. "Show me you want me."

"No, my sweet boy," Rex whispered, his arms sliding around my back. He pulled easily out of my grip and turned me sideways to hug me, my hard-on pressing uselessly at my shorts and thin air. "I want you, body and soul, but I'm not going to do that."

He spoke like he knew something I didn't. I wrapped my arms around myself, finally pulling away from him. "Shit," I whispered. "Why not?"

Rex spoke softly and clearly, steadying me. "Because you're in subspace, honey."

"I'm not," I whispered, a chill running down my spine. I didn't want anyone else to overhear that, but I was desperate to tell him what was wrong. He wanted the truth? He was going to get it. "I'm fucking not, and you know who—you know why."

Another glance around, but Isaac was nowhere to be seen. Seb was watching, one thumb hooked in his belt, but he was keeping his distance. He couldn't overhear.

I turned back to Rex. "This will help, Daddy," I begged. "Please. Help me."

For a moment, I felt bad. Pain flashed across Rex's face, his forehead creasing and lips turning down. "Oh, darling," he whispered, his touch gentle. He gripped my shoulders, making me look at him. "Listen to Daddy. Can you do that?"

I gulped for breath but nodded.

"I can't help you the way you're asking for," Rex continued. "It's not because I don't want you. It's because I know what you need, and it's not this. I'm not going to make our first time because you're trying to…" He trailed off, like he was choosing the right words.

"Trying to what?" I whispered. "Prove to *him* that someone loves me? That he hasn't broken me forever?"

Rex's fingers trailed through my hair, and he pulled me into him for a hug. His arms were tight and safe, but however much I relaxed in his hold, a few words were enough to bring the dizzying fear flooding straight back through me.

"You know what you have to do."

Fuck, I did. I knew what Rex was about to say, and I squeezed my eyes shut like it would stop up my ears.

"Report him," Rex whispered. "Later. When you feel up to it. But before the next time we come here. Then you'll be safe next time, and we can do whatever I want to do."

"Why?" I breathed out. "Why can't he just…"

"Crawl out of here and get hit by a bus?" Rex muttered. "Dom Nation's owner, Brighton… he needs evidence to kick him out, sweetheart. You have more than enough. He's put you through hell. This Slate—the one I'm holding right now… is the same Slate I met that night. I want him to find peace."

I shook my head and pressed my face into Rex's shoulder, my arms rising to clutch him like he was about to march me straight to the office.

Rex didn't get it. At the end of the night, even if Isaac was banned, *I* was the one he would keep tormenting. Maybe forever. Nowhere was safe.

Before I could say anything, Rex spoke. "I know how much it's asking, boy. But do you trust Daddy?"

Hesitantly, I nodded.

"Then I want you to move in with me," Rex told me.

I pulled back sharply, my jaw dropping. I hadn't expected him to say that. Okay, maybe he *did* get it... but I wasn't sure I wanted him to.

"I know it's sudden," Rex murmured. "And this isn't the right moment to discuss it. We have plenty of time to talk later. But I want you to know that you're safe, okay? No matter what, you'll be safe."

I knew he was trying to calm me down, but I shook my head slowly.

Rex would protect me, yes. I trusted Daddy. But I couldn't trust Brighton and Seb and others—people I barely knew—who could only protect me within these four walls.

My boyfriend couldn't protect me forever. At work? Hanging out with friends? I didn't know when Isaac would strike. But sooner or later, there would be a crack in even the highest walls Rex tried to put around me.

And it would be me facing down all of Isaac's rage alone, while trying not to break into a thousand little pieces of hot-edged shame.

The same bile of shame boiled in my stomach at the memory of just minutes ago—Isaac's single, cruel smile through a crowd. A split-second and he could pull me into his orbit again, away from the best thing I'd ever known.

But if I reported him, moved in with my new Daddy, and trusted a bunch of strangers to listen and believe me... wasn't I just jumping from living my life under one iron-clad thumb to another?

The choice was unfair and cruel, and *I* was still the problem. Me and my fucking curse: the insatiable need to be broken which, like a stone in a windshield, just shattered everything in my life sooner or later.

I shook my head numbly and pulled away from Rex, batting at his hand when he tried to touch me. My throat was too full of the lump I couldn't quite swallow down, and my cheeks burned fiercely.

I'd been so sure that I was invincible from Isaac now that Rex was with me, but not even he could protect me from myself. Even being claimed in public and beaten to tears in front of a room full of hungry men wasn't enough for me. How much deeper did this fucked-up part of me run?

I didn't mean to, but I looked over Rex's shoulder and saw Seb shifting to attention, watching us closely with an expression of studied neutrality.

He wouldn't let Rex follow me or make a grab for me if I just said one word. Fuck, guilt throbbed through every atom of my being, but I had to do it.

So I said, "No."

And then I fled from everything I wanted, toward the darkness and pain, because every breath hurt like I was breaking into pieces. Worse still, with every step, the padlock jingled softly around my neck like a millstone.

I didn't know how to fix any of this.

15

REX

"You know I can't let you do that."

I'd never fought so hard to keep my face blank. The need was overwhelming: I had to rescue Slate from the demons that had just chased him away.

But I also recognized the stance Seb had adopted—a forty-five-degree angle to me so he was imposing but not threatening, legs spread and hands behind his back.

If I moved to chase Slate, Seb would block my path.

Don't you dare, I thought. *Nothing gets between me and Slate.* Fire flooded my veins as I stared at my friend. I'd burn down anything that threatened my boy—or stopped me getting to him. But before I could do anything reckless, Seb spoke again.

"Not while he's in here, anyway," Seb told me gently. "Club rules apply. You know I have to enforce them."

I both hated and begrudgingly respected him for saying that. I wanted to snarl and throw myself past him—to make a break for it and chase my boy to the ends of the Earth.

But I wasn't giving up just like that. Not ever.

"This is sub drop," I told him fiercely. I bent over to grab my duffel bag and slung it over my shoulder. "He doesn't think it is, but he's wrong. Slate *needs* me."

Seb's answer surprised me. It was gentle and quiet, and he turned to face me, dropping the confrontational pose. "I can't disagree. What happened?"

"No idea," I whispered, but the icy tendrils of fear yanked suddenly at my gut.

I crossed a line somewhere. I finally went too far, and I hurt him. Maybe for good.

I swallowed the thought, my nails digging into the strap of the duffel. "No idea," I said again, louder. "Fuck. Did you let Isaac near us?" That was the only thing I could think of. One thought of Isaac could chase away the sweet, bold man I loved and leave in his place the deer in the headlights who had just fled.

I hated him for having that power.

"Don't take this out on me," Seb warned, bristling. "I can't keep him out of the room. Only away from you. This is between you and your play partner."

My gut roiled again. This was more than one session between us. More than a short-lived fling. It had to be. I'd given my word.

Unless I'd just screwed everything up, and I couldn't bear that thought. I didn't know what I'd do if I was too fucked-up to even keep safe the one man I'd promised that to.

The need to look after Slate—to comfort and calm him, and to drive off the nightmare that had closed in around him again—pulled at me, sharp and urgent.

"Not play partner," I corrected heatedly. "He's my boy, and he fucking needs me. I'm not waiting around any longer." How could I stand here talking when Slate was wrapped up in his fears, lost and alone and in need of his Daddy to take care of him? "I promised," I whispered fiercely, stepping up to Seb and staring him in the eye. "I *promised*, Seb."

My friend dipped his head slightly. He signaled another DM and then said, "Let's move. We'll talk to Tony and see if he's left."

For once, our slim, snarky friend didn't have a razor-eyed glance for me. "Yeah, he left a few minutes ago," he told us, his eyes on me rather than Seb, who had asked. "Everything okay?"

"That depends," Seb said gravely. "Did Isaac leave, too?"

Shit. My guts froze as I turned to look over my shoulder, like I'd find him standing there, leering in victory. I'd just assumed he was still lurking here, like a tiger circling the herd to pick out the weak prey.

"Yeah." Tony glanced at the curb. "You just missed him. He called a taxi."

"Fuck," I hissed. I turned to the barrier, but before I could step over it, Seb grabbed my arm.

"Think carefully," Seb told me quietly. He stepped between me and the line of guys waiting to get in and casting me curious glances. "If you think Isaac is capable of harm…"

I folded my arms over my chest, shivering as the night air cooled the frantic sweat from my forehead. "Then I can't let him get a head start. He's a possessive creep. He saw us together, and now he's going after Slate. I know it." I fished out my phone and stabbed for the taxi number.

Seb pressed his lips together hard and then nodded. "Call for help if you need it. And go straight to Slate's. No delays."

He had a point. The last thing I wanted was to be cornered by Isaac in some dark alley without help.

"Fine. Shit," I swore, my gaze fixed on the corner like the taxi would come reversing around the corner with a furious Isaac in it. Okay, maybe I needed a shirt, too. And sensible shoes. Although these stilettos *would* put a hole somewhere Isaac needed one.

When I hung up with the taxi on the way, Seb watched me. "Don't get caught up in Isaac. Fix this between you and Slate," he told me.

"I don't know if I can." I shook my head. Defending Slate from Isaac? Easy. Talking to Slate, begging his forgiveness for failing *so badly* as his Dom on our first public outing? God, it was scary.

"If being his Daddy hurts too much, be Master X," Seb told me quietly. "I don't care who you want to tell yourself you are—underneath, it's always the same man. And I know you're capable of this. Human to human, he needs you, Rex."

My throat was too tight. I couldn't speak. I just nodded, the strap digging into my hand as I clutched my bag close to me. "Thank you."

Seb nodded and detached the barrier for me to walk through. I sprinted for the taxi and climbed in, already kicking my heels off as I buckled up my seatbelt.

I gave Slate's address and then thrashed around the back seat to get into my jeans and sneakers while the bored-looking cabbie fiddled with the music.

Two blocks from Slate's house, I spotted another taxi in front of us, and I immediately knew who it was. "Oh, shit," I whispered and leaned forward, between the seats. "Follow him, but not too close."

"Sure, bud," the cab driver sighed, cracking his gum as the light turned to green. He let the other taxi have space and cruised down the street after him while my heart thudded.

Yes. Just as I'd thought, the taxi pulled to a halt outside Slate's house.

"Here," I urged him, keeping a few driveways between us. But it was too late for him not to notice me if he were looking to see if he was followed. The street was too quiet at this time of night to try any super-secret spy bullshit.

A minute passed. Seconds dragging by in the darkness, each an eternity long and laced with the deadly potential.

What was Isaac *doing* in the other taxi?

"Meter's running."

"I know," I whispered. "I'll pay. No problem."

"Sure." The guy turned the phone stuck to his windshield on its side and switched from a street map to a sports channel. The glare was hard to ignore as I peered across the phone and out the front window.

Finally, there was movement. Isaac—unmistakably him—in a dark suit, some obnoxious name-brand bag on his shoulder. He stepped out and faced Slate's house.

Thankfully this ride was on my account, so I didn't have to waste a moment paying. "Thanks!" I whispered and jumped out of the taxi, shouldering my bag.

The closing car door made Isaac turn my way, and under the streetlight, I suddenly realized he wasn't empty-handed. In the hand *not* holding his bag, he held a bullwhip, the coils loose and large in his fingers.

Fuck, I thought, steeling myself. Those things were dangerous —a skilled sadist like Isaac could take an eye out, break a bone, or knock me unconscious.

Both taxis pulled away from the curb as we stood facing one another, forty feet apart or so. When we were alone, Isaac slowly set down his bag. "Should have known you'd come crawling here," he greeted me. "I saw you hurt him back there. Did you like it?" A slow, unpleasant smile crept over his face as he licked his lips.

Just like he knew how to win over people, he knew how to go for the jugular. It took all my strength not to launch myself blindly at him, because he'd struck a nerve.

I *had* liked it—until I'd realized that something had happened. A line had been crossed, and I still didn't know where or how.

"Guilty conscience bring you here?" I retorted. "Or looking for an easy mark tonight? Cut the crap. You aren't here to defend his honor. Not with *that*."

"Oh, this?" Isaac lazily swished it in circles around his hand. "I find he needs to hurt to remember a lesson. I'm sure you've discovered this, too."

I gritted my teeth, trying not to imagine Slate on his knees for *this* psycho. "What do you want?"

"Nobody imagines for a moment *you're* really interested in a dried-up, untrained old thing like him."

Fuck you! Heat flushed my cheeks as my gut clenched. I lurched forward onto my toes but stopped myself before I sprinted close. I couldn't let him see he was getting to me. Instead, I put down my bag like I wasn't planning the best way to turn his face to pulp.

"You're loaded, so he's not paying you. So what is it? A guilty conscience or an easy mark?" Isaac flung my words back in my face almost effortlessly, like a man who was used to talking his way through the cracks in anyone's armor.

But I wasn't some vulnerable boy in need of his approval, or even his enmity. As far as I was concerned, Isaac was standing between me and Slate—and our future together. So his fucking mind games wouldn't work on me.

"If you think so little of him, why are you here?" I asked, my gaze fixed on the whip as he whirled it around. Estimating its length. I'd seen him use it in the club, on rare occasion. Playing with whips that long required a lot of space to do safely.

I knew the answer, so I was just stalling for time. He was obsessed—he thought he owned him. He thought every boy belonged to him on sight. I'd bet my eyeteeth he was one of those assholes who thought any sub should submit to him.

"Some call it love." Isaac smirked, making it perfectly clear that he wasn't one of those people. Instead, he was willing to use the word—defile it—to get what he wanted.

I laughed. "You wouldn't understand love if it spat in your face and called you a gutter worm."

"Is that what you tell him?" Isaac clicked his tongue. "And yet you think *your* love is different from mine? Let's face it: we're apex predators. We're bred for something different, you and me."

My heart hammered in my ears as Isaac started walking toward me, still casually playing with the whip to keep the threat fresh in my mind.

"And what's that?" I refused to back up a step, but I calculated the distance in my mind.

"To *take*." Isaac's eyes gleamed with a savagery that chilled me to the bone. He was talking about Slate that way—the man who had unlocked the tender side of me I hadn't even dared to acknowledge. "To *have*. And I had him first. You lost." Isaac raised his whip overhead, and with one flick, circled the tails around himself. "If I want him, he's mine. That's how it works."

No. I'd walk into a fire for Slate. It was nothing to face down this piece of shit who thought he owned the man who had pledged himself in all faith and innocence to me.

I'd keep my boy safe at any cost.

"Leave now."

I didn't have weapons to back up my words—just the flogger in my bag. Even if I did, it would be stupid to get into a hand-to-hand fight here on the street.

The whip wasn't my first choice in the dungeon, much less right now. I was relying on instinct I'd learned from watching others with far more experience.

Isaac said nothing, lazily flicking the whip around his head once more. Like he was waiting for me to come to my senses and leave. *As if*, I thought and stared him down.

"Fine. You had your chance." Isaac's eyes narrowed, and he stepped forward.

It was on… and seconds from now it would be over. I had to make sure this ended the right way, for Slate's sake.

The whip arced through the air toward me. The tip seemed to shimmer in the lamplight, and I heard it cut through the air with a keen whine as I jumped out of the way. Isaac's arm flexed and he turned side-on, bringing it up and around.

Before he could aim it my way again, I dodged and rushed forward, stripping him of the use of the weapon. I was too close now. That was the trouble with bullwhips—they needed space in the dungeon as well as on the street.

"Shit," Isaac hissed. His arm was up in the air, so he brought the handle down toward the top of my head.

I grabbed his arm above the elbow, forcing it back so I could twist and get a grip on his wrist, too. He yelped as I forced his hand open, and the handle clattered roughly on the ground.

I hated every moment of contact I had to make with the sick motherfucker—and disabling him required me to get closer than I'd ever wanted to be.

But I asked myself what Seb would do and then moved on autopilot to do exactly that. I pretended I was trying to mollify someone at the club who was too amped up to listen to common sense.

I jammed my foot in the back of Isaac's knee and the flat of my palm to his shoulder blade, bringing him down to the concrete sidewalk. I didn't let him slip from my grasp, though. I had him exactly where I wanted him.

"Fuck you!" Isaac hissed and writhed, but with his arm behind his back, he couldn't do much more than flail at the air and curse my name.

He wanted a fight—to cause a scene he could twist for his own purposes. But I wouldn't give him the satisfaction.

"Isaac?"

At the sound of Slate's beautiful voice, low and urgent, we both froze like boys caught with our hands in the cookie jar.

When I looked toward his house, he stood just on the other side of the front gate, still in his little leather shorts and dull black harness. The padlock dangling from his collar made my whole chest knot with pain. Metal glinted in Slate's hand, catching my eye. He was holding a kitchen knife.

Isaac saw it at the same moment. He thrashed, nearly getting free. "Get off!"

I leaned my knee against his back and gripped his other bicep to keep him exactly where he was. "He's not going to hurt you, you idiot," I hissed. If Isaac thought that Slate was capable of it, he'd never truly known him—and that made me glad. "Even if you deserve it," I added under my breath.

"Bastard," Isaac hissed, twisting this way and that. No doubt it was humiliating, finding himself subordinate to me in front of Slate. I wanted to ask how that felt for the apex predator, but I had bigger concerns than gloating.

"Slate?" I questioned, frowning his way. I wanted to urge him to get back inside, afraid that Isaac would break loose from me —get to Slate and the knife he held, and hurt him.

But Slate was looking at me like he wanted permission, eyes wide and sorrowful. "Daddy?" His voice was a whisper. "Can I come over there?"

Oh, God. It's not over between us.

Relief hit me, hot and hard and all at once. "Yes," I murmured. "Tell him what you need to say."

Isaac's body was stiff as a board and trembling with adrenaline, but he stopped fighting. He looked up from the sidewalk. "What? Come to rub my face in it? Get your revenge?"

Slate shook his head, his gaze fixed on me instead of Isaac. "I saw—heard—all of that. I have nothing to say to him." He could have sneered it, the way a Dom would when looking at a squirming sub underfoot. But he didn't. It was pure and simple and sweet. "I wanted to tell you that I love you." Only I could hear the waver in his voice—the way he gazed at me, reaching out for support. "That you're my Daddy, no matter what. And I'm going to trust you and report Isaac to Brighton."

Oh, my God. He loves me, too.

We'd danced around the word. In aftercare, it was one thing. He needed to know that I was there for him, to protect him and cherish him. But neither of us had said it like this—boldly, out of the blue, seeking something quite different.

"I love you, too, my boy," I murmured at last, beaming at him over Isaac's bowed head of black hair. Slate's shoulders sank, and a smile crossed his face. He pinched the bridge of his nose, like he was barely holding it together.

Isaac twisted away and finally broke my hold. I stepped back quickly, but he was slow to get up.

"Hear that?" I said as he stumbled to his feet and backed away from me, his chest heaving. "There's nowhere you can run. Word will get out to other clubs in other cities. Your reign of terror is over. Go crawl home and be grateful I'm not leaving bruises. I save those for boys who deserve it."

I swapped a grin with Slate, who stepped closer and opened the front gate.

"Fine." Isaac's face was twisted in a jealous rage. "Fine," he repeated. "Doesn't matter. You're nothing to me," he spat at Slate. "Nothing to *anyone.*"

Like he couldn't hear him, Slate still watched me. He tilted his head, so I nodded, hoping to give him confidence to do whatever he needed to do now.

"One more thing…" Slate stepped barefoot onto the sidewalk to grab the bullwhip that lay on the ground.

Isaac gasped sharply. "Don't you dare—"

Too late. He'd cleanly sliced the whip from the handle. Slate's grin only grew wider as he hauled the rest of the length of leather in, coiled it around, and drew the knife along the coils to slice it into a handful of pieces.

"Fuck you!" Isaac spat. "Do you know how much that cost?"

I didn't even need to tell Slate to ignore him. My boy just dropped the pieces again and looked up at me with a smile, like he was asking if he'd done well.

"Head inside," I instructed him, still aware that this knife was the most dangerous object in the situation, and Isaac was off his leash. "I'll be there in a minute."

"Yes, Daddy."

Slate's smile—less wavering than a few moments ago, now certain and trusting—made my whole world steady again. I wasn't sure I deserved his faith, but by God, I was going to cling to it tonight.

When he was inside the house, I looked back at Isaac, who was ranting. I cut him off with an outstretched hand. He stopped talking and then cringed, no doubt realizing that he'd given up the power to me.

"You broke the man I love just for sport," I told him, my hands curling into fists. I wasn't used to the rage inside me bubbling over its careful containment. It flowed through me now, tinged every breath with pain. "And I'm putting him back together, so don't count it as a victory. He's stronger than you'll ever be. But if I ever get the slightest wind you're hurting him, or stalking me, or treating anyone else that way, I'll put a stop to it. Understand?"

Isaac spat in my direction and said nothing. Instead, he dug out his phone to call a taxi.

I stood there with my arms folded and my duffel by my feet, silently waiting. The short minutes felt like hours, especially when Isaac was pacing back and forth, every curse imaginable falling from his mouth.

When the taxi finally arrived and he threw himself into the back seat, I watched until it disappeared around the corner and then stood there for another minute just to make sure.

It's over.

I let my breath go and braced myself on the white picket fence behind me as the tension sank out of my body. "Shit," I breathed out quietly and turned my face to the night sky.

The stars shone on, telling their stories from millions of years ago, and suddenly my problems seemed… tiny. Like I could get a hold of them, if I just took a deep breath and *tried*.

Slate and I had to talk.

So I gulped and focused on putting one foot in front of the other until I was inside Slate's house, and he pressed a cup of tea into my hands and guided me to the couch.

Aftercare, I dully realized when he wrapped a blanket around both of our shoulders. *That's what he's doing for me. Oh, God, I needed it.*

"Thank you," I whispered at last. "If you want, I... I have the keys." To the padlock around his neck, I should have said, but he knew what I meant.

Slate snorted softly. "No. I should be thanking you," he said, rubbing my thigh as he tried to keep the blanket closed but also held in place so I was free to drink tea. "I don't want you to take it off."

I could breathe easier knowing that. I reached up and touched his collar gently, stroking a finger over his throat, and then settled my hand on the cup of tea again.

At first, we just held each other for a long time. When the beast inside had coiled up and closed its eyes to sleep, I was finally free to speak. "I'm glad I followed you home. You gave me a real scare."

Slate gulped and rested his head on my shoulder. "I'm sorry, Daddy. I was afraid. I don't even know if I really... *got* to subspace tonight. Isaac looked at me, while we were in the middle of it. I just... realized he'd never stop haunting me. And I had to get out. I was afraid I was jumping from the kettle into the fire."

"And are you?"

The world might as well have stopped turning as I waited for the answer. After all, maybe there was truth in what Isaac had said. Maybe we *were* birds of a feather, searching for someone who wanted to be hurt...

"No," Slate murmured. He pressed his warm, rough lips to my cheek. "I'm going from a forest fire to a hearth."

That made me smile. I set down my cup of tea and took over blanket duty, shifting it around both of us as I drew his legs into my lap and wrapped my arms around him. "It was my mistake," I murmured. "I should have seen you were going too far. And then telling you to move in with me... that was too much, while you were in that state."

It had been foolish and impulsive—a chance to grab something good while it was going. An amateur move, not a real Daddy's patience. I could wait as long as I had to for him to be ready.

Slate nodded slightly. "But I want to. Even if Isaac flees town. Not for protection—for the future."

"You do?" My breath hitched. I hadn't fucked it up after all, or read him wrong! Slate wanted me—wanted the same future I did. The days in bed together, the mornings cooking each other breakfast, the nights... well, in every position imaginable.

Slate nodded once, his smile growing. "You're adorable when you do that."

I cleared my throat and blushed furiously. God, if I looked like half the lovestruck boy I'd suddenly felt like... "Do what?"

"Nothing," Slate teased.

He kissed my cheek again, but I growled and turned my head to make his lips land on mine instead.

God, his lips were everything I needed. Heat surged between us as I gripped him tightly, my tongue dancing across his until his lips parted. I sucked the tip of his tongue into my mouth, and suddenly the kiss became openmouthed and heavy.

My cock grew thick under all my layers—satin thong, latex briefs, jeans. I was panting for breath by the time I remembered that I *wasn't* allowed to do this. Not yet, anyway. There was still too much to talk about.

Slate gave me a hazy, wide-eyed stare as I pulled away. "Yes, Daddy?" His voice was hoarse, but he smiled like he knew just what he was doing to me.

Oh, you insatiable boy. My *insatiable boy.* I smiled at him and shook my head, trying to clear it. "I can't wait to rescue you from the tragic coffee maker situation next," I teased him right back.

Slate nodded once, searching my face. "I hope you aren't beating yourself up about tonight."

I winced. "Damn it. How can you read me so well?" I complained. I prided myself on being inscrutable. Master X was going to need a downgrade to Master Open Book at this rate.

Slate chuckled quietly. "Don't worry. I think it's just my talent," he murmured. "One of my two." His eyes glinted with amusement.

I desperately wanted to ask about the other, but I resisted. "I… I am, a bit," I admitted. "It was my job to protect you and keep you safe, and I failed at that. Maybe you weren't ready for baring yourself to the room—to Isaac, too."

"I was ready," Slate told me, shaking his head. "And it wasn't to the room. It was just to you. *Then* he came along…" Slate trailed off before resuming. "You can't read my mind. I said green."

I still should have known. Guilt was a steady drumbeat in my chest, and like he sensed it, Slate rocked into me, swaying back and forth.

"Green's supposed to mean yes," he carried on stubbornly. "Even when my no doesn't always mean no. I *wanted* you to hurt me, Rex," he said slowly, emphasizing each word.

I nodded, trying to get myself to accept his forgiveness. "And… did you get what you needed?"

It was easy to tell in the constraints of a scene—carefully planned beforehand and measured afterward. But a relation-ship? That was messy and organic and full of risks. It was hard work digging into the soft parts of Slate, knowing which ones were ready to be prodded and which might never be.

"Yes," Slate nodded. "It was fine until I saw Isaac. And then suddenly I felt…" He cleared his throat and looked at me like he wasn't sure he was allowed to mention that name again.

I nodded slightly, encouraging him. "You can tell me anything in the world, my boy."

Slate relaxed and breathed out quietly, nodding once. "I felt ashamed again. Dirty and used and discarded. And I kind of *like* feeling like that… but not the same way anymore. Not now that I know there's better. You make me feel all the best parts of those feelings, and then you make me feel loved. It was hard to accept at first that I could get all of that at once."

I blinked back the heat in the corners of my eyes, gratitude thick in my chest. "Good," I whispered. Slate deserved to feel like the king of my heart, because he was. Forever.

"I had to calm down and remember that you do mean it—that you're not just trying to get into my pants and then fuck off again after you blow your load." Slate swallowed hard. "I trust you. So I'm going to trust the people you trust, too."

That was it. That was what I needed to hear—the glue that would turn into cement. How could I be his Daddy if he was forever second-guessing me? But now... he understood what I needed and what I wanted to give him.

"Oh, Slate. I'm so proud of you," I whispered, hugging him so hard that he squeaked. All I wanted was to hold him night after night and remind him of how much he deserved a happy life.

There and then, I promised myself that I would make Slate's every dream come true. No less.

"You're surprisingly strong," Slate mumbled when I let go, his smile shaky as he looked out the door like he was planning a trip to Dom Nation right now. "So, should we... when can we tell Brighton?"

"Not tonight." I reached out of our little blanket cocoon to grip the tea and offered him a sip. Then I took one before setting it down again. "We're going to rest tonight and go to bed. In the morning, we'll report him." And then it would all be over.

Slate perked up, his smile relieved. "Tomorrow morning? So tonight, it's just us?"

"Just us, my boy," I whispered. "Let Daddy take care of you."

16

SLATE

At last, I felt like everything was going to be okay.

Sunshine streamed through the living room windows. I was cooking toast and eggs for breakfast, wearing nothing but a huge grin.

The kettle clicked just as the newspaper landed on my front porch, so before I poured the mixed-up eggs into the pan, I grabbed a blanket to wrap myself up and grab the paper.

"Newspaper delivery?" Rex was standing at the bottom of the stairs when I shut the door again. "Is it the nineties?"

I scoffed, adjusting my blanket toga as I moved back to the kitchen. I'd been planning to sneak upstairs and bring him breakfast in bed, but he must have heard me. "Good morning, Daddy. I prefer my news physical, thank you. Call me old-fashioned."

Rex held up a finger. "That blanket's a fire hazard. Sit down and read your old-fashioned news. I'll do the eggs."

"Big Safety Daddy energy," I teased, clutching the blanket to my chest. I settled on the couch, the blanket across my lap, and unfolded the paper.

It might have been just a few minutes of reading headlines out loud as Rex cooked breakfast, but this contented feeling would be engraved in my memory for years to come. By the time he coaxed me to the table, whipping away my blanket playfully, I was glowing with happiness.

This was what I'd been missing all along. A man who knew when I needed a soft touch, and when I craved something… altogether harder.

"Thank you," I murmured as I gazed over my plate of toast and eggs.

Rex looked startled, accidentally dumping too much pepper on his eggs as he looked up at me. "For what? Oh, shit."

I stifled a giggle. "For being patient with me."

"I could say the same," Rex told me, reaching over the table to rest his hand on mine for a moment. "Now, look away while I cry into these spicy eggs."

Despite our banter, these precious morning hours slipped away under the growing haze of anxiety about what we had to do next. Yesterday had seemed so far away, but the more I thought about the trip to Dom Nation, the more unpleasant details I remembered from that night.

Thank God I'd seen the whole exchange between Isaac and Rex. I'd watched Rex put himself in danger for me and defy Isaac like he was nothing. It had been impossible, after that point, to think that he didn't care. That he'd use me and leave me all over again.

Rex was different. He was the one. So I had to trust Rex's judgment, and have faith in him.

Still, the voice whispered, what would happen if Brighton *didn't* listen to me? After all, I was here, wasn't I? I was just fine. It wasn't like Isaac had left bruises I hadn't wanted. I wasn't some poor, pitiful victim. What if Brighton took one look at me and decided I was lying?

By the time I was dressed and ready to leave, my guts were a knot of anxiety.

"Should I drive?" I fidgeted with my car keys, swiveling each of them around until the keychain hung correctly from my forefinger.

Rex nodded and put his hand on my shoulder, a reassuring presence. "If you feel up to it."

"I want something to keep me busy." This way, I wouldn't have to think about where we were going until we'd arrived.

Rex winked. "One of these car trips, we'll explore other options." Then he opened the door and strode outside like he lived here, leaving me gasping in his wake.

"What does *that* mean, Daddy?" I asked once we were in the car, but he gave me an enigmatic smile and said nothing. Goddamn, it distracted me wondering what exactly he meant.

Which was probably the point, I realized only once I parked outside Dom Nation. Rex was trying to keep me in good spirits.

But sitting here in the driver's seat of my car, I shrank back into it. I didn't want to unbuckle the belt, or walk in there, or talk to anyone at all.

"What's up, baby boy?" Rex's pet names never sounded ridiculous. They slipped from his mouth like he'd practiced them all of his life. As he spoke, he unbuckled and slid closer, then laid a hand on my cheek and cupped it gently.

I closed my eyes and leaned into the touch, focusing on this one solid, grounding point. Well, counting my feet on the car floor, there were two more. And my hands on the wheel. But soon I was going to be out there, back in the club I'd fled from last night.

Honesty, I reminded myself. That was Rex's number one rule. So I murmured, "I'm afraid he won't take me seriously."

"He will," Rex promised solemnly. "I swear to you. We don't take this kind of thing lightly in the scene."

This scene let Isaac in, night after night, for years, I thought, biting my lip. *All the while, he was fucking with my mind. Was I the only one, then? Was he nice to everyone else? Is it me?*

I blinked back the tears that threatened to fall, bowing my head over the steering wheel.

It wasn't just me. I didn't deserve any of the ways Isaac had treated me—Rex had made me believe that in these last few days. I deserved love and pain on *my* terms, not his.

"Let go of the secret. You don't owe him any kind of protection," Rex told me, his thumb stroking the corner of my jaw where my stubble was starting to turn silver. "He sure as hell never offered you any."

From myself, from him, or from the world. I nodded and unbuckled, then reached out to take his hand as it glided down my shoulder to my arm.

We sat there for a minute like that, me quietly gathering my strength, him gazing at me like the whole world revolved around me.

I can do this.

I don't know how he got me out of the car and into Dom Nation, but it struck me immediately how different it looked in the daytime. How ordinary.

Hand in hand, we walked past the shuttered bar to a steel door with *Staff Only* engraved on it. I hadn't noticed it before.

"Right this way," Rex said as he held the door open after himself, leading the way inside. There was a short hallway with three doors, one of which was open.

Rex rapped lightly on it and poked his head in. "Brighton? Can I have a word?"

"Uh-huh."

Rex stepped into the office and gestured for me to follow. Then he took my hand when I joined him. "Brighton, this is Slate. Slate, the club owner, Brighton."

I didn't expect the man behind the desk to look so... well, *flamboyant.* I'd expected a big gruff man like Seb, maybe dressed in all leather and carrying a whip or something. Which was silly now that I thought about it. They had to wear other clothes sometimes.

Instead, Brighton was about Rex's size, if not slighter. He wore a pink T-shirt and jeans, and a dramatic undercut with bleach-blond tips.

"Hello, Slate. Pleasure to meet you."

"You, too," I told him.

Brighton rubbed his eyes with the back of his hand and pushed the paperwork on his desk away, folding his hands. "Why don't you take a seat?"

I swallowed hard and chose one of the chairs, while Rex sat in the other and reached for my hand again. I let him take it and work his magic, rubbing his fingers along my veins until the prickling anxiety settled in my chest.

"What's this about?" Brighton asked Rex, but there was a grim resignation in his voice that told me he already knew.

"Isaac," Rex said simply. Then he squeezed my hand between both of his, a silent prompt to talk when I wished.

I had no idea what to say. I'd planned for this moment since Rex first tried to drag me in here—imagining it playing out different ways. How I'd be calm and composed and relate just the facts, or maybe an emotional mess.

But I took a breath, and suddenly the words came out. "He abused me for years, outside the scene. He lied and said he didn't come to any kink clubs. I think it was because he didn't want me to report him here. When I finally came to Dom Nation for the first time, he approached me and grabbed my ass. Said I should take it as a compliment, that I should be glad for..." The words died on my lips. I made myself swallow hard so I could finish. "The *attention*."

I could *feel* Rex holding back his growl from his seat next to me, his grip suddenly tightening to a crush around my fingers. His whole body quivered, every muscle taut like he was about to spring out of his seat.

"This was in my club?" Brighton's eyes were sharp. He leaned forward, folding his hands and resting them on the desk.

I nodded. As I held my breath, Brighton let his out and closed his eyes, and a few long moments passed. Jesus, they were more like decades. I wanted to press fast-forward to the end of this scene and find out if Brighton was going to laugh me off or not.

Please believe me, I wanted to say. I didn't know who the DMs had been that night. I hadn't even known what DMs were.

"I—he's done worse stuff, too. Outside the club. He—he never taught me about consent or safewords or boundaries. I've learned all of that from Rex."

Rex stroked my wrist gently with just one finger, and that tiny touch was all it took to quell the anxious outburst of words that threatened to pour from me: more explanations, defenses, pleas.

Help me. Help us.

"Okay," Brighton said evenly and opened his eyes again. "Thank you for trusting me, Slate. I believe you."

Oh, thank God. I pressed my hand to my chest as my throat went tight with relief.

Rex kept his grip on my hand but leaned forward. "Thank you, Brighton," he murmured. "I didn't want to break Slate's trust, but... things escalated. Last night, Slate and I were in the middle of a scene, and Isaac psyched him out." I smiled with gratitude. The way he said it, it didn't sound like my fault. "He followed Slate home. Trying to break him—get him to shut up and not report him."

Brighton's lips tightened into a harsh line, and he looked at me. "Is that so?"

I quivered, the images flooding my mind once again. The handle of my kitchen knife clutched tightly as I crept out of the house, watching the two men square off against each other.

Watching Isaac raise the whip effortlessly around his head— imagining the damage he'd been planning to do to me. *Fuck*, I was lucky to have a Daddy like Rex to look after me, whether or not I was prepared to accept his care.

Kicking the cut-up pieces of his whip into the gutter this morning had been deeply satisfying.

"Yes," I murmured, my voice rough. "That's what he would always do. If he had a bad day, he'd just drop by and expect me to be home. His own punching bag." I cleared my throat, but I was too raw to pull myself together and sit up straight, so I stared at Brighton's desk.

The shame was no longer about *me*, but somehow it still bled into my gut. Instead of being ashamed that I'd wanted those things from Isaac, I was ashamed that I'd let *him* be the one to do it.

But none of it was mine. It was *Isaac* who had been abusive, and his ban was his own fault.

"I think he was coming to scare me away from seeing Rex, because he knew..." I trailed off, my mouth dry.

"I'd encourage you to report him?" Rex asked, gazing intently at me.

"No." I shook my head and then paused. Actually, now that he said it... "Well, yes. But more than that. He knew you'd show me what a real Daddy looks like. And he worked hard to make sure I didn't know anything outside of what he taught me."

I shifted uncomfortably. I didn't want to be all forty-year-old virgin in front of guys who had seen and done a lot more than I'd even daydreamed.

But Brighton didn't judge me. He just shook his head slightly. "I'm withdrawing his membership effective immediately. With your permission, I'm also going to contact some of the other clubs around here to report this behavior. If he did it to you..."

He didn't have to finish. All of us were thinking it as we exchanged glances. No doubt there were others—or would be.

"Thank you," I whispered, finally looking him in the eye again. "I didn't think the infraction was serious enough."

"It's serious, all right. *Anyone* grabs someone without permission, they get banned on the spot. I don't care who they are," Brighton rumbled in a surprisingly deep voice for that slender man. Was he a Dom, too? He sure looked like it right now.

Rex nodded once, sharply. "Consent is serious. If someone's willing to ignore it in what seems like a minor way, they'll ignore it when the scene gets heavy," he told me, his voice soft. "And if you're trained to believe your consent doesn't matter..." He trailed off, letting me finish that in my own head.

You'll think it never matters. I licked my lips and slid my fingers between his, holding his hand tightly as I looked over at Brighton again. "Okay," I said and let out a breath.

"Come on, Slate. We've got cupcakes to frost. I'll leave you to deal with that," Rex told Brighton with a smile. "Good luck."

I added my thanks again and clung to Rex as we left, my anxiety slowly creeping up. Brighton was such a tiny thing, and if Isaac took it badly…

Rex gave me a perceptive glance. "Don't worry for him," he murmured. "Brighton's a lot tougher than he looks. This isn't the first rogue Dom he's thrown out."

I nodded, wrapping my arm around Rex's. "Okay," I murmured. "Are you serious about the cupcakes?"

"Do you want me to be?" Rex tilted his head as we reached the front hallway and then stepped out onto the street.

It was odd to see the urban cityscape in the daytime. Concrete and steel and drabness, without the red velvet ropes, the allure of a shared secret, the tinge of excitement in the air.

I shook my head. Nothing felt real right now. I'd never even considered the possibility that Isaac was *in* the scene until that first night I came here. Then I'd just assumed he was so entrenched, like a part of the walls, that I'd always have to deal with him.

Daddy had told me to trust him, that Brighton would listen. And of course he was right. But now I could hardly think straight with the knowledge of what I'd done.

"I don't know," I admitted at last.

I didn't even have to ask him to, of course; Rex took over. "Okay," Rex told me, patting my hand as he led me toward his storefront. "We're going inside, I'm going to make you a cup of tea, and we'll make our own dessert for later."

Good. No pressure to get picture-perfect designs worthy of being sold. Just the two of us having fun on our own little date. "There's a date idea," I murmured. "Could charge hipsters a fortune."

Rex's eyes lit up as he considered me. "Not bad at all. That clever brain of yours never stops."

"You know what else never stops?" I teased, bumping his hip with mine.

"Your hungry little hole?"

Right here in public! I gasped and looked around us, but there was nobody to overhear. Still, my cheeks flushed as I let go of Rex's arm and folded mine over my chest. "*Daddy*," I whispered, scandalized.

"Yes, boy?" Rex gave me a wicked grin, unlocking and pushing the door open. "In you go."

But he made me giggle and forget all the tension I'd been holding on to, in favor of a much more fun kind.

It had been days, after all, since Rex let me come. But I didn't dare complain, because I knew I wouldn't get the punishment I sought. I just had to squirm and try not to think about it.

"Who's that?" Rex asked suddenly as he handed me another cupcake. Most of mine so far had been random squiggles of icing colors, covered with tiny penis candies. He was probably glad he hadn't asked me to help make any for sale.

"Uh, who?" I looked up just in time to see Pam walking past the window. My coworker was "disguised" in big sunglasses and a silk scarf wrapped around her neck and head. It was the worst disguise ever. "Oh, God. Pretend you don't see her."

As Pam passed the window, we hastily looked down at our cupcakes. I snuck a glance, though, as she stopped at the window and bobbed her head like a pigeon trying to look inside.

Rex burst out laughing and ushered me out from behind the counter as Pam hurried off again. "Go."

I pulled open the door and leaned on the doorframe, shielding my eyes. "Iconic, if you're auditioning for the gay best friend role. It's already taken, though."

Pam sheepishly turned and pushed her hands into her coat pockets. "Oh, hey, Slate. Fancy seeing you here."

"Stop lurking outside like an old man with binoculars at the swimming pool." I grinned at the snort of laughter from behind me, as well as Pam's stifled giggle.

"Sorry." Pam scratched her head. "I was curious and I didn't think anyone would be here."

"You want to meet my boyfriend?"

Pam's eyes flew open. "Your—*yes!*" she told me, grinning. "The boyfriend who owns a cupcake shop, absolutely."

"Good thing he's not like, a dentist or something boring," I murmured, holding the door for her. "Welcome to Daddy Cakes."

Pam grinned as she tucked her sunglasses in the pocket of her long black coat. "Oh, it's so cute in here!" Then she noticed the bondage gear put up on the walls. It was all high enough that it couldn't be spirited away, I realized in that moment. "Ohhh," Pam repeated. "*Wow.*"

I glanced at Rex for reassurance, nervously folding my arms. It was one thing to talk about it at work—or avoid talking about it. It was another to be here in plain daylight.

"Thank you. I'm Rex Black. Pleasure to meet you," my Daddy introduced himself as he came around the counter to shake hands. Then he rested a hand on my shoulder, calming me down.

It made me smile now that I knew his full name, Tyrus. He'd told me last night, and said he always hated it. Rex was the name he'd chosen, and I had to agree that it fit him.

"Pam. I work with Slate. I've heard a lot about you," Pam greeted, which sent me into a horrified silence. "And your cupcakes."

Good things! I tried to project to Rex, but I was blushing furiously. *Not sexy things, but good things!*

"Is that so," Rex said softly, his lips flickering into a smile as he looked at me.

I blushed and cleared my throat. "Yes, D—Rex," I corrected myself, checking the floor in hopes of a sinkhole. No such luck.

It was impossible to miss the light bulb that went on in Pam's head, or the way she silently looked at us both. "*Oh,*" she said again.

"I'm not giving you any state secrets," Rex teased me, and my blush only made him grin more.

"Please don't." I pulled out a chair from the table nearest and sank into it, propping my chin on my hands. "I'm done with secrets."

To Pam's credit, she recovered from the shock quickly. "Well, you're good for him, Rex. He's been smiling through lunch hours lately, not just appointments. It's wonderful to see. So I really am pleased to meet you for more than your cupcakes," she told Rex with a grin.

"It's a good thing I made so many and sold so few last night." Thankfully, Rex *didn't* explain to her that he'd closed early so I could go to Dom Nation with him. "Choose your flavor."

"Oh my God, they all look amazing." Pam dug out her wallet, even though Rex tried to wave it off, and paid for a red velvet cupcake and a cup of coffee. "And you do look happier," Pam told me out of nowhere once we'd made the obligatory small talk. "Even if your Friday nights are reserved now."

"Oh, crap." I buried my face in my hands. Movie nights had always been Fridays—but I hadn't even thought to check the listings, much less text and ask if we could move the day.

"It's okay," Pam chuckled. "I took my husband, and we had a real date night. Who knows—maybe he'll get bold enough to try *your* kind of date."

I tried not to choke on my tea. "Uh-huh" was all I managed, my cheeks hotter than the cup in my hands.

"There's some really good clubs in town," Rex said as he joined us with a cup of tea for himself, and before I knew it he was chatting to Pam about them.

I knew nothing, of course. The only club Isaac had told me about when I'd asked was Dom Nation, before saying it wasn't his thing. Liar. But now I was quite happy to stay here since it was clearly where Rex felt most comfortable. And I trusted the staff, and I had a Daddy to collar me and show me the ropes, literally and figuratively... I couldn't wait to come here more often.

"I'll put you in touch," Rex told Pam, grinning over at me. "Earth to Slate."

"Sorry," I mumbled and pinched myself. "My life just flipped upside down. My coworker and friend is talking to my..." I hesitated and swallowed hard, then finished, "my Daddy, about things I barely know. Or admit to knowing."

Pam grinned. "You'll have to work to keep up, then. I'm sure Rex has you covered." She stood up. "That was an excellent cupcake. I'll definitely be back here more often. You should do delivery or pickup or something. Or an app."

I winced and cast a look at Rex, who was trying for his inscrutable but agreeable face. "Yes," Rex murmured, and only I picked up that note of longing—or knew what it was about. "I should."

By the time Pam left, I found myself breathing easier. I wasn't hiding anything anymore. I could trust everyone around me with the real me, and it felt… like stepping out the front door into a huge, wild world.

"You're opening normal hours tonight, aren't you? I'll stay with you today," I offered. "If I won't be in the way." I wanted Rex's dreams to come true, starting with Daddy Cakes. No doubt I could find some sneaky ways to help out later.

Rex gave me a fond smile. "You won't be," he promised. "And you have to stay for supper with me anyway. My rules. More tea, my boy?"

"More tea," I agreed and settled in to keep my Daddy company. I didn't even need his hands on me to have a good time—not yet, anyway. The promise of later was worth waiting for, because I knew Rex would always follow through.

And I couldn't wait to find out what he had planned.

17

SLATE

The clouds stretched along the horizon in shades of cotton-candy pink and '80s carpet orange. Behind them, the sun sank, disappearing behind darkened skyscrapers. Soon, the streets below would be dark, leaving only the tops of the buildings aglow.

From out here on the balcony of Rex's apartment—well, soon to be mine, too—I could see it all. And I couldn't stop looking.

"Okay, here's the wine…"

I smiled and turned back-on to the railing, leaning against it. Rex and I had showered and changed. I hadn't questioned why he had some clothes for me in his wardrobe, but he'd explained anyway. He'd ordered new clothes in my size to make sure I could stay as long as I needed without going back to my house.

It sounded like a little white lie to cover up his worry that Isaac wasn't done with me yet. And he was right to be worried, because crawling away with his tail between his legs wasn't Isaac's style. Public confrontation was.

I'd worked out that Isaac must be a regular at Dom Nation on both Friday and Saturday nights, because he'd so often shown up at my house at 2:00 a.m. afterward. It was Saturday now. Could he stay away? I doubted it.

But my Daddy didn't know the most important thing of all: I didn't give a shit if he tried. Because my heart and soul were finally in agreement.

I trusted Rex with everything, and he'd never let me down. In his hands, I couldn't fall. I could only fly.

"Thank you," I murmured and took the wineglass. It was hard to breathe or stand still or look at him without growing distracted by the joy thudding against my rib cage, trying to burst out.

Rex came to lean next to me. "What a gorgeous view. The sunset's not bad, either. Supper's all ready, my boy," he murmured with a fond smile.

"What? Now?" I blinked at him.

It *had* smelled pretty good when we got into the penthouse, and I'd asked Rex why. Instead of answering, my Daddy had ushered me straight outside to the balcony.

It had taken me by surprise to find it all set up. The table was draped in a white cloth, silverware set out, a vase of flowers… the whole nine yards. We must be too high up for the pigeons to wreck everything.

Rex had been with me the whole time—unless he'd been very stealthy last night and figured out a way to keep dinner fresh all this time. Had he hired a caterer for this one romantic dinner?

My jaw dropped as I finally worked it out. "Are you spoiling me?"

"Okay, so maybe I had Jens let in a few people," Rex murmured, gazing at me the same way he'd just looked at the sunset—like he couldn't quite believe the beauty he'd been treated to. "You're worth spoiling."

I didn't know what to do with that. So I blushed—well, I was going to whether I liked it or not—and stared up. It was as much a shock to the system to see open sky above as it was to look down and realize how many floors up we were.

Rex shifted to face me and held up his glass. "A toast."

"What to, Daddy?" I straightened up and moved my glass until they almost touched.

"To… us." Rex tilted his head and caught my gaze with those pretty, deep green eyes that had ensnared me from the first moment we met. And then he smiled.

God, he was gorgeous. Fading orange rays brought out every streak of blond in his hair, and his cheekbones were razor-sharp.

"To us," I murmured and clinked my glass against his before taking a sip of the wine. Smooth, delicious, and no doubt expensive.

Then I took his hand and sank to my knees, and pressed my forehead against his thigh. He often stood with one leg cocked, his toes barely brushing the ground, so his thigh made the perfect pillow.

I felt strong here on the ground in front of him. Safe, with his hand on my shoulder and his slender body filling my frame of vision. Secure in the knowledge of who I was—with or without him. I'd never felt quite this way before.

I was at peace.

"Slate?"

I turned my head until I could see him and my cheek pressed into his thigh, even though my neck was at an odd angle. "Yes, Daddy?"

Rex's eyes were bright and—were they wet? "I love you."

I couldn't stop my grin as I buried my face in his thigh. He scratched his fingers along my scalp, but even that couldn't soothe my excited quiver. My wineglass almost sloshed onto my chest. "I love you, too."

We stood like that for a while, and for the first time, it didn't even feel like a test. He wasn't testing my boundaries, and I wasn't exploring them. We just *were*, like a symbiotic pair of animals. Each knew exactly who the other was, and in that knowledge, they knew themselves. There was no one without the other. There was only us.

"All right, I'm hungry," Rex finally said briskly and offered me his hand. "Dinner time. Sit down. I'll get you on your knees again later."

I grinned, making a mental note that Daddy became efficient while hungry. "Yes, sir," I teased. "I'll take that to the table," I offered and lifted his wineglass from him, then set them both down on the table.

It didn't take long before Rex joined me. Both plates were loaded down with food—chicken with white sauce, broccoli spears, fancy garnish on the plate and all. Suddenly I was just as hungry, my stomach growling like I hadn't eaten all day.

"Bon appetit," Rex murmured, raising his wineglass. We settled into a comfortable routine of eating, giggling together as we made up stories about people far below us and the lights that flickered on in the buildings nearby.

Once we were stuffed, Rex brought his chair around to my side so we could both watch the last few minutes of the sunset. "I want you to move in starting now."

I blinked and looked quickly at him, catching my breath. "Really?" He'd made the offer sound immediate before, but it hadn't been so direct.

I'd done a lot of thinking last night, while we slept uneasily in my house. It had once felt cozy to me—my own personal kingdom—but now it just felt lonely without Rex there. Even when he was in bed with me, it hadn't felt right.

No, *I* hadn't felt right. But here, there were no memories. The guilt I hadn't needed to carry and the shame I'd finally let go of didn't get a chance to creep back in. I was me, and I was loved for me when I was here.

"Yes," I whispered and smiled at him. I leaned in to kiss him. "I'd love that, Daddy."

Rex grinned. "It's settled." His chest got all puffed up like he was proud of himself.

"I could enjoy this view every day," I told him and winked. "And I can't wait for all the little perks of living together. And some not so little."

"Your subtlety astounds me, boy."

"Thank you, Daddy." I fought to keep my laughter contained, and I felt his shoulder vibrating slightly, too.

Rex cleared his throat and smoothed a hand over his face. "Right here one night, I think," he mused. I waited, but he gave no more context.

Did he mean...? *Oh, man!* I sat up straight as a rod, and so did my dick. "Yes...?" I was met only with Rex's enigmatic smile, so I groaned and nodded. "Of course, Daddy. I'll wait and find out what you want to do with me."

And that felt good. Not worrying or pushing or endlessly trying. With him, I could just *be*.

"Good boy," Daddy murmured and took my hand. I trembled as arousal steadily throbbed through me, but he didn't make another move on me. So, I resolved, I'd have to be patient for a little longer.

I could afford to be patient now: I was his.

The night was young, but my cupcake pieces were disappearing fast, and the compliments were racking up.

I loved the cool air against my bare back, and the pressure of the harness against my chest and shoulders, and the barely there shorts that kept my libido in check when I saw Rex in his sexy collared white shirt, cuffs rolled up, and leather apron.

Tonight was perfect.

Until the air was shattered by a raised voice. "And why not? Huh? Is this because of that little bitch Slate? Or that twisted fucking Rex?"

Just as I'd thought, Isaac was trying to slink inside like nothing had happened.

A few of the guys standing around nearby cast me concerned looks, but I brushed off their concern and walked toward the entrance of Dom Nation, still carrying the cupcake tray on one forearm.

There he was—staring down Tony, who looked strangely unconcerned for a guy even smaller than Brighton. He just twirled a finger through his hair and looked bored, though I noticed he had adopted a fighting stance, and there was a DM in a fluorescent jacket standing next to him now.

Was this a haven for superconfident Dom twinks?

"Yes, it is," I said, raising my voice to catch Isaac's attention. "Or rather, it's because of Rex that I realized what you did to me—for years—was wrong. That you lied to me when you said I was the only one, for two years straight. That you were just stopping by my house on the way home from here to let off steam, while telling me you didn't like the scene, all so I wouldn't come here and tell your friends that you pretend you don't know what consent is."

A crowd was gathering, murmuring with surprise and interest. Everyone loved a good gossip-rich story.

"Fuck you," Isaac spat.

I didn't even flinch. I wasn't afraid anymore. "You should be so lucky. You were, once. And you threw it away—threw *me* away. Thank God for that. Now I know what submission is supposed to be like. Now I have a choice."

Isaac snarled. He looked at Tony and then around at everyone else. "It's a pack of lies. You all know I wouldn't do that. I've never hurt anyone who didn't want to be hurt."

"*Technically* true," I said with an ice-cold smile. "Which has nothing in common with the truth."

"You guys have known me—" Isaac started, slipping into an oily voice I recognized. He could charm his way into bed and out of trouble with that voice.

"Save it," said one of the guys nearby, hands on his hips. "You're blacklisted. Get over it."

"I'll leave the city, you know!" Isaac snapped. "You'll never find another Dom like me, none of you. I'm the best at what I do." Insulting the people he was trying to win over—not the best strategy. I fought back a laugh as the scoffs and jeers grew louder.

"Listen," Tony cut in with a wave of his hand. His eyes flicked coldly up and down Isaac as he sneered. "You're not getting in, buddy. Nowhere in the city will have you. You broke the rules, and it wasn't even an accident. No second chances."

"Fuck you!" Isaac snarled at Tony, and then turned to me. "And fuck you in your pathetic little saggy ass." He took a step forward and then tripped over the black cloth barrier, hands and legs flailing everywhere as he hit the sidewalk.

I burst out laughing. "Really? That's the best you can do?" He sounded like a petulant child—not the larger-than-life villain who had haunted my fantasies and then my nightmares. Sprawled out on the pavement, he was just human—and a pathetic human at that.

"You'll regret this!"

"No," I said softly and smiled. "I don't even regret being with you. I just don't care anymore. So I sure as hell won't regret being in love."

And I turned and walked away, heading straight to Daddy Cakes, my heart lighter than ever. Behind me, I heard Tony calling a taxi for Isaac while the guys around me murmured and touched my arm in passing, giving me respectful and concerned nods. I gave them all my *I'm fine* smile while encouraging them to take the last few cupcake samples.

"All done," I announced as I pushed open the door of the cupcake shop, presenting my empty platter. "With this and with Isaac."

Rex was wiping the work surfaces down, but at my words, he sucked in a harsh breath and came out from behind the counter. He looked like the king of the jungle all of a sudden, prepared to hunt down and destroy anyone muscling in on his territory. On his mate.

"Where is he?"

It made me shiver with pleasure, an electric shiver dancing along my bare skin and straight to the tip of my cock. *I* was his mate.

I blocked his path and set the tray on the counter so I could take his hands. "Tony's calling a cab. Everyone told him to fuck off."

Rex's eyes widened as he looked through the plate glass window behind me. "Everyone?"

My grin widened. "Mmhmm." I was touched that they were standing up for me. I'd been so afraid that they'd take his side, since they'd known him for so much longer.

"Finally," Rex whispered. "I want to see this." He led me to the door and stood at my shoulder, his hand on my back. Behind me, the customers at tables craned their necks to get a good look, too.

The taxi was sitting there idle while Isaac paced back and forth, throwing his hands in the air and ranting.

We didn't need to hear his words to see how people were reacting to his breakdown. There was no other word but ostracization. There were even guys standing between the cupcake shop and Isaac, in case he tried to come this way.

My heart squeezed and I raised my hand to my throat, which suddenly felt tight. They were protecting us. Not that I felt like I needed protection anymore—I'd just found the confidence that he'd kept ground down for so long.

With my Daddy at my side—whether physically or not—there was nothing Isaac could say to upset me anymore.

Finally Isaac lurched into the taxi, flipping everyone off dramatically. When he slammed the car door, a spontaneous cheer went up. Rex grinned and pushed the door open, leading me outside to enjoy the moment.

"It's over," I said quietly and then grinned at Rex. "Well and truly over." Humiliation wasn't Isaac's thing. Not being on this end of it, anyway. No way would he risk coming back for another round of it.

"No, it's not," Rex whispered, and I instantly knew he wasn't talking about the same thing I was. He gazed up at me with a fond smile and leaned in to press his lips, warm and firm, against my cheek. "It's just beginning," he whispered, his breath ghosting along sensitive skin until my whole body shivered in pleasure.

I whimpered softly and wrapped an arm around Rex's waist, tipping my head to the side so Rex could keep pressing kisses along my neck. "Yes, Daddy."

A throat-clearing interrupted us, and I groaned as Rex pulled away. "Well, I was coming to check on you." It was Brighton in a bright shirt made of fluorescent patches of pink, blue, and yellow, skinny black jeans, and suspenders. "But I take it you're fine."

Rex laughed, his arm firmly settling around my shoulders. He pulled me into him and nodded. "We're fine," he agreed. "More than fine... great."

Brighton gestured behind us to the shop. "Are you out of cupcakes already?"

"Just about."

"Phew." Brighton shook his head. "You know, this business is doing a lot better than I thought it would."

"Well..." Rex murmured and squeezed me tightly. "I want to do even better," he told Brighton. "Do you think it's a good idea if

I offered the place in the daytime for private date space, and maybe did an app for pickup?"

I pressed my lips together and nodded hard. Rex eyed me, and I blinked innocently up at him.

Brighton laughed. "If you don't, I'll personally teach Slate how to whip you."

"Okay, okay!" Rex held up his hands. "I'll get right on that, then."

But I could hardly breathe. An app? He'd spent so long nursing the wound of having the joint venture with his friends ripped away. Hiring people to help him once again… that wasn't an idea Rex would say lightly.

He'd agreed to trust people—and he'd wanted me to hear that.

"You could get big if you do deliveries," Brighton suggested. "Way bigger."

"I'm up for it. Thanks to Slate, I'm starting to think bigger," Rex said softly, and though he didn't look at me, his grin turned affectionate again. "And maybe believe in people a little bit more."

"Good." Brighton scratched his chin thoughtfully. "We'll talk next week," he promised Rex and then smiled at me. "See you later, Slate."

I raised my hand for a little wave and saw him off, then turned to Rex. "Really?" I whispered. "You're going to go for it?"

"My boy," Rex murmured, resting his forehead on my shoulder, "with you here, I feel like I could move the world."

I could honestly say that I knew exactly what he meant.

"But first, let's close up," Rex said briskly. "I have other plans for you tonight."

"Yes, *sir*."

It didn't take long before we were walking to Dom Nation, hand in hand, to join the short lineup waiting outside. I was starting to feel like this costume was my second skin—or maybe my first skin. Like this was the truth of who I was, and everything I'd learned throughout my life was just a disguise.

But I didn't need those costumes anymore. I could bare my heart and soul, leave my very essence exposed to the world, and I was stronger for it.

When we reached the front, Tony just grinned as he looked me up and down. "You're good upstairs and downstairs, cutie." He jerked his thumb toward the building. "Go enjoy yourselves."

"I've got to change," Rex told me as we reached the darkened hallway between the dance floor and the bar.

I grinned. "You aren't wearing your corset underneath? I'll wait out here, it's fine."

"Okay. Don't let any other Daddies steal you away," Rex warned.

"I'll keep an eye on him." Seb appeared in the same head-to-toe leather outfit he'd worn the first night I'd been here, his eyes twinkling as he winked at Rex. When my lover disappeared into the change room, he looked at me. "How are you doing? I heard about your... moment with Isaac."

I scoffed as I grinned at him. "A moment? Oh, he only *wishes* it were a moment." I flicked my hand the way Rex might. "He can fuck off."

Seb laughed richly. "Good," he told me. "Well done. You needed to find that strength, and you did."

"I can't believe it," I said as I shook my head, leaning sideways against the wall. "All thanks to Rex, really."

"No," Seb said softly. "He brought out what was already there. That's what a Daddy does. You're a far cry from the man I first met. Be proud of yourself."

I swallowed hard and looked down, letting myself accept the compliment, as foreign as it felt. Rex was starting to help me get used to it. "Thank you."

"Of course, you've got yourself a damn fine Dom there, and a good Daddy now, too. You've made him better. Which is good, since he needed a slap upside the head and he got prickly when I tried."

I laughed. "Oh, I have my ways." I winked mischievously, just as Rex appeared. God, my blood ran hotter at a single glance of my Daddy in his sleek red corset, black briefs, and black heels. He had no gear at all, but I trusted that he didn't need it to make me submit. I stood a little straighter and licked my lips, instinctively waiting for my orders.

Rex tilted his head and glided over to me, wrapping an arm around my shoulders. "I don't know what you're up to, but you'd better not be teaching my boy to brat."

"Never," Seb pledged solemnly and crossed his heart, then melted into the crowd by the bar.

I bit back a smile and leaned into Rex. "Your wish is my command tonight," I assured him.

"Good," Rex murmured. "Then kiss me."

And I turned my head to do so gladly, pressing my lips against my Daddy's. I let him take control until his teeth scraped my bottom lip, my knees melted, and I had to clutch the wall and his shoulder for support.

Tonight was for us. Nobody else.

18

REX

"Relax," I whispered. "Daddy's got you now."

I ran my palm along Slate's bare back, over the leather strap, all the way to his hairline. I closed my thumb and fingers gently around the nape of his neck, watching him closely for his reaction.

Slate's back rippled, and then he relaxed, his chest resting against the raised and padded black board. "Yes, sir." Slate sounded faraway already, his voice a contented, low hum.

His spirit called for the meticulous detail only I could provide, and I'd be damned if I'd miss the chance to answer. I let go of his neck and brought my fingertips to his shoulder blades, scratching my nails down his back—across the leather straps and all.

The whimper he gave in answer was guttural, and it brought a grin to my face. I loved hearing him lose control.

Something deep and primal wanted to push it further, but not here. I didn't want the DMs coming to check on us. *Later*, I promised myself. It felt like every session with Slate, I stored up more plans for later.

I'd never get bored of picking this man apart and letting him twist and turn and beg in the wind.

"Please," Slate moaned, low and urgent. He shifted on his knees against the lower level of the two-tiered bench, but there was little room for him to move without sliding off.

I lifted one hand from his back and kept my fingertips in the hollow at the base of his spine, just above his bare buttocks. His shorts were tight around his thighs, keeping his knees forced together.

I sensed the storm inside him, and how badly it needed to break. Was tonight going to bring tears again? If so, I reassured myself that I could handle it.

Master X knew what he was doing.

"You remember the safeword?"

"Red. Pineapple. Safeword. I have a whole buffet of options," Slate murmured back.

Since he couldn't see me, I grinned. "Good." To keep him on his toes—metaphorically, at the moment—I gave him a light, stinging slap across his thighs.

"Oof!" Slate squeaked with surprise, his body going rigid before he settled against the bench and gripped the edges again. "No, Daddy. I've been a good boy."

"Have you?" I teased. I circled him, dragging my nails in lazy loops around his skin as I walked. Under my touch, Slate squirmed. His muscles tensed as his breathing deepened. Even his calves were hard now, on the lowest level of the bench where he knelt to await my punishment.

"Y-Yes?" Slate sounded uncertain now.

"Then your reward, my boy," I leaned down to murmur as I took up a position to his side, "is my pleasure."

Despite my words, every ounce of my focus was on Slate. Insofar as the room existed around us, it was only so I could ensure nobody else was too close for safety or comfort.

"Fuck," Slate hissed. He quivered in tiny, gorgeous ripples of goosebumps along his pale skin. I could watch him react to my words all day—but why, when I could also watch him react to my firm hand?

I knew how Slate felt, set adrift in a haze of pleasure and unmoored from everyday life's reference points. My worries were gone, the scope of my thoughts narrowed to Slate.

It was the closest I'd ever come to subspace. But compared to what I observed in boys, top space came with all of the power I craved. With everything in my hands—quite literally—I was a better person. Calm and focused, zoned in on every little move or breath.

Slate's body was a text in an obscure language that only I could read, and I jealously guarded that knowledge with the last breath in my body. I knew I was enough when I was with him; I could give Slate everything he needed and teach him more than he could ever imagine.

"My beautiful boy," I whispered. And then I raised my hand and brought my palm down sharply on the curve of his ass.

Smack.

"Mmmph!" Slate pressed his lips together to muffle his grunt, but the sound was sharp and immediate.

God, the sounds were beautiful. I repeated the slap on the other side, calmly placing my excitement in a mental box. As much as it thrilled me, I had to save that for later. Right now, I couldn't afford distraction for even a moment.

My focus stayed laser-sharp as I spanked Slate four more times, watching as his skin started to turn pink. I kept my palm curved gently and softened the blows at the last moment. All I wanted—yet—was to stir up the blood flow in the area.

My rhythm was steady and soothing, and I wasn't the only one relaxing into it. Slate's shoulders unknitted, and his breathing deepened. Slate's eyes were closed, and his head was turned just toward me enough that I could see a faint smile on his lips.

Like he's asleep, but awake. The bliss on his face kept me gentle for far longer than usual, but I couldn't hold off forever. His whole bottom was pink now, down to his thighs. Before long, no matter where my palm made contact, it would sting sharper than before. That was where the fun turned into something more raw and real.

So I chose my moment and finally shattered the peace, bringing my hand down hard and fast on his ass. At the same moment, I pushed his back down, knowing that his instinct would be to sit upright.

"Nnnnh! Fuck!" Slate struggled against my hand, his eyes dark and wild all of a sudden.

I grinned, the wolfish pleasure sharp and satisfied within me. I wanted to see him driven past the edge of endurance, beyond the bounds of language and thought, into the space where we could only be our purest, rawest selves.

I smacked his thighs, one at a time, hard and fast. Then I turned my back on him, laying my forearm down his back with my elbow closest to his neck to keep him flat on the bench so I could deliver a few more punishing blows.

"Daddy! No," Slate whimpered behind me. "Please, I'll—oh! Fuck! I'll be good, sir. Oh, God!"

He thrashed less than I would have expected, considering I didn't even have his hands tied together.

Very good, I approved mentally, but I wasn't about to reward him yet.

I dug my nails into his skin until white crescents appeared and then raked them down his back alongside my forearm.

Slate's cry was harsh and sudden, and then it turned silent like he was choking back a noise he knew was far too loud to be appropriate. I glanced over my shoulder, and the agonized pleasure across his face made me grin again as I turned side-on to him.

Oh, he was so responsive. The lightest touch or the harshest blow, he could feel them all—and he endured them with equal steadfast resolve.

Slate's vulnerability was utterly intoxicating. I couldn't imagine ever being in that position, much less enjoying it. Not just that. Those words were inadequate. Like a piece of my spirit had slid into Slate's heart, demanding the very same control that Slate needed to give up.

He was blissed-out despite everything that had happened just yesterday. And he kept his noises quiet, not struggling or begging for mercy too loudly. He knew what was allowed here.

I admired Slate's trust in me and his pure courage more than anyone on Earth. That defiant spark of his spirit shone as brightly as it did the moment I met him. But now, I felt up to the task: taming Slate, breaking him, and bringing him back to life again.

"Very good," I finally whispered when my nails reached the gentle mounds of his gorgeous butt. I moved behind him, pressing the heels of my hands into his ass. I kneaded before letting my fingertips drag closer to the sensitive little hole that pulsated with every touch.

Slate's breath was short and shallow all of a sudden. "D-Daddy," he gasped, twisting to look back across his shoulder.

"No," I told him sharply, pausing to stare him down. I wasn't going to let him get in that habit. One day, I'd be wielding a whip or flogger and that much movement would put him in danger. "Head *down*."

Slate blushed and quickly pushed his forehead against the bench again. "Sorry, Master X."

I smiled and dragged my thumbs down, across his hole. "Good boy." My words were almost muffled by how loudly he cried out, pushing back into my hands before his thighs trembled and he stilled himself again. "That's it. Stay still."

"More," Slate begged.

"Sounds like an order," I murmured. I circled to his other side and brought my hand down sharply, just once.

Slate's voice was hoarse as he clung to the bench for all he was worth. "That's too good, Daddy. N-No. Just a…" He trailed off, unable to even think of an excuse.

I chuckled. He was too new to push him for much longer, so I only spanked him lightly using my non-dominant hand now. With his ass red and sore, I needed much less force. I even paused after every few blows to rub down the hot skin, but it wasn't entirely kind. The other purpose besides soothing him was to keep him on his toes, never warning him when the next blow would come.

At last I let my caresses continue for longer than before, rubbing in broad circles over his hips and down his thighs, all the way up his back to his neck. "Good boy," I praised softly. "You've been a very good boy for your Daddy. I think you've earned a reward, hm?"

"Y-Yes, sir?" Slate held perfectly still, his head turned slightly to the side like he didn't want to miss a word.

I kept one hand on his back as I came around his side and crouched, making eye contact. His eyes were wide and wet, but his smile was impossible to miss. "How are you, my love?"

"Happy," Slate whispered. He blew out a quick, hot laugh. "So happy. Can't describe it. Floating."

"Mmhmm." I grinned, rubbing between his shoulder blades lightly.

"I loved it. The more you hurt me, the harder I got."

I raised a brow, my grin spreading as I trailed two fingers down his spine, never stopping despite the thin, desperate noise he made when I glided over his tight little hole. Then I reached his balls, a thick handful, and the hard line of his shaft.

"Mmm," I purred, squeezing Slate's cock as his jaw dropped. He whined with pleasure, his shaft jumping in my hand. "I see," I told him.

"All week, Daddy." Slate was fighting instinct, doing his best to beg me instead of commanding. It made me smile to hear his plaintive tone. "I've followed the rules all week."

"I know you have," I whispered. I let go of the stiff erection and trailed my fingertips around his balls again, then swept them up his thigh and hip. I was saving *that* for later. Slate gazed at me plaintively, his fingertips still curled around the edge of the bench. I might have to pry him off. "I want more pain next time, Daddy. Is that… weird?"

"Not at all," I whispered, rubbing his lower back again. "I'm easing you into it. But I love that you're telling me what you want now. That's good. That's what I want."

"Good. I haven't screwed up." Slate sighed with relief and closed his eyes.

"Not even a little," I promised. "You did well, my precious boy."

"Okay, Daddy," Slate whispered, that smile back on his lips again.

I smiled as I watched him, all too aware that others would want to use this bench soon. I had to ease him gently out of subspace—just for long enough to bring him home, anyway.

Finally, I leaned in to press our lips together, and Slate responded hungrily. He moaned against my mouth, seeking my lower lip and sucking hard. At last, he mumbled against my mouth, "Can we go home, Daddy?"

"We're going home right now," I promised. "I have so much more I want to do to you before I get to come. And then I might even let you spill that heavy load I feel you carrying around, too. What do you say?"

Slate's eyes flew open, and the grin of delight made my spirit soar. "Okay," he whispered. I had to hurry to support him as he scrambled to his feet, making sure he had his balance before cleaning up the equipment.

By the time we got in the taxi, I had gathered my wits enough to make sure we'd collected everything before we left. To get us outside and call a taxi. To keep us both safe and sound. But Slate was still smiling at me, giddy and soft, eyes alight with wonder.

I smiled until it hurt before finally looking out the window to try to get a hold of myself.

Slate would never know what he'd done for me. I was no longer afraid of showing my vulnerable spots, like it would mean I was a bad Dom or Daddy. I knew who I was, and I was the man Slate needed me to be—just like he was the man I needed.

It was like I'd found the missing half of myself, and with my eyes wide open, I could never go back to the darkness. He was the ocean and I was the moon, and the moon wasn't *wrong* to control the tides every day. What Slate needed, I gave gladly.

I was his, completely.

19

———

SLATE

As the elevator glided to a halt at the penthouse floor, I smiled and let go of Rex's hand. It felt like coming home.

"In you go," Rex directed me. Although he held the door for me, he slapped my butt, making me jump and laugh.

I loved the way he treated me with such respect, yet casually made it clear that he found me hot. And I'd never felt more attractive than when I'd walked out of Dom Nation arm in arm with Rex, head held high, while people I didn't even know yet wished us good night.

"I'm in, Daddy." I kicked off my shoes and turned to him, swaying on the spot as I lifted my T-shirt. "And I want *you* to be in, too."

"Jesus." Rex threw his shoulder against the door to slam it closed and then emptied his pockets onto the hallway table. His eyes never left me, hungry and dark. "You know what you're doing to me, don't you?"

He made me feel like prey, and I fucking loved it.

"I do," I whispered, breathless with excitement. "It was fun letting you show me off, but there's more."

"What are you thinking?"

I swallowed hard as I peeled my T-shirt off and dropped it on the floor, rubbing a hand along the buckles and loops of my harness. Then I dropped my hands to my jeans. "I don't want to think about who's watching, and how loud or quiet I should be, and whether I can beg you to stop without making the DMs think I mean it."

Rex's grin was all teeth and raw warning. He slid his finger over the front door, locking it smoothly. I was trapped in here with him, and he'd never looked so perfect.

The wildness within me yearned for his touch, like it could undo the layers of civility and bring me down to the level I needed to be at. The rabbit to his wolf.

"Yes?" Rex purred.

I stepped out of my jeans, my heart thudding behind my ribs as my hands trembled. I unfastened the catch on my harness. "And… I want us naked."

"Oh," Rex murmured, tilting his head as he looked down at himself. He was wearing a collared shirt and trousers over his latex outfit. For a moment, he didn't say anything.

"Not that I don't find that corset sexy," I rushed to reassure him, licking my lips. "But I want nothing between us tonight. No games, no clothes, no words. Just… instinct. I want to act and feel and *be*, not think. Like—like the other day, when you chased me into the bedroom…"

I bit my lip, heat flushing my cheeks as I played with the hem of my shorts. My fidgeting drew his gaze, and I waited for him to stare before I slowly pulled my shorts down. My semi sprang free, bobbing in midair with desperate relief, but I wasn't foolish enough to think it would get more attention yet.

Rex liked to make me wait.

"There's a name for that, you know," Rex murmured, his look dragging up my body like his fingertips had done not too long ago. It was my turn to stare as he bent over and slowly took off his shoes and socks. Then he curled his bare toes into the ground and straightened up, balancing his weight in an even stance I recognized.

It was the way Dominants stood, effortlessly radiating a confidence I yearned to get closer to. And he never stopped looking me up and down like he was memorizing every detail.

"There is?" I whispered. I shrank into myself under his inspection, folding my hands over my cock playfully.

Rex's lip curled like he wanted to tell me to stand still and stop hiding myself away from him, but then he took a breath and his eyes met mine instead. "Yes. It's called primal play."

"Uh-huh?" It sounded good already—instinctive and raw. That was what I needed.

"I've been suspecting you'd like it." Rex's smile was knowing, and I blushed under his look.

"Oh," I whispered. Did he know all of my kinks? Even the ones I didn't know yet? I loved it—in a way, it was its own form of humiliation. Being taught how my own libido worked, and what felt good.

"Are you ready to embrace pure subspace?" Rex whispered. He flicked his fingers along the buttons of his shirt and then arched toward me, his gorgeously lean body rippling out of the garment to leave it a pooled heap on the floor.

He had the body of a hunter, sleek and agile.

I nodded and bit back my whimper, shifting from foot to foot as my dick grew hard. I pressed both hands against myself, squeezing and rolling the shaft between my palms.

"Let's play, then," Rex murmured, unlacing his corset. "But I need to know your limits."

Not this again. I shook my head breathlessly. "I'm not sure yet," I admitted. "I… I wasn't allowed to have them, you know?"

Rex paused, eyeing me thoughtfully before he squirmed out of the corset. He fiddled with it and laid it carefully on the ground on top of his shirt. "All right. Then we're going to explore later, you and me. I won't draw blood or choke you or anything too risky."

Do I want him to? I had no idea. My stomach churned with pent-up tension, and I gave a nervous giggle. "Okay. But…"

Damn it, how did I put it without being cheeky? I didn't want to sass him, but I also didn't quite understand. I bit my lip and looked at the floor as I tried to put words to it.

Rex raised a brow and waited.

"But I like it when you're in charge," I murmured. "And that's what you want, too. If I'm telling you that I want to… play primally, or whatever… isn't that me topping from the bottom?"

Rex smiled. "No, sweetheart," he told me as his hands went to the button of his jeans.

Okay, I might be busy trying to figure out how to submit to my Daddy, but I was still horny as hell. He didn't keep stripping, and I shifted impatiently, biting my lower lip. "Mmm?"

"You're not allowed to steer me into doing what you want," Rex said, his tone soft and clear. This was the instructive voice I was getting so used to, soothing and wise and calm. I drew strength from it as well as knowledge. "But the whole point of this—look at me, boy." His tone was sharp for just a moment.

I responded to him before I even thought about it: I quickly met his stormy, demanding, and endlessly green gaze. "Yes, Daddy?" I whispered.

"Good boy," Rex said and smiled, his tone gentle again. "The whole point—the *whole* point," he said and stepped closer, his hands resting on my biceps, "is that you're the one in charge. It's *your* needs I'm meeting, not mine. So you tell me what to do, and I choose how to do it."

"But I need you to hurt me," I whispered, shaking my head. I wasn't telling him what to do, was I? "To take charge. To do what you want with me."

"You need to be hurt, just like I need to give you what you need. That's okay. It's more than okay. As long as you like what I'm giving you. And I do it *because* you want it." Rex cupped my cheeks and stroked my jaw with his thumbs, his warm palms caressing my neck before wandering across my collarbones and down to my chest. "The moment you stop wanting it, I stop."

I blinked several times as the weight of his words settled in. "But in the heat of the moment…"

"Doesn't matter," Rex cut me off, still perfectly calm. "I can be as animalistic and cruel as you can imagine, but it's my job to snap out of that in a second if I've gone too far."

How the hell could he even do that? When I was in subspace, it took so long to come out of it. Even when it went bad, like it had the first night I'd seen Isaac at Dom Nation, it took minutes or hours to feel like myself again.

Subspace must be different from… Domspace? Topspace? But however it worked, I trusted that he could do it. I swallowed hard and nodded. "Okay," I whispered. "I trust you."

And Rex smiled, wrapping his hands around the back of my neck as our lips met in a long, slow kiss.

His lips were sweet and deceptively soft, but nothing about the way he kissed was gentle. It was hot and demanding, a storm breaking free from its leash. His tongue slid along my lower lip and then into my mouth, demanding and possessive.

Fuck, I just want to give in right here. But Rex wouldn't give it to me that easily. He'd make me wait and wait until the last shred of sanity had fled before satisfying me in ways that words could never describe.

The heat of Rex's kiss made my dick stiffen under my hands. I let go so I could grip his waist, pulling my Daddy into me and grinding the throbbing heat of my erection against his stomach. Showing him how much I wanted him.

He pulled back sharply and grinned in that animalistic way again. The warning and the promise in his eyes were impossible to separate, so I didn't even try.

"Catch me," I whispered and scampered out of reach, then grinned playfully at him.

"Oh, I will." The promise of punishment in his voice made me weak at the knees. Rex didn't look away as he stepped out of his trousers and then pulled the shining, black latex down to reveal his bulge straining at the satin thong.

I wanted to touch—wanted to feel the smoothness of the satin and his skin against my palms. I swayed toward him before stopping myself. If I got any closer, he could catch me on the spot.

Damn it, was this a ploy? The sparkle in his eyes confirmed my suspicion.

I huffed and stepped backward again, even as I licked my lips. "You won't get me that easily."

"Oh, you're easy for me," Rex told me. And sure enough, I couldn't resist watching as he ran his palm over the tip of the tented thong, rubbing himself with a sensual moan.

I choked back a groan of my own, imagining him pulling his underwear to the side so his shaft could spill out and spear me...

"Nope," I gasped, like I was trying to remind myself. I was dizzy with desire, but I fought it with all I had. Tonight, I was going to make him work for it.

But the look Rex gave me as he peeled off his underwear and tossed it aside—hot and hungry and triumphant—told me that I was never going to win. He was going to fuck me tonight, at long *long* last. No matter what I did, he would have his way.

His cock already stood proud, pointing toward me like a compass finding north, and I could just imagine the thick length filling me up. Completing me at last, surging into me with merciless thrusts.

It made me throb from head to toe, pulses of electric desire lighting up every inch of my bare body. They shivered along my heavy, swollen shaft straight to the tip. With both of us this hard, running was going to be a challenge.

Rex approached, but not straight on. He circled me, his eyes dark and hungry. The calm, soothing Daddy was gone, and in his place he'd left the hard-edged Dom I needed.

I turned on the spot and shuffled to the side, finding myself drawn into circling him. Negotiating without words what would happen between us: the degree of play in tonight's hunt, and how hard I'd fight back.

We already knew how sexual it would be: Rex was going to have me at the end of this. But whether it would be rough or tender remained to be seen.

Wait—was he *sniffing* me?

Rex's nostrils flared as he dipped his head toward me. He leaned closer to me, his eyes bright as a near-smile played across his lips. Then he made a sudden swipe for my wrist, and I gasped and stepped out of reach just in time.

The mischief became something darker, like the territorial aggression of an animal denied. Rex growled, a low warning rumble in his chest.

Fuck. *Fuck*, that shouldn't be so hot, but I burned from head to toe at that one simple sound. Suddenly I was breathless, and it was impossible to distinguish between the adrenaline of fear and arousal.

I tried to hold my ground, raising my chin in a silent challenge. *Come and get me.*

Rex made another lunge. This time, he tried to grab my shoulder, but he was holding back. Testing me. I swayed out of reach again, shuffling backward toward the living room.

That was it. He wanted to see when my nerve would break and I'd make a run for it. I didn't let down my guard for a moment; there was no room for error when I wanted to be his match in every way.

Rex snarled and lunged for me, and my calm shattered. I yelped and scampered backward, the floor cool underfoot as I ran for the spacious, open combination kitchen-living room.

His strides were even and certain, approaching with a steady tempo however quickly I moved. Like he knew that all he had to do was corner me and he'd win.

I swallowed hard, but I used the time wisely. I darted around the edge of the kitchen island and kept it between us, then grinned at him when he appeared around the corner.

Rex's gaze narrowed. He didn't slow down—in fact, his strides grew longer, and in a few swift movements, he placed his hands on the edge of the counter.

"Fuck!" I whimpered, backing up as he sprang onto the counter like it was nothing, and then stood. With his cool stare pinning me to the ground from above, there was nowhere I could hide.

I wavered on the spot, my thighs quivering. I couldn't tear my gaze from his erection, straight and huge and swaying in midair just above my eyes.

Rex grinned down at me. The tip of his tongue dragged along his lower lip and then back across the top lip.

He wrapped his slender fingers around himself, pulling the silken skin down his shaft and back up again. As he stroked himself, he looked at me like a raw piece of meat and traced the vein along his dick with his thumb. Taunting me by forcing me to watch his silent promise.

But he hadn't won the struggle yet.

I circled the counter carefully, facing him the whole time while he turned on his heel. The taut silence lingered for seconds, but then it broke.

I made a dash for the bedroom, and behind me, a snarl and thump announced Rex rejoining my level. Which meant he had to be close.

Adrenaline made my heart jump into my throat. I swallowed the dizzying rush, risking a glance back as I scrambled down the steps.

There he was, silently appearing in the doorway already—even closer than I'd thought.

I whimpered, grabbing the bedpost as I flung myself around it.

Shit. Now he had me trapped against the wall in the corner. My palms grew damp, and I choked back another groan as Rex meticulously closed the bedroom door behind himself.

Then my Daddy turned to look at me, strolling closer like he had all the time in the world. He picked a careful path down the center of the empty space between the foot of the bed and the wall, so there was no escape toward the door.

This was the same place he'd caught me before, with the wall at my back and the dresser blocking my escape route to the side.

As difficult as it was, I gulped and edged forward. I had to ignore the instinct to flatten myself against the wall and whimper, bare my throat and body—to submit to his will.

I had one more trick up my sleeve. I waited with bated breath for my moment…

Rex walked down the steps toward me with a slow, certain stride, snarling with bared teeth in victory. It must only have been seconds that passed, but time itself seemed to open up, revealing lifetimes in every moment as the walls closed in around me and he stared me down.

Now!

With a frantic whine, I sprang toward him, but as he stared and reached out for me, I dodged around him. My palms pressed into the bedspread as I reached the bed in seconds, scrambling to get my foot up on it and launch myself across it…

But my foot caught in the duvet, and I cried out as I went face-first onto the bed. I flailed to scramble across the bed, but with a yowl, Rex sprang onto the bed and straddled me.

Daddy was upon me, snarling close to my ear as he shoved my head into the bed and dragged his nails down my back.

"*Mine.*"

Rex's snarl was the first word he'd spoken in long, heart-pounding minutes of adrenaline. And my body understood it in a way that surpassed language itself.

He was claiming me as his property, his prey, his helpless little fucktoy. I needed this harsh dominance like I needed oxygen, and I gasped for breath.

Hot lines of pain sprang up along my skin, igniting my nipples and shivering through my torso until a rush of heat hit my stomach. It coursed through my erection, throbbing all the way to the tip as I clenched and gasped.

Words failed me now, even curse words. The guttural whine that escaped my throat was close to a snarl. I threw my weight back into him, but he just pressed himself smoothly against my body to turn the blow into a smooth ride instead.

Rex's cock slid neatly between my cheeks, which still tingled from the punishment he'd delivered at Dom Nation. The hard line of him dragged along the most sensitive spot of my body.

He had yet to fill me, and *boy* did my body know it. I craved it like nothing else—almost enough to give up the struggle here and now.

I whimpered and bucked against him, but all it did was force his shaft to slide up and down between my cheeks, sending another ripple of painfully desperate sparks through my aching dick.

I twisted sideways instead, throwing my weight into it, and I caught him by surprise. The wrestling match was quick and intense as he locked his leg around my ankles to keep me from flipping over fully. With my lower half trapped down against the bed, I didn't have a lot of leverage.

Rex slid an arm around my chest, twisting me back down until I lost my grip on the bed and collapsed on my face again.

I reached behind me, scratching and flailing at anything I could reach, but my hands only made glancing contact with his skin.

I'd lost, and the animal inside me wanted to pay the price—now.

Rex grabbed my wrists and yanked them above my head, then pressed against them with one palm to keep my hands trapped there. "Mine," he hissed again, his teeth closing around my earlobe.

I whimpered, my whole body trembling as I held still. Then he bit the back of my neck hard, and the tension in my muscles eased like he'd pressed the *off* switch.

I went limp all over—well, everywhere but my dick, which was painfully hard and sensitive.

A long, low whine slipped from my throat as I resigned myself to submission, offered myself to the beast who had conquered me. I would have rolled onto my back and bared my throat, if I could have moved. But he had control of me, body and soul.

The stiff heat of my erection pressed against the smooth sheets underneath, sending sparks through me, but they were too shallow. The tiny movements of my hips weren't enough. Whether his touch or my own, I needed *something* more.

Rex had mounted me like the king of the pride, grabbing a fistful of my back and kneading my skin. He growled, the triumphant noise a low and deep shudder that vibrated through my ribcage. One hand still kept my wrists pinned above my head, but the other glided down my side at half the speed I might have expected.

He luxuriated in my submission, drinking me in like a prize.

"Fuck," I choked and thrashed—not for escape this time, but because my muscles suddenly went taut with the burst of heat that radiated from every inch of skin he touched.

"I will," Rex growled behind my neck, nipping my shoulder. He pressed his face next to mine, and suddenly his tongue ran around the rim of my ear. "I'll fuck you senseless. Use your body as my own personal fucktoy until I come. You like that, my boy? My filthy, slutty boy?"

Yes! I whimpered my agreement and nodded as hard as I dared. There was no hiding it. My treacherous body vibrated with tension, and I grew tight until my opening fluttered under his shaft. The duvet under my face stifled my breaths and even my sounds, but Rex never let up his grip. "P-Please, Daddy," I mumbled. My body rippled and heat pulsed through me as I pushed back against him. *"Please…"*

Rex's throbbing shaft dragged along my sensitive hole, waking up every dormant nerve I'd ever forgotten about. Instinct could take care of this, too.

I wanted him to pin me down and slide into me, fill me with his very essence and pound me until I trembled from head to toe.

"What do you want?" Rex purred, his voice deceptively soft again. He was still savoring the victory, rubbing my face in it—quite literally. I couldn't see anything as he pressed me into the duvet, my breaths hot on my own face.

"Fuck me," I gasped. I didn't care about the rules or anything else right now. I was going to *die* if I didn't get his cock in me *right now*. "Please, sir, Daddy, *please*. I need this…!"

The knowing, dark chuckle Rex gave only made me burn through the last of my patience. I lived for the pure, confident dominance that radiated from Rex at every moment.

No—not even confident. That was the wrong word, like it was a deliberate act. And while my Daddy was meticulously deliberate about everything he did, dominance wasn't just something he *did*. It was who he *was*. Unfiltered, natural, pure.

So filthy and so pure.

"Not dry, you little pain slut," Rex purred, his body trembling in a chuckle. "Not until you're *much* more used to me."

Although I moaned at the idea of him stretching me with his fingers and tormenting me, making me wait for his cock, I appreciated it. I wanted to hurt, but not beyond endurance. As long as he didn't make me wait longer just for *that*.

"Wait." Rex's voice was a sharp snarl of instruction.

I could hardly breathe. I trembled from head to foot as I obeyed, freezing exactly where I was. I didn't even dare to curl my fingers.

The bed dipped on my left side, and his knee brushed against my thighs as he dismounted.

No. Stay over me. I choked back a whine as I listened to him rummage, but I waited. I half expected Rex to cuff me or tie me down somehow, but he didn't. He just let go of me and trusted me to obey.

So I did.

Seconds later, the bed dipped and his weight settled on top of me again, soothing away the hot flush of anxiety. With Daddy here, everything was right in the world. This time, he knelt between my legs, though, so I spread my knees and raised my hips off the bed slightly.

"Good boy," Rex murmured, and I smiled to myself. I was safe to sink even further into the fog of ecstasy. It was his job to take care of me, and all I had to do was obey.

Slick fingers trailed between my cheeks, swirling in broad, prickly strokes over and around my tightness. The flashes of pleasure were intoxicating, but however much I moaned and begged for it, Rex took his own time.

Finally, a starburst of heat flushed through me as his fingers pressed into me. I stifled my moan, glad to press my face into the bed. I felt too tight and full already. How on earth was I going to handle Rex's cock?

But that was why Rex was stretching me first, making sure I was ready. I trusted him to take care of me.

"I know, beautiful boy," Rex whispered. "You're doing so good."

Gradually, the uncomfortable tightness slid further into me, opening me up and leaving me slick. Then, his fingers did something and a dull throb of arousal pounded through me like the beat of a drum.

I held my breath, my thighs quivering. Oh, he'd found my prostate, all right.

He stroked it gently, sliding his fingers in and out with ease. Back and forth, the tips of his fingers warmed up the spot inside me until my erection started to come back to life—hotter and harder than before.

Fuck, this was a whole different kind of pleasure. One that had been rare for me in the last few years—without the prospect of sex, I'd barely even fingered myself.

But having my Daddy already inside me, slick and demanding, made me whimper and squeeze my eyes shut with pleasure.

"Better, hm?" Rex growled. "Almost ready for my cock?"

I shook my head wordlessly. I was floating too high on the cloud all of a sudden, my thoughts coming in distracted little bursts in between waves of pleasure that washed through me.

I was tense, my muscles hard with arousal as I struggled to breathe.

"Oh, yes, you are," Rex chuckled deeply. His other hand cupped my balls and slid up my shaft, tight and hot, and I threw my head back and cried out. "See?" Rex whispered. "Don't think you can trick me into letting you come first, boy."

I shook my head. "N-No, sir," I whispered. "Of course not."

"So, let's try that again." Rex squeezed my shaft, sending another violent pulse of *yes* and *oh God more please* through my whole body. Then he let go and pulled his fingers free from me.

I gasped, my thighs trembling with how much I needed him. Fuck, I felt empty all of a sudden, and my very toes curled with how fucking badly I needed him.

"Are you ready for my cock inside you, my boy?"

This time I nodded so hard that my nose crushed into the bedspread. "Yes, Daddy," I whimpered. "Please!" My breathing grew sharp with nervous anticipation. It had been so long, after all.

Would I still like it? Would it hurt too much? Was that enough preparation? Was Rex too big to fit? Then, abruptly, a sigh escaped and the tension melted away as I remembered that none of that was mine to worry about. It was Daddy's job to take care of the details.

Rex chuckled, the noise warm and comforting. "Don't worry, love," he murmured. "I've got you."

I know you do. I smiled so hard my cheeks hurt, until my bliss was interrupted by the thick weight pressing into me—past the tight ring of muscle at my entrance and inside.

"Ah… hah! Fuck!" I cursed sharply, my throat closing as my eyes squeezed shut. Fuck, he was *big*!

I couldn't pretend I didn't like the burst of pain a little bit. It was just more central than the blows he'd landed on my sensitive skin earlier—and deeper, shivering straight down to my core.

"Good boy," Rex whispered, kissing my shoulder blade and then my neck. He draped himself along me, his weight surprisingly solid on my back. "You're such a good boy for your Daddy. So strong, so sexy…"

I gritted my teeth and whimpered as he pushed inside me, praising me in soft whispers, but the sparks that abruptly started to course down my shaft brought me out of the trance.

Oh, shit, that felt good all of a sudden. He filled me up, stretched me just to the point of endurance, but no further. The pain was pleasurable, and the stinging nerves changed their minds until pleasure blazed straight to my core.

"Y-Yes," I choked out, digging my knees and fingertips into the bedspread. "Oh, fuck. Better now…"

Rex chuckled softly and pressed his lips against the back of my neck, right where he'd bitten the scruff of my neck earlier. "Yes, it is," he whispered. His voice sounded strained. "You're so fucking *tight*."

"Sorry," I mumbled, dazed and breathless.

"No, my darling," Rex whispered, petting my arm gently before he stroked my hair. "No, it's good. It's fucking wonderful."

And I knew what he meant. Rex was finally inside me, our bodies and spirits locked together. The struggle between us had ended in this bliss, and so much more lay ahead.

"Fuck me," I whispered, my voice hoarse and my breathing harsh. "Please."

I didn't need to ask twice. Rex slid out and pushed back in, the first move drawing moans from both of us at once. But he kept going, staying slow and careful at first. The whole time, he kept kissing me, his touches just as tender as his voice.

But his words turned rough and hot.

"Going to fill you up with my load, my filthy boy. My precious cumslut."

My whole body went taut with desire as I whimpered and threw myself back into him. "Yes," I gasped. *Yes, I am! I'm yours, sir. Use me and hurt me and blow my mind. My Daddy. My Daddy,* I thought, a grin spreading over my face.

Reality faded in a heartbeat. His thrusts turned rough and fast, the mattress under me creaking in a steady rhythm as he started to throw his weight into it.

"Yes, Daddy!" I groaned as primal noises spilled from my throat again—yelps and whimpers, and even a snarl.

And the whole time, Rex rode me like a wild beast, the calm facade falling away as he embraced the Dom I'd sensed inside him from the very first night.

Grunts and growls from us both filled the air, along with the slick noises of his body slamming into mine. Words had vanished again, and the unspoken language of raw desire sufficed.

I begged him for more, throwing my weight back as he pushed into me, and he pounded me until I couldn't even hold myself up on my arms. I collapsed onto the bed again, desperately reaching under myself...

"No," Rex snarled and slapped my hand away.

I whimpered, reeling from shock and the plateau of ecstasy that had grown almost painful. I needed more, and I needed it now. "B-But—!"

Rex pulled out and I gasped sharply, my whole world spinning from the shock. I was empty all of a sudden, clenching tightly around nothing at all. *No!*

It wasn't just my world spinning. Rex had flipped me onto my back, and I reeled with the shock.

"Please!"

"Oh, I'm not stopping now," Rex growled at me, baring his teeth in a wicked grin. "Don't worry your pretty little head."

I gasped and threw my head back, my body rippling as he smoothly guided himself back into me. My knees rose and brushed his sides, and he hoisted them up until my legs locked around his waist.

That drove him deep inside me, straight over the spot that made pleasure pulse through me unbearably.

My cock was still neglected, shuddering hard and a handful of skilled strokes away from bliss. The edge was looming close, like it or not, and after being denied all week, I couldn't handle one more brush against the edge without release.

"Please, please, please," I mumbled breathlessly before I found his mouth on mine, hot and hungry.

"Please, what?" Rex snarled and sucked my lower lip into his mouth. He bit down and I gasped, trembling with how fucking good it felt. That ought to be illegal! His tongue swiped harshly across my lip, soothing the stings before he let me speak again.

"P-Please let me come, Daddy. I'm so close."

"So am I, boy." Rex dragged his nails along my scalp, cupping the back of my head. "I'm going to fill you up and mark you as mine, just like I promised. Leave you dripping wet."

"Yes!" I gasped, clenching around his pulsating shaft. "Yes, please, Rex. Please, *yes*! I need to come. Am I allowed?"

I needed to see his ecstasy and know that I was the one who'd caused it—needed to satisfy my Daddy and satiate him. I quivered on the edge, suddenly realizing how fucking close I was to losing control.

"I want to feel it," Rex whispered against my lips, his kiss suddenly long and slow and tender.

I closed my eyes and gave in with nothing more than a whimper, breathless and consumed by the fire that raged in the pit of my belly. At least, until his hand slid between our bellies and closed around me. My shaft suddenly pulsated in the tight circle of his fingers, quivering and thick and full all of a sudden.

Rex kissed the strangled cry from my lips. "I'm going to watch you come undone," he promised, his thrusts rough and deep. "I feel you, getting all tight around me. You can't hold back, baby. Not anymore, my boy. You have permission to come now."

But he didn't get it—I didn't want this to end! I needed him inside me, our spirits as bare as our bodies, our limbs tangled and skin hot and wet against one another.

I whimpered in protest, but there was nothing I could do. I was helpless in his hands and swept away by the lightning storm of desire that ravaged my body.

He stroked me fast and hard, keeping pace with the thrusts into me, and I cried out again.

Fuck. Fuck, I was past the point of no return already, my body quivering as every muscle pulled tight and the air itself burned in my lungs.

"I-I'm going…!"

"Yes, boy," Rex gasped against my mouth, his gaze dark and demanding. "Come!"

And I came with a single, breathless cry as the stars above my eyes spun out of control and exploded into a tremendous burst of heat that spilled from every inch of me.

The universe itself knitted together as Rex's cock swelled inside me. He grabbed my hip and cried out rough and low, spilling his seed just as I coated my own stomach and his with my mess.

Yes!

Everything was perfect, achingly and blindingly beautiful in a way we could never again recreate—but just as abruptly as I'd lost control and spilled into pleasure, I realized that this was just the beginning.

We had a whole lifetime of these moments to experience together. There were a thousand new and precious ways to submit to Rex and the ecstasy he showed me, for so many years to come.

My eyes grew wet as I clutched Rex against me, my lungs raw as I gasped for breath and whispered his name.

Wait, he was speaking, too. "Yes, my beautiful Slate," Rex whispered, stroking my chest in long, careful strokes as our bodies stilled. He was still buried deep inside me, twitching as he grew soft. "I know, baby. It's so good it hurts."

I nodded jerkily, my eyelids fluttering open again. Rex, too, was flushed with pleasure, his eyes glassy as sweat shone on his face and ecstasy lit him up from the inside out.

I clung to him with all of my limbs and buried my face into his neck as he petted my skin and ran his hand along my head, praising me.

"I… I love you," I finally mumbled into him. "So much."

Rex's chuckle shivered through me. "Yes, my love," he whispered as he finally slid free from me. "I love you too, Slate. My beautiful boy."

"Yours," I agreed dizzily. "And you're mine." I was the luckiest boy ever. I grinned at the ceiling as I closed my eyes. At first, I thought it would take a lot of persuading before I'd let him go even long enough to clean us both up.

But then he whispered the magic words, and I went limp against the bed, sighing contentedly.

"Let Daddy take care of you."

"Always," I promised and basked in the afterglow, grinning triumphantly. We'd both won the biggest gift of all: a love that I had no doubt could endure anything.

EPILOGUE

REX, THREE MONTHS LATER

The afterglow of tonight's scene had faded, but as Slate came out of subspace to drink and dance with me like he hadn't a care in the world, I'd only grown more excited.

My hands were actually shaking now. *Inconceivable!* I thought, hiding my smile. I certainly wouldn't have believed anyone who told me I'd lose my cool over one little plan.

Or one big, big plan, as the case may be.

The sweat beading my forehead wasn't just from the summer heat pressing in from all sides in Dom Nation. I dabbed my forehead and leaned in so Slate could hear me over the thumping music, the lights glimmering off his skin and the silver buckles of his harness. "Shall we get some fresh air?"

"I don't know, Daddy. Shall we?" Slate beamed at me, leaving the decisions up to me as always.

I flashed him a grin. He was cute, and I was wound up as hell. I'd let him get away with the sass. "Come," I ordered instead and offered him my arm.

"Yes, *sir*. I think I just did that, though," Slate giggled as he wrapped his hand around my bicep.

I elbowed him lightly. "There's always time for more."

Slate grinned at everyone we passed, nodding at a few of them. Ever since Isaac had been kicked out, he'd come out of his shell. Or maybe it had to do with my claiming him as my own. Either way, he'd blossomed into the man and the sub he'd always been supposed to be.

Isaac hadn't shown up here since that night. In fact, reliable intelligence had it that he'd found himself ostracized from everywhere in town overnight, and he'd moved away—far away.

By now, those early nights of fear and uncertainty seemed as far away as the faint pinpricks of stars that greeted us when we got outside and I turned my face up to the sky. The summer air was cool compared to the air inside Dom Nation, and I shivered.

"Are you going to howl? Give me warning if you do," Slate teased me, letting go of me so he could wrap his arm around my waist. He cast me an extra look, like he sensed the energy vibrating through me and wanted to help calm it down with his jokes.

"Oh, I'm saving that for later," I promised. Little did Slate know what was in store.

Slate had hinted earlier this month that he would like this. It was just up to me to actually do it, and I was finally ready. We both were. I needed it as much as Slate did.

I swallowed and stepped over the barrier with my boy, nodding at Tony on the way by, to find a quiet spot among the men mingling and chatting outside.

We were just a few steps away from Daddy Cakes, the light spilling onto the sidewalk and street from the brightly lit shop.

My new employees had helped ramp up the business quickly, so we could open both day and night to completely different crowds. And now I could come to Dom Nation any night I wanted, without waiting to sell out the day's batch of cupcakes.

Here, I thought and stopped, turning to Slate and taking his hands as I swallowed back the lump of excitement in my throat.

The confusion in Slate's eyes only grew when I sank to my knees on the sidewalk in front of him. "Daddy?" Slate whispered.

I smiled up at him, my hands trembling in his grip. "I first saw you right here," I said, my voice hoarse. My mouth was dry, and the rush of adrenaline made it hard to speak clearly. "Outside Daddy Cakes. Standing outside my door and my life, waiting to walk in and change my whole world. If you'd allow me..."

I fumbled inside the armband where I kept loose change, my locker key, and tonight, something else entirely. I closed the zipper again once I drew out the thin silver necklace and dangled it from my thumbs, gazing up at Slate.

"There's a matching ring, but I think—I think this part is more important," I laughed breathlessly. "There's a lock." I turned it to show him. "With a three-digit code that only I know."

Nobody would think twice about the thin, discreet silver chain. He could wear it at work and at home, and when we let the animals inside us out, I could take it off for the evening. Safety first, after all.

Slate's beautiful blue eyes opened wide and then grew wet. "Rex…?" he whispered.

I smiled up at him and let go of one hand so I could dab the corner of my eye with my thumb. "If you'll allow me, I'd like you to be mine—not just this once, but forever."

"Are you…?" Slate looked almost afraid to finish the words, in case this was all a dream. He even pinched his arm lightly, like he thought I wouldn't notice the movement.

Yeah, I couldn't believe it, either. But Slate had seen every part of me—even the parts that scared me—and he loved them all. So yeah, I was ready to spend my life with this boy, and I wanted him to know that.

I beamed up at him. "I'm proposing," I said and nodded as I took his other hand again. "I'm collaring you and marrying you and in every single way, making you mine for life."

"Oh, my God," Slate whispered, bouncing on his toes like he was trying to keep it together. He looked away and cleared his throat, then squeezed my hands. "Oh my God, Daddy. You want—you want…"

"I want you," I murmured up at him. "So, my boy… will you be mine?"

Slate crashed down onto his knees in front of me and flung his arms around my neck, his weight slamming into me. "*Yes!* Yes, yes, Daddy, oh, *yes!*"

I laughed as I pushed him upright again. He didn't know his own strength sometimes—he never quite had, but that was okay. I knew.

Slate clasped his hands in front of his chest and knelt there as I stood up again. I squinted in the faint light and spun the dial to the right code, opening the clasp.

5/05. The day we met. One day, I might even tell him that.

My fingertips trailed along his bare skin as I draped the chain around his neck and clicked it shut. Then, my hands still shaking, I spun the dial with one thumb and brushed my hands over his bare shoulders.

"Done," I whispered, and a wave of pure emotion struck me, swelling my chest until I puffed up with the pride I felt at finally having done it. *This is it*, I thought. *The rest of my life. And I can't wait.*

I took Slate's arms, pulling him to his feet. He beamed at me, not even bothering to hide the tears in his eyes, and I grinned back.

And then, while the applause and hollers from our friends nearby rang in our ears, I kissed him like the world was ending and we'd never get another chance. But really, it was just Slate making my world turn once again.

The tears spilled down my cheeks, and at last, I let them fall without shame.

Being Slate's Daddy had meant losing my fear of being vulnerable or hurt ever again. The day we met, I'd started learning to submit to my own feelings and to Slate's needs.

In letting go of my fearful grip on power, I'd found more strength and control than I'd ever dreamed of. I'd found my other half, the man who fit the parts of me I'd once thought was broken.

And best of all, I'd found someone who could help me learn to be a better man, a better Dom, and a better Daddy every single day.

AFTERWORD

If you enjoyed *Exposed*, please consider leaving a review and don't miss Seb's story, coming up next in the Dom Nation series...

You may also enjoy Barely Regal, a Daddy/boy MM royal romance.

Want to read more?

Sign up for my newsletter and be the first to know about my new books, discounts, giveaways, and more:

edaviesbooks.com/subscribe

Join my reader group on Facebook to catch up on my books with a whole bunch of lovely readers:

facebook.com/groups/edavies

Always be you!

~Ed

ABOUT THE AUTHOR

E. Davies grew up moving constantly, which taught him what people have in common, the ways relationships are formed, and the dangers of "miscellaneous" boxes. As a young gay author, Ed prefers to tell feel-good stories that are brimming with hope.

He writes full-time, goes on long nature walks, tries to fill his passport, drinks piña coladas on the beach, flees from cute guys, coos over fuzzy animals (especially bees), and is liable to tilt his head and click his tongue if you don't use your turn signal.

facebook.com/edaviesbooks

twitter.com/edaviesauthor

instagram.com/thisboyisstrange

bookbub.com/authors/e-davies

Brooklyn Boys

Electric Sunshine

Live Wire

Boiling Point

F-Word

Flaunt

Freak

Faux

Forever

Freedom

After

Afterburn

Afterglow

Aftermath

Rosavia Royals

Barely Regal

Men of Hidden Creek

Shelter

Adore

Miracle

Redemption